THE VOYAGE THAT CHANGED THE WORLD

S OME WERE RELIGIOUS FANATICS, SOME WERE brave souls, others crooks and cowards. One was a murderer. Many died within days of landing in New England. No one was spared famine or disease.

Voices of the Mayflower is the story of a disparate bunch who sailed from Europe to New England 400 years ago – some in pursuit of religious freedom but most in the quest for riches. The book uses contemporary accounts and uses the actual words of the protagonists where possible.

We know little of the actual players. There is only one portrait of a *Mayflower* passenger. What were they like? Why did they behave as they did? What drove them? The book tries to answer those questions in the voices of six of the individuals who founded the settlement.

None of them could have known that the moment they dropped anchor off Cape Cod in a new England they would set in train events which were to transform the United States and therefore the world.

A contract, something like the US Constitution, was drawn up on the ship; the foundations of a free economy were laid in New Plymouth; the destruction of the Native American population was set in train within fifty-five years of their landing. And that great symbol of US independence, the Thanksgiving Dinner, was held in the first October.

History does not confirm if they ate turkey or feasted on pumpkin.

THE AUTHOR

RICHARD HOLLEDGE is a journalist who worked for many UK newspapers: former assistant editor of *The Sunday Mirror*, editor of *Wales on Sunday*, assistant editor of *The Independent* and executive editor of the *Times of London*. He has freelanced for several newspapers including *The Wall Street Journal*, *New York Times*, *Financial Times*, *Daily Mail*, *The New European* and *Gulf News*. His books include *The Scattered*, an account of the ethnic cleansing of French-speaking people from Nova Scotia by the British; *Reverse Ferret*, a satire on the British press (under the witty pseudonym W.H. Boot); and *Life and Chimes*, a collection of football columns.

VOICES

OF THE

MAYFLOWER

THE SAINTS, STRANGERS AND SLY KNAVES WHO CHANGED THE WORLD

RICHARD HOLLEDGE

Matador
9 Priory Business Park,
Wistow Road, Kibworth Beauchamp,
Leicestershire, LE8 0RX
Tel: 0116 279 2299
Email: books@troubador.co.uk
Web: www.troubador.co.uk/matador
Twitter: @matadorbooks

ISBN 978 1838592 523

British Library Cataloguing in Publication Data.
A catalogue record for this book is available from the British Library.

Printed and bound in the UK by TJ International, Padstow, Cornwall
Typeset in 12pt Adobe Jenson Pro by Troubador Publishing Ltd, Leicester, UK

Matador is an imprint of Troubador Publishing Ltd

MIX
Paper from
responsible sources
FSC
www.fsc.org
FSC® C013056

My thanks to Jim and Peg Baker, Darius Coombs, Carolyn Cavele, Lea Sinclair Filson, Eldon Gay, Kristen Larson, Ginny Mucciaccio, Nigel Overton, Richard Pickering, and Susan E. Roser.

The Main Protagonists as They Appear in the Narrative

Book I

Scrooby, Nottinghamshire. William Bradford's story.

William Bradford, the troubled orphan who joins the Separatist movement.

Francyse Wright, the older boy who leads him astray.

William Brewster, lord of the manor, religious leader, mentor to Bradford. His wife Mary.

John Robinson, preacher and leading dissenter. Mary, his anxious maid.

Tobias Matthew, Archbishop of York.

Thomas Helwys, dashing religious leader. His wife Joan.

Richard Clyfton, charismatic preacher.

Book II
Leiden, Netherlands. William Brewster's story.

Myles Standish, former soldier and enthusiastic supporter of
   the cause.
Isaac Allerton, Leiden businessman who later cheats his comrades.
Edward Winslow, a printer. Later, a major player in Plymouth's
   fortunes.
Robert Cushman, hapless negotiator for the voyage.
John Carver, leading light in Leiden, the first governor of New
   Plymouth.
Edwin Sandys, treasurer of the Virginia Company.
Thomas Weston, deal maker.
Christopher Jones, skipper of the *Mayflower*.

Book III
On board the Mayflower. *Susanna White's story.*

The wife of William White who is widowed soon after the
   ship reaches New Plymouth and swiftly remarries – to
   Edward Winslow. She gives birth to the first child born
   in the colony.
Mary Allerton, wife of Isaac and mother of three. She dies
   soon after the still birth of her fourth child.
Stephen Hopkins, businessman and braggart.
The four orphaned More children.
Desire, John Carver's woebegone maid.
John Howland, Carver's servant.
John Alden, a cooper.
Clarke and Coppins, the *Mayflower's* first mates.

Book IV
Cape Cod. Squanto's story.

Tisquantum – or Squanto – a Native American, once
  kidnapped by the English who becomes the settlement's
  saviour.
Samoset, a tribal chieftain.
Massasoit, chief of the Wampanoag and ally to the English.
Hobbamock, a tribesman who settles in the Plantation.

Book V
New Plymouth. Edward Winslow's story.

James Sherley, London financier of the Merchant Adventurers.
Thomas Morton, mischief maker.
Thomas Billington, murderer.
Fear Brewster, daughter of William, unhappily married to
  Isaac Allerton.

Book VI
Up country. John Howland's story.

John Hocking, trespasser, murderer and victim.
John Winthrop, Governor of Boston and prime mover in
  Puritan settlement of the region.

NEW ENGLAND IN 1620

The Mayflower landed at the tip of Cape Cod - known today as Provincetown. Their expeditions to find a suitable settlement took place inside the curve of the Cape. They sailed across the Bay to Plymouth.

Merry Mount is just to the north of Wessagusset; Massasoit's camp in Sowans (Warren, Rhode Island) is north of Bristol.

The Pokanokets were the leaders of the tribes which included the Wampanoag.

Copyright: The Handbook of the North American Indian, Northeast, Bruce Trigger, ed. Washington DC: Smithsonian Institution, 1978.

Dates: The Gregorian calendar is used here - 13 days ahead of the Julian calendar which was used in the 17th century.

PROLOGUE

JUNE 1620

AN ARRANGEMENT IS MADE

Also Mr Thomas Weston, a merchant of London, came to Leiden about the same time, being well acquainted with some of them.

William Bradford, *Of Plymouth Plantation*.

"CAN WE TRUST HIM?"

"Well…" Winslow hesitated. "I am told he has wealthy friends."

"So I hear. But can we trust him?" repeated Robinson.

"Surely we can judge the p—p—probity of any man." Bradford chewed at his fingernails.

The three men sat on a bench on one side of the long table that faced the door. Robinson poked at the fire – more to fill the silence that had fallen between them than to revive the flames.

A knock. They paused for a second, as if reluctant to let the visitor in, but stood in clumsy unison as Mary the maidservant opened the door.

"Master Weston, welcome." Robinson shook the newcomer's hand.

"Thomas, please," he murmured, removing his cloak with a swirl and handing it to the girl without looking at her.

"You know William Bradford." Robinson introduced his

companions. "This is Edward Winslow."

"Gentlemen. A pleasure." His eyes were hard and alert but his handshake was softly perfunctory, reluctant to admit to any familiarity.

"Sit yourself down, Master Thomas," invited Bradford, a lean, priestly man of about thirty. "You must be weary after the journey."

Weston coughed as the smoke from the burning peat caught his throat. "The journey down the Rhine is always delightful and Leiden is a beautiful city. Beautiful."

"Mary, pour Master Weston a beer and get him a plate of herring," ordered Robinson.

He sat on one side of the table, his hosts on the other. An incongruous gathering: the newcomer with his carefully clipped beard and expensive linen, the others in their shabby fustian jackets, patched and made to last. They may eschew any show of vanity, but Weston knew that their humility veiled a core of belief so fierce that they had left the comfort of their English homes to establish a Church in a foreign country.

He had met Robinson – John Robinson, the group's pastor – and Winslow too when he had arranged the passage to England of some contentious religious tracts – a transaction imbued with righteousness for them; for him, a tidy profit. Nonetheless his hosts made him uneasy, particularly Robinson, who radiated a daunting moral certainty in the way he talked quietly and insistently, his dark eyes rarely leaving the person he was addressing.

Robinson came to the point. "I am informed you can help us."

"Tell me what you want to achieve and I shall endeavour to assist," replied Weston, as smooth as honey, smoothing his beard like it was the finest beaver.

"We must leave Leiden," interjected Bradford in an unexpectedly high voice. "This city is gripped with such an eruption of sin that our children are being led into bad habits. They live in danger to their souls."

Curious cove, thought Weston.

Robinson said, "Our future is elsewhere – Guyana, Bermuda, perhaps Virginia – it doesn't matter as long as it is a place where we are free to follow our faith."

So, reflected Weston, nodding in grave agreement and taking a mouthful of herring, *I can make the most of this. They want to go; I will supply the means.*

Robinson continued, "We are too poor to fund a voyage across the Atlantic. The Virginia Company in London has been granted a royal charter for us to settle in a new England, but now its leaders say they no longer have the capital to support us."

"The Company is bankrupt." Weston was blunt. "Bankrupt. They are no use to you, but I, my friends, I am." A stroke of the beard. "I know how business works, how deals are made. I have access to the most respected and wealthiest investors in the City of London."

He paused, his eye caught by the drawings on the tiles above the stove – a crude house with two chimneys, a stick-like child rolling a hoop and a ship cresting the waves.

"My friends." More honey. "My dear friends. I so admire the way you have left behind one home in the quest to live according to your beliefs, but this... to leave another..." He gestured at the etching of the house as if it was a symbol of their very existence. "This is remarkable. Here is what I suggest. I will effect an introduction to my affluent friends. They are known as the Merchant Adventurers and they have the money that the Virginia Company so sorely lacks. We – I mean you and they – can come to an arrangement that will suit both parties."

"What arrangement will that be?" asked Bradford. Suspicious.

"Details, details. To be sorted in good time. All you need to know is that they will supply whatever you need to build a new settlement, which, I suggest, should indeed be in Virginia. Quite the most suitable place for a new, unfettered life. This is where trade will flow, profits be made and their investment repaid. I hear the beavers are so tame that they wait by the riverside to be caught, and the fish leap into nets. The opportunities are incredible. Incredible."

"There is much to be done before we think of fishing," said Robinson dryly. And then, "Master Weston, can we trust you?"

Weston blinked at his forthrightness. He took a mouthful of beer, taking his time to muster the proper degree of sincerity.

"As the Lord is my witness," he intoned solemnly, "I swear that you can have every confidence that I will meet your ambitions."

"I am glad of it." Bradford got to his feet and shook the merchant's hand. "Though I fear it will be a desperate adventure."

"Rather, I say, hopeful," contradicted Weston.

"When can we expect to finalise arrangements with these Merchant Adventurers of yours?" asked Robinson.

"Soon, soon. The moment I get back to London," the businessman assured him. "One more thing – and I pray you will not find this forward of me – but I have made enquiries about a ship. You will need a ship, I imagine."

"You have found one already?" Robinson ignored the sarcasm.

"The opportunity arose," he retorted glibly. "Take my advice: do not encumber yourself with the expense and worry of buying a vessel. No, the solution is to hire one, and I have my eyes on a sweet craft which will fly across the ocean."

"Its name?" asked Bradford.

Weston put down his jug with an air of quiet complacency. "*Mayflower*," he declared. "The *Mayflower*."

BOOK I

1602–1608

THE VOICE OF WILLIAM BRADFORD

A GOSPEL OF SIMPLICITY

First I will unfold the causes that led to the foundation of the New Plymouth Settlement, and the motives of those concerned in it.

William Bradford, *Of Plymouth Plantation*.

CHAPTER ONE

SCORNED BUT SAVED

HE WOULD NOT DIE, DAMN THE MAN. His curses had been cut off in a ghastly gurgle when the bench was kicked away but still he clung to life. His mouth twisted as he gasped for air, his hands which he had torn from their bindings scrabbled at the sky in a parody of prayer until his son leapt from the hushed crowd. He tugged at his twitching legs as if he was pulling an unborn calf from its mother. A click of the neck.

The blank eyes of the hanged man stared up to a heaven he did not deserve to reach before his head slumped onto his chest. Spittle and snot frothed with blood and coursed down his chin.

Standish rasped, "Good riddance," and thumped the butt of his musket on the ground in grim celebration.

Yes, good riddance. John Billington had poured scorn on our dream of a home for true believers from the moment he stepped on board the *Mayflower* ten years before. Always the

3

troublemaker. Blasphemy, theft, slander, I expected that of him... but murder? It was hard to believe that even he had committed so heinous a crime.

He claimed it had been a hunting accident, but witnesses insisted that he had argued with his neighbour, sought him out and blasted him with his blunderbuss.

Billington laughed when the council brought him to trial. He taunted us that we did not have the authority and he boasted that he was too valuable working in the fields to be punished with more than a whipping or a spell in the stocks. The arrogance of the man. The foolishness.

His blusterousness turned to whimpering pleas as I reached for my quill and scratched the death warrant.

Billington's family wanted to cut down his body and take it away but I ruled, "Leave him there. No one must forget that he was a wretch who brought shame on our community."

His wife, usually as profane a woman as one could meet, called on God to soften my heart and the son abused me for my lack of pity. I ignored them. There could be no mercy.

Later though, when I was walking by the shore, the waves ruffled by the evening wind, I found myself reflecting on the execution. Had I done God's will?

Surely I had. The execution was more than retribution for one crime; his deed mocked the deaths of those who had perished in the weeks after we landed. Almost fifty of us were lost, about half our number. My wife too, her body never found.

Nonetheless, standing by the shore on that cloudless September day, I was gripped with foreboding. Maybe this murder – and the punishment I had put my name to – was a presentiment that our dream of an Eden where all lived in fellowship and love of God was coming to an end. Maybe now, because I had condemned a man to death, He would banish us to a life of relentless toil.

For just a second the ghost of my fractured childhood, with all its insecurity and pain, hovered over me and I resolved to write an account of my life and the brave endeavours of my comrades to ensure that the generations would know the truth of our desperate adventure.

I know the villagers said I was odd. Always reading the Bible, they scoffed. Always sick. No friends.

Maybe they were right but, until the autumn morning when Mother called me and my sister Alice in from the yard, I had been as happy and untroubled as any other four-year-old. Not odd at all.

She stood us side by side in front of her, the way we lined up to take Communion. "Children, I have something to tell you." She bit her lip and smoothed her petticoats awkwardly. "I am getting married again."

Alice held my hand so tightly that her nails dug into my palm.

"To Mr Briggs," Mother added, almost as an afterthought.

We stood in stricken silence. All I had known was the three of us living contentedly together on the farm, but now Mother was to belong to someone else.

How could that be? Why should a stranger be allowed to share my happy life?

I was barely one year old when Father was taken by the plague. "He was a yeoman," Mother would tell me proudly. "He left you land." But he wasn't as much as a shadow to me. I felt no loss. No, my life was blessed. When Alice and I weren't playing nine pins together or rolling our hoops, I chased the geese around the yard to Mother's feigned annoyance and flew my kite. We had created our own private fiefdom. We did not need the company of other children; we had Mother and the women who called by her small store in a comforting eddy of gossip and spoiled us with gingerbread biscuits.

But now that small, familiar world was to be torn apart.

This Briggs, this Robert Briggs, how would he fit into my life?

I found out soon enough. I was the one for whom there was no place. I was to be sent away.

"You will live with Grandfather," said Mother. "He is fond of you and will look after you well."

Fond? Apart from a tap on the head when he came calling, he had never shown any interest in me. I could not understand this rejection, by my mother of all people, the one I loved more than any. I wept, I stormed, but she would not, could not, change her mind. Maybe if I had not been so caught up with my own wretchedness I would have realised that she was as distraught as I was.

My stomach ached with the dread of my expulsion. I had never been anxious about anything until that moment but now I was wheezing with anxiety and my breathing was so tortured I was sure my chest would burst. I slunk off to hide in the barn and whimpered like a whipped dog, biting my nails and praying I would be spared my exile.

A forlorn hope. A cart came next day and we stood – me, Mother and Alice – in the yard. The racket of the farm – the hens, the pigs, the lowing of the cattle – seemed louder than usual, but we were silent, disconcerted by the awkwardness of parting.

Mother looked past me to where Briggs lurked by the gate. He stared through me with a faint sneer, of, yes, triumph. He was not the kind of man who would relent and allow me to stay in what was now *his* family.

"God bless you, son." Her smile was taut with misery as the carter threw my trunk onto the pile of beet he was carrying.

"Grandfather has plenty of room in the manor and it's not far away. You will be happy enough there." Her face contorted in ugly contradiction of her own words.

The cart trundled out of the yard and down the track. I looked back to see Mother holding her apron to her face. Alice gave a little wave, we rounded the corner and they were gone.

To my surprise the old man was waiting for me. He welcomed me with an awkward arm around my shoulders. "Come in, come in, my boy. Dry those tears. I have barley sugar for you."

I had assumed that he would dismiss me to the servants' quarters and have little to do with me. After all, he was sixty years old at least and had lived alone for ages, so he would be set in his ways. What would he want with a needy child? But no, he made me feel at home by kicking the dogs off the settle so I had somewhere to sit and whistled up a brew to warm me.

He let me have a room to myself in the attic and as we got to know each other he encouraged me to join in with life on the estate, feeding the chickens and mucking out the byres.

But that was nothing to the joy I discovered when he sat me down by the fire at the end of the day, picked up his threadbare Bible and painstakingly read to me, tracing the words with fingernails still grimy from the farmyard and translating from the Latin as he went.

How strange it would have seemed, had anyone peered through the manor window, to see this earnest child and elderly gentleman lit by capricious candlelight as we pored over the Bible. What tales unfolded, what adventures we shared: city walls that fell at the blast of trumpets, a sea that divided at the stamp of a staff, a prophet swallowed by a whale... I could never hear enough of these tumultuous sagas.

"Now," he would say, winking from underneath lowering eyebrows, "now for Master Foxe." And he would reach for our favourite book, which recounted the agonies of the Protestant martyrs persecuted by Catholic Queen Mary a century before.

The book's grisly accounts of hangings, burnings and crucifixions horrified and, I confess, thrilled me, but, more, filled my head with both a dread and contempt of popery that never left me.

We had been reading about a priest whose right hand had been cut off, blood spurting in crimson gouts before he was tied by the other arm to the stake. The lower part of his body was burnt to a horrible mess of singed flesh and bone but inexplicably – and just as ghastly – the rest of him remained untouched. At the end, as he finally surrendered, onlookers saw his tongue moving as he cried out, "O thou son of God, receive my soul."

I was haunted by burning bodies that night. Disembodied tongues that shrieked warnings of damnation, a devil brandishing a blazing ember who became transformed into an angry, snarling, Briggs. I woke with a scream, convinced that flames were licking at my feet, and even the realisation that it was only the early shaft of sun streaming through the window did nothing to calm me. I wrapped myself in a blanket and went quietly downstairs. The old man was still sat by the fading embers of the fire where he had dozed off the night before and I was eager to tell him about my dream, but as I went to wake him I saw that the Bible had slipped from his hands. His lifeless hands.

For several minutes I sat in baffled silence. I did not know what to do or what to feel. I was trembling with grief. But I was angry too. Why had such a good man been taken from me? And I was resentful. Why me? Why should I be left to suffer? I could not help such selfishness.

Maybe he would wake up and demand his morning bread and ale before stomping off into the yard as usual.

No. He had gone.

I picked up the Bible with shaking hands and the pages fell open at Saint John's gospel: 'In the beginning was the Word, and the Word was with God, and the Word was God.' I could hear Grandfather's voice: "You will be faced with many obstacles in life, my boy, but if you follow God's word you will overcome them."

Still I sat in silent anguish until laughter from the maids in the kitchen started me back to cold reality.

"Grandfather," I whispered. I was scared I might disturb him. I mustered my courage and cried out, "It's Grandfather. Help."

"Such a fine man," they exclaimed as they busied around his body. "Poor boy," they clucked as they banished me upstairs to let me struggle with my loss without getting in their way.

All day I stayed hidden in my attic trying to shut out the sound of the church bell as it rang out to signal the death of a parishioner. I watched from the window as the carpenter called to measure him for the coffin and the vicar came to pray for his soul.

I had been under his roof for only two years, a time of security and warmth that had taught me all I knew, but now… now what? Who could I turn to for comfort?

I was not given the time to languish in my misery. His body was still laid out in the hall waiting to be taken to the graveyard when Mother rattled up in the cart to take me away.

For a while I was happy. Happy enough. Master Briggs ignored me with a baleful indifference, but sister Alice was her sweet self. And whenever Mother saw me succumbing to sadness, she would spoil me with sugared almonds and jelly and, a rare treat, marzipan shaped like castles and animals.

But death came calling once more. A year after we buried Grandfather, it was Mother who was taken from us, giving birth to a boy. Her body was scarcely in the grave, our tears were still streaming, when Briggs declared that Alice and I were "nowt but a botheration, a pesky botheration" and "nowt to do with me". He sent us to live with my uncles, Thomas and Robert, both remote figures who were as hostile to us as Briggs had been.

"Two more mouths to feed," grumbled Robert, glowering at us as if we were a pair of sheep ticks. "I've got enough to fret about." From Thomas, not a word.

I was bewildered by a world that could cheat me of my mother's love and grandfather's tetchy tenderness and instead inflict on me the selfish indifference of Briggs and the uncles. They were from the same mould: coarse men, rustily dressed, who neither asked for nor expected any kind of closeness. It was only later that I came to understand that the three of them were gripped by the cheerlessness of an existence in which the only respite from the grind of hard labour was getting drunk at the tavern once a week and seeking redemption in the church on Sundays.

Life with the uncles taught me a painful truth: that to rely on anyone was the way to disappointment. It was a lesson I never forgot.

CHAPTER TWO

FRIEND AND PROTECTOR

I CREPT INTO MY SHELL, SEEKING CONSOLATION in the Bible, reliving the adventures I had shared with Grandfather and trying to understand the word of God, as he had encouraged.

I wanted nothing to do with the lads of my age, who spent their spare time catching eels or setting traps for rabbits – and even if I had been tempted by such childish pursuits, I was stricken by an illness so crippling that I took to my bed for weeks on end. It started with a headache, then a cough which tore at my innards. Soon I was racked by cramps that made the bones in my body burn and my brain reel from pains as sharp as if I was being jabbed by woolsack needles.

Uncle Robert dismissed me as a lazy lolloper and though Alice did care, nursing me with bowls of pottage and easing my headaches with the bitter leaves of feverfew, she was kept busy doing woman's work around the farm. If I am honest, it suited me to be struck down. That way I could hide away from scornful eyes and spend the day studying without being asked to do this or told to do that.

On the few occasions I felt well enough there would be lessons at the Dame school, which was run by the local women. They could teach knitting and weaving well enough but knew so little of Latin and Greek that I could not help myself from correcting their mistakes.

"That will have endeared you," commented Alice tartly.

I should have bitten my tongue, I knew that. Instead, my cleverness irritated the teachers and riled my fellow pupils. After all, none of them could read or write or saw the need for it. What was the point? Did Latin help plough a straighter furrow or Greek shear a lamb more closely? Not one jot.

Most days after school I would be surrounded by the village gang, eager to bring me down a peg or two with such japes as tripping me up so that I fell into a pile of cow dung or making me hop as stones from their catapults rained around my feet. Insults. Well, they were the least of it.

One day, like any other, I was greeted with the familiar chorus: "Look who's here. Bradford, the pious prig."

I had to duck as a stone whistled past my head.

"Milksop."

I stood, abjectly waiting for the torment to end.

"Don't worry, young Bradford." One of them patted me on the back. I flinched but he continued, "We've decided to treat you. I got my mother to make this stew."

"Thank you." I knew it was a trick but I was so desperate for any kindness that I ignored the sniggers.

He thrust the bowl and a spoon at me. It was a dirt pie. Crusts of cow shit floated on the surface.

"Eat, eat, eat," they chanted.

Gagging, I threw the bowl to the ground.

"You ingrate, Bradford," sneered one. "After all that trouble my mother went to."

"Let's give him a taste of knuckle pie instead."

They yelped with vicious glee and gathered around me in a menacing circle.

My legs were buckling with fear, my mouth was dry and the cough came spluttering back. I was about to collapse when a shout from Long Meadow made them pull back. "Leave 'im alone, you clotpoles."

It was Francyse Wright. He ran across the field, vaulted over the wall and pushed them apart.

"Shog off, you lot. Come on, Bradford."

He bundled me to the church porch and took me by the shoulders to calm me down. A balloon of snot popped from my nose and I wiped it with my sleeve.

My persecutors stood open-mouthed. Francyse Wright, the most popular boy in the village, the leader of my tormentors, the Achilles who carried all before him by force of his muscles and charisma was standing by my side. Not only that, but he was protecting me from his own gang. But why?

Our paths rarely crossed. He worked in his father's fields by day and spent his spare time fishing and snaring rabbits. He was two years older than me but he looked much older, with a lively, quick face, and a mop of black hair always topped with a jaunty red cap. He was a bad lad, everyone knew that, who spent many hours carousing in the tavern.

We could hardly be more different.

"You dropped this." He handed me a book. "Fell out of your knapsack."

"Th-th-thank you." I was reeling at his presence.

"What's it about?" he demanded.

"Sermons." I expected him to mock me or tear it from my fingers and throw it onto the dung heap.

He fingered it thoughtfully, peered uncomprehendingly at the words.

"Where d'you get it?" he asked. "I hadn't had your uncles as learnin' men."

"A gentleman called William B—B—Brewster came to the Dame school today and asked if anyone could read Latin or G—G—Greek, and after I read a chapter to him he gave it to me. Sort of a prize."

"Why was he there?"

"He came to talk to the headmistress."

"What did he say?"

The interrogation was making me nervous. "I d—d—don't know."

"Probably nothing," he muttered. "I know Brewster, proper gent. Lord of the manor in Scrooby. Worth knowing." He picked up the volume again and thumbed clumsily through the pages, tearing a few as he went.

He shot me a look that was somewhere between cunning and embarrassed. "I know folk mock you for your reading and that, but that's 'cos they're scared you know too much and might make fools of them. I never bothered to learn to read, but I want to. I want to be clever. Like you."

Like me? I could not believe what I was hearing.

"So here's what we'll do. I'll look after you, keep those idiots off your back, and you can teach me to read and… you know, understand stuff."

The next evening, he was by my side struggling with Matthew's Gospel. "*In principio erat verbum*," he managed. 'In the beginning was the word.' He was amazed that there were different tongues that could be translated to make sense in ours.

For a while he was a model student, attentive and eager, surprisingly humble at my superior knowledge, but after a month he missed a lesson, and then another. I plunged into my familiar abyss of self-doubt, only for him to return a few days later with a clap around the shoulders and a litany of excuses: "Sorry but the beet had to be brought in... my old man doesn't approve of all this learnin'... we had a leaking roof..."

Alice loathed him. "He's a braggart," she spat. "I don't know what his game is, but I do know he is too fond of himself to care about anyone else. Just beware."

My misgivings deepened everytime I saw him back with his old gang, and like a pathetic cur starved of its owner's affection I slunk along behind them and watched them going into the tavern on the Great Road. I peered through the window and there was my pupil, mug of ale in hand, surrounded by his laughing acolytes, regaling them with jokes. Mocking me, perhaps. I was in despair that he had deserted me for his real friends and had returned to his bad old ways. But more, I was mortified by the way I had demeaned myself.

But he did come back – keener than before, he insisted – flattering me on my brilliance, and once again I was disarmed. But not for long. Once again, I found myself checking up on him in the tavern, drawn by my insecurity but more, by my jealousy of the effortless way he gathered friends around him; young women too, giggling and flirting. To my self-disgust I was enticed by the scent of sin, but reduced to a tumult of baffled emotion at the tangles of lust that played out before my eyes.

Weeping with confusion, I would creep home and read about Christ's temptations to clear my mind and steer me away from this wickedness. 'Watch and pray so that you will not fall into temptation,' wrote Matthew in his gospel. 'The spirit is willing, but the flesh is weak.'

My shame was that my spirit was not strong enough, and my body was afflicted with fiercer aches and fevers than before. A judgement on me, I knew.

CHAPTER THREE

SPARKLES OF AFFECTION

SOMETIMES WHEN THE WEATHER WAS WARM and I was feeling strong enough, I would take a few faltering steps from the house to the churchyard, where I sat on the low limestone wall and read.

"It's such a lovely view," said Alice, pleased that I was getting out of the house and into the sunshine. "Look at the way the fields seem to stretch forever to the wolds. Do you ever wonder what lies beyond?"

But no, I did not. All I saw was the straggle of stone and timber homes of our village, Austerfield, which was marooned on the borders of Nottinghamshire and Lincolnshire – both flat, inconsequential corners of the realm. Through it ran the River Idle, which lived up to its name by dawdling its way to the River Trent and out to sea and faraway places that I would never visit.

There were about 120 folk living there, many whose roots went back for generations, united by their refusal to be cowed by the poverty and the meanness of their surroundings and oblivious to the permanent haze of smoke that wafted through the thatched roofs and seeped into their lungs. They no longer questioned, if they ever did, the beggarliness of their smallholdings, where pigs and chickens rootled away amid the clutter of ploughs, rakes and hoes.

We all knew our place: the noble in his vast estates who owed his pre-eminence to the king, the landlord with his manor, the yeoman with a few acres and, at the bottom, the destitute workers who lived from day to day, from scrap to scrap. Above everyone, the firm hand of the Church, presided over by the bishops and the monarch.

If anyone strayed from their diktats, punishment was swift: a whipping, a turn in the stocks or a dousing in the river at the end of a cucking stool.

Only the witch who lived in a cave of branches and moss in King's Wood refused to accept the order of things. A filthy, untamed creature, she was an object of fun and trepidation for the village children, who claimed to have seen her write the Lord's Prayer on a piece of cheese and feed it to mad dogs to cure them of rabies.

I admit that I was so eager to curry favour with my new champion that I joined Francyse and the gang when they crept up on her, shouting obscenities and throwing sticks at her before running for our lives.

I was not proud of myself. I resolved to tear myself away from the older boy's influence, resist the lure of the tavern and its shameful mysteries, and instead work all the harder at my studies.

Inevitably, my resolve was swiftly broken. One bright morning in April, I was perched on my familiar spot on the church wall when a hollering jolted me from my studies. It was Francyse.

"The King. The new King. He's on the Great Road. Come on, don't waste time with a stupid book." Then, in case he unsettled the ghosts of the recently grieved or the long forgotten, he lowered his voice. "King James, he's riding past on his way to be crowned in London. Oliver the tanner has come that way and says hundreds of people have gathered to greet him. There are lords, ladies, all sorts. And maids, lots of maids. Quick."

Before I could insist that my reading was more important than waving at the King, let alone lords and ladies, he had dragged me to my feet and half-pushed, half-carried me across High Common and through the undergrowth of the woods, toward Bawtry and the road that led to the capital.

Too late. All that we could see of the entourage were the backsides of the baggage men pushing overloaded carts out of the ruts where they had become stuck.

"They'll be going to Scrooby, to the manor." Francyse grabbed me by the arm. "We can take a ride on one of the carts."

We arrived as the manor door opened to reveal a tall, broad-shouldered figure with a strangely orange beard. His Majesty, King James the First of England, the Sixth of Scotland, no less. And alongside him, William Brewster, the man who had given me the book at the Dame school.

The crowd bowed and gave a ragged cheer.

What a strange fellow, I thought. Was this really our lord and master? I had to strain to hear what he was saying because, as well as his jarring accent – Scotch, reckoned Francyse – he chewed his words as if his tongue was too large for his mouth.

"My people," he declaimed. "Since my journey south started, the people of all sorts have ridden and run – nay, rather flown – to meet me, their eyes flaming nothing but sparkles of affection."

He took a draught of wine but it dribbled out of each side of his mouth.

"They utter nothing but sounds of joy, discovering a passionate longing and earnestness to meet and embrace their new sovereign."

We cheered dutifully. He wrapped his cloak around himself, snapped his fingers for his carriage and was gone. A brief glimpse of heaven-sent glory, despite his stumbling manner and curious speech, and one never likely to touch my life again.

"Let's say hello to Master Brewster," suggested Francyse.

I gulped nervously. He was the daunting figure who had entertained the King, no less – surely he would not remember me, and if he did, why would he want to talk to us?

"'Course he will." Nothing deterred my companion. "He's over there talking to those two gents."

They were obviously part of the royal entourage and I hung back awkwardly until Master Brewster caught sight of us.

"Master Bradford, so pleased to see you," he called out. "And you too… er, Master Wright. Come and join us."

Goodness, he did remember me.

One of the entourage, a man of the cloth, glared at me suspiciously.

"Aha, are these youngsters your new disciples, Master Brewster? I trust you are guiding them in the way of the true church, the King's Church."

The second man laughed knowingly. He was a slight figure with disconcerting bulbous eyes who, judging by his linen shirt and cape, was a gentleman, despite the mud that spattered his breeches and boots. "We cannot be too careful with so many damned dissenters around." He downed his cider. "His Majesty owns land near here and I have to make sure all is in order."

"If I can help in any way do let me know." Master Brewster was all easy charm. "We have been honoured to salute our new monarch. We have high hopes of him." He signalled to the valets to bring up their horses. "As for you, my friends, you must hurry to catch up with him. Have a safe journey. Keep us posted with news from London."

"Who were they?" I asked once the two men had galloped away over the ridge.

"The gentleman was Edwin Sandys, whose father was Archbishop of York until his death five or six years ago. Soon to be made a knight, I hear. The other is Tobias Matthew, the Bishop of Durham, and one who has made it his business to keep in with the King. No friend of ours, I suspect."

CHAPTER FOUR

ABOMINABLE CARCASSES

W HAT DID HE MEAN, HE WAS NO FRIEND OF ours? Before I could pluck up the courage to ask, Brewster slapped me on the back. "You look fair clemmed, young Bradford. Come inside, we have plenty of mutton and capers left over."

Once we had polished off our food, he fetched a pile of books from his library. "You are obviously a lad who enjoys reading; here are some sermons and a work by the King himself. They will help you understand that he believes the Church is his to do with as he wishes but that there are many of us in this very county who would rather put our trust in the scriptures. That's where we find the word of God, not with the fiddle-faddle of the bishops who think they know better than our Lord. As you may imagine, it brings us into conflict with the Church and no mistake."

He paused, realising he had been too forceful about a subject that meant nothing to me, and sighed. "The King thinks those who share our convictions that the truth is in the Bible are fanatics. He does not mince his words; he says that we are pests, rash and brainsick."

I was taken aback at such language. "And from a man who can barely string a sentence together."

"Don't be misled." Brewster parcelled up the books. "His convictions are as strong as ours and he has the power to enforce them. Here's an idea. If you get permission from your uncles, why not come with us next Sunday to Babworth? There is a preacher there by name of Richard Clyfton who is possessed by such fervour that he will send your soul soaring to heaven."

"I cannot." How inadequate I felt rejecting such a well-meant offer. "Babworth is twelve miles from Austerfield and I am too sick to walk that far."

But Francyse declared, "We must go. I will borrow Father's cart."

When she heard what I intended to do, Alice begged me to stay at home resting while Uncle Robert, who despite his curmudgeonly behaviour was, improbably, a churchwarden, threatened me with the fires of damnation. The vicar of my church, St Helena's, the amiable but ineffectual Reverend Fletcher, murmured something about the dangers of mixing with 'fantastical schismatics', but he did not explain what those perils might be.

In truth, I could hardly believe that I of all people could even consider leaving my place in the pew empty. I had been praying there since my baptism twelve years before and the church had always been at the core of my life, but come dawn the following Sunday, I had plucked up my courage and waited in the rain to ride to Babworth.

"Where is the cart?" I asked when Francyse arrived without as much as a barrow.

"The wheel's come off. Can't be helped."

Alice's reproach turned to anger. "You cannot go. You can hardly breathe now, just think how you will suffer in weather like this. Don't think I am going to spend next week nursing you again. Look at the state of him." She rounded on Francyse. "The boy is so poorly he can barely stand."

"Don't you worry, you lovely lady, you." He pushed back his cap and leered at her. "All this mollycoddling ain't good for him."

She flushed at his familiarity but before she could stop us, he pulled my arm around his shoulders and we set off. Five hours it took, stumbling across the meadows and through the woods until, soaked and breathless, chests heaving and legs like wool, we reached the church at Babworth.

I saw his father trundling past on the cart, laden down with beet.

"He must have fixed it." The youth spoke rather too quickly. "Anyway, we're here now."

The moment Clyfton began to speak, I forgot my aches and pains. A slight figure with a beard as long as those of the Old Testament prophets of my imagination, the preacher did not climb into the pulpit to talk down at us or wear a surplice like the Reverend Fletcher, but stood in the aisle and spoke, calmly at first, his voice rising with an intensity that was intimidating.

He attacked the folly of the clergy who wanted to stifle the truths of the gospel because they had been driven by Satanic forces to indulge in 'vile ceremonies and vain canons and decrees'.

Vain? Vile? Did he mean dull, dutiful Fletcher?

"For it is the conscience and not the power of man that will drive us to seek the Lord's kingdom," he declaimed. He stared hard at the roof of the church, looking beyond to the heavens, and lowered his voice so that we in his small audience had to strain to hear. "Anyone who dares to usurp the authority of Jesus Christ shall be brought down to the dust as abominable carcasses."

Abominable carcasses. For weeks I was haunted by images of worms wriggling through the eye sockets of ghastly, grinning skulls, but more, much more, I was possessed by a dizzying truth that was both compelling and dangerous.

I was still reeling from the sermon, if such a tirade could be dubbed as such, when I joined Master Brewster outside talking to a handsome woman in her thirties, lightly freckled, bright-eyed and friendly.

"My wife Mary." Brewster introduced me. "I am glad you were able to come. You too, Master Wright."

My protector was enthusiastic, perhaps too much so. "What words, Master Brewster. What inspiration."

I think Brewster expected me to chime in with similar ardour, but before I could open my mouth Francyse continued. "Bradford and I are reading the gospels and those books you gave him. Very interestin'. Life changin'."

"That's admirable," declared Brewster. He flickered an eyebrow at his wife so slightly I almost missed it.

I collected my thoughts enough to say, "I had not realised how corrupt the Church has become and how far it has strayed from the truth. All I have to judge by is the Reverend Fletcher, who I have never deemed a bad man."

"No, he is not a bad man, not at all," interrupted Brewster. "But the simple facts that he uses the Book of Common Prayer for his guidance and that he dresses up in such fripperies as a cap and surplice means that he is standing between you and your god. Despite his innocence he has fallen foul of those Satanic forces Master Clyfton warned us about."

Alice was waiting for me when I finally limped home. She was a generous soul, more likely to smile than to frown, but not that day. She had found the books that Brewster had given me and was in a fury of indignation.

"This man claims that children should not be confirmed because they cannot answer questions about the Bible and do not understand what is being taught them. And here." She jabbed at an offending paragraph. "The sign of the cross is meaningless, akin to popery rearing its blasphemous head again."

She dropped the book as though it was the apple from the Garden of Eden. "You must take it back to Master Brewster and never see him again, or I shall tell the Reverend Fletcher."

"But these works are so inspiring," I insisted. "If you had heard the sermon that I have just been listening to you would have no doubt."

"Inspiring? Pah." She pushed the hair out of her face, where it had become loosened during her outburst. "No doubt? Fiddlesticks. I shudder for your soul, William, I really do. You're twelve years old, old enough to decide what kind of person you want to be; will it be a follower of the most despicable person in the village, a reprobate who skulks around as hungry for mischief as a starved dog sniffing out his next bone, or will you abase yourself as the disciple of an old man who preaches the destruction of the Church that we know and love? I will tell you what to choose; go to church – the King's Church – take your communion and obey the commandments. I need no more and nor should you."

If only it was that easy. Thanks to Grandfather and now Master Brewster, my passion for the scriptures and learning burned as fiercely as the bush that the Lord kindled to inspire Moses.

But Alice was right about one thing. I was torn. What

Francyse offered was a world of friendship which kept me from falling deeper into the kind of lonely despair that had embraced me so completely before. Loneliness like that cannot be cured when it grips you; not even a musket blast can shake you out of it. So yes, I was divided between my compulsion to embrace the scriptures and be a worthy Christian and a world of feckless daring, which I battled to suppress but which excited me strangely.

There was something else. I hoped that if my teaching made Francyse a better person, it would redound to my credit. Vanity, I know. I should have heeded Saint Paul's letter to the Galatians: 'Brothers and sisters, if someone is caught in a sin, you who live by the Spirit should restore that person gently. But watch yourselves, or you also may be tempted.'

CHAPTER FIVE

VANITIES OF YOUTH

I SPENT EVERY SUNDAY REVELLING IN MASTER Clyfton's sermons and later, after walking across the fields, would stay at the manor, partly to recover my strength but mainly to discuss what we had just heard.

Francyse often joined me and I was surprised to see how eager he was to impress Master Brewster. He talked a little too fast and quoted pieces from the scriptures, pretending he had known them all his life but which I had taught him the day before. It was, to be honest, embarrassing.

Brewster made no comment, merely smiled and made encouraging noises about the importance of study, but the moment Francyse left Brewster would take me off to the library, where shelf after shelf bowed under the weight of books.

"My grandfather would have loved this." I felt the leather bindings with a reverence that was almost religious. "He had only the one battered Bible and a handful of books with lettering so faded we could hardly make out the words, but somehow he opened my eyes to a world that most boys cannot imagine."

"I met him once or twice," recalled Brewster. "A good soul. He would be proud of you. It seems he turned your years of loneliness into a time of learning and now, I reckon, you are one of the wisest youngsters in the county. You know, your years of sickness may well turn out to be a blessing."

"A blessing? It hardly feels that way."

"They have kept you from the vanities of youth," he continued. "No idling, no unholy behaviour. God made you suffer so that you could become a better person. Yes, a blessing."

He was diverted by one of his farriers, who I assumed was concerned about a horse that had shed a shoe or needed a cure for colic.

"How long have you been friendly with Francyse Wright?" he asked once the farrier had left.

"Only a few months. He has protected me from the bullies and in return I try to teach him Latin and Greek." I blushed. "I am grateful to him."

"Of course, but be careful," warned Brewster. "He does seem eager to learn but believe me, I have seen many a young person start out full of good intentions only to be deflected by other temptations."

Was he talking about me? Had he heard of my nights loitering around the tavern?

"You are bright." He smiled reassuringly. "Too sensible to be drawn from the right way. But may I suggest you spend more time with us? I can help you with your learning better than the Dame school and, more important, we enjoy your company."

I was made so welcome that within days I felt I was one of the family. Mary reminded me of Mother, the way she worried about my health, and fed me up on bowls of pottage full of vegetables and mutton; while their son, ten-year-old Jonathan, and his younger sister Patience treated me like an older, if slightly eccentric, brother.

"I don't know why you don't move in permanently," suggested Jonathan impulsively. "You're almost one of the family."

"Indeed you are," laughed his father.

First I had to tell Alice, who wept a little and stormed more. Uncle Robert shrugged. I braced myself for an outburst from Francyse when I stammered out the news on one of our walks to Babworth. Instead, he stared at me pityingly.

"What do you mean? How will you survive without me? Who will keep the lads at bay when they hear the news?"

"I shall be safe in the m—m—manor."

"Don't be so sure." He cocked his head to one side as if sizing up a sheep for market. "Why do you think I bothered with you?"

"B—b—because I could help you with your learning."

He sneered contemptuously. "Help me? You were just a game as far as I was concerned. But don't forget this." He pushed his face so close his chin scratched mine. "You would never have heard of Richard Clyfton or met Master Brewster if I hadn't pushed you into their company."

It wasn't true but he made me feel guilty, as though I was betraying him. For a second I was tempted to change my mind and stay under his protection.

"But, you know, Bradford, I don't care." He had not finished with me. "You are all hypocrites – you, that puffed up phoney Brewster, every one of you – all wrapped up in a parcel of self-righteous humbug."

"It's not like that," I protested. "They are good people who want the b—b—best for me – and for you."

"Good? They are anti-Christs and traitors. I find more honest folk in the tavern – real people, not those prattling gabblers in the manor who you think are so clever."

I was seeing the second person, the dangerous one who lurked behind the devil-go-hang eyes.

He leered at me. "There's some frothy maids in the tavern these days. That Maggie Idle, have you seen her recently? Quite growed up, if you know what I mean. And Janne Ryall. Now that's a wench."

I did not see him for a few weeks after our confrontation – in fact, not until the very day I left Austerfield for my new home – when I came across him in the lower meadow with the Ryall girl. She was sitting on a fallen tree trunk watching him saw firewood. Despite the chill of the day he was sweating; his shirt had come out of the top of his breeches to reveal a muscular stomach. As for the girl, her kerchief was askew, showing the upper swell of her chest, and her skirts were hitched to display more of a woman's leg than I had ever seen. The two of them together in such reckless closeness disquieted me, but she shocked me the most, flaunting herself next to a half-dressed man. He kept his eyes on me as he ran a hand up her leg and I shivered with shame at the way I felt so agitated.

The world of men and women was a mystery to me, so dark, stirring and discomfiting. Once I caught Alice in her shift and was so abashed I could not look at her for a week. Being Alice, she had just laughed.

"What are you staring at?" Janne taunted me.

"I d—d—don't think you should behave like that. Not in p—p—public for all to see. Not even if you were w—w—wed."

"I don't hear you stammering when you're in company

with the Helwys woman,' sneered Francyse.

"M—M—Mistress Joan?"

"The very one. The bedswerver." He took a swing with his axe, splitting a log as if stunning a sheep for slaughter. Is that what he would do to those who crossed him? "She and Master Thomas are not married; no priest has blessed their union. They've been summoned at least twice by the bishop's court for their lawless strumming."

Thomas and Joan Helwys were close friends of the Brewsters and regular visitors to the manor. He was a dashing fellow, clearly of some wealth, judging by his jerkins of soft leather, fashionably cut capes and fresh linen. When I first met him I considered him rather too worldly to be serious, especially as he spoke his mind with alarming frankness and peppered his language with oaths, but I soon realised he was a man of deep faith who led a group of like-minded believers in Gainsborough, twenty miles distant. He was as passionate about reforming the Church as any of us in Scrooby and Joan was a spirit as dauntless as he, though I have to confess her boldness made me nervous. I was speechless to hear of such scandalous behaviour.

Her accuser smirked. "She's like the filly Father owns. They both need a stallion to tame 'em."

"All us lasses love a bit of taming." Janne licked her lips in a deliberately crude manner that made me feel faint with confusion. I could think of nothing to say and made to leave but Francyse blocked my way. He had not finished with me.

"You think you're so clever but look at your tattered jerkin, those boots… you've as many holes in them as I have. You're really just another village lad – just more pathetic because you have deluded yourself that you are better than the rest of us. Don't you know that's why all the neighbours scoff at you, you prig? Get off to your books and prayers with those creepy old men and shameless women. You'll come running back to me."

"While you're prayin' we'll be at the cock fighting in the tavern." The girl hitched her skirts higher up her legs and taunted. "Too exciting for a pansy like you. There'll be dancing too – a hop merchant is coming up from Doncaster."

"Preparing for life after death is one thing," jeered Francyse. "But what about life itself? It's for living."

I was sick to the stomach. How could I have been deluded by such falseness? I turned my back on the pair and trudged along the river bank to Scrooby.

Brewster saw I was troubled and put his arm around my shoulders.

"From what you are telling me, Master Wright has been too easily deflected from God's purpose by this maid and chosen instead a life of sin. I am disappointed; I hoped he would change his ways and be as faithful as you, Will. Put him behind you. He was desperate to be part of our household, always pestering me for work because his family farm has fallen into decay. Hardly surprising – the father is a drunken sot."

I admitted nothing about the way I too had craved Francyse's goodwill or how I had fooled myself that by my teaching he might become a God-fearing citizen.

Brewster seemed to divine my feelings. "I should not tell you this, but one of my duties as lord of the manor is to solve disputes between neighbours. Your sometime friend was accused of stealing from the farm of the Dame school's headmistress."

"So that is why you were there?"

"Indeed. A happy chance, otherwise you and I would not have met. He ransacked their stables of hoof nippers and clinchers, as well as a clutch of knives. We know that because he tried to sell them to my farrier. Not very bright, our Master Wright. We let him off with a warning because he insisted he had mended his ways and boasted that you and he were studying the Bible together. He reckoned if he was friendly with a clever, respectable lad like you, he would stand a better chance of being acquitted. I am afraid he was using you."

He paused, shot me a knowing glance. "To your credit, you stayed true to yourself while he returned back to his bad old ways. In the Bible he would be damned as a profane and wicked apostate – harsh, but close to the truth."

But I had not been true to myself. I had been a gullible fool, seduced by the longing to be accepted by the most charismatic person in the village. It was the older boy who had stayed true to himself, however despicable that self might be.

Brewster put both his hands on my shoulders and held my gaze. "I think you will find that this experience has prepared you for what God intends."

Chapter Six

Dumb dogs

I HAD BEEN OVERAWED BY WILLIAM BREWSTER when I first met him.

He was one of the most influential men in the area thanks to the patronage of the Archbishop of York, who had appointed him postmaster of Scrooby, a role that meant he was endowed with the manor and its many acres of farmland. His duties included bailiff, receiver and, as I had discovered, the arbitrator of disputes between neighbours.

But for all his importance he made time for me. He invited me into the great hall with its timbered ceiling, so high it seemed to arc to the heavens, and there we would read from his well-used volumes.

As the months in my new home turned into years scarcely a day passed when he and I did not spend time together. When the evenings were warm we would wander around the estate, checking all was well with the stables, the granary and the kennels, calling in on the village's few homes before wandering along the banks of the Ryton back to the manor, its red brick walls glowing comfortingly in the sunset. A small world but one that he made stretch to distant horizons for as we walked, we talked. My, how we talked!

He radiated a hard core of self-belief about the meaning of the scriptures and the path we were to tread, which was intimidating to a boy of twelve, yet for all the passion of his beliefs there was something worldly about him. His oilskin doublets, often in bright colours, hung smartly on his slight frame and he wore polished Norwich gaiters, the height of fashion to us country folk. He was well educated too – he had studied Latin and Greek at Cambridge University with the finest minds in England.

He gave ironic accounts about his early life, when he danced attendance on the royal whims of Queen Elizabeth and served with her army in the Low Country.

"Twenty years back, it was." He paused to examine the horseshoes being hammered into shape in the estate's small smithy. "I was secretary to a courtier called William Davison who was the old Queen's Secretary of State. Poor Davison was blamed by Her Majesty for issuing the death warrant on the Scottish Queen Mary for her treachery. Elizabeth denied she had signed it – afflicted by guilt, I've always maintained – but she had Davison tried and, though he was spared execution, that was the end of his career – and mine, for that matter." He gave a wry laugh. "Father was the postmaster here until 1590 so it was the most natural thing for me to take over."

He fished the mangled corpse of a carp, which had been feasted on by a heron, from the moat. "I prefer this to my old life. I'm paid more than £30 a year and I'm rarely troubled by the machinations of the court, except when a spy reports me to the Archbishop of York for sermon gadding." He shrugged. "That usually earns me a fine."

"Sermon g—g—gadding?"

"It's when we go to another parish to hear a preacher rather than stay in our own as the King's Church dictates. I am sure the archbishop's agents will have reported me for turning my back on St Wilfrid's here and going to Babworth to listen to Richard Clyfton. Maybe you too, youthful as you are, will have been spotted and your name recorded. The church wardens have to disclose the smallest misdemeanour by the congregation even as petty as someone wearing a hat in church."

"My Uncle Robert is churchwarden at St Helena's," I said nervously. "Do you think he might report me?"

"I cannot believe he would betray his own flesh and blood. Still, make no mistake, the very pews are alive with spies and they will stay so unless the King rules that we are free to follow our beliefs in our own way."

"And will he?" I asked.

"I fear not. His Majesty has called a conference at his palace of Hampton Court. He sees himself as the 'nation's physician' who can heal our spiritual ills, but. I am sure the demands of folk like us will be too much for him to stomach. We want an end to bowing when the name of Jesus is used and to stop using the sign of the cross in baptism. We say there are too many priests and that the services are too long. He will not tolerate such heresies."

"What if he rejects your demands?" My stomach tightened with apprehension. "What can we do about it?"

"We will have no option but to throw off the chains of the Church. To separate." He frowned and held his Bible like a talisman to give him strength. "It will be hard. The bishops and their followers prefer the old popish ways – the base and beggarly ceremonies, the money, and the trappings of servants and underlings. To be blunt, they are hypocrites and renegades who uphold a church which is a huge mass of old and stinking works."

I was struck dumb by the outburst. The Master Brewster I knew was a benign gentleman, quietly spoken and humorous; I had no idea that he was driven by an anger that ripped straight from the heart of his beliefs.

He blinked at me, almost apologetic for speaking so fiercely. "You need to understand that above all, they enjoy the power, and to keep it they will persecute us with greater zeal. They will fine us for breaking their rules, drive us from our parishes and put us in prison. Maybe worse. That's why you are brave to join us."

Join. Brave. How honoured I felt. It filled me with both foreboding and elation to be enlisted in such a crusade. Above all, it brought meaning to my existence. It cured me of the virus of solitude that had so cursed me.

Yet I could not grasp how these threats from a king who had appeared such an awkward, dribbling figure could affect our small congregation in this far corner of his kingdom.

I had my answer a few months later after morning prayers, when I found Brewster clutching a message, his brows furrowed with concern.

"Clyfton has been excommunicated and expelled from his living so I have invited him to stay here. But he is not alone; my good friend Richard Jackson from this very parish has been threatened with prison and Robert Southworth of Headon has been removed from his living for his 'disobedience.'" He spat out the word contemptuously.

Clyfton arrived, clutching his knapsack and breathing defiance. "At least seventeen of our brethren have been deprived of their livings in recent months, scores have been fined or thrown into prison, but the King sorely misjudges us if he thinks we will surrender."

"The net is closing in." Brewster pursed his lips. "This is the work of Tobias Matthew. You probably won't remember him,

Will, after all, it has been three years since the King stopped at the manor but he was in his Majesty's retinue and now has been rewarded for his loyalty to the King by being elevated to Archbishop of York."

"As dark as winter, that one," grunted Clyfton.

Now we lived in constant anxiety. Any unexpected noise – the neigh of a horse in the orchard, the barking of dogs, the hoot of an owl – made our stomachs lurch. Any stranger in the lane or unfamiliar face seen loitering around the manor gates made us hold our breath. Could he be a spy or an archbishop's man come to arrest us?

"I have news of another victim called John Robinson," announced Brewster. "His congregation in Norwich loved him but he has been thrown out of his living and excommunicated."

"He is by all accounts a fine preacher," pronounced Clyfton. "He is speaking just down the road in Sturton in Lound this Pentecost."

"We must go," insisted William. "There will be spies looking out for us and it could be dangerous, but we have a duty to show our solidarity."

Come Pentecost, we crowded into the village's ancient church to listen to the preacher. I marvelled at the clarity of his vision. A tall, angular figure with unwavering brown eyes, he spoke quietly but emphatically; very different to the histrionics of Master Clyfton. He attacked the incompetent ministers of the established church and the negligence of the magistrates – 'dumb dogs', he called them, which made us listeners gasp.

"They are contemptuous of our beliefs, but it is religion itself that has been disgraced." He paused for effect. "The godly amongst us have been persecuted and imprisoned; all have suffered for our faith while the Church of King James, little better than the Papists of old, has encouraged ignorance, profanity and, yes, atheism."

I introduced myself nervously after the service. If he was surprised at my youth, he disguised it by treating me like an equal, while I, with the naivety of a fifteen-year-old – some might call it arrogance – thanked him for his bravery speaking out for the cause.

Brewster hurried up to us.

"I think we should move on." I had not seen him so anxious. "There are two men over in the copse who I am sure are spying on us. We should go our different ways before they get a good description of us to give the archbishop. They know me and you, Master Robinson, but there are many good souls here who do not deserve a knock about the head and a few months in jail."

CHAPTER SEVEN

BONDS OF FLESH AND BLOOD

I was dreaming. I had been seized by the constables and Francyse was wrestling me on to a cucking stool so that they could plunge me into the river. Janne Ryall was egging him on with obscene cackles that rose to screams of pain. I started to awake to discover the noise was coming from the Brewster family bedroom. It was Mary crying out in agony, but instead of finding her husband in a panic, I found him in the corridor calmly smoking a pipe, a new-fangled – and filthy – habit that he had taken to with relish.

"It's Mary." He was unconcerned. "She is having the baby."

"Oh." I had not realised she was pregnant.

A flushed maid emerged and, quite forgetting her station, ordered the nonchalant husband to 'get quick to the kitchen for a brew of laurel, pepper and sage'.

By morning all was quiet.

"A girl." Brewster did not appear to have moved from his place, still smoking meditatively.

"Congratulations," I murmured uncertainly. "The Lord be p—p—praised."

"Thank you." The new father was oddly melancholy. "Mary wants to name her Fear."

Too close to the emotion that grips us all, I thought, but managed, "A powerful name."

"It is how Mary feels. She fears for the future of this little one. In fact, she fears for us all."

Fear in her crib. Fear in the shadows. Fear.

Brewster reflected, "Her name challenges us to look peril in the face. That's how we become strong enough to defeat whatever evil comes our way."

He drew on his pipe.

"God willing, we will give the next child a more hopeful name. Love, perhaps."

We celebrated with pastries and sweetmeats washed down with warm wine spiced with borage, though that was not to my taste.

For a while the new birth filled the household with cheer, until early in the January of 1607, one of Uncle Robert's labourers came knocking.

"It's your sister Alice," he muttered. "Come quick."

As I drew near to Austerfield the still of the day was disturbed by the tolling of the bells from St Helena's. It meant one thing: another victim had been claimed by the plague, which had been quietly, malevolently, seeking out its victims, defying the usually cleansing chill of winter. The fields were deserted by the parishioners, who were frantically scrubbing and smoking out their pitiful homes to rid them from disease.

I paused to greet a man who I assumed was digging his allotment, only to find he was burying a dog that he had killed in case it was carrying an infection. In the churchyard there were two fresh mounds of earth. One belonged to Thomas

Hanson, I found out later, about my age; the other to Robert Smith. Both had been in Francyse's gang and had made my life a misery.

Instead of outside feeding the chickens or the pigs, Alice was indoors lying on a straw palliasse that had been made up by the fire. Her face was a mottled grey.

"Just feeling tired," she whispered feebly. "I'm getting to be like you were and you are more the way I was. Look at you – you've got colour in your cheeks, there's flesh on your bones and you haven't coughed once. Don't let Uncle catch you, he'll have you in the fields in no time."

It was true. I was almost seventeen, the aches in my bones had eased, the coughing that had so wracked me had all but disappeared and I had put on weight.

"Thanks to my mutton pottage," Mary Brewster would chuckle, and how could I argue? Good food, tender care and the sheer pleasure of living with people who shared the same purpose had made quite the man of me. Now it was my sister, usually so full of vim and vigour, who was stricken.

I held her hand and we sat in silence. How little had changed in that room since we had been sent there five years before as unwanted orphans – the fire that was always burning, the blackened kettle on the hob, the bench along the wall and the stained oak table.

"Have you heard that pest Francyse Wright and Janne Ryall are to be married next week? She is with child, I hear." I must have flinched because she continued, "I did warn you about him. You were a game to him. A plaything to be exploited."

"I had hoped to save him from himself," I protested feebly. "I convinced myself that if I taught him to read the Bible he would become a better person. And a friend."

"A friend!" Her bitter laugh turned into a ferocious bout

of coughing. "He's a weasel. Beyond saving. He would make lewd comments about me to my face, call me a darling, say how much he wanted me. Disgusting. Now he is back with his own low sort. He and Mistress Ryall deserve each other."

I fiddled with a frayed edge of her blanket. "I still cannot accept that he has given up everything that truly matters for the passing flame of lust."

She shook her head in mock sorrow at my naivety. "Dear Will, you are a little different."

She was overwhelmed by another paroxysm.

"I wish I saw more of you," she whispered.

"I am sorry, but you know where my path leads."

"It is so dangerous though." She reached for my hand again. "I hear dissenters are being hunted down and imprisoned."

I had to make her understand what drove me. "It is important that we live according to our lights. The truth is to be found in the gospels and not in the edicts of bishops. They want to use their tyrannous power to persecute poor servants of God like us and they want dedicated reformers to become slaves to them and their popish profanities."

She was not impressed, I could tell, but I carried on. "People like William Brewster and John Robinson are the men to show us the way. If only you would get to know them, you would understand why our struggle is so important."

She grimaced. "You and words. You sound like the preachers who come to Bawtry market and harangue the passers-by. Dear Will, you know so much of the scriptures, but so little of life. Maybe if Mother had not died when you were so young, maybe if you had not kept yourself apart…" She could not finish the sentence because she choked and spat blood-tinged phlegm into a cloth. "I know it is important but I don't feel strong enough to argue with you."

"I'm sorry, I do talk too much." I was mortified by my self-indulgence. "I will stay until you get better."

"Please do." Her voice was so weak that I had to lean close to hear. In the short time I had been by her side, her face had become as pale as the snow outside, and I had to mop away crimson trails that ran from her nose and mouth. The tips of her fingers that clutched the blanket were turning a ghastly black.

"I am glad you got here in time," she gasped. "Pray for me."

I stayed to help with the funeral arrangements. The Reverend Fletcher and Uncle Robert, doing his duty as churchwarden, ignored me but I stood by her grave and prayed for her soul, certain that she was safe with God.

After the service I walked through the wood on my way to Scrooby and the witch came cackling from her lair.

"Young Bradford. I know you," she screeched. "Too holy for your own good. There's nowt for anyone as strange as you in this country. Get thee hence, arsworm."

I dashed out of the coppice into the bright light of the meadows. If only Alice had been there, she would have humoured the crone, given her bread and cheese and told me to ignore her ramblings. She was mad, I knew that, but her words made me feel twelve years old again. Spurned and mocked.

Strange? Maybe I was.

Chapter Eight

Harbinger of hope

THERE WAS A NEW FACE BY THE MANOR FIRE. John Robinson. He had been invited by Brewster to become one of our growing community along with his wife Bridget and their family.

They brought with them a maidservant called Mary Hardy, a sturdy lass with untamed red hair. She was rather too chirping-merry, if I'm honest, always trilling away tunelessly, though it seemed the only song she knew was 'By A Bank As I Lay'.

"Mary, some hush please," I would beg her. "I am trying to study." But she would tease me – "Come, Master Will, all work and no play, you know what they say!" – and I would hear her imitating me when she was larking about with the other servants in the kitchen, talking in a rather silly high-pitched voice.

A little mockery, albeit from a servant, was a small price to pay for the inspiration of the company of Master Robinson, who I so wanted to impress that I gave a talk on lines taken from Saint John's gospel, 'In the beginning was the Word'.

"How well you express our gospel of simplicity." He actually shook my hand in congratulation.

A preacher of his prestige attracted scores of fellow believers. Every Sabbath, forty or sometimes fifty worshippers crept across the fields, along the lanes and by the river banks to the manor for a day of prayer and revelation, which started at eight in the morning and continued until five or six in the evening. For me, time sped.

But all the time, an unceasing flow of travellers broke into our peaceful meditations, indifferent to the time of day or night. There was nothing we could do about these interruptions; one of Brewster's many duties as postmaster was to provide for riders on king's business as they headed north to Edinburgh or raced in the opposite direction to London.

We would hear the blast of a horn from the Great Road and minutes later the horsemen would gallop up in a tremendous pell-mell demanding a fresh steed, which the stable hands always had ready for them. The ones with time to spare stayed the night eating, drinking and singing songs that had some maids blocking their ears in embarrassment and the others giggling guiltily.

One group of riders, hell-bent on reaching the royal court in Edinburgh, stopped long enough to report an assassination attempt on the King himself. Eight conspirators, led by Papist fanatics called Robert Catesby and Guy Fawkes, had been caught after they had smuggled barrels of gunpowder into the cellars of Parliament and placed them right below the throne where James was to sit. They were about to blow the place up when they were seized.

"The traitors were hanged and cut down before they died, their balls chopped off and their bowels ripped out," related one of the messengers.

"Their remains were burned before their faces," reported another with unwonted enthusiasm. "Their heads were cut off, the bodies quartered and set high for all to see."

I blanched. "Who were they?"

"A bunch of mangy pope-blowers. God rot 'em."

I was disconcerted by Brewster's dismay at the news. "I have no sympathy for any Catholics and less for traitors," he pronounced, "but mark my words, James will now clamp down harder on all dissenters – and that means us."

His forecast was soon proved correct. Our outspoken comrade Thomas Helwys arrived at the back gate having spent the best part of two days walking from his mansion in Broxtowe, a way off near Nottingham. His breeches were soaking wet and his ruff askew.

"Joan and I cannot step out of the gate without a pesky constable asking us where we're going and what we are doing, so I reckoned it safest to come across the fields," he explained. "I tried to jump across the river but I fell in." He patted ineffectually at his wet clothes.

"Have you seen this?" He produced a damp sheaf of papers. "It is a proclamation from the King ordering the churchwardens and constables of every parish to keep a monthly record of any dissenters, be they Papists or true believers like us, and present it once a year to the justice of the peace. Anyone not attending the King's Church will be put in jail to await a hearing, and if they don't appear they will be found guilty and fined £20 a month."

"Our poor folk do not have that kind of money." I knew that from studying Uncle's accounts. "The farmers are lucky if they earn £15 a year and the labourers get a miserable one shilling a day – that's if there is work for them."

"Mark this." Helwys prodded at the document. "The archbishop is offering a reward of forty shillings to any informant."

"So many good folk will be forced to choose between their faith and starvation," said Brewster. "I cannot blame them if they beat their way to his vestry for a sum as tempting as that."

Mary broke in. "Did I tell you that only the other day a stranger offered widow Hanson twenty shillings to tell what was happening here? He wanted to know if we wore hats when we prayed."

"Oh dear." Robinson managed a thin-lipped smile. "It has come to this; the menace of our faith is judged by our taste in headgear."

Brewster sighed. "It is all so hard. Persecution is not too strong a word. Our people are being clapped into jail, their houses and lands have been confiscated. Many are leaving all that they own behind and fleeing to safety – wherever that might be. How can we continue like this?"

"I can understand why many of our brethren are talking of settling in the Netherlands," said Robinson.

"It's a fine place with admirable people." Brewster recovered his spirits. "I must have told you about serving the Queen there in the '80s and how impressed I was by the liberal thinking of the Netherlanders. Furthermore, their cities are nobly built and the skies soar over a countryside as gentle and cultivated as here."

It crossed my mind that this was not the first time the two men had held this conversation. There was something awkward about the exchange, like they were floating a thought, just a notion, that there was a solution to our plight which the rest of us had not considered.

Robinson started, "Maybe that is a sacrifice..." but he was interrupted by the maid Mary who came dashing in, still clutching the chamber pot she had been emptying into the river.

"Master, mistress, the sky is on fire."

We humoured her by going outside and were astonished to witness a mighty arc of flame soaring across the heavens. It was an awe-inspiring moment. But was it sent by God or the Devil?

"Plague and terror," squeaked the maid. "Doom, we're doomed."

"Not so." Brewster was all calm reassurance. "I have read the works of the astronomers who have studied these comets and they judge that they are harbingers not of doom, but of great world change. It is not too fanciful to claim that we are among the architects of that change. We have no need to tremble at that gaudy firework."

From the diocese records of Archbishop Tobias Matthew, 1607

From my window I watch a comet as it blazes between the two great towers of the Minster. It leaves a beautiful trail of gold, blue and green. I have no doubt; it is a harbinger sent by God to tell me that those who reject the teachings of the Church must be destroyed.

Who are these people who spurn the bishops and the wisdom of the King? Let me tell you: the Papists, argumentative Puritans and the sect I despise the most, the Separatists, a gang of dangerous and malicious hypocrites. They pretend to follow the scriptures, but they insist we bishops should have no say in the way our Lord is followed. How can that be? We alone have the education, the skills and the power to interpret His teachings.

I was at the splendid gathering at Hampton Court in 1604 when all matters of religion were discussed, so I know His Majesty's mind. He told the Puritans that if they demanded an end to the power of the bishops, he would see it as an attack on himself and the monarchy. "No bishop, no king," he cried. "The very idea that elders, as they call their benighted preachers, should run the church agrees with me as well as I agree with the Devil."

He warned all extremists, "I shall make you conform or I will harry you out of the land — or worse."

So, naturally, when the King so generously elevated me to be Archbishop of York, I promised that I would be most industrious rooting out the pests.

I have already banned their prayer meetings, excommunicated their preachers and flung many in prison. My network of spies is bringing wayward congregations to heel and compelling them to return to their village churches where they will kneel to pray, the preachers will dress as the Lord intends in surplice and cap, and the Book of Common Prayer will be their only guide.

Mark my words, I shall force them to sign an oath of allegiance to His Majesty alone.

I have ordered my Court of High Commission to draw up a list of the men who must be taken in hand. One is a fanatic named Robinson, who we have excommunicated. I shall deal once and for all with Master Helwys and his shameless woman – I cannot call her wife. They have both had a taste of York's cold prison walls but still they flout the marriage vows. Imagine, seven children and every one a bastard.

The most dangerous offender is William Brewster, the postmaster. The brazenness of the man. He lives in great comfort in a manor house that is actually owned by this very diocese.

I met him once when I was travelling with the King from Edinburgh on his way to be crowned. Very pleased with himself, I thought. Surrounded by unbelievers and acolytes and worse, callow youths whose minds he was poisoning with his dangerous cant.

No more. £37 a year I pay him to do his duties, and he insults me by harbouring traitors. I will teach him the lesson he richly deserves by fining him £20 and suggesting he resigns – an invitation he will not be able to resist because I shall send my man Thomas Southworth to kick him out and treat him to a spell in jail if he protests.

I will scatter these people like sheep without a shepherd.

My rheumatism cripples me, my catarrh often keeps me in bed, but that will not stop me. Only last month I visited Bawtry, a few miles from the nest of vipers in Scrooby, where crowds flocked to hear me preach. I told them the straight unvarnished truth about these traitors and their childish fallacies; that they are proud without learning, presumptuous without authority, zealous without knowledge and holy without religion.

The people – good, honest salt of the earth – came up to me afterwards to thank me for my determination to remove this blight from their devout lives.

This comet has inspired me. For my next sermon I shall read from the Book of Revelations. 'The third angel sounded his trumpet and a great star, blazing like a torch, fell from the sky – the name of the star is Wormwood. A third of the waters turned bitter and many people died from those waters.'

Wormwood. Bitterness. Grief. That will be the fate of Brewster and his brainsick conspirators.

CHAPTER NINE

A DESPERATE ADVENTURE

I WAS ABOUT TO TAKE MYSELF TO BED AND SNUFF out the candle when I glimpsed a shadow flit through the gate that led from the vegetable garden. A fox? A pig escaped from the pen? But then another. And another. These shadows were made by men and they meant danger.

"Help! Wake up! Thieves!" I ran from my room but before I reached the top of the stairs there was a ferocious hammering, a crash and the sound of splintering as the door was shaken from its hinges and men in masks carrying pistols and knives burst in. They raced upstairs, shoved me to the ground and dragged Master Brewster from his bedchamber.

Mary was screaming, more in anger than fright, "Villains! Swine! Stop them. Save him." But by the time I staggered to my feet he had been manacled and bundled into a cart that lay waiting in the drive. We were left dazed and helpless in the doorway looking on as the men galloped away. A shot thudded into the door and one of the men yelled, "It will be your turn next, you heathen swine. Beware, John Robinson. Watch out, young Bradford. We know about you and your damnable blasphemies."

The household gathered in the library. While her mistress was shivering with the shock, Mary the maid, alternately snuffling and sounding off about the attackers in a most unmaidenly way, scurried around lighting candles. Robinson poured us all a tumbler of brandy.

"My, it makes my head spin." Mary Brewster gave a little gulp, somewhere between a giggle and a convulsive sob and held her baby close. "William will be back tomorrow, just you see."

But there was no welcome sound of the postmaster's boots on the manor drive, only the news from a loyal ally that he was being kept in Retford jail and a warning that the archbishop planned to seize us as well.

Fear in the shadows.

One week later, William walked through the door as blithely as a man who had been on a stroll around the estate but sporting a bruise above his right eye. "I tripped over a Book of Common Prayer," he joked as Mary bathed the wound with warm water and pigeon's blood. "My hosts needed to consult with me on the finer points of theology."

Later, over supper he gathered us together to announce, "Our time here is up. The archbishop has evicted me from this old home of mine. I have been sent my last two payments, a princely £74, and we shall have to move out by the end of September. A replacement has already been found who, no doubt, will be more pliant."

Mary gripped her husband's hand. She understood what a blow this was to him.

Robinson, however, drew himself up as he did when he gave a sermon, when every word had a meaning and every sentence was a call to spiritual arms.

"This proves that we have reached a tipping point." He had the air, I thought, almost of relief, as though he welcomed the news. "We are beset on all sides – the bishops hate us, the nobility is scared by us, the poor folk resent us. We dare not wait for the next knock on the door.

"You will know that I was reluctant to break with the established church even when I criticised it and though I was excommunicated for my pains. My hope was that it could be reformed from within because I had never been able to break the bonds of flesh and blood that tied me to it. But time, these few years, has proved me wrong; we cannot cure the cancer that afflicts the King's Church."

He held our gaze, his eyes black with certainty. "Now, the truth is like a burning fire in my heart; I know what we have to do. We must find a home far from the hatred that surrounds us."

"True, there is nothing to keep us here anymore." Brewster reflected for a second or two and took his Bible in his hands, balancing it like scales, weighing the options. "It will be hard to leave what has been my home for forty years or more. I have been lord of the manor and postmaster here since 1590 – the year you were born, I think, young Will – and Mary has been with me for most of that time. I know she loves the place as much as I."

I assumed he was going to argue that we stayed to continue the struggle somewhere else in the county. But no.

"I am with Master Robinson. We leave Scrooby. Leave Nottinghamshire. Leave England."

"Leave England?" I asked. "Is there n—n—nowhere safe in our own c—c—country?"

"Sadly not." Robinson was adamant. "We must go abroad. That is the sacrifice we have to make."

I felt myself spiralling down into the darkness of my childhood anxieties, so much so that my chest tightened like it used to when Uncle harangued me for my laziness, and the cough that afflicted me as a boy returned.

"This sounds an almost d—d—desperate adventure that could end in m—m—misery worse than d—d—death." I was gasping so much I could hardly get the words out.

Robinson shook his head. "It might be desperate but it will not end in misery because we have right on our side. Yes, we will have to leave behind much of what we hold dear without any hope of return, but if we leave as exiles we will find a city where we can be free men."

"And that is all that matters, is it not?" averred Brewster. "That we are free to believe in God without let or hindrance."

I pulled myself together. He was right. Of course he was right.

Brewster continued. "As you know, I am an admirer of the Dutch. Many good people fleeing the wrath of the King have already gone to Amsterdam and I hear they have been made welcome and encouraged to follow their beliefs in peace."

I fought back another nervous cough and swallowed hard. "F—f—forgive me for speaking the way I did before. I have regained my courage. The sufferings our people have endured are mere flea b—b—bites compared to what we might face if we stay here. I may be inexperienced and know little of the world, but I do know that together we can bear whatever is thrown at us."

I was charged with the intoxication of the moment. "God will guide us to freedom like the Israelites. Hear the words of Moses: 'Thou in thy mercy hast led forth the people which thou hast redeemed, thou hast guided them in thy strength unto thy holy habitation.'"

No more the stammering, insecure boy. No more to be scoffed at for my infirmities or for my milksop embrace of the scriptures. Just for a moment, I felt I was the match of my elders. My own man.

"Bravely spoken." Brewster thumped me on the back. "You are right. This is the only way for us." Robinson gazed around the room. "Now, are we in agreement to settle in Amsterdam?"

There was a chorus of yeas.

"We are all of one voice," pronounced Brewster. "I still have a fair few comrades in that city and I will write to seek their advice and ask them to find work and rooms for us."

Robinson chimed in, "I have sounded out a trustworthy captain who has agreed to sail us across the North Sea."

So he and Brewster *had* been planning the venture for some time, long before the postmaster had been arrested.

The die was cast. The manor became a bedlam of activity as the congregation gathered to receive their instructions. Some were boldly optimistic but most were alarmed at leaving their homes; after all, they had rarely strayed beyond the countryside around Scrooby. Gainsborough and Doncaster, they were far enough, but how, they asked, would they get to this Amsterdam? How could they hide from the constables when they came hunting for them? There was no answer except to be alert, tell no one of our plans and put our trust in God.

We sold what we could: livestock, farm tools, saddles and horses, anything and everything, and invariably for less than they were worth. We set free the animals we could not sell; unlocked the pigs from the pen next to the church, opened the gates to let the cattle roam and left the chickens to chance their luck with the foxes.

Helwys, busy man, had arranged for boats to be moored on the Ryton, ready for our escape. "The craft are small," he warned, "but they will carry us to the coast near a town called Boston, where we will be picked up. We must travel light, which means no great trunks of clothes and, Master Brewster, no books."

"Of course," he agreed, but later I caught him climbing down from the attic looking guilty. "Sssh," he begged. "I've stored most of my books up there until I can send for them, but I am smuggling out a handful of the ones that mean the most to me. Don't tell Master Helwys."

I did not confess that in my change of clothes I had hidden my Bible and the battered *Foxe's Book of Martyrs*. I reckoned my resolve would be bolstered by tales of popish cruelty and Protestant courage.

But as we prepared for our escape there came the sound of horsemen galloping down the lane from the Great Road.

"Just what we need," grumbled Mary resignedly. "Hungry travellers. At this time of night too."

But instead it was a gentleman with two constables who came hammering at the manor door.

"My name is Thomas Southworth," he declared. "I am from the High Court of Commission. I come from Archbishop Matthew to see Master Brewster."

He stationed the guards at the door and, holding up a parchment as though he was the Bawtry town crier, proclaimed, "The office versus William Brewster of Scrooby; information is given that he is disobedient in matters of religion. Process is served. A fine of £20 and an order from the court officer to arrest him."

Brewster gave a grim laugh. "So they haven't given up on me yet." Switching to the disarmingly friendly manner I knew so well, he cried, "Come in, come in. You must be a relation to our dear friend Robert Southworth from Headon, a man of staunch faith."

We could hear the murmur of voices from the library and we listened in the corridor, taut with apprehension. Was this the end for him? For us? But when Brewster sent out for more ale and a platter of cold meats, we prayed that the danger was passing.

We heard the sound of farewells in the hall followed by the clatter of hooves, and Brewster came back into the parlour wreathed in smiles. "I don't think we'll be seeing him or any of the archbishop's men for a while."

"What did you tell him?" asked Mary.

"I can be very convincing, you know," replied her husband blithely. "Don't breathe a word, but I actually believe I made a convert to the cause."

A few days later in the darkest days of late December, when the snow was falling and the moat had become a skating rink, Thomas Helwys came by, clapping his frozen hands and chuckling with glee.

"Damn me, Brewster, I don't know what alchemy you summoned up to baffle the good Southworth, but he has told the magistrates that he cannot find you or understand where you could have gone to."

"They will be back," asserted Brewster. "The Archbishop will send more constables, be sure of that, and they will not be as persuadable as our Master Southworth. We cannot delay. We leave at dawn."

CHAPTER TEN

BETRAYAL

THERE WAS NO SLEEP THAT NIGHT. LONG before sunrise, fifteen or so folk crept out of the darkness to join us, shivering with cold and clutching lamps that lit up faces pinched with anxiety. The snow crunched under our feet and a freezing mist rose from the river. A woman gave a little scream when a pig bumped up against her.

"Come on," whispered Brewster. "Let's go." As we pushed off from the jetty, water leaked into my boots. I never did get the holes repaired.

Only the cawing of crows disturbed the stillness as we sailed toward Bawtry. There were shadows that looked like dragons and the monsters that the vicar insisted would devour us sinners in Hell, but as the black of the night turned into a streaky grey the dragons became trees and the monsters merely cows chewing the cud. The fish began to leap and the birds to twitter. A marsh harrier swooped down on an unlucky vole that squealed and wriggled in its claws.

We floated down the Ryton, so narrow we could almost touch each bank, and into the River Idle that skirted one of Uncle's fields. I had an unexpected ache watching my old life slip away and bid a silent farewell to Mother, Grandfather and Alice – the few I had loved and had loved me in return – but when we reached the wide grey waters of the Trent, the powerful current and the wind in our sails fair raced us along and the past was left behind me.

Mary the maid blithered away, worrying about the state of the coppers in the kitchen, who would collect the hens' eggs and prattling on about seeing Francyse with his bairn – "such a sweet little thing" – until she caught my eye and blushed with embarrassment. Goodness, she could talk as carelessly as she could sing but, perversely, I found her mindless monologue comforting because I too was scared.

We paused to pick up more fugitives in Gainsborough and sailed along a canal as straight as a die.

"It's called Fosse Dyke, built by the Romans," explained Brewster. "Isn't it wondrous to think we are travelling on a waterway carved out of the land so many hundreds of years ago, and which so many have sailed. It puts our small adventure into perspective."

I should have been more interested but I was gripped with an anxiety made worse by the bleak emptiness of the countryside with its trees frozen into eery stillness. Every now and then men would gallop out of the desolation and ride alongside us, their horses' hooves muffled by the snow. The archbishop's spies? Constables? Who could tell? They disappeared as inscrutably as they had come.

What a relief it was to reach Lincoln, where we could lose ourselves in the crowds. And what crowds. Lincoln was a very Babel of commotion: wharves lined with ships taking wool to the continent, stevedores loading and unloading to a chorus of cusses, merchants haggling at the top of their voices; and in glorious serenity, a cathedral high on the hill that filled the sky with its towers, the setting sun shimmering in the great window like a thousand beacons.

"Only God could have inspired such a building," I murmured to myself, but Brewster overheard.

"How wrong it was to use his name to allow such extravagance. The vanity of bishops was sated but many poor folk perished in its making. Four plain walls and a roof – that is all the Lord requires."

I was taken aback by his anger but before he could continue his onslaught on such popish flummery, Master Helwys interrupted.

"There are too many of us; we are a sitting target for the constables. We must split up. Half must take to the byways, the rest stay on the boats."

I set off with the party that sailed through the fens toward our rendezvous in Boston. We left the boats before we reached the town and skulked past its unlit houses, terrified of waking guard dogs or disturbing a sleepy constable, before trudging across ploughed fields to a desolate spot on the estuary where we found a dilapidated jetty. This must be the spot where we would meet the ship that was to take us away.

The waterway was restless with fishing boats tracking their way out to sea and returning with their catch but the only sign of life on land was a farmer driving his cattle home. We asked him for milk but he shook his head and without a word strode away into the dusk, turning round once to stare suspiciously at us.

After two nights by the river bank, chilled to the marrow but not daring to light a fire in case we alerted vigilant constables, the rest of our fugitive band came creeping across the fields to join us and barely had we greeted each other than a ship came buffeting up the channel and tied alongside us. The captain greeted us warmly and there was much slapping on the back when Brewster handed over the payment for his services, a satchel full of sovereigns that glinted in the pale morning light.

"Come on board," shouted the skipper. "Get below and make yourselves comfortable. We shall sail with the night tide."

No sooner had we settled in than we were startled by a tremendous banging on the deck.

"Get yourselves up 'ere, you arsworms. Come on. Get a move on, treacherous scum."

Bewildered, we climbed on deck to find ourselves face to face with a score of muskets. Constables. We had been betrayed.

The skipper jingled the money contemptuously in William's face. "Did you really think you would get away with it?"

The soldiers pinned us up at the point of their halberds and we men were stripped to our shirts and searched for money. Once they found we had nothing to hide, they started on the women. They put their hands under their shifts and shoved their hands between their legs. It was horrible. How could they behave like that?

"Give us a smooch," shouted one as he grabbed Mistress Mary.

"I fancy a go with this one," cried another, thrusting himself at his victim like a dog in heat.

They cheered each other on with filthy insults but we men were powerless against the sharp end of a pike.

"That's enough, lads," shouted the chief of the constables. "You've had your entertainment. Let's get this rotten lot locked away."

They tied our hands and manhandled us into boats that

63

took us back to Boston, where a small crowd had gathered to gawk and jeer but mostly to watch curiously, as though we were a troupe of mummers. To my surprise some cried, "God bless you!"

"There are many like-minded folk in this city," reckoned Brewster, but there was nothing they could do to prevent us being locked away in the Guildhall's three tiny cells while we waited to be called before the justice. For four weeks we endured the sweat and stink of it until we were charged with holding 'unlawful assemblies, maliciously and with seditious intent'.

"The women can go," ruled the judges. "But you men are going to Lincoln prison to stand trial."

All of us, even Jonathan Brewster – poor lad, he was only fourteen – were manacled together and marched down to the wharf and back we sailed to Lincoln, but there was no respite for us there. The moment the boats docked, we were jabbed at gunpoint into a column and ordered to march on.

"It's York for you, my friends," announced a constable. "A spell between those prison walls will soon cure you of your treachery."

"A fine city," remarked Thomas Helwys sardonically. "I know it well. Joan and I find the prison one of our favourite spots for rest and contemplation."

For three days we stumbled along roads which were so iron-hard with frost that our legs ached and our feet were covered with blisters. A savage wind cloaked us in a layer of ice like a stiff white overcoat, our faces were blue and our hands so numbed we could barely move our fingers.

There was no respite in the stony chill of the jail. I told myself I should have been able to cope with imprisonment after my solitary years as a boy, but ghosts of past prisoners, whether sinners or the falsely accused, walked the prison corridors. I saw shapeless wraiths that took the form of Alice, waxy and bloodied, and Grandfather, who mutated into a spiteful Briggs. The witch slithered into my fevered mind. "Strange, you're strange," she hissed.

If my soul was tortured, my very being recoiled at the stench of bodies and the indignity of using the bucket that made do as a privy – if we were lucky enough to have one; most of us had to relieve ourselves in our cells.

The constables talked noisily and longingly of hangings they had witnessed. I was frightened and I was ashamed of being frightened. I was like the vole on the river bank – I had seen snatched by a hawk, but in the claws of a predatory archbishop who would stop at nothing to crush us.

For weeks we languished until we were summoned before another judge, who harangued us for our 'beef-witted blasphemy,' not to mention our 'disloyalty to King and Archbishop' but, nonetheless, released us on bail on condition that we agreed to attend the assizes. Which, of course, we had no intention of doing.

The women had waited outside the prison walls and for a brief moment we were cheered by being together again, but what now? We had failed to escape. We would be pursued wherever we went, except we had nowhere to go. The manor was closed to us; many villagers were eager to claim their reward by betraying us and constables harassed us continually, accusing us of vagrancy or trespass – anything they could do to make our life as unbearable outside prison as it was inside.

We had to keep moving. We scuttled like rats along ditches, crawled behind hedges, waded along streams – children held high to keep them dry – and slunk past busy farmsteads. We hid in outhouses, pig pens, cow byres, anything with a roof, but as often as not we slept in the open air.

We foraged the fields for food – early kale that was forcing its way through the frost or old potatoes that had been left in the earth by a careless farmer. Once we chased off a fox which had been feeding on a dead deer and lived on it for a week. Brewster displayed an unexpected skill by setting traps for rabbits and someone caught a rat which we skinned and roasted over the fire.

We discovered how much the ordinary folk hated us when a gang of vicious youths attacked us and destroyed a pathetic shelter of branches and twigs we had put together in a copse a few miles from Gainsborough. I could have sworn I saw a youth wearing a red cap throw a burning torch into one encampment. Was it Francyse? Maybe hunger and despair made me hallucinate, for we were all a little deranged, never knowing what the next day would bring except more misery.

Thank the Lord, a friendly farmer known to Master Helwys let us settle in his barn on the edge of the wetlands between Doncaster and Gainsborough, where we waited while he and Brewster came and went, always insisting that we would escape but never telling us how.

"God will guide us to freedom like the Israelites," I had declaimed. Oh, the arrogance of youth.

Chapter Eleven

Outwitted

Master Helwys sidled into our hiding place.

"I have arranged to meet a Dutch skipper who I know we can trust to take us to Amsterdam. I have new boats and I have bought more oars and sails. This time, though, we will not be caught."

He could see the doubt on our faces; after all he had been just as confident before the betrayal in Boston.

"Believe me, God is on our side this time. But just to be extra prudent we should split up; most of the men should go on foot and the women by river. That will confuse any spies who might take an interest in us."

It was forty miles to our rendezvous on the River Humber and despite my lack of sailing skill, I agreed to help the women by taking the tiller on one of the boats. All went well until a few miles into the Humber when we were plunged into a thunder storm, the like of which would have had the ghosts of St Wilfrid's out of their graves and dancing a jig. The wind tore at us, the rain flooded the boat so fast that we had to bail it out with our hands, and the rudder was torn from my grasp. The sails came tumbling down and the current drove us into a mud flat.

"We'll have to wait for high tide to float us off," I gasped.

Mary the maid gave me a look to say, '*You might know your scriptures but you have no idea how to cope with the real world.*' She grabbed a rope, hitched up her skirts and leapt out of the boat up to her thighs before squelching her way to shore.

The women laughed and cheered as she pulled us free, but to me it sounded like mockery of my own inadequate skills.

"Perhaps you should learn to walk on water," joked Mary, in what I considered a tasteless blasphemy, but the others all found it great sport and were still poking fun at me when the rest of our band caught up with us.

Robinson called us all together. "This is Killingholme Creek. We are a few miles upstream from Grimsby, a small port that's seen better days. This is where we will be picked up."

We had another night in that forlorn spot; a blackness that sapped the soul followed by the pale, dead light of dawn. The east wind lashed the rain into us, water leaked through the holes in my boots and my soaking jerkin weighed as heavy as a stook of sodden wheat.

When it was becoming too much to bear, the lookout shouted, "There she comes."

At last.

The skipper rowed to the shore to greet us. "Sorry, *mijn Engelse vrienden*. You will have to wait until high tide tomorrow before we can sail. Be patient."

Waiting, worrying. Was this another trap? Early next

morning the tide rose enough for the captain to send his skiff to take the first batch of our men to safety – sixteen optimistic souls laughing and joking as they went.

"God is with us," rejoiced Mistress Mary. "We are next."

But in that very instant – a glint of sunlight on steel. Across the flats, from behind the hedgerows and out of ditches, poured the militia, some on horseback, all armed with billhooks and muskets. Betrayed again.

As I turned to run, I was transfixed by the sight of the men who had been taken to the ship. They were clustered by the railings, helpless as their women on land were rounded up. They began to clamber over the side to leap into the sea and swim to the rescue, but it was futile. They would have been swept away by the tide and drowned in an instant.

"Run!" shouted Brewster. "Don't stand there. Run!"

And run we did, floundering hither and thither in panic and shouting, "This way… no, that way! Over there."

I caught a glimpse of Master Robinson being grabbed by two constables before I tripped and fell into the slime of the river bank.

By the time I had staggered back to my feet, Mary the maid had been forced on the ground by a soldier. He had straddled her, forced her legs apart and was tearing at her skirts. There was a flash of her white skin as her stockings were torn from her legs. She was screaming, biting, scratching, but the more she struggled the more the brute seemed to like it.

I was seized by some spirit – was it the Devil or an avenging God? I grabbed an oar and hit him. I was not going to let her be defiled by a beast like that, even though she was only a serving girl. I hit him again. I stood over the bully. "This day will the Lord deliver thee into mine hand," I cried. "I will smite thee, and take thine head from thee." I lifted the oar high for one final blow. I was going to kill him.

I howled, "All the Earth may know that there is a God in Israel."

"No, no! Will, don't." It was Brewster. He grabbed me round the shoulders and dragged the oar from my grasp. "You must be mad," he gasped. "You'll make things worse."

In that instant, the constables launched themselves on the two us and charged us to the ground. The goatish lump I had laid low got to his feet and kicked me in the stomach and chest and crashed his boot into my head.

The archbishop had outwitted us again. We might have the strength of our beliefs, but what was that when set against the determination of the King and his Church to destroy us?

"Dear Lord," groaned Brewster, trying to wriggle free of the ropes that bound his hands. "Look." On the shore, heedless to the mayhem around them, stood the women whose husbands had boarded the ship. One moment they were happy and carefree, on their way to freedom; now they were like widows at a funeral, staring hopelessly as the ship, just a flutter of sail in the distance, took their men away.

We were a sorry bunch, muddied and covered in blood as we were dragooned back to prison. My ribs were sore and my head ached but this time I was determined not to surrender to despair. I conjured up the heroes I had discovered with Grandfather, the ones who had suffered but survived. *Let me be as intrepid as Noah*, I prayed, *as redoubtable as Joseph, and as brave as the martyrs who defied the Pope in Queen Mary's reign of terror.*

"Is this where we end our days?" Mary Brewster was struggling to hold back her weeping. We had gathered around a water pump in the prison yard but, in what felt like divine mockery, however hard we pumped, not a trickle came out. "Has the archbishop won?"

"No. Never." I spoke with as much authority as a seventeen-year-old could muster. "No. We shall find a way. We must keep our belief in God's mercy."

But did God have belief in us? He inspired Moses to lead his people to freedom but as the scriptures told us, he did not allow the prophet himself to reach the promised land.

BOOK II

1608-1620

THE VOICE OF
WILLIAM BREWSTER

A VERY CHEERFUL SPIRIT

It is not with us as with other men whom small things can discourage, or small discontentments cause to wish themselves at home again.

A letter from John Robinson and William Brewster in Leiden, to Sir Edwin Sandys in London. December 15, 1617.

BOOK II

1608–1624?

THE VOICE OF
WILLIAM BREWSTER
A VERY LIBERTY MAN

CHAPTER ONE

HOPES DASHED,
HOPE REKINDLED

FREEDOM. WE FELL TO OUR KNEES ON THE
filthy quayside, oblivious to the rank odour of rotting
fish and the pungent tang of hot tar that the sailors were
slopping on to caulk the ships. We ignored the stevedores, who
stopped shifting sacks of nutmeg to jeer at our motley band –
though in truth we must have looked as if we had escaped
from a lunatic asylum.

What did we care? We had escaped. We were free of the
King's tyranny, free of Archbishop Matthew and his spies, and
at liberty to praise God as we wished. We were in Amsterdam.

After all our hardships and disappointments I had to
pinch myself at how easy our flight had been. I had resigned
myself to another crushing spell in the dark, dank walls of
York prison but, to our astonishment, one morning we were
set free. With no explanation we were jostled through the gate
and into the street, and before the archbishop could change his

mind we slipped away into the countryside and hid ourselves in the shadows.

"It must be a ploy." John Robinson dampened any slight hope we might have had. "Matthew plans to lull us into holding a prayer meeting or for me to preach a sermon so that he can seize us again, and this time throw away the prison keys. Maybe worse."

"Hanging?" My Mary whispered the word.

"I would not put it past him." Robinson avoided her frightened gaze.

Helwys, as ever, saw it differently. "I have acquaintances in the archbishop's circle, good folk who I trust even though their faith is not as ours. Shall I say, we agree to differ. They take no pleasure in our suffering and they assure me that Matthew does not want blood on his hands – but more, they say, he does not want *us* on his hands. Of course, he hopes to rid himself of us as fiercely as ever, but he does not want the bother of chasing around the country after a few pesky conspirators."

"You might be right," I said. He was on to something. "There's the expense too. The word is the King has run out of money; there are food riots in the midlands and Ireland is in turmoil."

"Our mistake has been to try to leave in such large numbers." Helwys was pacing excitedly up and down the barn where we were sheltering. "Matthew cannot ignore such a provocation because he sees it as a challenge to his authority. But what if we break into small groups? His constables might not notice two or three people creeping on board a ship bound for the Netherlands, and the customs will find it easier to turn a blind eye."

"Out of sight, out of mind." I slapped him on the back. "Sound thinking, Master Thomas."

So, family by family our congregation simply disappeared. Five households left for the Low Country one week and a couple sailed a few days later, soon followed by Richard

Clyfton and his wife and children. Our turn came in the summer of 1608 when Mary, me and the three children, along with the Robinson family, were picked up by a Dutch skipper near Hull and made our getaway hidden among bales of wool.

Scores of familiar faces from the old congregation were waiting for us when we landed – young William Bradford, as eager and anxious as ever, Helwys and the spirited Joan, and Richard Clyfton, who had instantly made a name for himself with his blazing sermons. We were together and all was well.

But no. Our hopes were swiftly and cruelly dashed. Amsterdam was not the home of opportunity and freedom I had assured everyone it would be, and our small group was overwhelmed by the clamour and confusion of such a huge city. I was better prepared for such ugliness for I had seen something of the world – Cambridge, London and several of the Dutch cities – but most of our band of fugitives had never stirred far from Scrooby, where their horizon had been broken only by the smoke rising from the cottages dotted across the fields. Here they were hemmed in by the tight-packed rows of stern buildings, and instead of sweet-smelling meadows they had to breathe in the foul stench of the canals.

They had never visited anywhere busier than Bawtry on market day and, simple folk, they had known only the steeple of St Wilfrid's in Scrooby and were bewildered to discover God had so many churches in one place.

We found a hall for prayer in a district called Fleaborough. "Well named," joked Mary grimly, for it was in the most downtrodden part of the city and overflowing with thousands of refugees who, like us, had fled from intolerant regimes the world over.

Like them, we had nowhere to live. How could we? We could not pay for any kind of shelter because we could not find work. There was no demand for the talents of a retired postmaster and as for the rest of us, we soon discovered that the ability to sow a row of beet or shoe a horse was no use in a city where the artisans earned their living from metal work, textiles and leather-making. The only employment we could find was on the docks loading ships or stacking pallets in the warehouses.

When we did scrape together a few guilders we had to settle for rooms above taverns or sleep in unused sheds, where the smell of nutmeg from the Netherlanders' trade with the East was so sickly that we preferred to huddle outside in doorways until the city guards moved us on.

We were hungry despite the best efforts of the women, who spent hours scrabbling around the markets and the rubbish tips for cabbage stalks, potato peelings, morsels of meat from a butcher's stall – whatever they could find to make a stew. But it was never enough.

"How long can we go on like this?" Young Will slumped onto a bench after a fruitless day searching for work, and summoning up the direful turn of phrase he so cherished, "I see the grim and grisly face of poverty coming upon us like an armed man."

"Very colourful, Will." I had to encourage him. "But as Proverbs continues, we must buckle down and not admit defeat so soon. God will ensure our well-being."

I confess, I wished I believed it. I did not always feel the good Lord was on our side, especially after the hardship we had endured in our attempts to flee England, and I wondered, did He have other plans for us? My disquiet was heightened when our beliefs were repudiated – not by the King in England or the leaders of Amsterdam's Calvinist Church – but by the English congregations in the city. To our dismay, the very people like us who had fled persecution and who should have been united under the spiritual flag of Separatism and reform spent their days and nights in vicious disputes.

"What a babble of discontent there is," bemoaned Robinson. We had been talking so intensely that we had walked as far as the docks, where the bodies of criminals were hanged on gallows as a warning to all sinners. "Even our own folk from Scrooby are caught up in tortuous wrangles about the Bible. Some are saying that we must only read the Hebrew version, not the Latin or Greek. There are quarrels about baptism – no baby should be called a Christian because it cannot confess its sins and therefore has no understanding of what the ceremony entails."

"So who does the baptising?" I was irritated by such false logic. "By this reckoning, the holiest of preachers cannot baptise an infant because he himself would have been baptised before he understood the scriptures."

"Wait until you hear this," Robinson continued with a wry smile. "The preacher who was so exercised by the mystery of baptism has solved it by… guess what? By baptising himself."

"So there is at least one man with the power to make us Christians." My mockery was tinged with frustration at such nonsense.

"You hear how these so-called reformers are slandering us?" Will was choking with indignation. "They say that we have crept in like caterpillars and that we are two-faced and hollow-hearted."

Helwys dismissed the furore contemptuously. "What fools. They say we are so monstrous to look at that we wear broad hats and narrow ruffs to hide our pricked-up ears and sharp noses. They claim we have misshapen hands – a sure sign of possession by the Devil, apparently."

"Lucky I brought my old gloves with me." I tried to make light of it, but I was depressed by such ignorant abuse.

CHAPTER TWO

FLEEING THE CONTAGION

A T FIRST I DISMISSED THE GIGGLING CHATTER of Mary and the other maids as the repeating of silly rumours – but no, they were horribly true. Drinking and party-making, adultery and abuse were rife among the very men – and the shame of it, the women – we had considered our brethren, the ones who should be beyond reproach.

It was whispered that a leading light of a reformed church, no less, forced his maid to strip naked before he tied her up, beat her and had his way with her. A deacon was caught molesting his wife's daughter from a previous marriage and when the girl resisted, he gave her a black eye and a beating.

"He was caught hiding in the bedchamber of another man's wife." Robinson was appalled. "The same woman had been caught with other men, one who claimed he was just 'keeping her warm' and yet another who bragged he had lain with her 'night after night.'"

Her husband had her summoned before the elders for 'unnatural and unchristian behaviour' which, I considered, was remarkably restrained of him.

The scandalmongers wallowed delightedly in the antics of a brazen tavern landlady who sang ditties like a trollop until she was reported to the elders for crawling out of a whore house in an unseemly way. How such disgraceful goings-on could ever be conducted in a seemly way defeated me.

Wherever I turned, I saw the signs of moral abandon. How shocking to be confronted by women, little better than bouncing girls, wearing tightly laced bodices that were so low cut and revealed so much white breast that they might just as well have been naked.

Young Will, flustered with embarrassment, stammered, "So many f—f—flaunt themselves in a rich excess of l—l—lace and ruffs and often I have caught the sinful scent of musk. Such impiety, such l—l—lewdness, must be condemned."

One chill winter's afternoon when we were strolling along a canal side, Robinson paused, brow furrowed. "Have you heard that Richard Clyfton, such an inspiration to us in the early days, has thrown in his hand with that rum crowd of drinkers and whoremongers? He says he is prepared to forgive their sins and embrace their beliefs."

"How could he be so misguided?" I lamented. "I heard only yesterday that one of their number is an elder who taught vile songs at a children's catechism and forced himself on one of them. How did we come to these depths of depravity?"

We had reached Blood Street, where the cacophony from the drinkers and the prostitutes in the taverns confirmed our consternation.

"We cannot let the contagion spread." Robinson paused, as he often did before he emphasised a point. "We cannot stay here in Amsterdam. I think we should find another home."

I agreed without hesitation. "Where do you have in mind?"

"I confess, I do not know. Many cities have reputations for tolerance and learning, but then so did this benighted cesspit."

"As you know, I visited Leiden when I was serving in the old Queen's army and found it a fine place," I mused. "It has a first-rate university but above all, the people – whether Lutheran, Calvinist, or of the most radical churches – live together in harmony."

"Let us see if the city authorities will allow us to move there," decided Robinson.

I swiftly established that some of the city's councillors, whom I had known during my time with the army back in the 1580s, were still in office and wrote to them asking for a meeting.

Within weeks we were sitting in the mayor's offices in Leiden City Hall, where I met old faces, including – most usefully – the council's secretary Jan van Hout.

I shook him by the hand. "Twenty years since we last met, by my reckoning."

"More like twenty-five," he corrected me.

"What times," I recalled. "Remember how we celebrated the peace with Spain? Quite a party."

"And we shall drink to that again. But first, to business."

"What can we do for you gentlemen?" inquired the mayor.

"We beg free and unrestrained permission to come here." Robinson summoned the formality that the moment required. "We had high hopes of Amsterdam but we find the city is fractured with religious discord and sin. We did not flee the Sodom of England to find ourselves in a new Gomorrah."

"I have heard and seen nothing but good about Leiden." I reckoned a little flattery would help our cause. "I was impressed by its university and its civilised ways when I was here and already I can tell that has not changed."

"How many of you are there? The city is already too crowded."

"There are only a hundred of us," I replied. "Mostly families, all godly and law-abiding."

"When do you envisage coming here?"

"We would like to be settled by the first day of May."

"That is very soon," interrupted van Hout. "Barely five months."

"We will be ready and eager to earn our living in various trades the moment we arrive," Robinson assured them.

"And," I stressed, "without being a burden to you."

The mayor adjusted his spectacles and did not speak for what seemed several long moments. He shuffled his papers. Would he turn us down?

He pronounced, "We refuse no one who wants to live in the city, as long as they behave honestly and obey all the laws and ordinances."

I gave a sigh of relief. "Of course. That is our intention."

"In that case, you are welcome." The mayor beamed, we all shook hands again and he signalled to his servants to pour us a flagon of beer in celebration.

Before we caught the ship back to Amsterdam, van Hout took me to one side.

"I must warn you that you will find it hard to find somewhere to live and, like Amsterdam, work is difficult to come by. We have about 15,000 immigrants from all over Europe living here, and that is about one third of the population. The city elders have done their best, building alleys of new houses, but they are small – just two rooms and an attic – and they are so crammed together that we call the district the Ants' Nest. It will be a challenge for you – too many people chasing too few jobs."

Undeterred by his gloomy warnings, on a brisk February morning in 1609 we crammed onto the boats which sailed to Leiden and headed for yet another home.

What joy to be leaving the discord of the city for the countryside, where the fields were as flat and friendly as the land around the manor and the sky soared to the heavens just as it did over Scrooby. Our spirits rose and we were smiling again. Mary Hardy, who had become so downcast that she had ceased her tuneless trilling, was humming a tune that could have been '*The Country Lass*', though it was hard to be certain.

I had to confess to a pang of nostalgia as the morning mist swirled from the river banks the way it did on the Ryton and draped around the branches of the willows. A heron left its nest on a farm chimney and wheeled effortlessly across the water, snapping up a sluggardly fish with barely a break in its steady flight – like the herons that raided my old moat.

After several hours we reached the broad, steady flow of the River Rhine and there was Leiden with its windmills whirling on the horizon.

"That's St Peter's." I pointed to a grey hulk of a building. "And over there is St Pancras. Too grand for my taste; too stony and cold."

As we sailed nearer, the commotion of the city grew: farm hands rounding up their cattle in the fields, the shouts of the watermen as they steered their skiffs laden with poultry, fish and meat to market and the hubbub of the men carousing in the bank-side inns. The racket swelled until the boat bumped against a barge tied up to the quay at the Aalmarkt and earned us a volley of abuse from the skipper.

I grabbed Fear, who was heading for the water and as I lifted her to safety on to the wharf, there was van Hout.

"*Welkom, mein freund.*"

CHAPTER THREE

NEW FRIENDS

"COME WITH ME." VAN HOUT GUIDED ME through narrow cobbled streets lined with tall houses, and across bridges that passed over canals filled with a grey sludge that had a smell so pungent that it caught the back of my throat and made my eyes water.

"It's overflow from the dye works," explained my guide. "And shit. Best not to linger."

We skirted the grey bulk of St Peter's before cutting down an alley almost too narrow for two to walk side by side.

He opened a door that led straight on to a threadbare room with a big brick hearth, its oak mantel framed with blue and white tiles. There was a bedstead along the rear wall and stairs down to a cellar and up to an attic. An indoor privy too, I noted. Very refined.

"Welcome to Vico Chorali. I have to tell you though that the locals call it Stink Alley because the men stagger out of the tavern and piss up against the wall."

Perhaps not so refined after all.

"It's not much, is it?" Mary ruefully surveyed our new quarters with a handkerchief pressed against her nose. "It's smaller than the scullery at the manor."

But within weeks, she had transformed it into a home comfortable enough for the two of us and the three children, and had prepared a room for Will in the attic.

"We can't leave him on his own," she decided. "He'll never cope."

She had rescued a few sticks of furniture which had been repossessed from a house in the Ants' Nest – well named, it transpired – a box for linen, a rush-seated chair, a table and a bench – well, really it was nothing more than a plank balancing on barrels – and she even conjured up a throw for the bedstead.

But as van Hout had warned, life was as harsh as it had been in Amsterdam. We had to make money, but how? I could not compete for work with men whose skills in the silk and wool trade had made the city one of the leading weaving centres of the world. I did try to make ribbons, surely that could not be too difficult, but it was a toilsome business and time and time again I failed the test set by the wool guild, and without a certificate I was not permitted to work.

"I'm too old to learn new tricks," I grumbled to Mary, but she would have none of it.

"You have to persist. Look at our boy Jonathan, he is doing well with his ribbons. And Will, surely the most impractical person you could hope to meet, is learning how to handle a loom. You will master it eventually. Meanwhile I'll take in laundry, which will help pay for peat for the fire and maybe a few sacks of flour."

It was never enough, and after a few months I had to dip into my savings to pay the rent and keep us fed.

Every morning the women would set off to the markets to scavenge for what leftovers they could find. Mary the maid and Desire Minter, a servant girl whose mother was midwife to the burgeoning English contingent, made a canny team of foragers. It was quite a lesson to watch them exercising sharp elbows when the fishing boats came in or pushing prettily past tutting housewives to the front of the queue at the Pelhaus meat market for scrag end.

Now and then, our undaunted hunter-gatherers would come back with a lobster that they had 'just found', and occasionally Will would earn enough for a goose or a roundel of cheese, but usually we had to settle for a pan of thin vegetable soup and onions on bread.

As the oldest of our company, I always felt it my duty to cheer everyone up by pretending I did not have a care in the world, but when tragedy befell our little family I could not save myself from falling into a well of sadness.

After another fruitless day trudging the streets in search of work, I came home to find Mary sitting desolately in our decrepit rush chair with Fear grizzling, ignored, in her lap.

She gestured to the crib, a rough thing of oak that I had just finished nailing together. In it lay our fourth child, born only a few days before but now still and cold. We had yet to choose a name for her.

It was God's will, of course, but as we stood before her tiny grave with its cross inscribed with *Infant Brewster – June 12, 1609*, we shed bitter tears.

Mary spoke so softly I could hardly hear her. "So small, yet she took up so much of my heart."

She quickly picked herself up. "It is the living who need us," she declared in the practical way I had loved since we were married twenty years before. "We have a household here who need looking after."

I first saw her when she came to the manor with her father to arrange a sale of cattle feed, and was immediately struck by her grace. Her eyes were of a diverting amber colour, and she had chestnut hair and unfashionable but beguiling freckles around a mouth more given to laughter than frowns. It was the kind of beauty that did not need admiration to make it bloom and I was captivated. I was well into my twenties and, despite my travels and youthful opportunities, had found no one to match my desires until that serendipitous day.

It was the custom for the elders and leading lights in the church to advise those considering marriage, and I too had been drawn to one side by the vicar of St Wilfrid's to be warned about the dangers of becoming too inflamed or suddenly overwhelmed with emotion.

"It is best to cast on the cold water of forbearance," he advised me.

I needed none of that advice. My mind was made up. The week after Mary had visited the manor, I wrote a note to her father asking permission to call on her. I steadied my nerves and cantered across the fields to declare my feelings, and to prove my sincerity I gave her a gold ring – and not a cheap affair; it set me back ten shillings. She blushed as I had hoped but she liked to tease; on my next visit, when I gave her a pair of gloves she mocked me gently. "I see my value has gone down, Master Brewster." And she giggled at my confusion.

I could not wait for the year that the ritual of courtship demanded and after only a few months I sought her hand in marriage. Her father agreed but I knew it was her decision to accept me.

We gave each other a rare sense of worth that we could see reflected in each other's eyes and, as for our moments of fire and emotion... well, we neither needed nor wanted the warmth of our love to be doused with the cold water of restraint.

It was always like that, right to the end. What did I give her? Love, support, and my prayers, though I knew it was never enough, but Mary gave me so much more because she knew me better than I knew myself. She understood the dangerous path our little church travelled but she willingly joined me. God was always with me, but Mary made the way easier.

It was not long after the melancholy funeral for our little one that I had a change of luck. I had been introduced to a professor at the university with whom I had enjoyed many a joust interpreting the intricacies of the Bible, and he employed me to teach Latin and English to the sons of wealthy Dutch, Danish and German families. What a pleasure to be in the company of students eager to learn, and what a relief to have enough money to buy food and – joy of joys – to afford more books.

I was returning from a morning at the university, my brain buzzing from a stimulating debate on a minute aspect of Lutheran doctrine, when John Robinson caught up with me.

"I have something to show you." He took me by the arm along the Kloksteeg before halting by St Peter's graveyard.

"Look." He gestured at a solidly built house opposite. "Green Close. I have finally signed the deeds."

He showed me around what was a spacious dwelling, furnished simply like mine and decorated in the Dutch way, with blue and white tiles depicting charming scenes such as a ship on the high seas, a house and a stick-like child playing with a hoop.

"My plan is that we should also use this as a meeting place and that we should build homes on the land behind."

The new abodes were humble enough, to be sure, but it

did mean that most of the congregation had somewhere to live. And as a further sign of God's consoling justice, Mary gave birth to a boy who we called Love. Unlike his older sister, he came at a time of optimism.

Every month more comrades from England joined us. I bumped into Thomas Southworth, the archbishop's man who had been sent to arrest me in Scrooby and who I disconcerted by greeting him with extravagant warmth, though I was tactful enough not to refer to that night.

"You see," I joked to Will, who had been distinctly hostile when they met. "Such are my powers of persuasion that not only does he spare my life but he joins us here."

"I have little interest in that family," snapped the young man, which took me aback.

I mentioned his reaction to Robinson and he confided that another of the Southworth brothers, Edward, had also come to Leiden and brought with him a new wife named Alice. He had been told that a youthful Bradford had been sweet on this Alice and she on him, but the parents had forbidden the union. Robinson had naturally not pursued the gossip and I confess, the courtship – if there had been such a thing – must have been conducted with the utmost discretion. Neither Mary nor I had ever detected any signs of burning passion on the part of our callow lodger.

Discretion and reticence, these were not qualities of another of our new comrades, a swaggering gent called Myles Standish, who had a blaze of red hair and was as stocky as a bulldog.

He had come roaring unannounced into Green Close. "My dear Pastor Robinson, I have heard much about you and your brethren and by my troth, I so admire what you are doing. Now, I am a common straight-talking soldier who served as a captain at the siege of Ostende in '01. God's teeth, it was a bloody affair. But that was war and this is peace. I know you are doing a grand job here and I think I can be of service to you."

Robinson flinched at his language but I suppressed a smirk; it reminded me of my saltier days with the army.

"A soldier and a Christian are much the same," Standish would bellow when anyone questioned his right as a man with blood on his hands to join our movement. "One fights against the enemies of our country and the other, the enemies of our God."

I warmed to the soldier for all his bluntness – indeed, maybe *because* of his plain speaking – but I could not conjure up the same goodwill toward one Isaac Allerton, a tailor from Suffolk who had joined us a year or two after we arrived from Amsterdam. To be fair, he was a hard-working member of the congregation, but there was an air about him that made me uneasy – like the way his eyes darted restlessly over my shoulder when we met to check something or catch the gaze of someone, he deemed more important.

One small incident troubled me for many years. I had come across Desire comforting a weepy Mary Hardy returning from market. The maid told me that Allerton had persuaded her to buy some herrings he had with him. "Save yourself the trouble of scrabbling around the stalls," he had suggested. "I've bought too many, so you can have these cheaper than you would normally pay."

"I've just found out that the stuff 'e sold me was much more pricier than I could've bought," she sniffled. "What can I say to the mistress when she finds out I've spent too much? She'll say I was lazy and she'll be right. Oh my, I'm in trouble."

"Don't fret." I gave her a few guilders to make up the difference. "No need to tell the mistress."

Desire, I thought, was about to speak out, maybe tell of another low trick by the tailor, but Mary shushed her and hustled her away – though not before bursting into sobs of gratitude.

I did not challenge Allerton about the incident. Perhaps I should have.

CHAPTER FOUR

DARK CORNERS

ON THE SABBATH, AS MANY AS 300 OF US would gather in Green Close from eight in the morning until five in the evening. First we would hear a sermon from Robinson, who by now was unchallenged as our pastor, and we would stand in prayer and debate the scriptures – prophesying, we called it. For us the day was always one of pure delight, even though we stood most of the time and had no organ to give our singing a lift. The Devil's bagpipes had no place with us.

This purity of worship was what we had fled England for.

Will and I were crossing the square on our way home after the last amen had been uttered when he broke out, "You know, Master Brewster, the single-heartedness and sincere affection that the congregation has for each other proves that we have come as near the aims of the first churches, with their simple passions, as any other church has done. We have achieved our goal."

I said I agreed with him, partly because I admired his enthusiasm and was keen to encourage him, but I did not share his certainty. Only days before I had received news from Amsterdam that reminded me how fragile our world really was. Thomas Helwys had not come with us to Leiden but instead had done his best to further the Separatist movement in Amsterdam until, sickened by the turmoil among the religious factions, he had decided to return to England. The man who had done so much to help us flee the oppression of King James and his vindictive bishops now preferred to risk all at the hands of those same tormentors.

"There is no doubt, he will die in prison." I was dismayed by the futility of his decision. "I feel guilty that we have found peace of mind here while he has decided to fight a war of words he cannot win."

"There is no point brooding." Mary had tried to cheer me. "He and Joan have made a brave choice, but they would not deny us the chance to make the most of our existence here."

There were few happier proofs that the lives of we exiles were blossoming than the double wedding of Isaac Allerton – to a nineteen-year-old called Mary Norris – and his sister Sarah, who wed an amiable hat maker named Degory Priest.

What a day it was. I made a note in my journal; November 4, 1611. The ceremony was held at the city hall and we adjourned to the Dover Inn for our celebrations, where the brides sat at the head of two tables with wreaths above them in the Dutch manner.

We tucked into the finest feast we had known since arriving in the Netherlands – roast venison ribs with cloves and rosemary, chicken and eels fresh from the Rhine, followed by lemon pasties warmed in wine and sugar, with almonds, capers, olives and raisins; all washed down with ale, which I have to admit was more flavoursome than we were used to in England. A troupe of pipers added their jolly dissonance to the scene and Mary Hardy sang a sweet ballad unexpectedly well, which brought tears to my eyes.

Will sat in sullen silence. He had refused the pretty buttonhole of flowers Mary gave him to cheer his shabby serge suit, he picked at his venison, he barely spoke and he absolutely refused to join in the singing, blushing awkwardly. How graceless he could be. He was more than twenty-years-old, yet when he was not at our prayer meetings he became remote and monosyllabic. Secretive too. He would often disappear at night – for a walk, I presumed – only to return perturbed and wild-eyed many hours later.

The mystery deepened one night when I was sitting by candlelight engrossed in a work about herbs and their uses.

Bradford crept in and gave a start when he saw me and mumbled about having 'm—m—much to consider and losing track of the time', but instead of going to bed he sat down heavily in the rush chair. "You heard I received my inheritance."

I nodded.

"I decided to break with the past and sell my father's land, every single acre, and take all the money coming to me."

"It must give you great happiness to be free of money troubles."

"It fills me with anxiety to have so much." He stared at the dwindling flames of the fire. "I feel guilty. What have I done to deserve it?"

"The Lord never questioned the laws of inheritance," I reminded him. "Your father left you the bequest because that was the proper thing to do."

"And there are temptations," he added cryptically.

"God will help you resist them," I encouraged, but I did not pursue the subject.

He sat in silence biting his nails for several minutes. "I pray so." And he climbed the stairs to his bed in the attic.

"We never really know what lies in the dark corners of a man's heart," I reflected when I explained the strange encounter to Mary.

"I imagine it will be something to do with the service of Venus that has disturbed him." She was always more perceptive about human frailties than I. "We know that he cannot cope with the fair sex; just look how he behaves in their presence, he is at a loss."

"The youth Francyse rather turned his head," I said. "He gave him a glimpse of delights that were sinful but undoubtedly appealing, especially to an impressionable lad. He has yet to recover from the crippling self-absorption of his early years. He was excited by the goings-on at the Austerfield tavern but more than that, I rather think he was bewildered by the women who gathered there. I am sure they teased and tormented him, poor lad."

"And these days he's not helped by cheeky Mary Hardy." My wife smiled ruefully. "She gangs up with Desire to mock his high-pitched voice and his old-fashioned formality. It's galling to see how his stammer resurfaces and he blushes like a rose."

"The trouble is that he has little interest in everyday life," I ruminated. "He is so eloquent when it comes to our Bible readings, yet take him away from the Good Book and he is not much different from the nervy lad we first met... when was it? Nine years ago? I think the answer is to encourage him to discover a world beyond the pages of the scriptures and, indeed, beyond these four walls."

Mary nodded. "And one thing more: the boy needs a wife."

I don't know if he overheard our discussion but a few weeks later he looked up from his stew to say, "Now I have the money, I think I should move out and give you more space."

"Well, you know you have always been welcome here." I meant it. However odd – and that he was – he was part of our family. We loved him.

"I know and I am grateful, but I must be getting under your feet." He was embarrassed. Yes, I was sure he had heard us.

"But where will you go?" I asked.

"I have seen a tidy little place on Achtergracht. It has room for my loom and has enough light to work by."

"You know what you must also do?"

He shook his head.

"You must get spliced. You are a man of twenty-three now; it is your duty – and pleasure – to be looking out for a wife."

He blushed and stammered that he was 't—t—too young' and we did not refer to the matter again until several months later, when his lanky frame ducked into the house and, his voice rising a few flustered octaves, he announced, "I have taken your advice. I have proposed to a girl called Dorothy M—M—May. She seems well suited."

Of course, we congratulated him. I shook him by the hand and Mary poured him a small tot of juniper, which he sipped nervously. He did not appear as elated as he should and sat for a while in pensive quiet until Mary and the girls had gone to market.

"I first met her in Amsterdam when she was eleven. Her father is an elder there; you may have come across him."

Indeed I had. He visited me in the manor occasionally and we shared a philosophical joust or two. We agreed on more than we differed.

Will did not listen to my reply. He was too preoccupied. "I had to get his approval and we shall have to wait before, er, we m—m—marry, because she is only sixteen."

I murmured encouragingly about the delights of a joy delayed, but he had something else on his mind.

"Can I confide in you? I have never learnt what to expect of a woman, and as for l—l—love…" He trailed off uncertainly.

"Which of us does, however experienced?" I recalled the advice I had been given. "Couples should be about the same age," I continued but, remembering that he was several years older than his bride-to-be, went on swiftly. "They should share similar financial backgrounds and show the same amount of affection to each other. It's a matter of balance."

Poor lad – his face was set with anxiety, his cheeks were burning.

"Discuss it with Master Robinson," I suggested, realising I was not reassuring him. "He is so full of common sense on this matter."

A few days later he came knocking at the door but, in truth, he was considerably more perturbed.

"John had much sound advice." He could not look me in the face. "How the Lord requires in the man love and wisdom and in the woman subjection, that marriage is not to satisfy l—l—lust but to avoid it. He warned me against excess; that just as a man might drink too much in his own house, he might also be like an adulterer with his own wife if he overdoes the affection and the action. It is best, he assured me, to d—d—discourage her b—b—boiling lust by, er, coming t—t—together once a week at an ap—p—pointed hour."

I tried to soften the rigour of the pastor's guidance, which I considered was somewhat short of warmth and affection. No wonder the poor boy was babbling with anxiety.

"These days, in our Church, marriage is also an occasion for pleasure… within, er, reason," I tried to reassure him. "But also remember that to be sure children come along, you have to be a little bold, because that is expected in a man. You have to caress and arouse your wife."

"B—b—bold? Caress?"

"Maybe practical advice would help too." I called to mind my own confusion those many years before. "Here's a book by a noted physician, who recommends oysters with dill boiled in oil and carrots as an aid to happy procreation. He claims that if you eat a dog's cullions, you will beget sons, while if your wife partakes, she will have daughters."

The groom-in-waiting turned a faint shade of green so I changed tack. "Worry not. If you are as lucky as I have been with Mary, you will be content."

That November I heard that the banns had been read in Amsterdam's city hall, and soon enough he appeared at the house.

"This is Dorothy." He introduced a slip of a thing, a very tender sixteen to my eyes, but pretty enough in a pale way.

"A pleasure to meet you, sir." Her voice was so quiet I had to strain to hear.

"And you, my dear." Mary patted her gently on her arm. "If ever you need help or a sympathetic ear, you will be most welcome here."

The girl nodded politely and clutched William's hand. "I am sure I shall cope very well without having to trouble you."

"She's shy," I pronounced when they had gone.

Mary was offended. "I thought she could not wait to get away from us."

CHAPTER FIVE

TEMPTATIONS

FOLK FELT SORRY FOR ME BECAUSE MY FAMILY were quite a charge on me. They could not know that I had used up most of my savings, but they could see that my clothes, once the fashion – too bright, a tad gaudy, judged some – now hung threadbare, my beard had grown ragged and the grey hairs had begun to outnumber the brown.

I tried to stay cheerful but Mary understood that I was hiding my worries beneath a carapace of drollery and urged me to find consolation in my books, teaching my students and talking philosophy with Robinson.

It was not enough. For the first time in my life I was at a loss. I needed a challenge.

Robinson sensed my restlessness and revived an idea that he and I had been discussing for a while – the creation of a printing house. The pastor produced a veritable torrent of treatises, letters and essays, and he wanted to spread the word of Separatism to a wider audience, particularly in England. There was a problem, however. It was impossible to publish a word without it being registered with the Company of Stationers in London, and they would not permit publication without the agreement of the Church and the King. Would he tolerate the kind of dangerous works we had in mind? Indeed not.

"We should publish what we can and see if there are ways of circulating our writings without, er, involving the authorities," I proposed. "I have enough money from my teaching to afford typesetting equipment and there is room to set up a small press here at the back of the house now that Will has moved out."

My poor wife tutted with irritation at the clutter, especially as she had just given birth to our fifth child, who we named Wrestling, because, as she declared, "The Devil is always spoiling for a fight."

I promised to be as tidy as any man could possibly be, but I was in heaven. I loved the smell of the paper and the ink and the caress of the parchment under my hand. I thrilled at the feel of the long handle that turned the heavy wooden screw of the press down onto the paper and miraculously produced a sheet of paper full of words.

How proud I was with my first publication, a translation of a work by a Dutch theologian, which I inscribed with these words:

Lugundi Batavorum

Apud Guiljelmum Brewsterum

in Vico Chorali

It translated as: *In Leiden, at the home of William Brewster, in Choir Alley.* I could hardly admit that the home of our radical press was known as Stink Alley.

"We need to do more." Robinson was admiring a smart new translation of the Ten Commandments. "This is the way to tell the world about our beliefs."

"To spread the word further we require greater investment," I reminded him.

He scratched his head. "I have a businessman in mind who has made a fortune here in Leiden buying and selling anything from dates to timber. He has expressed an interest in our project."

That was good news indeed until I discovered our investor traded in saltpetre, the powder used to make explosives, which he acquired from an Amsterdam arms dealer. I was disturbed to learn he sold it in England with the help of a go-between called Thomas Weston, a London merchant of some kind.

"John, that means our godly work is to be financed by the trade in arms," I protested. "That cannot be right."

He would not be gainsaid. "Our message is the important thing and we have to compromise. After all, God used violence when it was necessary. Think of the fire and brimstone rained down on Sodom and Gomorrah, remember the violence of Jesus against the money changers in the temple. A small trade in weaponry signifies nothing when so much is at stake. I'm assured this Weston understands how the customs men operate. He knows the right people."

I pushed my disquiet to one side, especially as it meant that with the extra funds we were able to publish several more tracts, which earned us plaudits for their radical thinking.

But it was not until the day when there was a hearty knock on the door that our enterprise really began to flourish.

Mary opened it to a tall, curly-haired character with pink cheeks, a dashing moustache and a beard cut to a rakish point. He was aged, I guessed, about twenty-two.

"I am Edward Winslow," he announced. "From Droitwich

in Worcester. I gave up an apprenticeship with a London stationer to travel the world but heard about your cause and am eager to join. I hear you have a publishing house. I am a professional printer. Can I work for you?"

His zest and easy charm immediately won over Mary, who invited him to stay as our lodger. What a fine companion he turned out to be – not to mention an adroit word setter – and what a contrast to Will with his anxieties and febrile sensitivities, which he displayed yet again one summer's day in 1617 when he called by with Dorothy.

"She is expecting." He was matter-of-fact while his wife managed only a wan smile.

Mary embraced the girl warmly but she sat in stony silence while her husband toyed nervously with a lemon pasty that Mary had brought fresh from the oven. I wondered which of my advice William had taken to ensure the pregnancy, but I could hardly raise that delicate subject with Dorothy alongside him.

I poured them mead and saluted their happy news, but Will was clearly not in the mood for small talk.

"I have lost my money. All spent."

"My dear Will! How… why?"

"It is my fault." He had the look of sullen defensiveness that he used to hide behind when he was a boy.

He gnawed at his fingernails. "I was sure I could afford the house. I hoped I would earn enough to afford a few small comforts."

Dorothy pursed her lips.

"It is a correction bestowed by God for certain decays of internal piety," he muttered in one of his curious turns of phrase. "I have learnt a lesson."

Mary looked up from her knitting and held my eye. Dark corners indeed.

"Let us hope so." Dorothy spoke through gritted teeth.

"I will work harder. We might sell the house for something smaller."

"If we can help in any way…" Mary started, but the girl unexpectedly burst out.

"I fear for this unborn child. What future is there for him here? We live in poverty, we have always lived in poverty, and now we might soon be without a home."

Her husband stumbled on. "I will m—m—make it right but, even without my m—m—mistakes, life is hard. Too hard. We work all the hours we can, but wool combing and weaving earn us so little. You know that, Master Brewster."

Only too well. My latest ragged offering of ribbon lay draped over the back of a chair. No one would pay for that.

"Our only reward is to breathe in the fumes from the rinsing and dyeing," he continued. "There's hardly a person here without a cough or chest disease."

"It is no way to exist." Dorthy wrinkled her nose in distaste. "The canals are filled with so much waste they are like sewers."

"No wonder some of our brethren, particularly the older folk, no longer have the strength to resist the crosses and sorrows that bear down on them." Will had worked himself up into such indignation that he was gripped by a coughing fit. He took a sip of mead and grimaced. "They are thinking of returning to England, prepared to risk p—p—prison, ready to face death like Master Helwys."

Poor Thomas. He had continued his fight for religious liberty in London but, as we had feared, the King had short shrift with his sedition and imprisoned him in London's infamous Clink. And there he died, only forty. As for his wife Joan, always so intrepid, what of her? There was no news. Maybe she had gone into hiding with one of her many children; more like she perished in a lonely cell and was buried in a pauper's grave.

I shook myself back to the present to listen to Will, who by now was thoroughly agitated.

"What really concerns me is that so many of our youth are being influenced by the l-l-licentiousness of the Dutch youth and led into the t-t-temptations of the city and its dangerous ways. So many of them want to taste freedom, they want to leave their parents and become soldiers or sailors. Many have become so degenerate that their very souls are corrupted. If that is not bad enough, our people are marrying locals." He buried his head in his hands as if to suppress the idea of such unseemly intermingling.

Dorothy spoke up with uncharacteristic force. "A man was killed in the next street to us over an argument about the scriptures and was left lying by the gutter with no one coming to help him. That's not the world we want for our child."

Her husband took a listless bite of his pasty. "This is not me being new-fangled or giddy. I tell you, there are many weighty reasons for good men and their families to leave this city and find a new life."

CHAPTER SIX

FAREWELL TO BABYLON

A FEW DAYS LATER I WALKED DOWN THE ALLEY – which was filthier than ever, though that might just have been my jaundiced mood – and joined Will and John Robinson in Green Close. The strains of children singing wafted through the open window from the house of the music teacher who lived on the square, but they were abruptly drowned out by the discordant fracas of drums, shouts and gunfire.

"It's those trouble-making Arminians." Robinson made no attempt to hide his irritation. "They have been rioting outside city hall against the Dutch church, which, quite rightly, rejects their benighted beliefs about predestination. How can such otherwise intelligent people claim that every sinner has a free will to decide his eternal destiny? The burgomaster has set the Red and White Guards on them. That should clear their heads."

He closed the window to shut out the racket and sighed. "Did you hear that our old companion Richard Clyfton has died? He was broken by the scandals that enmeshed him."

"We must remember only his early days when he showed such bold vision and forgive his later foolishness," I declared.

"Amen to that." Will was deeply moved by the news. "I will always remember the first sermon I heard him give. 'Anyone who dares to usurp the authority of Jesus Christ shall be brought down to the dust as abominable c—c—carcasses.' I had never heard anything like it. He set me on this road."

"Perhaps the end of this particular road is near," ventured Robinson. "Clyfton's passing is, perhaps, a symbol of what has gone wrong with our mission. Good men have been led into iniquity, bad people have prospered, and our high hopes have been dragged down by dissension and, as we know, by sin. Many of the congregation agree with you, Will. They have also talked to me about moving away."

I had not realised that feeling was so strong because my head was stuck in my publishing work and I was oblivious to such talk amongst our people.

"Are you thinking of another town in the Netherlands? Zeeland, perhaps."

"No, I think we should look further afield."

"Back to England and risk the fate suffered by Master Helwys? Surely not."

"No, indeed." Robinson shook his head ruefully. "I was at a meeting when one of our brethren suggested that and, my word, what a fury it unleashed. They railed that such a move would be mightily displeasing to God because he had already rescued us from the Babylon that is England, the mother of all abominations, the habitation of devils and the hiding place of all foul spirits. So England, I think, is out of the question," he concluded dryly.

"Maybe we should be bold," suggested Will. "Go far from here, m—m—miles from England too, where we can be truly free."

His sudden impetuosity stirred me. "Indeed yes, how about Guiana or the Caribbean outposts that Sir Walter Raleigh has discovered? Maybe the island of Bermuda, which by all accounts is rich in tobacco."

"Perhaps." John leant forward to ensure our concentration. "But, rather, I think, Virginia. There is a settlement there called Jamestown. A Virginia Company arranges the royal patents for ownership and raises the money to fund such colonies. We should petition the King to discover if we can join them."

Will's eyes shone with the same fervour that he had shown in the manor at Scrooby when, as a nervy seventeen-year-old, he had urged us to flee like the Israelites to a promised land. "We could establish a perfect society, once and for all time. Throw off the disappointment we have encountered here and live at liberty from all interference in a land where God rules and everything is done in his name."

"There is one small impediment." I had to bring us all back to Earth. "King James. He harried us out of England; why would he want to waste his money on blaspheming fanatics like us, as I recall he dubbed us in one of his gentler insults?"

"It might suit his purpose to send us," offered John. "If we succeed, he profits; if we die in the attempt, he won't care very much."

"A good point, if a trifle pessimistic, Master John, but yes, maybe we should dip a toe in those uneasy waters." I was warming to the idea, albeit cautiously. "I know a man called Sir Edwin Sandys. I have not seen him for many years but I hear he is a leading light in the Virginia Company. You might remember Sandys, Will. He was at the manor the day the King called by."

William cast back. "I remember thinking how he seemed altogether more the gentleman than that poor creature, the King. It will be proof of God's favour should our paths cross again."

It was agreed. I sent a letter to Sandys, reminding him of our meeting, flattering him on his success with the Virginia Company (though I had little evidence of it) and outlining our desire to establish a small settlement.

His reply came surprisingly quickly. It was welcoming and positive but there were conditions, the kind of impediments we were to become used to.

I skimmed through the letter. "He has put our proposal before the Privy Council, but what a suspicious crew they are. They insist we explain where we stand on such contentious issues as the power of bishops and how we conduct our services."

"Why do they make such unjust insinuations?" Will was indignant. "We should tell them how grieved we are at their reaction."

"We must never forget how hostile the King has been to us," I reminded him. "We must tread carefully. Be humble – or at least, pretend to be. I suggest we write back to say that we are glad of the opportunity to clear matters up with such honourable personages."

"Master Brewster is correct," said Robinson. "We must not offend them. We should admit that there are some small accidental differences between our beliefs and the Church – the roles of the pastors and elders, for example – because, in faith, they will hardly matter when we are thousands of miles away. Above all, we have to affirm that we swear allegiance to the monarch as Supreme Governor of the Church of England."

"We have come a long way from Scrooby," I observed. "Monarch as Supreme Governor, eh?"

"A gesture, merely." Robinson was dismissive. "It is his church he rules, not ours."

Our conciliatory tone seemed to work, for within the month Sandys wrote to say the King and his bishops had accepted our appeal and that soon there would be 'something to communicate'.

But then, not a word.

Some months later I bumped into Will walking hastily through the hubbub of the Aalmarkt.

"We have had our baby." He showed no great emotion at such joyful news. "It is a boy. Dorothy wants to call him John after Master Robinson."

"Congratulations, Will. Mary will be delighted to hear your news."

"Thank you. It is God's blessing on us."

Robinson was flattered by the infant bearing his name, but he was preoccupied.

"We are not making fast enough progress with the Virginia Company. Writing letters, relying on go-betweens, waiting for replies. Nothing is happening."

"Perhaps we should send emissaries to London to put pressure on the Virginia Company?" suggested Will.

"But who?" I wondered. "Will has duties here as a new father. Master Winslow and I are finishing an important project, so that counts us out. And anyway, I rather believe my energetic assistant is quietly courting that jolly sprite Elizabeth Barker – more than a match for his derring-do, I'd say."

"John Carver would be a sound choice." Robinson ignored my frivolity. "He has the respect of the Church and we have known him from the days when he came to Scrooby to join our prayers. He is also my brother-in-law, as you know, but most importantly he is a prosperous businessman whose negotiating skills are well honed."

"Who will go with him?"

"I suggest Robert Cushman." There was a disconcerted silence at the pastor's suggestion. "He is a good man who has proved as a deacon that he is organised and clear in his beliefs."

I had bumped into Master Cushman only the day before in St Peter's Square. It was a freezing winter morning, the children were throwing snowballs and skipping precariously on the icy cobbles. He had been praying in St Peter's, as he did every morning, for his wife and two children, who had all died within a few months of each other that very year. A terrible burden and one he was not ashamed to admit had tested his faith.

"I know I must accept His judgement, but the Lord has yet to explain to me why he has inflicted this pain on me," he had confessed as we stood shivering. All I could do was murmur a feeble aphorism about time, the great executor, and how, no doubt, his wife's spirit lived on in his ten-year-old son and his infant daughter.

"Some blessing, at least," I suggested, but he was not moved.

"Are you sure he is the right choice?" Will expressed what was in my mind. "He has not been the same since tragedy afflicted him."

"Do you think he has the strength for such an endeavour?" The doubt must have shown on my face because Robinson spoke out firmly. "The very fact that he has suffered much should harden him to adversity. To help him recover his former serenity, I have suggested that he marries again. I have introduced him to Mary Shingleton, whose husband died some six months ago, and I expect a wedding in June. That should cheer him and sharpen his resolve."

Being men of duty, both of them agreed to the task; Carver with enthusiasm but Cushman reluctantly. For the first time I noticed he had a tic in his right eye, as he blinked around the room like a rabbit caught in the beam of a lamp before agreeing.

"I will do my best."

For me, I could return to my printing press. I was so emboldened by our successes that I published a work by a Scottish preacher entitled *Perth Assembly*. It was a denunciation of the way King James was imposing the power of the bishops on the Presbyterian Church in Scotland. It was a fierce work and I was proud to publish it.

The businessman Weston, who Robinson had hired to smuggle the copies out of the country, convinced him that the safest way to deceive customs was by hiding the copies in wine vats.

Robinson was impressed. "You see, I told you he was clever. The authorities will never think of looking in a barrel of port."

CHAPTER SEVEN

BRAVE NEW WORLD?

I ASSUMED I WOULD BE LEFT TO MY OWN DEVICES, happily printing pamphlets, reading my books and watching my family prosper, but no such luck. Some months later Robinson asked me if I could help Carver and Cushman in their negotiations, and I had little choice but to agree.

After all, I was the one man who had any knowledge of London and, more, knew how the court worked, how its officials and hangers-on manoeuvred, dissembled and boosted their esteem in the eyes of the King rather than doing anything worthwhile.

"Their talks started so well." Robinson was impatient. "The King did agree to grant us a patent but he changed his mind and changed it again, so now our hopes have become bogged down in a quagmire of delays and indecision. Carver and Cushman need your advice."

So it was that I sailed to London and joined the two men in their lodgings in the White Hart in Aldersgate, just inside the city walls. The street was so narrow that the eaves of the houses almost touched, reducing the daylight to a few feeble rays – just enough to pick my way through the filth underfoot. The putrid gutter that was the River Thames was just a short step away and brooding over us, the bulk of St Paul's Cathedral.

"Having to look at that every day is a constant reminder of the power of the King's Church," remarked Carver dryly.

"And what we are pitted against," added Cushman gloomily.

By chance, the tavern was a few doors down from the London house of Sir Edwin Sandys, the very place where the directors of the Virginia Company held their conferences.

I arranged a meeting the next day and we were ushered into his study, fashionably accoutred with an oak wainscot and Turkish carpets, where Sandys, now a corpulent figure in his forties, peered at me with oddly bulging eyes.

"Ah yes, Master Brewster, you owned the manor on the road to London where we stopped with our dear King. He commented on the tastiness of your capons. A pleasure to meet you again."

"A delight for me too," I replied. "It must be fifteen years ago."

"How time flies and circumstance changes," he remarked absently. "The King has seen fit to honour me with a knighthood since we met."

"Indeed. Congratulations."

"Well, we can reminisce later. We have much to discuss." He spun a globe and stopped it with his finger on New England. "Everyone knows that the Company has struggled financially. But now I have been appointed treasurer, I plan to make Virginia profitable – and to do that, the settlers must rely less on tobacco for trade and more on beaver and fish. We need many more recruits to increase the population and we need women." He raised a knowing eyebrow. "You cannot make a colony grow without women, can you?"

"We will be taking our families," I explained. "We are not a bunch of mercenaries going all that way merely to catch and sell fish. We will make our home there and future generations will flourish." And in case he had missed the point, I added, "There will be several single females."

"Good. Breeding stock. That will impress the men who matter."

He scanned a document we had drawn up for him to present to the Privy Council.

"Clever work," he acknowledged. "Of course, you have to say, as you do, that you will stay within the law, you accept His Majesty as Supreme Governor, only he can appoint bishops, and lastly you desire to give due honour to all your superiors, etc, etc, but I notice you add a proviso that the King's authority has to be within the rulings of God. Yes indeed, clever; acknowledges the power of the King while covering your conscience. Well, I have to admit it is sensibly worded, but remember there are many in high places opposed to dissenters like yourselves and they will be reluctant to let you roam the world spreading your particular brand of faith – or heresy, as they would call it."

Despite his note of caution, Carver and I were in such a confident mood when we returned to the tavern that we ordered special helpings of brawn pudding and sauce and jugs of ale.

"It will be settled within weeks." I really believed it.

"I pray so." Cushman was not convinced.

"It had better be," asserted Carver. "We cannot delay much longer."

I did not wish to remain in London any more than necessary either. I had forgotten what a ditch of depravity the city was. If Will had condemned Leiden as a den of licentiousness, what would he make of this horrible travesty of all God taught us?

In Aldersgate, where wealthy bankers and merchants rubbed shoulders with writers and poets, there were alehouses full of drunks fighting and vomiting in the street and Covent Garden nuns, as those particular ladies were called, in flagrant, foul-mouthed display outside the brothels that graced – rather, I should say shamed – the neighbourhood.

I was walking as fast as I could, averting my gaze from a couple drunkenly pawing each other outside the Cardinal's Cap, when a sedan almost knocked me over. Sandys leant out.

"Master Brewster, I have news. The King has deemed your petition a good and honest motion. He asked, 'What profits may arise in the parts to which they intend to go?' I told him, 'Fishing.' 'So God have my soul,' cried the King. ''Tis an honest trade! It was the Apostle's own calling.'"

"That is most encouraging," I enthused. I did not think it wise to confess to our complete lack of skill when it came to fishing.

"The King plans to consult with the Archbishops of Canterbury and London and other learned prelates, but I see no hindrance to our plans." With that, the sedan chair took him off into the hurly burly of the city.

"I will believe that when I see a signed document in front of me." Cushman had been so ground down by the dithering inaction over the months that he assumed every move would be checkmated by the Privy Council or the King. And with good reason; a few weeks later we heard that His Majesty had, after all, decided not to grant us a patent. His enthusiasm for fishing had apparently waned.

We heard nothing for months after that. Sandys reassured us one day that all was well; the next that the Privy Council had rejected another bid for a patent, and while we waited, rumours swirled around the tavern that the Virginia Company itself was threatened with bankruptcy. They were all dismissed by a breezy Sandys.

We kept up our spirits with prayer meetings and talks held with great secrecy in the homes of our fellow believers who lived in the city. I studied religious tracts and added to my library books on medicine and silk – I had a vague idea that Virginia might be just the place to breed the worms – and I acquired works by Aristotle and Macchiavelli. One salutary tome, *The Scourge of Drunkards*, was a selection of sermons on the sin of drinking. Quite a revelation.

Occasionally Carver and I entertained ourselves with trips to the Globe Theatre, where one of our favourites was *The Tempest* by Master Shakespeare. Like most of the audience, I revelled in the shenanigans of the monstrous Caliban and his drunken cohorts, but I was much taken by the words of Prospero's daughter Miranda after her shipwreck on the island:

> Oh, wonder!
> How many goodly creatures are there here!
> How beauteous mankind is! O brave new world,
> That has such people in 't!

Brave new world. What would we find on the other side of the Atlantic? Grotesques like the drunken Stephano or beings with the nobility of Prospero?

Cushman refused to 'waste his time' by joining me in such frivolity; instead he spent his days scribbling away in his chambers. "Just a few notes on our dealings here," he muttered. He seemed embarrassed at being found working on a project of his own and was reluctant to share his 'notes' with me.

He did, however, put down his quill when Master Carver suggested we made the acquaintance of the many merchants in the city who were seeking to invest their money in profitable projects.

"We are getting nowhere with Sandys, but he is not the only person with contacts in the court. I have heard many good things about an enterprising gentleman by the name of Sir Ferdinando Gorges who started a settlement in Virginia, and though it failed, he is always launching some new venture or other."

I remembered him from the Queen's court. A flamboyant personality who made much of the fact that he had raised the alarm in '88 when the Spanish armada threatened our shores. Rather pleased with himself.

Gorges was too preoccupied with his own schemes to rekindle our acquaintance, especially one as slight as mine, so instead we introduced ourselves to a businessman, Sir John Slaney, who was treasurer of the Newfoundland Company, a small trading centre to the north of New England.

He was no help, but he was most welcoming. "Have a taste of this latest vintage." He thrust a bottle at us. "I know a skipper in the wine trade who is just in from Bordeaux. Owns a ship called the *Gadfly*. No, that's not it… the *Mayflower*."

The wine was excellent, but we were more intrigued by his household. Slaney owned three Indian slaves who had been kidnapped from New England some three years or more before in 1614 and taken to Spain before fetching up in London. To my amazement, one of them – he was called Squanto – spoke very good English. Not only that, but the savage was polite, civilised and, I have to say, a cut above the ruffians who loitered on the city's streets.

The three of us were returning from Slaney one autumn afternoon when our coach was held up by a crowd of the city's dregs drinking and cheering, one holding the effigy of a head on a pole.

"What's amiss?" I asked.

"It's Walter Raleigh," cried one. "Justice has caught up with the bastard at last. 'E's been beheaded."

He was pushed aside by another from the mob. "He were a bleedin' 'ero. Should 'ave seen the way he took the axe in his own 'ands and shouted, 'Do you think I am afraid of it? This is a sharp medicine, but it is a physician for all diseases. Strike, man, strike.'"

His execution was no great shock. From my days in court I knew Raleigh to be a brave explorer and a champion of the late Queen Elizabeth, though prone to flout the proprieties of palace life. The charge was treachery – trumped up I had no doubt – but the execution was intended to prove to a sceptical country that King James was his own man and no longer in the shadow of good Queen Bess's glorious reign.

And that did not bode well for us.

CHAPTER EIGHT

HIDE AND SEEK

A S THOUGH THE WAITING, THE DASHED HOPES and false promises were not enough, it all went arsey-varsey, as Mary Hardy used to cry when the milk boiled over or pigs broke into the barn and ate the apples.

A courier from Leiden arrived with the news that the wine vats concealing our precious pamphlets had been seized and the King was demanding the heads of the perpetrators. All London knew he was gripped with a paranoia more consuming than at any other time in his reign. Any slight, let alone a hostile tract like the one I had printed, drove him to a fury.

He had been criticised for his drinking, and denounced for his passion for boys and an unhealthy 'love' for his chief adviser, the Duke of Buckingham, a gross aberration which made my flesh creep. His enemies satirised the slobbering way he talked and the way he constantly fiddled with his cod piece. Yes, His Majesty was hurt and angry, and he wanted his enemies rooted out.

Could I lie low and wait for the storm to pass? The answer was quick in coming. The King's ambassador in Holland, one Sir Dudley Carleton, discovered that I was the publisher of an 'atrocious and seditious libel' and announced that he was hot on my heels. Constables on both sides of the North Sea were on the lookout for me.

"I shall have to disappear," I told Cushman.

"What shall I do?" His tic was more vivid than ever. "How will I cope?"

"Tell Pastor Robinson I have gone away."

"Where to?"

"Anywhere. Write that Mr B is not well at this time; whether he will come back to you or not I don't know. Something like that. John will understand."

Like a homing pigeon, I headed toward Scrooby where I still knew scores of people and hoped I could disappear for a few months, but I had ridden to Nottingham when I was recognised by a farmer I used to do business with. I reckoned if I was known that far from my old home, news of my existence would be all over the parish in minutes, so I slipped back to London where one of our sympathisers hid me in his loft.

"If anyone asks who I am, say I am a Master Williamson in London on business," I told Cushman.

"Of course, of course," he gabbled. "But have you heard the latest? Carleton is claiming you left Leiden three weeks ago and are now in London."

"In that case, I will give his men the slip and return to Leiden. He won't think of looking for me so close to home."

If the customs men had been more alert, they might have stopped a Master Williamson and found his papers were not in order. Instead I tucked myself into the darkest corner of the ship and when I reached Leiden avoided the Aalmarkt, which was always patrolled by constables, and cut along the back streets into Stink Alley. Mary clung to me, weeping with relief.

"What is the news?" I asked. "The last I heard, Carleton claimed I was in London."

She poured me a mug of beer, with trembling hands and gave a strangled laugh. "He is baffled about your whereabouts. Last week he claimed to have seized you, only to find it was the wrong man."

"He blamed his bailiff for the mistake," chortled Winslow. "A dull drunk oaf, he called him."

"I shall do my best to add to his puzzlement." I felt sure I could escape his clumsy clutches. "They won't catch me, be sure of that, but you and the children must move somewhere safer and we will have to cease our printing."

I spoke too soon. There was a tremendous pounding on the door, which was sent crashing into the front room. A band of guards burst in; they thrust aside Mary and the children and shoved Winslow and me against the wall at the point of their halberds, and with savage glee smashed up the typesetting equipment, tore up our pamphlets, ripped apart the books and threw them on the fire.

I did not wait to find out what they had in mind for me. While they were revelling in the flames of their destruction, I dashed through the back door, leapt over the wall – almost knocking over two lovers in the alley – and ran to the university. I would be safe there; it was outside the jurisdiction of city law.

My students smuggled me to Amsterdam in a barge concealed under a pile of cabbages before I doubled back, first to Leiden and on to a village called Leiderdorp, just outside the city borders.

I was lurking in a barn that had been used all winter to shelter cattle and was now, in the heat of summer, as rancid as a dead badger when I heard voices. They had found me. I crouched behind a pile of hay stooks as the door creaked open and a thin shaft of sun picked out the eddy of insects that spiralled above rotting cowpats.

Should I stay and fight? My fists would have no chance against the swords of the guards. Best to make a run for it. Then, the oddest thing, a girl singing in tremulous tunelessness. *"Oh, for joy my spirits were quick. To hear the bird, how…"*

I knew that tune: 'By A Bank As I Lay'. Mary Hardy. I laughed out loud, threw aside my straw defences and flung the door wide open to find two figures standing there.

"Jonathan, my son. And Mary. I never thought I'd be pleased to hear you sing ever again." She looked hurt at my careless slight so I hastily added, "As soothing a signal of help that any man could wish for."

"Master reckoned it would alert you without anyone else knowing what it significated."

"That was very wise." I was suitably contrite. "Thank you."

"We've brought you food." She thrust a loaf of bread and cheese into my hands.

"And beer," said my lad.

"Even wiser. Get inside quick and shut the door. It was very brave of you to risk coming here. I'm sure Carleton's spies are everywhere."

"No one saw us, Father." Jonathan did his best to put on a brave face, but he kept darting frightened glances at the door. "And if they did, folk would think we were just a couple stepping out."

Mary giggled. "Fat chance."

I devoured the bread and cheese with the ferocity of a starved dog.

"Your mother, the children – how are they?"

"They are well, staying with friends," Jonathan reassured me. "But they are under watch. Carleton is still insisting that he will capture you and give you a thrashing, though he does seem to be in a muddle. One day he says you have been spotted in Leiden again and only fourteen days later he has to admit you have not returned. Then he claims you won't be coming back or that you have moved the family away. It's obvious he doesn't have a clue where you are."

"Well, that gives me time to find another hiding place."

"Master Allerton has a theory about Carleton's failure to find you. The good ambassador is spending most of his time collecting fine antiques and works of art for the King when he should be attending to matters of state."

"And runnin' after you, Master B," cackled Mary.

"He has become very close to a painter called Rubens who Master Allerton knows to be rich and successful. Apparently Carleton is busy doing deals with him."

"Well, let's hope he keeps still long enough to have his portrait painted by this Master Rubens." I made a joke of it but I knew sooner or later my luck would run out.

"Master Robinson says you should get back to London and vanish," said Jonathan. "He has hired a trawlerman to take you to Delfshaven and from there it should be easy enough to find a ship to smuggle you to England. Master Cushman can help you hide and stay undetected until everything cools down."

"My boy, bring me some fresh clothes and more food. This time tomorrow I shall disappear. Pfft. Just like that. I have a feeling, though, that it is Robert Cushman more than I who could do with help."

CHAPTER NINE

INTRODUCING
THOMAS WESTON

B Y THE TIME I REACHED LONDON, DEEP, DARK
winter gripped the city. A raw wind whistled off the
river, icicles hung from eaves and the smoke from well-
banked fires spiralled turgidly out of chimneys and became
a freezing fog which wreathed along the streets. Some days
I could only tell if anyone was close by the sound of their
coughing.

I kept on the move from safe house to safe house until
it became clear that the King had lost interest in me. Sandys
had stayed in his Kent estates hunting, and hopefully Master
Carleton was spending his time with this Rubens character, so
I was content to pass the days reading while Cushman spent
the hours working away at his mysterious 'scribblings'.

When Sandys did return, our hopes were raised – and
immediately dashed – with the rejection of another patent
by the Privy Council, only to be lifted once more when the

New Netherland Company in Amsterdam, something like our worthless Virginia Company, offered us free transport to New Amsterdam, their colony on the Hudson River. They sweetened the offer with a promise of cattle for every family.

It was too good to be true. Within weeks, a promise to provide two warships to protect us from pirates was broken and we were back where we started.

While we came to terms with those disappointments, we were driven into a fury of frustration by a decision by the Virginia Company to fund a rival. Bad enough that we had been disregarded, but what stuck in our craw was that the expedition was to be led by an elder named Francis Blackwell, a charlatan and a cheat. A few years before, he had been seized at an unlawful prayer meeting but saved his skin by betraying a fellow Separatist. Bradford had condemned him with unusual brevity: "He won the bishop's favour but not the Lord's."

Perhaps the Lord had taken note of his shameful behaviour, for Blackwell's expedition ended in tragedy. Packed in like herrings, they were stricken with dysentery and by the time they reached Virginia, the skipper and his crew were dead and only fifty of the 200 passengers survived.

"What of Blackwell?" I asked.

"Dead," stated Carver bluntly. "It is a miracle that so many survived."

With so little progress in London, I returned home to find the news of Blackwell's disastrous voyage had our people all a-jitter. Many were keen to abandon the flight to Virginia and rather remain in Leiden, however 'licentious' it might be. Why sail to an unknown land if the reward was drowning or disease? they demanded. Now the talk was not of the golden opportunities offered by a vast and fruitful land, but how we would freeze to death in winters of unbearable bitterness and struggle to survive in summers hotter than a furnace.

"Brutish men like wild beasts are waiting to kill us in the most barbarous manner," predicted one of the congregation.

"They flay their victims alive with the shells of fishes," claimed another.

"They cut off their members and limbs piece by piece and roast their flesh," asserted a third.

Who knew where they got these frenzied ideas from?

Robinson was shaken by the discord and blamed Master Cushman for everything that had gone wrong.

"He has proved himself to be brainless," he seethed. "All our difficulties are being made worse by his negligence. Fortunately I have found the solution." He was discomfited and, unusually, did not meet my gaze. "While you have been in London, we had a meeting with the businessman Thomas Weston. He is, er, to help us."

I was aghast. "The man whose crazy scheme had me hunted across two countries?"

"He has good contacts." Bradford, too, was embarrassed.

"We have to be realistic." Robinson had recovered from his momentary awkwardness. "He knows many wealthy businessmen, Merchant Adventurers he calls them, who have money to invest, and others who are eager to make their fortunes in Virginia."

"He says he has a ship ready for us," added Winslow.

"I was on the run for months because of his cocksure stupidity," I protested. "Clearly, he is not be trusted."

Robinson set his face. He was not to be deterred. "We have had several meetings with him and we have agreed to draw up a list of conditions so that his investors can understand our aims and provide us with shipping and money."

"Perhaps I could look at these 'arrangements.'" I was mightily exasperated.

There were ten points and, to be fair, they were sensible enough. Each person would have a share worth £10, which would be valued in money or the equivalent in materials. We would take part in a joint stock partnership with these Adventurers that would last for seven years, after which time all the benefits from trade and building houses would be owned by us settlers. The profits from fishing and tilling the land would also end up in our hands.

"And look here." Robinson pointed to a paragraph. "Everyone will be entitled to two days of rest a week for prayer and relaxation."

Isaac Allerton spoke up. "Once the seven years are up, we will be free from debt and able to lead our lives as we have dreamt of for many a year." I confess, I was irritated by the way he had worked his way into the inner circle while I had been away.

There was one more revelation for me.

"We have found a ship." Allerton was pleased with himself. "She's called the *Speedwell* and we will use her when we reach our new home for fishing and exploring. She is only small, about sixty tons, but she saw action against the Spanish at the Armada so she must be sound."

"That was thirty years ago." I was not impressed. "Isn't that rather old for a ship to cross the Atlantic?"

"I am assured that she is totally seaworthy," insisted Bradford. "She is being refitted in Delfshaven with taller masts and broader sails, which she will need to speed us along. The plan is to journey to Southampton and rendezvous there with these Merchant Adventurers from London, and sail on in convoy."

Robinson broke in. "I, by the by, have decided to wait

behind with my dear wife Bridget and the family to make sure all is in order here. We shall follow in a few months. The flock here needs as much care as you will on the brave adventure. More, perhaps, because you will have many leaders of our community with you."

Needless to say, Cushman was hurt – no, incensed – to have been sidelined in the decision to appoint Weston. "Never heard of him and I have met all the reputable merchants in the city. Let me see these so-called arrangements."

As I handed the papers over, I relayed a warning from Robinson. "He is adamant that you follow the plans that have been agreed with Weston to the letter. I cannot stress that enough, Master Cushman."

"I think that rather depends on this Weston," he replied with asperity. "He, too, must follow these conditions."

A few days later, a smartly dressed gent with an air of nonchalant superiority sauntered into the tavern.

"Weston," he murmured. "Thomas Weston." He proffered a much-ringed hand in a limp handshake.

Cushman bridled. Carver affected a cool politeness.

"How splendid to make your acquaintance. Splendid. I have met your people in Leiden, as you know. Good men all. Good. We have much to talk about, I deem."

Should I mention the wine vats and the turmoil he caused me? Best not; but I did resolve to watch him closely.

"Now, thanks to my friends in the city, you will have the backing you need," he continued. "There will be none of the shilly-shallying that you had to endure with the Virginia Company. Shilly-shallying. I and my people are sure that you will make a healthy profit out of fishing – and if you prosper, so do they."

He held the agreement in his palm as though he was

weighing a brace of mackerel. "I foresee no problems, Master, er, Williamson." I still felt it wise to keep up the pretence. "I will consult with my investors and come back to you in a blink. A blink." With that he bowed and slipped out of the tavern before I could inquire how many merchants he actually had waiting to invest in our fishing enterprise and, more important, when we could inspect the ship he claimed to have hired.

Cushman rubbed his eye to stop the tic. "He is not a man to trust."

I did not need convincing.

From the papers of
Robert Cushman, 1620

I do not know who is more troublesome, this Weston who is clearly an impostor or, forgive me, Pastor Robinson, admirable though he is, who constantly complains about my endeavours on his behalf.

He has put his trust in Weston but if he could see the way this ironmonger, for that is all he is, twists and turns, lies and cheats, he would think differently. Apparently Weston claimed months ago that he had hired a ship to take us to Virginia. But where is it? The man is obviously a scoundrel.

After weeks of silence he turns up at the tavern, disturbing my work on a treatise which I am writing to demonstrate why we Separatists are the noblest of the movements which oppose the established church. Without preamble he announces that the Adventurers have rejected the ten articles of the arrangement.

"But you promised me that they accepted them," I protest. "You boasted that there were seventy wealthy men ready to invest in us and our enterprise. £500 each, you told me."

He spreads his arms in that shifty way he has and gives a shrug of disavowal. "I am sorry. Sorry." How annoying it is, the way he repeats himself. "The investors do not accept that the homes and lands should remain wholly in your ownership come the end of the seven years. They must be shared between all. Nor do they agree that you should enjoy two days a week lolling about in rest."

I am furious. "You know that is an essential part of the deal."

He strokes his beard. "We shall not raise the money without these changes." Smooth-as-silk. "Already my colleagues are threatening to pull out — indeed, only yesterday one withdrew his £500. Others will follow. It's risky to ignore their wishes. Risky. They need to be sure they can make a profit."

What can I do? He is playing a game and I have no choice but to agree to his terms, otherwise the voyage is over before it starts. I know the congregation will not be pleased but I am deeply hurt — no, shocked — by a letter that Robinson, Master Bradford and Allerton send to Carver — not to me, I note — rejecting these new conditions.

Now it is they who threaten to pull out of the venture, and they accuse me of being too singular and 'full of presumptuous arguments.' Further, they malign me for making conditions more suitable for 'thieves and bond slaves' than honest men.

They actually write: 'Robert Cushman wants to know why we dislike these changes, saying we think he has no brains, but all we want him to do is exercise those brains and remember our instructions to you both that you must not exceed the bounds of the arrangement.'

To my utter mortification they add: 'Salute Master Weston. We hope he is not deceiving us. Tell him how much we rely on him and have confidence in him.'

Confidence! Rely! How easy it is for Bradford with his pedantic certainties, to pass judgement — though how a man who mysteriously lost all his money can consider himself qualified to do so beats me. And as for the tailor Allerton — too glib, too clever by half — and that roaring rabble-rouser

Standish... *I really cannot understand how they have inveigled their way into Robinson's trust.*

There is a complete schism between us here and in Leiden. Such clamours jangling.

While I digest this hateful missive, Weston flounces – that is the word for it – into the tavern and without preamble hisses, "Everything is in chaos. Chaos. Why are your people being so headstrong? What about the provisions? Some goods are being bought in Leiden, some by you here, others by Master Carver in Southampton."

I have to agree. It is a shambles. On the pretext that the **Speedwell** is to rendezvous with us in Southampton, Master Carver has taken himself off to the south coast to buy supplies. Heaven knows what and how much of our funds he is wasting because I most certainly do not.

To add to the confusion, he has written to Robinson full of complaints about me, actually accusing me of negligence. Pah. I marvel why so negligent a man as myself was given this undertaking.

I work myself up into quite a stew and write to Robinson, *'Let me have no more stir about these conditions. Let us have quietness.'*

Some hope. Weston sidles into the tavern to tell me – tell me! – that Leiden has appointed some businessman or other to raise funds and secure stores in what they describe as a fair and efficient way. And what is the result? Within weeks, Weston comes to me complaining that £700 has been spent in Southampton.

"But on what?" he demands to know. "On what?"

"I have to remind you that this was your appointment," I retort with asperity. "He is not under my control."

The shrug. The nothing-to-do-with-me.

"It would help if we could be sure there was a ship ready to transport us." My patience is shot through. "I believe you *promised one was ready for hire. A pledge you made many months ago."*

I had hoped to catch him off-guard but he is ready for that.

"Of course," he says and gestures as if it was there in front of us. "Of course. Let us meet tomorrow. Bring Master Williamson and I will introduce you to both ship and captain."

He finishes his Madeira and saunters out of the tavern.

The man is impossible.

Chapter Ten

Captain Jones
and other sea dogs

E ARLY START. CUSHMAN AND I MET WESTON AT Brooks Wharf, a few steps from the White Hart, and the wherryman sped us along with the tide until we reached Rotherhithe.

The water came over our boots as we walked along creaking wharves, past decaying boats lying moribund in sulphurous trenches of water and sewerage with anchors poking out of the mud – rusty memorials to lost seafarers.

Weston paused and pulled me back from the wharfside so that we were half concealed by a tower of brandy barrels. "Here she is. The *Mayflower*. Your ship."

To me, she looked weather-beaten and neglected, her paintwork peeling, ropes left unfurled on the deck and sails hanging raggedly off the masts.

"She has been well used on the wine route to Bordeaux." Weston tapped a barrel with the air of an expert in the drinks trade. "Looks a little rough and ready now but she's in good shape and the skipper is mightily experienced. Mightily. Nothing you can teach him about the sea."

"She looks very small." Cushman had kept a gloomy silence all morning. "Can this really cross the ocean?"

"She'll fly across the waves," Weston reassured him. "A hundred feet long, 180 tons – nothing to worry about."

Cushman cheered up a little. "At least I can write to Robinson to tell him that we have a fine ship, and if they don't like her or they think she is too small... well, if they are that easily deflected from our purpose, they should stay where they are."

Two men on deck peered down on us.

"The skipper and his first mate." Weston raised a hand in greeting.

They gestured for us to go on board, which was harder than it looked; the gangplank was so buckled it was like a corkscrew and with only a rope to cling to, I worried Cushman would slip and disappear into the filthy water, never to be seen again.

Weston made the introductions. "Meet Captain Christopher Jones, your skipper, and Master Robert Clarke, the pilot and first mate."

Jones was a slight, wiry, individual of about fifty years, with skin as tough as a leather bombard and a handshake like a vice.

He appraised me with disconcerting opaque eyes, no doubt bleached by scanning the horizon for pirates and flayed by the battering of gales and the glare of the sun.

"I've 'eard about you. Goin' west. It's as well you've got the good Lord on your side 'cos you're goin' to need Him." He gave a bark of a laugh and spat into the murky water, disturbing a rat that was scuttling along a floating timber.

"Master Clarke here owns the vessel with me," he continued. "Can't do better than Clarkie. He went to Virginia last year with a shipload of cattle. And 'e came back."

"Only just." Clarke gave a mirthless chuckle. "Only just."

"At least you will know the best place to land." I tried to be cheerful to hide my lack of confidence.

"There's a lot can go wrong when you're sixty days at sea." Clarke shook his head sombrely. "Who knows where we'll end up, eh, Jonesy?"

"Too right," he agreed.

"Gentlemen," interrupted Weston. "Gentlemen. There will be plenty of time to share your memories, but now I suggest we investigate what I am sure are the most congenial of quarters."

We clambered down into the hold, me bumping my head on the hatch door. "We'll keep all the vittals and the cargo here," explained Jones. "Normally it's filled to the top with barrels of the best Bordeaux. Have to keep Coppins off that – likes a drop, does our Bob. He's the ship's mate; you'll meet him soon."

"When he gets out of the tavern," smirked Clarke.

"If he gets out." And the two men guffawed like old chums who had shared the joke before.

"There's not much room, is there?" I could hardly stand upright. "How can we get our passengers into so little space?"

"Have to snuggle up close." Clarke was still chuckling. "Friendly-like."

"It'll be more crowded when we sail." Jones took a delight in our discomfort. "We'll have to make space for the powder and ammunition." He patted a cannon affectionately. "This little beauty can shoot a cannonball almost a mile. You'll be glad of it when the Frenchie pirates hove to."

And he let out that unnerving bark.

As we crouched in the lowest of the holds, he took me to one side.

"You know Master Weston well?"

"Hardly at all." I hesitated to tell him about his ludicrous attempt to hide my pamphlets in wine barrels. "Just the one business transaction a while back. It did not end well. My colleague, Master Cushman, has been dealing with him."

"Thought as much; he's got the nervy look of a man who's been in the company of that particular gent for too long. He talks a load of glib-glabbety, that Master Weston. Known him for years. He's the kind of cozenin' fox who 'as a finger in every pie – imports, exports, deals, double deals, anything for a sovereign and more."

Though I suspected we had little else in common, I warmed to Jones. They are a race apart, sailors. They face the seas with a bravado forged from the possibility, maybe the probability, that one day a storm will sweep them to their deaths, living each day as though it were their last – fiercely and in complete disregard to polite society.

He had no interest in why we were making the voyage. "As long as I get my cut it's no worry to me who you are or what you believe in. All I'll say is that it's a long sail and a hard one, the furthest me or this old girl *Mayflower* has attempted. Tell you what, come and meet Bob. I can tell by the snoring he's back from *The Angel*; he'll tell you what to expect."

Jones gave a hammock a shove, almost sending its occupant tumbling to the deck. As he scrambled to his feet, Jones clapped him on the shoulder.

"We've seen a bit of the world together, ain't we, Bob? Remember that jaunt to Norway?"

"Never forget it. Lucky to be alive after that." Coppins blinked and scratched like a dog disturbed from its sleep. "But nowt compared to the Atlantic run. I've been across the pond many a time, doin' a bit of whaling and scrabblin' around for cod. Now that's what I call rough. Seas as high as St Paul's." I thought he was looking over my shoulder as if a wave was about to sweep me off my feet, but it was a wildly wayward squint.

"A jealous husband hit him with a bottle in a tavern in Porto," explained Jones. "Always in trouble with the ladies."

Coppins hadn't finished. "You'll be sick from the moment we raise anchor. Puke everywhere. You'll be 'ungry, you'll be thirsty and, to top it all, you'll think you're goin' to drown every bleedin' day."

"Too right," barked Jones. "But you'll get used to it."

"If you're still alive," chipped in Clarke.

The three of them fell about.

Cushman reappeared from inspecting the ship's quarters and caught the end of the first mate's joke. He blanched but doggedly persevered with what was worrying him. Poor man, he was always worried.

"What's that boat doing there? It's all in pieces."

"It's the shallop," explained Clarke. "It's a lot bigger than the long boat which we keep on deck, so we have to take it apart and stow it in the hold. When we reach the other side, we'll stick her together again and you can use her to sail along the coast to do your explorin'."

"Takes up a lot of room." Cushman was finding problems wherever he looked.

"Can't be without it," replied Jones. "Your people can use it to sleep in."

"That means there's no space for anything big." Clarke became businesslike. "No furniture. It's not a floating withdrawin' room. Bring matting to lie on. You'll need blankets but only one change of clothes allowed. We ain't got the space. Bring your own spoons, knives, ladles, all that sort of thing. Beer mugs."

I had told Winslow to bring my smaller printing press on the *Speedwell* but I thought this not the best moment to mention it. Instead I asked, "Do you have a crew? Are they ready to sail?"

"No problem." Jones gestured to the busy dockside. "We'll need a minimum of thirty men and there's no shortage of good lads."

"And plenty of lazy louts who'd rather rob their grandmothers than swab the decks." Once more they fell about at Clarke's witty assessment. *Many a word spoken in jest,* I thought.

The sailors adjourned to *The Angel,* a less suitable name for such a noisome watering hole than I could imagine, where they pulled up a table and benches and Jones banged on the table with the side of a hammer and yelled, "Roll up, roll up, you lucky lads. Voyage of a lifetime. Enough money to keep you in tarts for the rest of your days."

"And nights," yelled Coppins.

Cushman and I spent several uncomfortable hours inhaling the stink of stale ale and sweat to witness a succession of scruffs and undoubted vagabonds parade past. Parade? In truth, most of them had been at the port and could barely stumble.

"You sure the lad we signed as bosun is up to it?" Clarke looked doubtful. "Struck me as a lubbardly lout. Trouble."

"But he knows his way round the rigging," insisted Jones. "He can look after the long boat."

I left them interviewing several more sailors, all of whom seemed as lubbardly and loutish as the next, and clambered back up the gangplank to have a quiet survey of the ship.

I banged my head again climbing down to the cargo hold, which smelt of sour wine and fetid water. Could we really fit ourselves and all our equipment into this? Would there be room for the barrels of beer, water and food we'd need? If we were going to bring goats, pigs and chickens, as Cushman planned, how could they possibly be crammed in here?

The bare timbers of the hold where we were to spend most of our days were splintered by careless use, rough, ready and unvarnished. Were we expected to sleep on that?

Maybe we could build small partitions for privacy, though quite how I was not sure. I made a note to bring a few empty crates on board despite Clarke's ruling.

I paced out the length of the deck from fore to aft; about eighty feet long and twenty-four feet at the widest, but the capstan and the main mast took up valuable space. A further twelve feet at the stern was given over to the gun room where our armour and weapons would be stored alongside the ship's cannon shot and powder. Above it were the staff's quarters and the captain's cabin – a modest room with a hammock, benches and a table. Not a man given to luxury, Captain Jones, I was pleased to see, though my eye was caught by a generous array of wine bottles and a barrel of beer.

In all, I reckoned, our ocean-going ship was not much longer than the great hall in Scrooby, and not as wide.

I confess my heart sank. This would be as desperate a venture as we had feared. Were we doing the right thing? But no, this was no time to be disheartened. God had tested us every day, every month and every year from the moment we had left Scrooby, but we had met those challenges and overcome them. He would not let us down now. I believed that with all my soul.

Jones and Clarke came up the gangplank and the skipper shouted, "Twenty-eight signed and sealed. Fine bunch of lads."

He saw my doubtful expression, barked and spat.

"You don't want milksops on this kind of venture. You

want tough bastards, sons of whores who beat their women."

"They know some of 'em won't be coming back." Clarke shrugged. "They live for the day."

"For the pay, more like," barked Jones.

And once more they laughed fit to bust.

Chapter Eleven

ON ROTHERHITHE WHARF

NEXT DAY WE MET WESTON AT THE QUAYSIDE where, to my surprise, Master Carver was waiting for us – he had been buying supplies in Southampton – as calm and dignified as ever, despite the turmoil around him.

He embraced me warmly. "Master William, what a pleasure to see you again."

Weston raised an eyebrow, Jones looked at me with suspicion. Cushman broke in with commendable quick thinking.

"William*son*. This is Master Williamson. From Kent."

Carver recovered quickly. "Master Williamson. Indeed, indeed. So similar to an old acquaintance of mine." He feigned a coughing fit and changed the subject by introducing a young man who had clearly been bemused by the exchange. "This is my trusted manservant, John Howland. He has been helping me with the plans for the voyage and is keen to prosper in the new settlement."

He seemed agreeable. Rather serious, but with an easy openness about him.

"Good day, sirs." He bowed politely. "I am honoured to be joining you on this great enterprise."

I was thinking how well it boded that a person of this calibre was coming with us when Jones exploded like cannon shot from his cabin.

"Gadsbobs. Gadsbobs with knobs on," he spat. "What's this? Women? Ankle snappers?"

He gesticulated angrily down the wharf where a group of strangers of all ages — at a guess from five to fifty — were stumbling toward us through the mire and the mess.

"Your companions on the voyage," explained Weston, unmoved by the skipper's outburst.

But Jones was incandescent. "And dogs! Bloody dogs. No one told me this was a family outing. Boating down the river to Vauxhall Gardens, I don't think. We can't have this. Oh no. They won't last two minutes. The women will be sick, the brats will fall overboard."

"But at least we can eat the dogs." I hoped Coppins was only joking.

"And there'll be trouble with the crew. They'll want to get their end away with the frothies on board and if they don't there'll be fights and all hell to pay."

"Or worse." Coppins scowled. "Remember La Rochelle?"

We never discovered what despicable deed had occurred in that French port because Jones glared some more, swore, and crashed back into his quarters. I could hear the three sailors fulminating angrily at such an incomprehensible state of affairs until there was the sound of a brandy bottle being uncorked. More cussing, another bottle and soon the sounds of merriment.

All the while our new companions had been left standing, gaping in trepidation at such a welcome.

Most of them seemed just the sort of respectable men and women who would grace our enterprise. But not all. I could not understand why one, an obstreperous oaf called John Billington, from Lincolnshire, who noisily introduced himself and his wife Elinor and their two lairy sons, had been allowed to join – or indeed, why he would want to. I took an instant dislike to a braggart called Stephen Hopkins, a tanner and a merchant, apparently, who hailed from Hampshire and was quick to tell me how much he had spent to join the voyage and why it entitled him to the best cabin on the ship.

"Cabin!" exclaimed Jones, whose spirits had been revived by several mugs of brandy. He fell about in mock astonishment. "Cabin! A few feet of timber to lie on and a blanket, which will be covered in vomit by the time we reach Gravesend – that's the best you'll get, matey."

To my astonishment, the Hopkins wife was obviously pregnant. "Is it wise to make the journey in such condition?" I wondered aloud. I should have kept my mouth shut. Jones exploded again.

"You must be mad. We can't have women in your condition on a voyage like this. You'll be hanging over the side, sick as a dog with distemper, and you'll stay there until you drops it. After all that, the poor little bleeder will die from scurvy."

"We Hopkins are made of stern stuff," boasted the father-to-be. "An Atlantic crossing is nothing to me. I've done it before."

"In that case, you won't mind being treated the same as everyone else – down in the shit of the hold," riposted Jones bluntly.

One couple I did warm to were the Whites, William and Susanna. She was familiar. Where had I seen her before? Not Leiden that was for sure. Maybe Amsterdam. Somewhere in England? As the new arrivals loaded their possessions I wracked my brains but, no, I could not remember. She showed no sign of knowing me so I left it there. There would be time enough for a trip down memory lane.

The husband struck me as an easy-going jack of many trades, happy to go where fate took him, but she appeared altogether more purposeful. She wasn't pretty – she had a chin that was too pronounced and eyes that protruded slightly – but her dark hair contrasted with pale, pale skin and there was a boldness about her which was striking. She reminded me of Joan Helwys, our audacious comrade from another life. They had a son, maybe about four or five years old, and I noticed that when Jones was ranting about the lunacy of a pregnant woman making the journey, she looked away and busied herself with her trunk. I rather thought I detected a blush.

If Jones was forthright about the Hopkins wife, he was speechless when Weston reappeared shepherding four children up the gangway.

Now this did need explaining.

A few days earlier, Weston had come to my quarters in the White Hart with this little group – and what a sad, dishevelled bunch they were, alternately mute with despair or wracked with tears of confusion.

Weston was unexpectedly flustered. He quite forgot his affectations, the stroking of the beard, the irritating repetition of a word.

"These poor infants – the oldest is only eight – have come into my care," he explained. "I know of their family. Ellen, Richard and Mary, meet Master Williamson and Master Cushman. Come along, Jasper." One by one, they solemnly shook our hands.

"Theirs is a sad story," he continued. "They are the victims of a lust that is not suitable for the ears of religious men like you two gentlemen. Suffice to say they are the bastard children of a wife who cuckolded her husband. There was a bitter divorce – is there any other kind? – and the father... well, not the father, if you see what I mean, decided to send them as far away as possible. He has paid me £100 to ship them on your voyage. He had heard of you people and trusts you as honest and religious folk."

"We must do the best we can for them," I offered.

"Thank you, both." Weston was genuinely grateful. "I have one more favour to beg of you: that you look after them until the voyage, when we can find them guardians."

What could I say other than 'of course'?

It was all too much for Jones. "Brats this age cause complete and utter bloody chaos," he fumed. "But four of them? Without parents to keep 'em tied down? Gadsbobs." He ordered them to be packed away in the darkest of corners, where they clung together in bewildered misery.

I joined Cushman on the wharf, where he was checking the inventory.

"Salt peas, wheat, rye, pork and salted cod. All safely loaded. Where are the barley and oats? Did anyone purchase them? Who knows?" He answered his own questions, exasperated. "We will be short of beer if the order has not been placed. Brass ladles and spoons. Surely we need more. Pewter bottles and copper kettles."

"There should be more nails and hammers," broke in Carver, which earned a dismissive tic of irritation.

"Indeed there should. I thought you had ordered them. Where are the blankets and the linen for towels? There should be more butter and dried mutton."

But before Carver could explain where the missing supplies were, Coppins hollered from the wharf, "Jonesy, come down 'ere."

The two of them stood on the quay, peering at the ship.

"I don't like the look of that," grumbled Jones. "Not one little bit."

"She's heeling to starboard." Coppins squinted through angles he made with his hands to size up the problem. "We know what that means."

"We do, Gawd save us." Jones sent a comet of phlegm into the water. "A sign of a bloody difficult voyage. We'll have to shift the load to the larboard and get her nice and lined up. We can't ignore an omen like that."

As I looked on from a bench outside *The Angel*, I made a note in my journal.

July 15, 1620, Rotherhithe, London. Tomorrow we leave with the tide. God and Captain Jones willing.

BOOK III

1620–1621

THE VOICE OF
SUSANNA WHITE
A WEIGHTY VOYAGE

*And after many storms, at length by God's providence,
upon the ninth of November following, by break of the
day we espied land which we deemed to be Cape Cod…*

Mourt's Relation, a journal of the Pilgrims at Plymouth.

BOOK III

1870-1881

THE VOICE OF SUSANNA WHITE

A WRIGHT TRILOGY

CHAPTER ONE

THE DIE IS CAST

I T WAS A STIFLING JULY DAY WHEN THE CART dropped us by the wharf in Rotherhithe.

"It must be here." Will's voice was muffled by the kerchief he held against his face to keep out the flies, which whirred up from the rivulets of wine that had escaped from broken barrels and trickled through a sludge of horse dung and rotting fish heads.

"He arranged to meet us by *The Angel*." We waited irresolutely. My, it was hot. The servant Edward dropped our trunk with a thump to catch the dog, which had taken off after a rat; our boy Resolved tottered off behind them. I grabbed him before he disappeared over the edge of the quay into the greasy water.

A man lurched out of the tavern and relieved himself against the wall right beside us, quickly followed by another, whose fashionable clothes stood out peacock-bright against the squalor.

"Welcome," he murmured, glancing with fastidious distaste at the vulgar exhibitionist. "Welcome, Master William. This must be your lovely lady wife. Lovely." And, to me, "Weston, Thomas Weston at your service."

He shook my hand with a flourish that was not matched by its firmness. My father always warned me against men with a weak grip.

"Here" – he gestured to a ship behind us – "is your vessel. The *Mayflower*. A fine ship. And that is your skipper." As he pointed, I noticed his shirt cuffs were frayed and in need of a wash. "Captain Christopher Jones. A sterling man of the sea. Sterling."

The object of his approval tipped his hat ironically at us and hawked into the waste that lapped around the hull.

For the first time since we had decided to join this madcap enterprise, I did have a qualm; were we doing the right thing?

My heart had sunk when Will, my husband, returned from London where he had spent some weeks trying to win over a wealthy contact or two in Leadenhall, the wool and leather market. Always eager for a deal, my Will, always looking for a bargain.

This time he was brimming with excitement.

"I have met this businessman. A real player. He has a scheme to make us wealthy."

I let him jabber on. Will was often caught up in money-making schemes; a few sensible, most hare-brained.

He had invested in the tobacco trade that the great explorer Walter Raleigh had made so popular, only for the King himself to condemn smoking as a loathsome custom. Harmful to the brain, dangerous to the lungs. The business collapsed and we lost a lot of money. Poor Will. It seemed no one else heeded the royal decree, for within months tobacco became one of the most profitable ventures imaginable.

He wasn't cast down for long; he never was. "The scheme cannot fail." He strode around the drawing room, restless with enthusiasm. "This gent, name of Weston, has already lined up an expedition to ferry a bunch of religious types from Holland to set up a plantation in Virginia."

"Virginia! Are you mad?"

"No. It's all sorted. His Majesty has given his blessing. He swears we shall catch lots of fish and make a splendid profit."

"But who are these devout Dutchmen we are getting mixed up with?" I demanded. "Are they heretics? I don't want to be excommunicated for helping people like that."

I'd had my share of god-fearing folk – so called – in Amsterdam when we moved to the city a few years before in search of a better life. I was never so unhappy, surrounded by zealots telling me what to do and how to do it. So much cant from so many – nothing more than fine words and false piety.

"It's not like that," reassured Will. "They're English, not Dutch, and they are just a harmless bunch who spend all their time reading the Bible. Decent folk, not like the ones we met before. They haven't a clue how to cope with everyday life let alone cross the ocean, so Weston needs sensible folk like us to help them make a success of the venture."

"I imagine you met this so-called gentleman in the White Hart and drank too much porter." I knew my husband.

"Not at all," he protested. "It was all very businesslike. The plan is that we invest £500 now and in seven years' time, we will have hundreds of acres to call our own. Do you know what the market for beaver is in London these days? Forty shillings for a hat. At least."

"My, who has that kind of money to spend on a hat?" I was impressed.

"The King for one. Everyone who is anyone. Think of the money we'll make."

But I was not impressed enough. "This is not the time." Honestly, he could be so thoughtless. "Perhaps you have forgotten that I am pregnant. Remember how sick I was with Resolved? Crossing the Atlantic – that's a tad more arduous than taking a wherry across the River Trent."

But then I decided, *why ever not?* What was there to keep us in England? Our lives were humdrum, despite Will's constant quest for half-cracked schemes, but more pressing, we needed the money. Without telling my husband I had inspected our books and discovered we were virtually bankrupt – and not for the first time. I could not rely on my father for yet another handout.

Fishing? What did we know about that? Just a few casts in the nearby streams. And beaver? Not a thing. But we could learn. How frightening could sailing the Atlantic be? It might be fun.

Once I made up my mind, there was no going back. Will was amazed at my acceptance and boasted to all and sundry about his powers of persuasion – I had to let him think he had made the decision – and galloped off to London to sign the agreement. Impetuous lad, he had brought the same spontaneous eagerness to the way he wooed me.

I had not been ready for matrimony, I enjoyed my independence, but as Mother insisted, "A woman needs a husband to be complete," so when Will boldly introduced himself one market day in Amsterdam's Fleaborough district where we were living in a grubby hovel, I decided to give him a chance.

The few female friends I had in that forsaken city took time from their daily struggles to admit they rather envied me for catching such a good-looking lad – curly hair, dangerous green-blue eyes and, it transpired, no slouch when it came to the bedchamber. He made me laugh as much as he made me fume at his fecklessness. I grew fond of him… no, I came to love him.

"Aha." Weston brought me back to reality. "Here come your fellow travellers." In a trice we were caught up in a blur of unfamiliar faces. There were about sixty of them and I forgot their names the moment the dance of introductions was over. There were several families, some with children as young as my Resolved, a brace of well-to-do types, a shoemaker and a carpenter, and several who were noisy and, frankly, boorish.

There was much huffing and puffing as my new companions loaded their possessions onto the ship. I waited our turn perched on the chest that held our few belongings. It was a wedding present made of fine black pine with Chinese lacquerwork inlaid with mother of pearl and it had a drawer for letters, though I did not suppose I would be writing many missives from the forests of Virginia. Still, I was proud of it; it spoke of a certain style.

I was interrupted by a spry character older than most in – I'd guess – his fifties, sporting a jaunty violet-coloured jacket and green trousers, who introduced himself as Master Williamson, and his two companions – one a tall, imposing gent called John Carver and the other a Robert Cushman. Where the former radiated a steady confidence, Cushman was an anxious soul with a tic that made one eye flutter in a most disconcerting manner.

"Welcome to our enterprise." Williamson doffed his cap. "We are the movers behind this great challenge. Our comrades are sailing on another ship from Holland and will meet us in Southampton. You must be one of the Adventurers."

I liked the sound of that. *Adventurers.*

Will enthused, "Indeed, sir. I am William White. What a pleasure. This is my wife Susanna and my boy Resolved."

"White," pondered Williamson. "We have comrades in Leiden by that name. Wool combers by trade. Any relation, perhaps?"

"I think not," replied Will. "We did spend a few months in Amsterdam but we did not go to Leiden. It was not the place for a man of my ambition. Which is why I have agreed to join this venture."

I let his boasting go – though Williamson smiled indulgently. Cushman, however, was too fretful for pleasantries. He glared reprovingly at the throng. "I cannot imagine how some of these have shuffled into our great venture," he grumbled. "They lack breeding and they are certainly strangers to the scriptures."

"Not you, of course, my dear." Williamson's smile served as an apology for his companion's irritability. "Your refinement is obvious. The important thing is that we are on our way. Whoever and whatever we are, God will steer a course for us all."

"Rum lot, these amen curlers," remarked Weston when the men had left. "Rum."

We set off to sail to the rendezvous with the other ship from where, Williamson explained, we would continue across the ocean in a convoy.

I will never forget my first taste of life at sea. The moment we hit the tides off Gravesend there was a stampede by the passengers to the rail, where they clutched their stomachs, moaned and groaned and almost in unison vomited over the side – to the great amusement of the crew.

But me, I loved it. The crash of the waves against the bow, the unpredictable lurches, the buffetings, the sheer exhilaration, blew away any lingering doubts I might have had about the enterprise. I thrilled to the space, the skies that reached to the far horizon, the taste of the spray on my lips. My spirits flew as unfettered as the wind.

"Dear Lord, save me," gasped a woman, who was hanging weakly over the rail. That was all she managed before sickness overwhelmed her.

She recovered enough to groan, "I'm Elizabeth Hopkins. I did not want to come but my husband would not change his mind. I have three children to look after and if that wasn't hard enough, I am expecting another."

"That makes two of us," I admitted.

"Best not tell the skipper until we are well out from land," she managed between bouts of puking. "He almost kicked me off."

I warmed to her but found her husband Stephen a preening sort who considered himself superior to the rest of us. Even before we had set sail, he fussed about the cramped conditions and insisted that he had paid enough to deserve a cabin.

"I know all about the high seas," he informed us grandly. "I was sailing to Jamestown – which as you should know is Virginia – in '09 as a minister's clerk when the ship was wrecked on Bermuda. We were stranded there for ten months but I was able to save our lives by trapping turtles, birds and wild pigs. I can't pretend it wasn't rough going, but we castaways stayed strong and built a boat sound enough to sail on to Jamestown, where we were greeted like heroes."

Clarke, the first mate, who was more amiable than his weather-hewn demeanour suggested, noticed me rolling my eyes.

"Hear this, mistress." He leant forward conspiratorially. "I'm chummy with quite a few folk who know the truth about Master 'opkins. What he does not tell you is that he led a mutiny against the gent who was about to take over as Governor of Jamestown. His plan was thwarted and our gallant 'opkins was sentenced to die. Then everyone saw what a hero he really was. He got down on his knees and wept for mercy. They let him go free." He gobbed. "Unfortunately."

I whispered, "He was boasting that he is the inspiration for a player in a work by Master Shakespeare."

Williamson, who had overheard Clarke's revelation, paused from helping to light the galley fire to add his own amused ha'porth.

"I saw the play in London quite recently. It's called *The Tempest*. Hopkins wants you to think he was the model for Prospero, a wise old duke with magical powers who was stranded on an island, like him. Instead, I consider our Master Stephen to be the inspiration for a disloyal, drunken serf by the name of Stephano. More fitting, methinks."

Will caught the end of the tale.

"They *are* a rum lot, aren't they? Weston was right."

We blustered down the Channel for a few days until we docked in Southampton and moored alongside the ship that was carrying the saintly sorts. *Speedwell*, it was named, which boded well for the adventure ahead. Or so I thought.

"God's hooks!" exclaimed Jones. "They're not going anywhere in this, surely. Hey, Reynolds." He shouted to the skipper of the other ship. "I'm carrying a shallop almost as big as this. It's the Atlantic you're meant to be crossing, not a dawdle to Dieppe."

Reynolds yelled back, "I've told 'em. But I'm being paid so that's good enough for me. If you want to know…" he started, but he was interrupted by a flurry of raised voices from the quayside.

Master Cushman, the anxious type we had met at Rotherhithe, was being confronted by an angry group of passengers. One was poking him in the chest.

"I don't owe the merchants a thing," he cried. "Not a pin."

"You simple man, of course you never made any deals with them, of course you never spoke with them." Cushman could not contain his raging sarcasm. "Ha. You spent our money buying provisions that do not exist. Where are they? All that money thrown away, was it your own?"

Another griped, "You betrayed us to these so-called Adventurers by accepting their terms."

Cushman ignored that. He had not finished. "Where is the cheese, the bread, the beer that you claimed to have bought?" he demanded of his critics, his tic a blur of indignation. "You spent £700 of our money rashly and lavishly and have never explained what you spent it on. £700!"

"Goodness," I whispered to Will, "I thought these were meant to be men of God, not brawling hooligans."

He rated it great sport. "It's like Leadenhall Market when the traders have been drinking all day."

"If anyone is to blame, it is Weston and the Adventurers." Spittle formed round Cushman's mouth. "They are no better than slave drivers."

As the men glowered at each other, Weston himself materialised out of the crowd and glided between them, his cane raised to keep them apart.

"Without those slave drivers – as you call them – you would not be here today." He tapped the *Mayflower's* hull with his cane. "You would not be comfortably quartered on such a well-equipped craft or enjoy the services of its admirable captain. Now, gentlemen, please." His voice did not lose its even, sibilant tenor, his face kept the same mild expression, but his eyes were unflinching. "Now, please concentrate. My colleagues in the city feel their investment is too big a risk and they worry that they will not get the return they deserve. They have decided that instead of letting you have the land to yourselves after seven years, they will share the benefits. Also…" He paused to let a growl of indignation die down. "Also, I am afraid your demand to have two days of rest and prayer every week is not acceptable."

Master Williamson stepped forward. "Our congregation will not accept this change." He was angry, but he spoke with calm assurance. "We demand that you stick to the original arrangement."

Weston was unmoved but his voice took on an edge. He was very different now from the soft-as-you-like gentleman I had first met. "The Merchant Adventurers will not change their minds at this late stage or give you more money. I have to inform you that they will pull out altogether – *altogether* – if you do not accept these minor alterations. Remember, it is their money that is paying for this escapade of yours."

"That means that we will be forced to sell our stocks before we can leave port, maybe as much as £60 worth," moaned Master Cushman. "We will have to sell most of our butter, we will be without oil, there won't be a sole to mend a shoe."

Weston shrugged. A gesture more final than a curse. "Then you must sell." He waited for another ripple of anger to die down. "As for me, I will return to London. If I do not receive a letter of agreement from you, you can assume there will be no more help from the Merchant Adventurers. No more."

He snapped his fingers and a carriage clattered through the crowd to take him away.

Cushman was almost in tears. "This is a disaster. Without more funds we will not be able to arm every man with a sword or musket. As it is, we will have to leave most of our armour behind."

I did not like the sound of that. In fact, I was appalled at the scene I had just witnessed. "I cannot believe we are scrabbling around on a jetty arguing about butter shortages and days of rest when we are already on our way."

"I understand your feelings." It was Master Williamson and he was as dispirited as me. "I too have wondered if it would be better to cancel the voyage than to suffer such misery. But, you know, the die is cast, armour or no armour. We must make the most of what we have."

He spread his hands in resigned acceptance. "By the way, my name is Brewster, William Brewster. I am an elder of our community."

"I thought it was Williamson." I blinked in surprise.

"You must have misheard, my dear. It was noisy on the quay." He seemed rather amused at my mistake. "But I do have another confession. We have met before. In Scrooby."

Now I was thoroughly taken aback.

"I've been wracking my brains since we met on the quay at Rotherhithe and it suddenly came to me," he continued. "Your dear father Richard Jackson, God rest him, was a friend of mine, a staunch believer in our mission and one who was pursued by Archbishop Matthew as fiercely as I was.

"You were young, perhaps only fifteen or sixteen, when our families fled to the Netherlands but now look at you, a wife and a mother, no wonder I didn't recognise you."

I cast my mind back; long evenings in Scrooby manor when Father and many others would talk and pray, talk and pray. And yes, Master Brewster did come into fuzzy focus. A passionate speaker as I recalled, the one the rest looked up to. Not that he made much of an impression on me. I was a good Christian but not that good. That's why Will's irreverence appealed to me so much.

A swirl of wind blew a speck of dry tar into my eye. I dabbed at it and Master Brewster, assuming I was grieving for my father who had died in Amsterdam, put a hand on my arm and murmured soothingly, "We must live by God's will to find the meaning of pain as well as pleasure."

161

But my tears were not for my father, I had shed them long since. I had moved on. I was eager to embrace whatever the future brought me.

"Perhaps you could introduce me to some of your friends," I asked.

"Of course. It must be difficult for you to be cast among so many strangers."

CHAPTER TWO

MEAT FOR THE FISH

WHEN WE REACHED THE TOP OF THE gangplank, he greeted a woman standing there. "This is Dorothy Bradford, she must be about your own age. I am sure you will be great friends."

Like me, she was in her twenties. She could have been pretty, dark brown hair against skin as fair as swan feathers, but she was listless; she did not smile when we met and her grey eyes, which on a more spirited person could have sent many a man spinning, were without expression.

I assumed that her half-hearted response was caused by sea sickness, but the moment she saw Resolved her face lit up and she knelt down to be at his level, gazing at him with such longing that I was convinced she would sweep him up and run away with him. Resolved must have felt the same unease for he wriggled out of her grasp.

"What a lovely boy." She wiped away the suspicion of a tear. "I have a son about his age."

"He's just five," I said.

She watched Resolved as he gambolled about the deck playing tag with the other children. I was surprised there were so many; I counted at least twenty. "My John is three. William decided it was best that he stayed behind." She grimaced.

"William?"

"My husband." She stared blankly at the dirty grey bilge water that washed between the ship's hull and the quay. "I am sure he is right. The journey so far has been frightening enough. I wouldn't wish it on the boy."

"Which is your husband?" I asked.

She pointed to a lean man of about thirty, slightly stooped with a receding hairline, who was in deep conversation with the man I now knew as William Brewster.

He was clearly angry, holding a Bible and making downward chopping movements to emphasise what he was saying.

"William and his companions accuse Master Cushman of failing to deal with the merchants the way he was instructed, and the merchants blame him for the problems with our brethren," explained Dorothy. "There is much bad feeling."

"I could tell." I tried to make light of it. "And no butter."

She allowed herself a strained smile.

"It will be a weighty voyage. But that is the price of achieving our destiny. So William tells me."

Reynolds, the *Speedwell* skipper, mentioned casually that there would be a brief delay for repairs because the ship had a problem with a leak. We thought nothing of it – just a routine hazard to be expected on the high seas – but it was ten days before the two ships sailed away from Southampton, a drab town best left to the down-and-outs who hung about its derelict docks.

Our gladness at finally getting underway was dashed only six days later when Skipper Jones summoned us on deck.

"It's no good." He struck the rail in anger. "Gadsbobs. Forgive my language, ladies. We've got to go back. The bloody *Speedwell*, leaking like a sieve."

We docked in a port called Dartmouth, a prosperous little place with a castle high on a bluff – to keep out the Spaniards, explained Master Brewster – and while we waited for the sailors to make the repairs I had the time to make friends with many of the women on board.

Master Brewster's wife Mary was quick and lively with unusual amber eyes and she greeted me with an open-hearted welcome. Sharp, too. She took a look at my expanding waistline and winked conspiratorially.

"I have two of our children with us, Love, who is nine, and her six-year-old brother, Wrestling. My other son and my two daughters Fear and Patience will be joining us on the next ship."

It transpired the couple had been apart for many months and, judging by the way they linked arms and joked together with an intimate ease, were more than pleased to be reunited.

"I was, er, detained." Brewster grinned but did not elaborate.

Mary took over the introductions. Mary Allerton already had three children under seven with her and blithely disclosed that she was expecting another. I could not comprehend how she would cope in the topsy-turvy, cheek-by-jowl world of the hold, especially as her husband Isaac did next to nothing to help, but preferred to stalk the deck deep in thought as if he was already calculating the profit he would make from the sale of beaver.

"This is Elizabeth Winslow, whose husband Edward is my William's partner in a printing business." The young wife must also have guessed my baby secret, for she cheerfully feigned guilt at not producing an heir after two years of marriage.

"Not for any lack of trying," she giggled and then blushed.

I could hardly not confess my own secret. I say confess because I was aware of Dorothy's pain and did not want to appear more blessed than her. Unhappy woman, she was sorely affected by there being so many children on board, but nothing gripped her more than four little brothers and sisters who did not join in the games with the others but stayed apart in a forlorn huddle.

I had noticed them when we boarded in Rotherhithe but no one was able, or willing, to tell me about them until Dorothy spoke up.

"Poor, sad things. How much they must miss their mother."

"But where is she?" I wondered.

"It is such a sad story," she gazed wistfully across the deck at them, "though William judges it one of scandal and shame. He says it is a wonder that they have been allowed to come on this voyage when our aim is to create a righteous and prayerful society."

"They are only children." I was taken aback by such intolerance. "What sin have they committed to deserve such condemnation?"

"They have done nothing wrong." Mary Brewster spoke out firmly. "Rather, they have been sinned against."

Dorothy lowered her voice. "William says their mother was nothing better than a trollop. Forgive my language."

"It is easy to judge others' mistakes," interrupted Mary briskly. "The mother was married to a respectable Shropshire landowner called Samuel More. He was often away in London on business but within a few months of their wedding, his wife gave birth to a daughter. The wife had three more children in three years. Understandably they had a likeness to each other, but what dawned on Master More was that they had no resemblance to him – instead, they were the very image of a farmer who worked on his land. They had no sooner baptised the fourth child when the mother confessed her transgressions, but insisted she had been married to this farmer all along because they had signed a contract. All the couple had to assert was 'I receive you as mine' and they were married. As simple as that. That meant her marriage to Master More was bigamy."

Bigamy. Goodness. It was hard not to be shocked at such behaviour.

"No doubt, the sinners deserve to be shamed, but my, what unhappiness is left in their wake," I wondered. "How come these innocents were condemned to be on this voyage?"

Mary was about to explain when Captain Jones shouted, "We leave tomorrow. Get yourselves sorted out and settled in."

I paused briefly by his cabin.

Reynolds and Jones were sat before jugs of ale, wreathed in clouds of tobacco. They were arguing.

"The masts and sails are too big," scoffed Jones. "Ridiculous for a ship that size."

Reynolds retorted, "They will speed us on."

"Or sink you. She's too small. That's why you've had all these leaks; the tub is being stretched and strained beyond redemption."

"Well, if she don't make it, it's no skin off my nose," grunted Reynolds. "I mean, no one would choose to sail the Atlantic at all, let alone this late in the year, but the amen curlers are determined. We won't get much profit out of it and frankly, Master Jones, I won't mind if we don't get beyond Land's End."

When I mentioned this to Will he was dismissive. "These sailors, either bragging about how dauntless they are or fretting about imagined dangers. We'll be fine." He patted my stomach.

Yet, once again, a hundred leagues out, Reynolds signalled to the *Mayflower* from the deck of his craft and Jones called us together. "The *Speedwell* is done for. Can't go no further," he announced to a chorus of groans.

Back we went and this time docked in the bay off Plymouth. We all knew about Francis Drake, the way he had seen off the Spanish Armada, and though the fort he had persuaded Queen Elizabeth to build had fallen into dereliction, we could only wonder at the huge citadel that now sat on a ridge overlooking the port's alleys of narrow brick houses.

Master Cushman was waiting on the quayside. "There was a gap in the hull as big as a mole hole." He was pale and despairing. "I'm sure if we had sailed three or four hours more she would have sunk."

I thought he was overreacting as usual, but he was right to be so dejected. Reynolds summoned us. "Sorry, folks." He showed not a hint of remorse. "We can't fix the leakage. This tub ain't going nowhere." With that, he and his crew stowed their gear and headed off to the Minerva, a tavern I'd noticed before for its crowds of drunken seamen and their dubious female company.

But even that hotbed of excess could not compare with the uproar that followed.

One enraged passenger almost pushed Captain Jones over with his finger prodding. "Look, my man, we cannot tolerate this incompetence. We are going to lose a fortune if we don't get this voyage underway."

Jones had clearly had words with him before because he let him rant, spat, then hissed, "The sailors are sick of your brazen ignorance. I warn you, watch out in case a mischief happens to you."

That quietened him but the altercation did not deter Master Bradford, who stepped forward. "There can be no giving up." He had a high, grating voice, which cut through the racket. "We have a destiny to fulfil."

Destiny or not, we had left Rotherhithe on July 16 and here we were one month later, still on English soil and showing no signs of going any further. I did somewhat agree with skipper Jones when he rolled his eyes and declared, "Destiny! The only destiny you'll have is with your maker if we don't get a move on."

He took control. "We can take a few of you on the *Mayflower*. Tight squeeze, though. Draw lots, play cards for the privilege, fight over it, but make your minds up and fast. We must sail now if we are to beat the storm season."

Master Cushman chose to stay behind. He was positively wailing with disappointment. "It may be that the Lord will help make a success of this venture, but I cannot see how we won't starve or end up as meat for the fish."

"His heart and courage failed him," I overheard Bradford say dismissively as the *Speedwell* passengers were ferried to the *Mayflower* and were counted on board.

"Thirty-five, thirty-six, thirty-seven, thirty-eight... there are thirty-nine of you." Jones was aghast. "That makes 102 in all. And all these brats, no use to anyone. No, there's too many." But seeing the obdurate expressions on the faces in front of him, he shrugged. "Just as well you are close companions because you're going to be hugger mugger for many a week. Don't complain to me if you run out of food. Don't bother me when the scurvy makes your bones ache so much you'll beg to be thrown overboard to be put out of your misery."

"Captain Jones, there is one thing." Brewster broke into his outburst. "My printing press. It is the express wish of the

Leiden congregation that we take it." He knew the skipper had
banned all furniture, let alone this hefty contrivance.

"You already have the largest trunk of anyone." Jones was
beside himself with impatience. "Gadsbobs, man, do you really
need all those books?"

The old chap maintained an expression of benign resolve
and gave the slightest of shrugs. The skipper shook his head in
exaggerated resignation, mumbled a string of oaths that Will
confessed were unknown to him, and waved it on board.

Once again, on September 6, the *Mayflower* unfurled her
sails and left for Virginia, and this time there was no going
back.

CHAPTER THREE

NEW FRIENDS

I RATHER ENVIED MASTER CUSHMAN'S DECISION to desert the voyage once the newcomers from the *Speedwell* had squashed and squabbled their way into a space meant for half the number.

Captain Jones had the foresight to rescue as many supplies as he could from the wounded vessel, but it was never enough for all of us. My, we were hungry.

"You're goin' to have to make do with half rations," he warned to a chorus of protest. "We should be arriving in your promised land by now, not setting off to it. We have been so delayed that the victuals are already half eaten and, mark me, if the weather is bad – and it will be – we will take longer to make the voyage and we'll barely have a month's provisions left when we get there. I have to tell you, the land will not be flowing with milk and honey, but it will be covered with ice and snow." He barked humourlessly. "That's if we get there. So 'alf rations it is. No argie bargie. Not even from you, Master

Billington." The tricky chap had already made a ruckus, blaming his sea-sickness on the poor cooking.

We did what we could, warming stews in a large copper cauldron that swayed precariously over a charcoal fire, but for the most part we had to make do with salt meat or fish infested with bugs; hard, dry biscuits, almost impossible to chew; dried peas and beans. The tiny supply of butter and cheese turned into a mouldy mess and was thrown overboard.

And as for hugger mugger? If only it was that genteel. I had to lay claim to our patch in the hold with the tenacity of a she-wolf defending her cubs. There was barely enough room to lie down but Will got hold of timbers from the shallop, a kind of boat that had been dismantled and stored for the voyage, and built a wall around us. At least it gave us a small oasis where we were spared the sharp elbows of our neighbours.

Hemmed in on either side, oppressed by a ceiling so low it was a wonder we didn't knock ourselves out every time we stood up, and plagued by the unrelenting noise, I was surprised more of us didn't end up gibbering like lunatics escaped from Bedlam.

By day, the bickering over how much space each family should have often ended in blows and competed with the shouting and the crying, not to mention the scolding of over-excited children by exasperated parents. The men – who, as ever, had to prove their manliness – fought over how many biscuits the other had taken or whether he had drunk one draught of beer or two.

By night, we would be awoken by the screams of sleepers in the throes of nightmares and we had to endure a chorus of snorts and groans, which broke into noisy cusses when one sleeping body accidentally rolled over and encroached on another's space.

Often, too, there would be muffled giggles and muted groans of pleasure as the men crept alongside their women for a swift taste of nug-a-nug. I could tell when Dorothy had endured a visit from her husband by her tight-lipped embarrassment the morning after, but for me, though my stomach was growing and I was afflicted with morning sickness, I did nothing to deter Will from his pleasure. It was mine too.

Or rather, it was at the beginning. This was not the place for love-making. The hold made a pig's pen smell like a perfumed garden with its sweaty, mildewed odour of damp, and we were crammed so close to each other that we could smell the fetid heat of our bodies and each other's foul breath. The uncomfortable truth was, we stank. Obviously, we never washed, and we had no spare clothes – so when the women suffered from the curse there was no way to prevent the tell-tale stains on their already dirty smocks.

Most days we perched perilously on the bowsprit to do our business but when it was too rough we had to stay under cover and use the buckets that served as chamber pots. Inevitably they were filled to the brim and slopped over onto the cabin floor. Worse, a few lazy, inconsiderate dolts simply relieved themselves where they were. The foulness caught the back of my throat and made me gag.

Whenever we left the teeming darkness of the holds and ventured onto the deck, we had to run the gauntlet of obscene yapping from the sailors, who would lounge about when the sea was calm and entertain themselves with ignorant abuse like, "Woah there, you bushel bubbies, fancy a docking?" and "What an arse, that deserves a good clipping."

They became most excited – and most offensive – when we relieved ourselves off the bowsprit. It was undignified enough, but to be exposed to such vulgarity when we were at our most vulnerable was, to say the least, distressing.

What dull-witted sots they were. The ringleader was one of the bosuns, whose favourite trick was to stand pissing off the side of the ship and turn round when we came near to shock us by waving his member at us.

"I've seen little fingers bigger than that," I jeered and though I pretended to laugh it off, I was deeply upset and complained to Jones. He would not listen.

"We're at sea, lady, and rules are different here. If I had my way, I wouldn't have any women on board. Not one. They're a damned nuisance."

I think we were all a little scared by the sailors but it was the youngest of the women who suffered the most. They had led sheltered lives; the language of the streets and the rawness of animal lust was unknown to them, so no wonder they were not just disgusted but dispirited by such demeaning antics.

Perhaps it was presumptuous of me, but I took it on myself to give them heart. They were likeable girls like Elizabeth Tilley, a pretty lass of thirteen whose parents had imbued in her the strictest of beliefs, and Mary Chilton, whose father James was the oldest on the ship. He had been stabbed in Leiden by a gang of fanatics, he told me, and worried all the more for the safety of his child.

The oldest was Priscilla Mullins, aged seventeen or eighteen, who was the daughter of a shoemaker and had, I sensed, awoken a spark of interest in the cooper John Alden, an eager young fellow, who had come on board in Southampton to look after the barrels of beer and help out as a carpenter. A relation of the skipper apparently.

First, I had to reassure them that there would be no foul-mouthed sailors to debase our new world, only fine young men like Howland and Alden. When I mentioned the latter's name I detected the slightest of blushes from Priscilla. *Hmm,* I thought, maybe the spark of interest flickered both ways. I could not blame her; Alden was a handsome devil, strongly built, with dancing blue eyes and a rollicking spirit to match.

I painted an alluring picture of their lives in the land of plenty we were sailing to and the privilege of being part of such a noble venture – though, to be honest, by then I needed to be persuaded about that myself.

I talked about their future as wives and mothers, how they would provide the children that future generations would admire, but they tittered nervously. Marriage and men meant little to them; they were, after all, still daughters.

One girl never accepted her lot and that was the maid, Desire, who had left home when her mother remarried, and though I tried to convince her that she could not be luckier than to be Master Carver's maidservant, she would have none of it.

"I can tell you, Mistress S, this pilgrimage business is not for me," she lamented. "I miss my ma and I want to be in a bed that stays still of a night. If only my friends from before were here. Mary Hardy, did you meet her? She could sing like a bird. We could cheer each other up 'cos I am scared of the sea and frit of what lies ahead. All them lions waiting to pounce."

Her worst horrors were confirmed when she woke to find a dead rat by her head.

We blamed the ship's mouser, but Will heard one of Master Billington's rascally boys boasting that he had done it for a prank and gave him a sound cuffing.

One evening, Mary, Dorothy and I were returning from our visit to the bowsprit when we heard a scuffle and a scream. We found Desire struggling to escape from the same creature who had abused us before. He had her pinned against a bulwark and was pulling up her petticoats, grunting obscenities. I threw myself at him, fists flailing, but to no effect – he grabbed my arms and forced me to the deck.

"That's where I like 'em," he sneered. "On their knees."

He was not going to get away with that. Out of the corner of my eye, I saw a hammer left lying on the deck by the ship's carpenter. I grabbed it and swung it round, hitting him on the head with all my force. He gave an astonished yelp and fell to his knees.

"That's where *I* like them." I was exultant.

He glared cross-eyed through the blood coursing down his face. "You..." But he keeled over before he could tell me what he would do to me.

"Have you killed him?" Mary did not know whether to share my jubilation at his humiliation or be frightened lest I had sent him to his maker.

"Serves him right," hissed Dorothy with unusual asperity.

The sailor groaned and staggered to his feet, his pain made infinitely worse by the shame of being routed by women.

We reported the attack to Jones who barked uproariously. "Sounds like you did for 'im already."

"He must be made an example of." I was not going to be denied justice, even if it was his word that ruled while we were at sea. "To stop the others. The insults, the foul language, we can cope with, but he attacked the girl. He might have killed her."

He sighed and spat. "Very well, lady. I'll give him a taste of the cat. Don't mind a bit of badinage and felonious sheet-shaking myself, forgive my language, but I've a wife and seven little 'uns at home and I don't like to see anyone get hurt."

By now we women had become close. We talked about our lives before, our beliefs, our men, and often we discussed the plight of the four abandoned children.

"I have real sympathy for the mother," I reflected.

"The husband, Samuel More, perhaps he too was remiss." Elizabeth Winslow, a gay spirit, had impressed me when she revealed that she and her husband Edward had agreed to be guardians to Ellen, the oldest of the children. "He spent most of their married life pursuing his ambitions in London – and, knowing some men, who knows what else."

"The mother craved love, not just a cold arrangement masquerading as a marriage." In case I seemed too forgiving of such a sin, I hastily added, "Though I do not condone her behaviour."

"I cannot persuade William to have any sympathy." Dorothy gave the slightest of frowns. "He says the children are beyond redemption."

Elizabeth Winslow could not suppress a tut of exasperation. "My Edward takes a different view. Look how troubled they are. They deserve our compassion."

Her husband was one of the sparkier of the Leiden contingent. Ruddy-faced and vigorous, he had an easy charm and naturally enough struck up a bond with the young men like Alden and Howland and, indeed, my Will. But there was a seriousness about him, judging by the way he spent hours pacing the deck discussing the mysteries of the world with William Brewster.

"He feels they were punished enough for the sin of the mother," continued Elizabeth. "She and the lover were found guilty of adultery and fined £25 for their iniquity, but the little ones, yes, they do warrant our understanding."

Mary, who explained that she and her husband were looking after two of the children, Richard and Mary, concurred. "No one knows what happened to the farmer, but the mother was divorced from Master More and denied the right to keep the children."

Dorothy was tremulous. "Enough that they are torn from their family, but to be condemned to this." Her hands fluttered as she gestured at the hold. "How did they end up here?"

"The father was an acquaintance of Thomas Weston." Mary was well-informed. "He wanted rid of all reminders of the shame and his embarrassment. He paid £25 for each child, as long as they were made full partners in the colony when they came of age and had enough money for food and clothing to last them for the seven years. Then, mark you, they would inherit fifty acres each."

"A generous enough arrangement," I considered. "But I think they would rather be with their mother."

Ah, the mother, what became of her? Exiled to a distant corner of the country, destitute and lonely, the gnawing pain of separation from her lover and the despair of losing her four infants never to be eased.

One of the children had banged her head so I dried her tears and we went on deck to play the best game of all, watching for whales. What a moment it had been the first time one of those mighty creatures slid silently to the surface and swam alongside the vessel. I think it was orphan Richard who was the first to see one and he came screaming to me, burying his head in my petticoats in terror.

Who knew such creatures existed? There were stories in the Bible and a depiction of a strange watery beast in the church window at home, but this monster, almost as long as the ship itself, its huge body covered in barnacles, flippers like wings, this was beyond the wildest imaginings. How did God create such a creature and why? What part did it play in our universe?

We crept tentatively to the ship's rail to wonder at the beast. Its stillness only emphasised its power as it looked back at us from one eye. A steady, incurious stare.

We grown-ups were as excited as the children when the creatures performed a dance for us – for that is how it seemed – swooping and sliding in and out of the swell, spouting fountains into the air and diving, without a trace left on the sea that frothed around them. They uttered alien noises like the confidential whispers of gossiping women and mewing sounds, howls and growls, which echoed from beneath the waves.

"They are talking to us." Resolved jumped up and down with the thrill of it.

Who was I to argue?

From the commonplace book of Dorothy Bradford, found among the possessions of the maid Desire Minter after her death

John would have loved the whales.

Oh, John, my dear boy. How I miss you. Your sobs were as bitter as mine as the Speedwell *sailed away. How rejected you must have felt.*

I stayed on deck until the dockside faded into the blur of the mist and you were lost to sight. My heart has hoarded you since I gave birth to you three years ago but now... will I ever see you again?

My desolation is total.

William had been matter-of-fact when he announced that 'the boy' could not come. He would be a liability on a voyage as perilous as this, he asserted. "When we land, there will be savages and wild creatures waiting to tear us to pieces, starvation, sickness. Do you want to inflict them on him?"

I pleaded, I begged. I reminded him that many children were going, that Isaac and Mary Allerton were taking their three and she was pregnant again. She might even give birth on the journey.

He was adamant. What others did was their business.

"But John needs a mother's love," I persevered. I offered to follow in a year's time with the other families, but he pursed his lips in that scolding way of his. My duty was to be with him, our obligation was to guarantee the future life of the Plantation. It would be for the best that John stayed behind and learnt his scriptures, his Latin and Greek, as his father had.

"Remember," he wagged a finger at me, "I grew up without a father or a mother and it did me no harm."

How torn apart by loss, how trapped by 'duty'. Not from my husband a loving softness or the sweet possibility that marriage could be more than an obligation.

I never forgot the way he stood in Father's front room cutting an awkward figure with his thinning hair and much-darned fustian. He fiddled with the buttons and I noticed how bitten his fingernails were as he stammered out a few words about marriage: best if based on affection and inclination, how the most appealing bride does not always make the ideal wife or the best man the fittest husband. Better to lower one's sights, he seemed to be suggesting.

I was only sixteen, I knew nothing of love, but I did think the proposal lacked the romance a bride should expect. Father, on the other hand, considered it an excellent summary of matrimony.

"You will have to wait until she is twenty-one," he had declared, shaking my suitor by the hand, "but in the meanwhile you have my blessing."

William was 'not a little joyful' at my acceptance – though I had done little more than sit in the corner like a mouse – and settled down for a conversation with Father about a pamphlet one of his colleagues in Leiden had published. I was struck by how full of certainty and clarity he was about the scriptures compared with the diffidence he had shown when asking me to be his wife.

Married life was not what I expected. Maybe it never is. William worked all day at his loom in the front room, turning out fustian jackets and leggings by the score. Labours completed, we would walk to Green Close, where he forgot about me, about everything to do with the grind of daily life, and threw himself into the passion of prayer and argument.

We were awkward in each other's company, there is no denying it. We had none of the easy familiarity of Mary and William, for example. Our love-making was perfunctory. "It has to be done," he told me awkwardly. "We must procreate."

I plucked up the courage to ask Mary if she had any pleasure from the act and, in her forthright way, she explained how she and Master Brewster did not deny the body but, as she put it, 'harness it in the service of God'. She patted me on the arm. "Be patient. Maybe you should set aside a special time every week. Treat him with hot food full of mustard, pepper and cinnamon to arouse him."

William's sense of 'necessity' did not leave him once we were on the Mayflower. *Despite the closeness of other bodies, he would take me from behind clumsily and – mercifully – briefly, leaving me in an uncomfortable state of uncleanness.*

This was not the way with the other women, judging by the stifled squeals that I could hear at night. Mistress Billington particularly combined pleasure and duty with considerable satisfaction, though I tried to block my ears to such wantonness.

I felt inadequate, a feeling made worse when Elizabeth Hopkins gave birth. I was much affected by her cries of pain and the sobs of joy. The parents christened the infant Oceanus and toasted him with noisy self-congratulation and tots of brandy, but I was envious at their happiness and bitter that they had been so blessed.

I knew such feelings were ignoble and became so low that I lay on my filthy blanket for hours on end to shut myself off from the horrible agitation around me.

Mary was sympathetic but she was a practical type with little time for self-pity. Susanna White though did not give up on me. She chivvied me to my feet and forced me on deck to breathe in the air and watch the whales perform.

I admired her. She was forthright and fearless, though I did think she had been too outspoken in her sympathy for the More orphans and their shameless mother.

How unlikely, then, that it was those poor mites who brought me consolation.

They would cluster round me, seeking reassurance and cheer. From me of all people. "Mistress Dorothy, can you tell us a story, can we play Fox in the Hole?" And off they would scurry, shrieking with delight around the nooks and crannies below deck.

Despite William's frowns, I did my best to comfort them, particularly seven-year-old Jasper who was always dizzy with headaches and coughs. In turn, in their sweet, unaffected way, they roused me from my apathy, but the more time I spent with them, the deeper I felt the loss of John. The pain would not go away.

The words of Pastor Robinson came back to me from the day we had gathered at Delfshaven to bid farewell to our old life. It was a warm summer's day and we were wearing our worn garments of grey, soft greens and faded brown. The more daring had added dashes of red and yellow. We were like autumn leaves that could be scattered with a single blast of a gale.

"Do not think about what might go wrong," his voice boomed above the racket of the docks. "Lift up your eyes to heaven and calm your fears. Lord knows whether we will see each other's faces again, indeed we may never meet again in this world."

Never meet again.

CHAPTER FOUR

MAN OVERBOARD

O NE BY ONE THE WHALES ARCHED THEIR backs, slid gracefully into the deep and were gone. Bradford was a man transfixed and for a moment I assumed that, like the rest of us, he had been gripped by simple wonder at the sight.

But he was not like us.

"Jonah and the whale was one of the first stories my grandfather read to me, and now I can see its truth." He paced the deck, half talking to himself. "The Lord spared Jonah for his disobedience by making a whale swallow him, but he had a purpose. Jonah lived and saved Nineveh from sin. It will be the same for us when we reach Virginia; we shall rescue the savages from their heathen practices and impose the will of the Lord."

Jones scratched his head. "If there's any swallowing going on, it should be by us. Quite tasty, whales, aren't they, Clarkie?"

"Too fat and gamey to my taste," dissented the first mate. "And just beware them if you fancy yourself as a second Jonah. They won't eat you, but one swish of a tail by these big buggers and that's the end of you."

"You're lucky to have seen so many of 'em." Jones peered into the distance as the last of the sleek black backs disappeared into the horizon. "They normally head south when the weather gets colder and the storms pile in." He sniffed the air. "Talkin' of which, I think we have one coming our way."

There had been a strong breeze all day fluttering the sails like washing on a line, but now the wind grew steadily fiercer and the sky became a forbidding granite, brightened only by a low moon that flitted through the clouds, its white light dancing off the crests of the waves. It was both frightening and intoxicating.

The skipper ordered the crew to tie up the ropes, which were thrashing around like snakes, draw down the sails and lash them to the skeleton of the masts. I dallied on deck to feel the first cleansing drops of rain on my face, but in an instant the splashes became a solid sheet of rain that soaked me as thoroughly as if I had dived into the sea itself.

The moment the hatch was slammed shut, we were hit by a wave that sent us tumbling. Then another, followed by an unceasing barrage that made the ship shudder, thrown this way and that, plummeting into chasms like a starving cormorant and lurching upright, every timber creaking.

We could see nothing in the pitch black. We screamed, we were sick, chamber pots were sent flying. I had splinters under my fingernails where I had torn at the timbers to stop myself being hurled across the hold. The noise of wailing within and the incessant tumult of the storm was like a discordant choir of devils.

The hatch burst open and a great gush of water poured in,

followed by a figure who crashed to the deck, straight down, with no chance to break his fall. He lay crumpled, arms and legs akimbo, covered in blood, wild-eyed and gasping for breath.

It was John Howland.

"Overboard," he gulped and spewed up a bellyful of ocean. "Wave. Tripped." He fell back, cracking his head on the steps.

Desire and Elizabeth Tilley were the first to his side, tearing up lengths of linen to bandage his head and staunch a mass of cuts on his arms and chest. They wrapped him in blankets and I steadied him with a mug of beer, which he could hardly hold for his shaking.

He gabbled, "I was tying up a loose rope when a wave, a bloody monster of a wave – sorry, forgive my cussing – swept across the deck and took me clean away. I grabbed a halyard as I went over but I was dragged under and smashed against the side of the ship. God's blood – sorry – those barnacles are like nails. I thought I'd had it, my lungs were bursting, but one of the lads threw me a rope and then fished me out with a boat hook."

"You don't know how damnably lucky you are." Jones had scrambled into the hold. "Normally we don't bother with men overboard, not when it's that rough. We let 'em go."

"I was trying to help," spluttered Howland.

"Well, don't."

After two, maybe three, nights – who could be sure in the chaos? – blessed relief. The storm passed and we clambered on deck, blinking in the daylight. The sky was a palette of pinks and angry purples streaked with inky blue, and the sea still a confusion of great white tops that foamed angrily against the prow.

Back in the hold, Will dashed a drop of water from his face. It happened again. And again. The drop became a steady trickle. "Look, there's a huge crack in that beam."

"Nowt to worry about." Jones was dismissive. "You might not have noticed but we have been in a bit of a blow. The beams are bound to be damp."

Nonetheless, he inspected the crack, prodded it, swore under his breath and sent for the carpenter and Master Alden.

"There's no use banging in a few nails and splashing on tar," judged the cooper. "We need stout timbers, really solid, to prop it up."

To no avail. One timber bent under the pressure; two others split. The men rolled barrels underneath but they did not reach high enough.

Jones and Clarke scratched their heads. The skipper muttered, "This is the main support for the deck, damn it."

"Too bloody right." Clarke was grey with anxiety. "If this breaks, it's curtains."

I clutched Will. So this was it. What had been Master Cushman's terror? That we would be meat for the fishes? Dear Lord, he was about to be proved right.

"Gentlemen, I have a suggestion." It was William Brewster, serene as you like, as if he was about to deliver a sermon. "If you remember, I persuaded you to bring the device that I use for my printing."

Jones scowled. "Not now."

"It might be useful," continued the older man steadily. "It's like a screw; you winch it up and it exerts pressure on the press like a vice. If you wind it up as far as it will go, I think it could be used to support a heavy weight like this."

"I think you're onto something, Master Brewster." Edward Winslow jumped up excitedly. "I have often wondered at how powerful it is when you think all we use it for is forcing ink onto paper."

"Well, we must try anything." Jones was not convinced, not at all, but he ordered his men below and, with much heaving and swearing, they manoeuvred this strange contraption into position. Winslow took hold of its long handle and levered the screw up until the top fitted snug to the beam.

He gave the screw a speculative shove. It stood firm. He heaved at the beam. Solid.

"I think that will do nicely, Master Brewster." Jones was sweating with tension and relief. "I am grateful to you, sir. I confess if I'd have my way this contraption would have been hurled into Plymouth Sound."

The old fellow merely spread his arms in a gesture that declared 'all's well that ends well', and returned to his book.

CHAPTER FIVE

LAND

JOHN HOWLAND HAD BEEN LUCKY BUT IT WAS not long before the Reaper came calling again, and this time he did not leave empty-handed. His victim was the foul-mouthed bosun who had attacked Desire. He was left on deck away from the other sailors as he moaned in agony while his one-time mates ignored him and went about their tasks. It could be their turn next, they understood that when they signed up, so why make a fuss? The moment he died, Jones grunted a perfunctory prayer and his body was thrown overboard, disappearing like a pebble in a pond.

I felt guilty that I had felt such scant pity for him and confessed as much to Dorothy.

"I agree, it feels unchristian, but..." she began, only for her husband to cut in.

"He deserved to die. The way he cursed others rebounded on his own head. You can see how horrified his mates are, they can see the just hand of God has struck him down, but we

189

have been spared. Further proof, I think, of the rightness of our venture."

For me, 'rightness' had long been replaced by weariness. I was tired of the battering by the elements and worn down by the terror of being swept overboard from the lurching deck. I had lost the enthusiasm that had buoyed me up at the start of the voyage, when I loved to stand recklessly on deck breathing in the salty tang of the waves as they splashed over the prow. Now I was more likely to cower miserably below.

We were weak, hungry and filthy. There was hardly one of us who did not suffer from a hacking cough that infected our chests and became a fever. Most of us were afflicted by constipation, though, as Mary remarked wryly, "It's better that than diarrhoea."

I was covered in lice, which bred in the damp and drove me crazy with itching until I scraped them off my body, but that was nothing compared with the scurvy that made my joints ache. Small red-blue spots appeared on my skin, which turned into the sickly yellow of jaundice, my gums swelled and my teeth came loose, filling my mouth with blood. We all suffered the same.

To make it all the more unbearable, eight months of carrying the baby was taking its toll. My ankles had swollen, I felt nauseous and bloated, my thighs were gripped with cramp and I could not get comfortable on the mat that was my bed. Every now and then I was sure I felt the kick of the baby, but I told myself it was just the heartburn. *Not yet*, I beseeched it. *Not here. Wait until we reach land.*

Desire comforted me, cooling me down with wet rags and massaging my belly.

"She helped deliver my John." Dorothy gave a rueful smile.

"You made such a racket." The maid was more cheerful than I had seen her all voyage. "Never heard the like."

I remembered my own time with Resolved. *Never again,* I swore, but as Desire reminded me, "They all say that – and back they come, year after year."

And, of course, she was right.

While I fretted about the life I was about to bring into the world, a servant lad called William Butten, who had been ailing for most of the voyage, died on November 6. I had hardly noticed him during our time on board but, I judged, his death did contradict Master Bradford's confident claim that only the ungodly would be punished.

As his shrouded body was dropped into the deep, a flock of birds wheeled over the ship.

Jones sniffed the air. "What do you think, Clarkie? If I'm not mistaken, these feathered friends mean we are close to land."

Could it be? Spirits rose and we clustered on deck, chattering, full of hope and anticipation and, above all, relief.

Two days later – two long, long days – there came the cry we had waited for.

"Land hoy."

Coppins shouted down from the forward deck. "This is it, ladies and gents. Cape Cod."

We clustered on deck to see a grey blur on the horizon come tantalisingly into focus – low brown cliffs, mile after mile of sand and, behind, thick black forest. The waves surged relentlessly onto the shore, breaking into a never-ending ribbon of white surf that reminded me of the garland of lace I had worn at my wedding.

"It's a wilderness." What had I been expecting? Something greener, prettier? Somewhere that was like the village I grew up in? A place to lift the spirits? "Is that what we have come all this way for?"

"At least it's land." Will put his arms round me. "It means we can get off this wretched ship."

"We have sailed too far north." Jones and Clarke had been brooding over their charts. "We shall have to tack along the coast and head south to the Hudson River and make land there. Not many days now."

Not many days. Dear Lord, one more hour was too much.

Hardly had we changed course than the ship was seized by churning currents.

"Pull to port," yelled Clarkie. "Quick about it. Rocks."

So it was to end here. That garland of lace concealed a deadly danger that would shatter the ship into pieces and sweep us ashore, where our bones would be picked clean by crows and whitened by time.

The ship tipped and yawed as it fought the current in a frantic attempt to escape the deadly pull of the tide and sail away from peril, back the way we had come. So loud was the creaking of the timbers and the anguished squeal of the whipstaff that I felt sure the ship was tearing itself in two.

But the *Mayflower* and its flinty skipper were made of sterner stuff. By dawn, the ship was sailing away from the rocks and into the safety of blessedly peaceful waters until we rounded a long curved outcrop of sandy land shaped like the claw of a huge lobster and glided into a bay. The leadsmen dropped the lines overboard to gauge the depth.

"Three hundred feet deep, 250, 200, 120."

"Anchors away," shouted Jones.

November 11, 1620. Our voyage was over.

It had been sixty-six days since we left Plymouth, ninety-eight from Southampton, and for the exhausted folk from Holland, almost four months. Wives and husbands embraced, the sailors gave a cheer and the children dashed around the deck in sheer high spirits.

As for me, I flinched as the baby kicked, and kicked hard. It was as though he sensed the world was ready for him.

William Brewster stood apart, his face working with emotion.

"This is a day I will never forget." He rubbed his eyes. "We have fulfilled God's will."

"My, Master Brewster, how content you must be." I could not find anything more eloquent to say, but I did understand how much the moment meant to him.

"I am. I am." He nodded emphatically. "More than content. I have worked to achieve this for many years. We all have. God has delivered us to the destiny we sought. But first, excuse me – I have business to attend to."

He ducked into the captain's cabin, clutching several sheafs of parchment. One by one, the rest of the men joined him. Billington was making a nuisance of himself but Master Standish gave him a shove and the door was slammed behind them.

"What's going on?" I asked Mary.

"William and Master Carver are determined that the men sign an agreement to make sure that from the moment we step ashore, we are all united in a common purpose. He is concerned that some among our number are little better than mutineers who prefer a free-for-all – everyone to his own without a care for the others."

We could hear a low rumble of voices and once I was sure I heard Standish yell 'traitor'.

"How predictable that we have to wait while the men decide our fate." All I wanted was to get off the damnable ship.

But Mary shook her head reprovingly. "They know best. They have been planning this for weeks. Our survival depends on everyone signing."

So we stood at the prow watching the setting sun make long shadows of the trees on the shore. How strange it was without the constant movement of the vessel, and how I longed to walk on dry land. Dry land! The reassuring smell of earth and trees, no more the bitter tang of salt on my lips.

Dusk settled, rain spattered on the deck and the birds stopped their screeching. In that briefest of moments, an outlandish howling echoed from across the bay. Dorothy grabbed my arm in fright. I shivered and pulled my shawl around me.

Our fear fell away when the door to the captain's cabin swung open and the men trooped noisily out. William Brewster had an expression of quiet satisfaction on his face but Billington brushed past me, treading on my toe as he went and muttering, "Sanctimonious, self-regarding, canting clique. Damn them all."

The signing of the compact. As told by John Billington and preserved by his wife

The very second Jones turns the ship round and heads north to get out of them currents, I know we're in a new game. He tells us as much one night when he has been at the port; if the ship doesn't make the Hudson River, he says, we won't be under the rule of the King.

"How come?" I ask.

"Because the patent for the settlement has been made out for Virginia and not territory to the north. It won't apply."

He winks and it takes me a while to realise that it means the country is up for grabs. We don't have to obey any patent, we don't have to follow the Bible thumpers. No, it will be first come, first served. We can go where we want, trade as much as we like and make as much money as we fancy.

I get plotting with the London lads long before the anchor drops – 'Hoppy' Hopkins, his two servants Doty and Leister, a couple of wild 'uns if ever there are, and the other like-minders.

"This is our chance to get away from these moaning joltheads," I tell them. "Stake a claim to the best land. But we must move fast."

Doty reckons, "Hold 'em at gun point."

Another, "Grab the longboat. Leave 'em stranded."

But just as we think to help ourselves to a musket in the gun store – to help our argument along, you understand – up struts the dwarf Standish.

"Meeting in the captain's cabin." An order. Bloody cheek.

"What's it to do with us?" I ask.

"Find out."

"Shog off, drummer boy," I riposte. "You have your own meeting. We'll have ours."

The dwarf edges his sword an inch from its sheaf. Laughing boy Winslow sidles up. He trims his nails with a knife.

Leaves me with little choice; my blade is below decks.

They are all there: Bradford, Brewster, Carver, all the pleased-with-themselves Leiden clique.

Carver's like a jumped-up town crier. "Our great voyage is over now, praise be. Tomorrow we begin the life we have come all this way to forge."

Brewster chimes in, "It is essential we speak and act with one voice."

"Not I," retorts Doty.

"Nor me," says Leister.

Hopkins shifts about a bit and keeps his trap shut.

I speak up. "We want nothing to do with you schism-mongers." I'm encouraged by a round of hear-hears.

"Traitor. Backstabber. Apostate." Standish is incapable of civilised manners.

"You have no right to insult me." I stay unruffled. "I stand for the rights of them who aren't in your gang."

"You are a mutinous mob." Has a silly high voice, Master Bradford. Like an angry mouse.

Carver tries to calm things. "Be sensible. All of you. Our women and children are ill. We are all so exhausted we can go no further. We must work as one."

Jones breaks in. "And get a bloody move on. We ain't got barely enough food and drink for the voyage back 'ome and I don't want to lose money on this venture."

Brewster again. "We are in a wild land, we have little food, there are savages in the forests waiting to strike at us. Are you really suggesting, Master Billington, that we split into separate groups?"

That's exactly what I am saying.

"Remember the words of our pastor when we left Southampton," he continues.

"No," riposte I. "Your pastor, nothing to do with us."

But the interfering old fool won't be silenced. "I happen to have kept his message." He leafs through sheafs of parchment. "'You are now the citizens of the same body politic so bear in mind, there is no one more special than any other to be in charge. Be wise – and godly – only choose people who will promote the common good. And then, honour and obey them.'"

He looks up from reading. Keeps his trap shut for a bit of drama. Milking the silence. Trying to intimidate us.

"We may not need a king, but we do need a governor."

So that's the game.

Hopkins finds his voice. "Honour and obedience is all very well, but the man in charge would be one of you Leiden lot. Your aims are different. You want to be good Christians living in sin-free perfection – nothing wrong with that, but we've come for the profit, not the prophet."

"Nice one," I chuckle. Hoppy is pleased with himself.

Brewster is polite but cold as ice. "Master Stephen, you know well what it is like to be disloyal to your peers and betters, do you not?"

Hopkins blinks.

"Shall I remind everyone about your time in Bermuda? How you were sentenced to death for mutiny. Do you want that to be your epitaph, as a man who betrays his companions?"

Damnit, he has him there.

"That was a long time ago," *flusters Hoppy.* "I am wiser now and now that I, er, hear your arguments, I have decided, er, yes, that I am with you. I concur, we should, er, unite."

Craven turncoat.

"I am glad to hear it." *Brewster reaches into a satchel and brings out another sheet of paper.*

He's already prepared a document. It's all there, ready to be signed. The brass of it.

"In the name of God, amen." *He's more pompous than a bishop.* "We, whose names are underwritten, the loyal subjects of our dread Sovereign Lord King James of Great Britain, France, and Ireland, defender of the Faith, etc, etc…"

"I like the etcetera, etcetera," *mocks Leister.* "All la-di-dah, la-di-dah." *We fall about.*

The old bore drones on. "Having undertaken, for the glory of God, a voyage to plant the first colony in the northern parts of Virginia, do solemnly and mutually, in the presence of God and one another, covenant and combine ourselves into a civil body politic."

"Words. Just words." *I've had enough.*

"To order, preserve and enact, constitute and frame such just and equal laws, acts and offices, from time to time…"

"Time's up," *I remark smartly. Doty snorts.*

Brewster raises one eyebrow. Patronising old fart. "To which we promise all due submission and obedience."

"Not us," *chorus Doty, Leister and me. A few of the servants mumble support.*

"As witness to that, we have subscribed our names at Cape Cod the 11th of November, in the seventeenth year of the reign of our Sovereign Lord King James."

Flatulent rubbish, I reckon, and I am about to take a step forward and tear it from him but that pesky Standish gets so close to me I can smell his noxious breath.

LAND

Brewster speaks up. "I propose Master Carver as our first governor."

"Aye. Aye." The toadies are of one voice. Of course they are.

I take a count of the men in the cabin. Damn me, there are many more of those in support of the pesky pilgrims than against.

"This is solemn and binding," squeaks Bradford. "This compact will guide the way we govern the settlement forever and furthermore, I believe future generations will study this and follow our example."

"Let me sign." Carver steps forward, and with a great flourish writes his name. Bradford follows, then Winslow, Brewster, the dwarf, William White and then Hopkins. The snake.

When John Howland, only a manservant, reaches for the pen, I have to object. "Surely only men of breeding should sign."

"We have made this great voyage as equals," pronounces Brewster. "We must all sign, whatever our station – gentlemen, servants, even the labourers. Even you, Master Billington."

Forty-one sign. Twenty-seven refuse.

No point flogging a dead horse. We aren't going to win this one. Me, Doty and Leister are the last to scrawl our names.

As soon as we can, we'll break away and do our own deals with Thomas Weston. He has the same contempt for these scurvy sneaksbies as I do.

CHAPTER SIX

PEREGRINATIONS

WHAT BLISS. WE WERE LOWERED BY ROPES into the sea. My, it was cold. Clean and clear. Glorious. I gasped at the shock of it and whooped with the sheer delight of being out of the stale fug of the hold.

Unexpectedly, the water was so shallow we could wade to the shore, the salt pricking our feet, which were crusted in a stubborn mix of dirt and tar, and I submerged myself up to my neck. I never bathed from one year to the next – a damp linen cloth did nicely – but now I splashed water on my face and head and crouched down to slip off my shift to let it surge around my naked body, washing away the rankness of weeks afloat. My stomach, like a balloon, floated above the gentle ripples. It was all so delightfully daring.

Mary Brewster was horrified at my lack of inhibition but gingerly waded in as high as the top of her thighs. Only Dorothy – sad, lost Dorothy – stayed on the shore holding the orphan Jasper More, who was slumped across her lap in feeble surrender.

"He's on fire." She cooled his brow with a cloth but he did not stir.

Back on deck, the snow cloaking us like nuns in their white cowls, Master Carver called us round.

"We men must begin the exploration. I need volunteers for a reconnaissance party."

Sixteen men stepped forward and, despite me hanging onto his arm, Will was one of them.

"Please don't go," I begged. "You might be killed by the savages or eaten by the lions we've been warned about. What will happen to us, to me and Resolved?"

"I must." He pulled his arm away. "It will be an adventure."

"How selfish. How typically selfish," I snapped. "You are going in pursuit of excitement when you should be by my side. And what about this?" I patted my stomach. "Are you going to leave me alone with your unborn child?"

"It is my duty. You should be proud that I have been chosen. We are ready for anything. We have muskets that will blow the head off any marauder and we are led by Captain Standish. What a heroic figure he cuts. One sight of him and the savages will flee and lions cower."

I wondered about that. Standish did not make me quake with dread; rather, with his sturdy frame and red hair poking from his helmet, he looked more like a pugnacious ginger mongrel.

The men lined up on the shore. For all the armour and the muskets, all the braggadocio, nothing could disguise the fact that they were stooped with fatigue and limp with hunger. They would be no match for a hostile savage.

Will blew me a kiss as they trudged away through the sandy hillocks, which tugged at their boots and made them stumble.

Dorothy gave her William a tentative wave but he was oblivious. Always the man on a mission.

Late next day, they shuffled back, exhausted but buzzing with excitement.

"Savages. We saw them. We had marched about one mile when, bold as brass, there they were, cutting up a whale."

The first sign of life, alien and, no doubt, dangerous. I had heard so many tales from Coppins about the way the savages skinned their enemies alive and cut off their limbs that I was gripped with terror, but the men were flushed with the thrill of the exploit.

"They did not flee when they saw us but stood tall and black in their furs. They even waved at us. Before we could load our muskets, they disappeared into the forest as fast as the ferrets we keep for ratting at home."

They were like boys in a playground, but within days the mood changed. Will muttered about walking for hours, wading through rivers, squelching through mud and getting lost on tracks that led nowhere.

They were wet through, faces inflamed and lips cracked by the remorseless wind. They were worn out and discouraged. Most of them refused food – though not because their hunger pangs had been eased in some miraculous way, but because, as an embarrassed Will revealed, they had been so hungry that they had eaten mussels and been gut-wrenchingly sick.

Edward Winslow was spitting blood and Will had traces of red on his kerchief. He dismissed it. "Cut myself on a bramble." But he did confess, "The truth is, we are worn down. We have no strength. We cannot sleep because the ground is too hard and too cold, but what really troubles us is that the nights are filled with strange howls and cries. We have to be on guard all the time." He saw the dismay on my face. "Nothing to worry about," he blustered. "We're not frightened. We know we have a mission to accomplish and we cannot falter."

I was not convinced by his bravado. Of course, he could not admit to any kind of foreboding, typical man, so it took me a while to realise that he and the others were not just enfeebled by lack of sleep and constant marching, but that they were disturbed – more, depressed – by what they were finding.

"We came across an abandoned house where a pot still hung over the fireplace." Will was uncharacteristically subdued. "The leftovers of a meal were still in it – looked like dried fish and acorns. A haunch of venison too. We dug up mats, which hid a mortar and an earthenware pot, bushels of corn. A kettle. Just left there."

"They must belong to someone." I was strangely moved by these simple signs of everyday life but I shuddered when Will described how they had uncovered a bundle of bones and the skull of a man.

"It still had flesh hanging to it." He grimaced.

"European, judging by the yellow hair," reckoned Winslow. "Had a pair of breeches like you'd see being worn on any high street at home."

"We also discovered the bones and head of a child," stated Bradford in his meticulous way. "It was wrapped in a sailor's canvas coat and wore a pair of cloth breeches. In the grave were bowls, trays, trinkets and a knife. There was even a string of white beads."

Dorothy hid her face in her hands. She was thinking of her boy.

Will thoughtlessly added to her pain by reaching into a knapsack and spreading out an array of 'treats' for the children.

They gathered around in fascination as he held out brass arrow heads carved with macabre shapes made from eagles' claws and stag antlers, and squealed with delight when he tipped out a sack full of bracelets and beads, coloured bone, shells and a brass earring. Gruesome tokens from the grave.

While the children played with their new toys, the rest of us lapsed into a dejected silence until Will – it had to be him – suddenly brightened up.

"Shall I tell them?" He positively chortled. There was muted sniggering. "Bradford put his foot into a deer trap and was whisked arse over cop into the air. Such a joke. He was upside down, shouting and twisting to get free, and when I cut him down he landed head first in a muddy heap."

Yes, we roared at that, but more out of a nervy need for release than real amusement. Bad enough they had failed to find a place to settle, but more upsetting, for me at any rate, was the awful notion that somewhere in this wasteland there were folk whose lives we were interfering with; the owners of the corn, the kettle, the pot of food; the parents of the dead child. How would we feel if a stranger despoiled the graves in our village churches?

The object of their mirth stayed stony faced.

"We have a task to complete. This is no time for merriment."

"Master Bradford makes a serious point, a deadly serious point." Standish had joined in the merriment as loudly as the next man but now he became businesslike. "The trap must have been the work of the savages. I reckon they know where we are every single moment of the day. They are playing with us, flitting in and out of the shadows like ghosts at a funeral – though not, by my sword, our funeral."

Jones broke in. "At last. Sense. Now perhaps you'll realise that we are in constant danger. But not just from the Indians. Unless you want to perish here, you need to find a fresh-water spring, you need to plant crops, and you must find a deeper bay than this where we can bring the ship close to land and unload."

"Can't get anywhere without the blasted shallop." Clarke was testier than usual. "How are you lazy so-and-sos getting on with it? My mother could have banged it together quicker than you lot."

"Be ready tomorrow," promised Howland, who had been working with Alden to reassemble the craft. "Just the last of the caulking to be done."

"Well, go to it," barked Jones.

They toiled all night and by dawn, the shallop was loaded and the sail raised for another perilous exploration. I would have happily donned armour and joined them, but all we women could do was wait helplessly and worry. That was our role.

The very moment Will was lost to sight I felt a sharp stab of pain. The warm flow down my thighs. The deep, fierce cramp in my belly.

"Dorothy," I quavered.

One glance. She did not need an explanation. She steered the children into the hold and half carried me down the ladder.

And there in the squalor, behind a sagging curtain held by willing helpers, I screamed, I pushed and I begged to be spared such torture, until I held him. He was perfect. Ten fingers, ten toes, a beating heart and a red-faced squeal of indignation. All the pain was forgotten. Peregrine.

What else could I call him after carrying him for every day of the voyage, the first baby to be born in this scary world? The women joined in sisterly celebration, even the sailors congratulated me, but Dorothy gazed on him with an intensity that was disquieting.

"Everything is so precarious," she murmured. "But your boy, he is a symbol of hope."

CHAPTER SEVEN

A RESTLESS SPIRIT

OUR SERVANT EDWARD HAD COMPLAINED OF feeling 'queer in the head'. He was trembling and coughing up gobs of bloodstained mucus, his breathing was erratic, he was sweating and shivering.

"My chest," he groaned. "The pain."

I dabbed at his head with a wet cloth.

"Don't give up," I exhorted. "Fight. You'll get better."

But I didn't believe it. He gave a convulsive jerk and was gone. It was so quick.

"We have to get him off the ship as soon as possible," ordered Jones. "That's pneumonia, if I'm not mistaken, and the germs that cause it will spread like wildfire."

His body was loaded onto the long boat and I clutched Peregrine close as it was ferried ashore, where prayers were offered up and he was buried in a hollow in the dunes. And that was that. I grieved for the futility of his short life and felt guilty for bringing him on our adventure. Adventure! Was that what it was?

Resolved tugged at my arm. "It's Jasper, he won't wake up."

Dorothy was bent over the boy, her mouth like a vice as she mopped his forehead. His face was blemished by ugly spots and his limbs twisted with the last contortions of his agonised body.

"If God withholds his compassion from this child, what will become of the rest of us?" she cried bitterly. "What kind of life was that? Born out of sin and rejected by all."

I struggled for consoling words. "He would never have had a chance to prosper here, so maybe this is God's way of sparing him further suffering."

But she shook her head and clutched his cold body to her. The small bundle was buried next to Edward.

Dorothy stumbled slightly as she clambered back on board and she disappeared into the hold without a word.

I expected to find her the next morning standing by the prow, where she used to gaze into the swirling snow, mesmerised by the way the flakes hissed and vanished as they hit the water, but she wasn't there. I thought nothing of it; I was kept busy with the baby.

Richard, the eldest of the More children, sought me out.

"Mistress Susanna, where is Dorothy?" he asked.

"Have you not seen her?"

He shook his head dumbly.

I asked the sailors. Nothing. None of the passengers had seen her.

We searched the ship from the lowest, darkest hold to the gun room. No sign.

"Perhaps she lowered herself down the side and waded to the shore," suggested Mary.

"She was in a distracted mood," offered Elizabeth. "More than usual. She must have decided to visit Jasper's grave."

"We should check. She was greatly affected by his passing."

But as I spoke, one of the sailors shouted, "There. On the anchor chain."

Just above the waterline, a shred of white cotton had been snagged on the rusty iron.

It was from her dress. She had washed it only two days before.

The men belayed down the side of the ship to see if they could find her trapped under the hull while the rest waded to the shore and scoured the scrub.

"Sorry, missus." The search party gave up. "She must have fallen over, maybe banged her head and drowned. The tide will have dragged her out."

Poor, forlorn, Dorothy. She had been denied the love of her boy and maybe too, she had been denied the pull of affection between a man and a woman. Her life had been mapped out for her and she never had the chance to follow the compass of her dreams.

She was only twenty-three. I don't think she had laughed once in all the time I had known her.

I hugged Peregrine tightly and pulled Resolved close as we stood by the graves where now there were three crosses – but only two bodies.

The snow fell and as it settled, the atmosphere became eerily deadened. The world beyond the ship was silent, the birds had taken cover and stopped their singing. On board, we spoke in hushed voices and tip-toed about in case we somehow disturbed the memory of her.

We stayed in that same state, strangely removed from the reality that lay hidden from us by the mist, until a great clamour from way out in the bay had us rushing to the rails. Out of the gloom appeared the men in noisy triumph.

Carver dropped his customary punctilious manner to shout from the shallop, "Home! We have found the place for our new home."

Will bounced across the deck and kissed me. He grabbed Peregrine from my arms and whirled him around, but stopped when he noticed our sombre expressions. He looked at me questioningly.

Brewster took Bradford to one side.

The younger man stared around, nonplussed. He had not noticed that his wife was not waiting for him.

He remained expressionless as Brewster pulled him down to his knees in prayer. After a few minutes, he got to his feet, jaw working, fists clenching and unclenching.

"God's will be done. I am used to this. It is my lot." He stood alone at the rail, oblivious to the rest of us who looked on in anguished silence, gripping it until his knuckles were white.

"We have made a cross for her." Brewster put his arm around him.

"It signifies nothing without a body beneath. Her spirit has not been drowned, so to that extent she is still with me."

He walked stiffly across the deck and into the hold, reappearing with a small bundle of clothes, a small embroidered purse and what looked like the commonplace book I had seen her writing in on many an evening.

"Here." He thrust the few belongings into Desire's hands. "Dorothy would have wanted you to have them." Once again, he stared around sightlessly, picked up his Bible and began to read.

We might have stayed in our inarticulate sorrow, unsure how to react, had Jones not barked, "We must get moving. Get that shallop tied up safe. We'll be on our way tomorrow."

As the ship's company bestirred itself, Mary Brewster reflected.

"When the one person you love is missing, the universe seems empty, but I think for young Bradford, orphaned, often bereft of love and kinship, he has come to believe that loss is the natural order. Only the death of his sister upset him – or perhaps I should say, it was the only time he showed he was troubled – but as always, he was able to reach out to the scriptures and find a meaning. They inspired him to find a cause, this cause to which he has dedicated himself."

"Perhaps that explains why he did not seek her out the moment he got back on the ship." Elizabeth Winslow, in marked contrast, had been embraced by her Edward in a lively display of affection.

"I thought it strange." I too was trying to make sense of his curious detached behaviour.

"But what of Dorothy, what if she is still alive?" wondered Mary Allerton. "Taken by the tide and abandoned on a distant shore. How terrible if she is crying out for rescue and no one can hear."

"A restless spirit, denied her peace." Mary Brewster wiped away a tear.

"Do you think…" I stumbled to express what was troubling me – that her sadness had made her careless of life.

Mary Brewster shook her head fiercely. "Do not begin to consider it."

Our time for mourning was brief. With a great hustle and bustle the anchor was raised, the sails unfurled and the *Mayflower* set sail across a wide bay, leaving the lonely graves behind.

Our plucky explorers were once again in good heart and only too eager to tell us about their heroic adventures.

"We were attacked by savages." Will had Resolved on his knee, who listened agog. I disapproved mightly of such boastful talk but let him chatter on. "Forty of them. Imagine that."

"More." Standish was not to be outdone. "Fifty at least."

"What a huggery it was. There were arrows whizzing everywhere." Yes, my husband was back to his spirited self. "They thunked into the trees by our ears but we had our muskets ready in a flash and fired back. We winged one. You should have heard him screaming as he ran for it."

"We showed them what to expect from the power of England." Standish pulled himself up proudly.

Will confessed to me later, "Fact is, we were getting mighty anxious. No place we landed in was right for a settlement. If there was a spring the land was too rocky; if we found a nice stretch to plant in, there was no water. The longer we wandered about, we knew the Indians were never far away and could have wiped us out any time they fancied. It was looking pretty hopeless until Coppins suggested we head to a safe harbour where he had sheltered years back."

"Thievish Harbour, I calls it," said the mate. "Some bastard we was trading with last year stole my 'arpoon."

"The seas got up and we were in a right pickle. The rudder broke, which had Clarkie cursing Howland and Alden for being lousy workmen, then the mast shattered, which made him as mad as a trapped badger. The language."

"Hardly our fault," objected Howland. "We were short of nails and ropes and you know it was a rushed job because Captain Jones was so impatient."

"Excuses, excuses," joshed Will. "All I know is that I reckoned we'd had it."

"Damned close-run thing." Coppins puffed on his pipe and spat. "Too damn close."

"And the so-called island you landed us on was just rock and sand."

"You'd have ended up as fish food without me," riposted the mate, glaring at him with his good eye while the one with the squint focused on a horizon way beyond the Cape. Maybe he was longing to be reunited with his wife in London. *More like*, I reckoned, *the amorous lady from Oporto.*

"Or eaten by wild animals," chipped in Clarke. "And don't forget, that lump of rock and sand turned out to be an easy row to your new 'ome. So less of it."

Far from cheering me, this banter and Will's guileless enthusiasm dismayed me. I hated how much he was enjoying these scrapes – yes, enjoying – without a care for his family. I'd be having words with my wayward husband. No more daft exploits. No more Indian arrows whizzing our way, thank you.

And then without fanfare: "Welcome to New England."

The ship had come gently to a halt.

Governor Carver stood at the prow. "The maps call this harbour Plymouth and that, I suggest, will be good enough for us. Perhaps more dignified than Thievish Harbour." He gave Coppins a good-natured nod. "It will remind us of the last place we knew in the old country."

We gave a ragged cheer.

It was December 16, 1620.

CHAPTER EIGHT

A ROOF OVER OUR HEADS

W E WERE IN A BAY BRACKETED BY TWO spits of sandy dunes topped with spiky brown grass. The terrain immediately in front of us was flat and empty, overrun by tangled brambles and stalks of withered maize, and it rose steadily before disappearing into a wall of foreboding forest.

It should have felt momentous, but I had never felt so oppressed. Was this to be our home? A life in this wilderness? Surely not. But the anchor rattled and splashed, the sails were furled and the gangplank manhandled to the shore. There was no going back.

Mary Chilton was the first to bound down the gangplank and leap onto a huge boulder by the shore, and from there she hopped to land. We gave her a cheer and she curtsied in mock thanks before, one by one, we shuffled after her, me holding Peregrine and clutching Resolved by his jerkin to stop him falling in.

We stood irresolutely, overawed by a cheerlessness heightened by the wash of waves and the wind whistling through the bare branches of the trees. The stillness was broken by the shrill piping of a grey and white bird that hopped along the shore. It was oddly comforting, like the dippers on the muddy banks of the River Nene near my village at home.

The rain became snow, darkening the sky and turning the forest into a wall of blackness. Shadows moved and flickered with the wind and I swore I heard the same unearthly howl that had so alarmed Dorothy and me the night we first made land on Cape Cod.

Standish strutted to the front. "Let's go. Keep close. Men, keep your muskets primed and dry. You women stay close."

We shuffled in single file, feet crunching on the sand, voices lowered to a whisper in case we alerted the savages – though, as Will pointed out, they were bound to be watching our every move however quiet we were.

We crept forward until out of the murk emerged a ghostly skeleton of branches, which had been bowed and tied to make a shelter. Rushes that must have been used for the roof but had decayed and dropped like the blackened remains of prehistoric birds were strewn on the floor. The poignant signs of domestic life lay about: scattered beads, pots and pans and bowls that must have once been full of food. A family haven, perhaps, where children had played.

My foot stubbed against a branch bleached by salt and sun, or so I reckoned, then another. I went to pick it up. Not a branch. A bone. A human bone. I screamed and covered my eyes until Will threw it into the trees.

There were more, many more bones scattered in that forlorn wasteland. Skulls grinned vacantly into the grey sky in a horrible memorial to the families that had perished, their bodies left where they fell for the wolves to tear apart and birds to pick at.

I was trembling. That men and women and their children had been left unburied, without the proper rituals, chilled my soul. Was that to be our fate? To be cut down like them and abandoned in this field of death?

"Here." Master Carver came to a halt by a spring that danced its way merrily to the shore. He thrust the butt of his musket onto the ground. "Just here." He held out his arms parallel to the ground. "We will build two rows of houses on this slight incline."

All I saw was snow-covered nothingness. Two rows of houses, just like that?

"We must not allow strange fancies and terrors to stop us now," he pronounced. "We cannot delay."

My, we worked hard, men and women alike. It was December 25, Christmas Day, but there was no time to celebrate, no time for seasonal greetings or even quiet meditation – no, we had to carve this New Plymouth out of nothing – and anyway, as Master Bradford informed me brusquely, "We do not acknowledge Christmas. It is a vulgar Papist corruption."

We dragged ourselves awake every morning, sunken-cheeked and dull-eyed, still in the wet clothes we had worn the day before, grabbed a mouthful of dried biscuit, and with hoe and axe did battle with the land, struggling against the sleet that stung our faces and froze our fingers. We wheezed, we coughed, we struggled for breath. Every limb ached.

Even the Billington family buckled down and helped with clearing the ground, chopping down trees and sawing them into planks. No one stinted. Brewster, more comfortable with a book in his hand, took his turn hammering in nails.

"I used to help shoe the horses at the manor." He was gasping for breath.

To my surprise – and admiration – Bradford was as active as any, working like a demon from dawn to dusk, but he was not the practical sort. He was tugging a beam into position, pulled a muscle and fell, clutching his hip in great pain.

And then, the miracle. By the end of January, only four weeks after landing, we had done as Master Carver had demanded – we had built two rows of houses. Nineteen of them. Rough and ready, to be sure, made of timber and patched up with wattle and daub, but even if the wind blew off the rushes or the rain washed away the mud foundations, we did not care. We had a home.

We cast lots to see who would have which plot. Will and I were given a patch in the lee of the hill. The Standishes and John Alden took root on the north side of the settlement, Edward and Elizabeth Winslow were opposite and Bradford in the centre. I did wonder quite how Mary and William Brewster felt about living next to the Billington family.

My spirits rose as I unpacked my trusty chest and tucked Peregrine into his cradle.

Will chanced on a lone herring flapping on the shore and gave it to Master Carver to eat, which he did with gusto. As he ate, Brewster told us a convoluted tale about the negotiations with King James for the right to live in New England.

"'What profits may arise?' asked His Majesty. When he was told they would be from fishing, he cried, 'Tis an honest trade! It was the Apostle's own calling.'"

Will made light of the old man's meanderings. "Even Christ would find it difficult to feed us all with one herring," he laughed. "How disappointed the King will be."

It was the briefest moment of gaiety.

As Jones had warned, we were too late to plant any crops, the birds had flown south and the deer stayed hidden in the forest. What little food we had left from the voyage was so stale it was barely edible.

But that was nothing to what was in store for us.

Starvation, disease, death. Remorseless and unescapable.

In December, six of us died.

In January, eight more.

We quickly learnt to recognise the symptoms of scurvy, for that, combined with debilitating months in the ship's germ-ridden holds, was what afflicted us.

We tried to ignore the lack of appetite and dismissed the loss of weight, the diarrhoea and the fever as 'just a passing ailment'. We'd reassure each other with 'we'll soon be up and about', but when the blisters turned to ulcers and gums putrefied, we knew there was no escape. Bones that had previously broken fractured again; old wounds opened up and discharged pus and blood.

Mary Brewster noticed it first. "This might sound odd, but have you noticed how the dying actually smell?"

"It's a well-known fact, missus," explained Jones. "And I'll tell you another thing. Scurvy weakens the muscles and makes the bodies of the victims sound like they are creaking and rattling."

That January, Ellen More, only eight, slipped away followed by her four-year-old sister Mary. They never understood what they had done to deserve such cruelty at the hands of humankind.

Death was routine. It was left to the women to clean the bodies and wrap them in shrouds while the men dug graves near the top of the mount – Burial Hill, Will dubbed it – and we listened to the consoling tones of Master Brewster reading out the prayers as we stood by the fresh mounds of earth.

"We must bury them here out of sight to make sure the Indians cannot see how many of us are dying, how weak the rest of us are and realise we are easy targets," decreed Carver. "We should plant corn on the graves so it seems we are tilling the earth to grow our vegetables."

The good, the not-so good, the folk I had got to know well, others I had not particularly liked – the plague was no respecter of the worthy or the sinful. In all the blur of death, one gentleman's going stuck incongruously in my mind – that of Degory Priest, who had been a hat maker in Leiden.

"It's a nice view from up there on Burial Hill," he joked as he gasped his last. "Remember our big day?" He grasped Mary Allerton by the arm.

"How could I forget?" She half sobbed, half laughed as she explained. "We had a double wedding. I married Isaac and Degory was hitched to Isaac's sister. What a day it was. We ate, we drank, how we danced. Degory made toppers for all the men."

As we stood by his grave, Desire choked, "How strange to think his wife and the two bairns back in Leiden will be going to market as they do every day, while he lies under this cold earth."

Forgive me; I had a less charitable conclusion. Degory was a jolly enough soul, but what help had he been building our shelters? How useful was a nicely turned tricorn with a feather when it came to tilling the fields? Very little. Come to that, what use were any of us? There were not enough men with the skills to make anything. How could we possibly succeed in this desperate enterprise?

"Mary Allerton," cried Elizabeth. "She needs help."

At last, the baby was coming. Mary Brewster and Rose Standish dashed in and out of the ship's cabin where the pregnant woman lay with hot water and cool rags, but it was Desire who was in charge.

"Learnt all this from Ma," she declared. "She was the best midwife in Leiden."

For seven agonising hours Mary laboured, and then it was all over with a cry of relief and joy. She reached for her baby, only to see the expression in our eyes. The child was dead. At first she would not let go of the infant, but husband Isaac gently prised it from her arms. She stared at us numbly, sank back onto the filthy blanket and turned her head to the wall. Nine months of hope and hardship had ended in inconsolable bitterness.

She never recovered. Whether it was from the heartbreak or the suffering she endured on the voyage, she died a few days later. She was holding my hand when she went. "Bless you and your child," were her last words.

There was no respite. Mary Brewster came running. "It's Rose."

Poor Rose. Poor Master Myles.

He did not bother to wipe away the tears as he stood silently by the mound where his dead wife lay. The tough little Captain Standish, as vulnerable as the rest of us – except the very next day he was back at his station, corselet polished like the sun.

"It is what God asks of his warriors," he proclaimed. "Every moment is a struggle. Now we must take action. We must discover how strong the savages are, find their encampments and parley with them. If necessary, we must fight them."

"Above all," interjected Brewster with his habitual sound sense, "we need to know if they are friend or foe."

CHAPTER NINE

CLOUDS

THE MEN STRAPPED ON THEIR ARMOUR, PRIMED their muskets and plunged into the forest to flush out the natives. Day after day they scoured the land, but the savages were too clever. They would light a fire at one end of the forest but when our men dashed through the trees to follow the plume of smoke, they found only embers. Immediately a spiral of smoke would rise from the other direction. Cries from the north of the bay sent them racing that way, only for taunting shouts to echo from the south.

"They are mocking us." Standish was beside himself with frustration. "Damn them."

"Maybe the Indians are playing these games to weigh up our strength." Will was polishing his musket. "They might be more frightened of us than we are of them."

"I think not," retorted Standish. "They are biding their time."

That time came a few days later.

A shout echoed from Burial Hill. "Over there. At the forest edge."

Two savages had materialised out of the shadow of the trees. What a moment, one I remembered to the end of my days. We had heard so much about them, how they ate raw flesh and killed for sport, and now they stood as bold as you like before us. They were tall and muscular, so athletic compared with our sickly men, but what I had not been prepared for was their strange dark skin. So black, so foreign.

They stood on the knoll and stared down at us. They gestured for us to go near.

Desire and Priscilla – all the girls – squealed in terror, though I did wonder if there was a hint of embarrassment behind their squawks, perhaps even a shameful thrill, at the sight of men who were wearing the briefest of deerskin cloths around their midriffs. It was not often, if at all, that we had seen a man naked – not even our own husbands.

The Indians had the skin of a wild creature draped around their shoulders, a feather stood out from hair which hung down to their shoulders and their faces were decorated with a thick indigo stripe. Knives swung from string around their necks.

We watched each other, we waited. Not a twitch of a muscle or a change of expression on either side.

"Prime the muskets," ordered Standish. He gestured to Stephen Hopkins to join him, and the two men took ten steps forward before standing defiantly eye to eye with the savages. Slowly, deliberately, he placed his weapon on the ground.

The two men stood to attention for two, maybe three, minutes. Standish took half a step forward, but Hopkins tugged him back. Standish carefully retrieved his weapon and the two men turned their backs on the Indians and steadily returned to the settlement. I held my breath at such a display of bravado. Would savages erupt from the shadows of the forest and attack the retreating men? We waited for blood-curdling cries and the swish of an arrow, but nothing. The Indians had disappeared like phantoms, barely disturbing the leaves as they glided back into the forest.

Standish sat down heavily on a log, beads of sweat on his forehead mingling with the drizzling rain. "I don't understand their game, but we need to frighten them so much that they come to us begging for mercy. Tomorrow we take a cannon from the ship and set it on the hill. One blast from that will show them who rules here."

What a to-do. Winching the weapon onto the deck, hauling it onto shore and lugging it along the beach and up to its vantage point took the men a day of aching muscle. We celebrated at the top, deed done, by tucking into a very fat goose that Will had shot.

Needless to say, Bradford had a message from the scriptures to explain this welcome treat.

"This is manna from heaven," he declared. "Remember how the Israelites travelled in the desert for forty years following the Exodus from Egypt, living only on this food. Remember too that they conquered Canaan and set up their homes there. We are stepping in their footsteps."

"But a goose tastes better than the bread of heaven," joked Will, throwing a well-chewed bone onto the fire.

Will was exhausted. "My arms are aching. And my legs. Bit of a headache too. I'll have a lie down."

Dear Lord, not him. Not my Will. My prayers were answered. Next morning he pronounced himself 'fit as a fiddle' and set off with his axe to clear another swathe of forest.

I was collecting driftwood with Resolved, who had been helping by taking each stick of wood off the stack and starting his own little pile, when Alden shouted across the fields.

"It's Will. Come quick."

He was slumped at the foot of a sassafras tree. Ulcers, those familiar heralds of doom, had already burst out; his skin was yellow. The gasping, the dribbling. My bold young lover was falling apart before my eyes.

"Food, I can see food." He was hallucinating. In the bright light of the winter sun I saw for the first time how he had lost as much weight as a man can lose and still be alive. Except he was not going to live. His eyes were set deep in a face that was once so bold, but now disfigured by ulcers and as old and wizened as a death mask.

"A haunch of venison, pigeon. I can see them. Fruit tart and Madeira."

He reached out, not for me or the children but for the food he imagined was in front of him. Then he was no more.

Next morning, we congregated on Burial Hill. I had stood there so often consoling widows, mothers and despairing husbands; now it was my turn to listen to the grate of the shovel as it dug into the stony ground, looking on as the corn was sown on the disturbed earth. A futile gesture. Resolved with puzzled tears and snot running down his face faster than I could clean it, Peregrine wriggling and crying. And me? How long would it be before I accepted that the man whose existence had been part of my own had departed forever?

"It's odd," I mused as the women comforted me. "People die every day and the world goes on like nothing happened. But when it's a person you love, you think everyone should stop and take notice. That they ought to cry and light candles and tell you that you're not alone."

"You aren't." Mary put an arm around me. "We are all here."

It was a small but precious comfort that I could trust them with my despair but that night, my first night as a widow, I could not imagine how I would ever climb out of the void.

My heart was ready to break – no, my heart had broken – but I had no choice, I had to live as normally as I could, despite normal being a desolate place where evil held sway. Yes, evil – surely a caring god would not have allowed this pain?

On the day Will was buried, three other graves had been dug and welcomed their victims. It was selfish of me, I know, but I had no sadness left to share with the families left behind.

Still the death toll rose. Seventeen were struck down in February but I could muster only a passing regret for their going. I should have cared more for the thirteen who choked their last in March, but the night of my soul was too black.

I did shed a tear when Elizabeth Winslow died, sweet-natured Elizabeth, always preferring to laugh than lament our plight. It was toward the end of March; the weather was warmer and we thought – we hoped, we prayed – the worst was behind us. But no. God took her vibrant spirit from us.

By then half of us had died. Forty-eight of the optimistic voyagers who had gathered on the Plymouth quayside lay on Burial Hill. Almost half of the crew had joined them. Many of them had been obnoxious, hateful to us, but they left behind wives and children who would mourn their deaths.

As for me – for some reason I had been spared. Why? I could not make sense of anything. When I was a girl agonising over an impossible problem, I would lie outside and stare at the stars until I felt at peace and the answer came to me.

I did it again that night but all I saw were clouds.

The next morning, Resolved was by my side begging for food and Peregrine was still wailing. There was no time to indulge in grief. It was my duty to buckle down and survive this cursed wilderness.

BOOK IV

1620–1622

THE VOICE OF SQUANTO, INDIAN GUIDE

RIPE-WITTED AND JUST

... but Squanto stayed with them and was their interpreter and became a special instrument sent of God for their good, beyond their expectation.

William Bradford, *Of Plymouth Plantation.*

BOOK IV

1620-1622

THE VOICE OF SQUANTO INDIAN GUIDE

SCATTERED AND LOST

CHAPTER ONE

FRIEND OR FOE?

W E WATCH. WE WAIT. WE SEE THE SHIP when it is many leagues out, its sails flitting in and out of view like a flock of gulls that have been carried far from land by the wind.

We follow it from the heights as it struggles through the shoals of Monomoy. Not many survive those waters and the skipper must know he is in mortal danger because the vessel swings back and heads to the north. It sails along the Back Side, rounds the curve of the cape and drops anchor in the bay. Night falls. Candlelight flickers though the cabin windows and shimmers across the waves.

In the morning I creep close enough to decipher the name on the poop, salt-stained and peeling though it is. *Mayflower*. Rotherhithe. I know Rotherhithe. Filthy place. But *Mayflower*? Didn't my English hosts buy their wine from a skipper who owned a ship of that name? My memory must be playing tricks.

The passengers are on the deck. A low babble of voices as they stare and point at the great bay with its long sandy shore lined by dark forest; the emptiness, for that is what it seems to them. They will be happy that their ordeal is over – because an ordeal is what it has been, I know, I have made that journey. They will be frightened. They gather in a circle while one of their number reads from a book. Praying.

Why do they make landfall here at Meeshawn? Cape Cod, the white men call it. They should know this is no place for a ship that size; the sea is knee-deep for half a league from the shore. Desperation, perhaps. Too weak to go further.

"Look," exclaims one of the braves. "Women and children."

I squint against the falling snow. I have sailed on the ships of white men and seen many hove to on our shores, but they never carry women unless they are a low sort forced to pleasure the sailors.

But here, by the great god Kiehtan, children as young as five. Mothers, fathers, not just men eager to fight. What does it mean? We hunker down in the woods on the shore's edge, wrapping our deerskins around our shoulders against the chill. We are ghosts, invisible in the shadows. Still as stones.

After two days, men are lowered down the side of the ship by rope and wade to shore, joshing and splashing each other. A skiff carries the children. Some women are up to their necks in water. They must be mad. The little ones have runny noses and vomit on their jerkins, their mothers are worn down with the burden of keeping them alive. Themselves too.

A brave nudges me. "Those two, they are with child. Can that be?"

Surely not. But yes, I believe they are.

The men shiver in the sleet as they kit themselves out in armour and make sure their gunpowder is dry. They might tell themselves they look bold and ready for action, but they are round-shouldered and weak-kneed with exhaustion. Easy prey.

I count about sixteen of them as they stand on the dunes and murmur incantations. Giving thanks to their god. Begging for his support. They find out soon enough how much help they need and how little they have to be thankful for.

They set off along the shore and pass close to where we hide. *Chobocco?* Yes, English.

We track them. We dart like birds, we slither around rocks like snakes, we stand still as trees when they come too close. I can almost touch the one who seems to be in command. A short man, hair as red as a Scarlet Tanager. Always bawling, "Heads up, stay alert, weapons ready, muskets dry."

I feel sorry for them, poor devils, as they trudge along, heads down against the sleet, struggling through the shifting sand and muddy water of the estuaries. They slip, they slide, water comes over their clumsy leather boots. Many are wracked by a cough and some spit blood. They won't have eaten properly for months. They have dogs with them. They might have to eat them.

They find a spring and drink from it as if they never taste water before and clap each other on the back like drinkers in a tavern when they take too much beer. One prises a mussel from a rock. He gulps it back. The others do the same. Within seconds they are puking and pulling down their breeches to rid themselves of the poison.

"*Matchanni.*" We laugh. "Very sick."

That they are.

We follow them into the woods. They beat a way through the scrub, get lost and retrace their steps, take another turning which ends in a dead end. If only they stop and use their eyes they would see the paths we have used for many lifetimes through the sassafras trees and the pines. But how could they know the ways of the Wampanoag? We understand the language of the land.

They startle a deer and that has them reaching for their muskets, but they are too slow. We can kill the beast and eat it in the time they take to pour the gunpowder down the barrel.

One of the chief's men slips alongside. He has run all the way from Pamet and he is panting.

"Tisquantum, what think you? *Netop? Matwaûog?* Friend or enemy warrior? Do they seek to destroy us and carry us away into slavery?"

"Too soon to tell," I say. These are not like the white men who come here before. Not like the villains who pretend to truck with us only to sell us into slavery. Not like the devil who seizes me.

"We should test their mettle," I say. "Let's show ourselves where the pines meet the dunes, on the ridge over there."

Six of us step out of the shelter of the trees. The English do not see us until the dogs bark and one looks up, wipes the sweat from his eyes.

He yells, "There, savages."

They duck for cover behind the dunes and charge their muskets, they run toward us, boots flapping, helmets falling into their eyes. Too clumsy, too slow. Their armour might protect them against our arrows and knives, but they will find it hard to get close enough to hit us with their bullets.

"*Moos.* Go." We lead them on, through woods, up hill, down. Darting in and out of shadows. We run three leagues or more. Dusk falls and they stop their pursuit, exhausted, coughing as if to throw up their very innards. They light a fire and set three guards. We are a few yards away.

We watch. We wait. We keep them awake with howls, shrieks and roars. They are scared and huddle together, guns ready.

They do not give up. Next day, they are greatly excited when they find corn buried by careful tribesmen the year before. They dig up mats lying under the sand that cover a mortar and an earthenware pot. They hold them up as if they have never seen such things before. They root around an abandoned wetu and are baffled by a kettle.

After much talk, they fill it with corn.

They are excited by a hoard of arrows. But they should not touch. We bury our dead with our possessions. The arrows will be needed in the afterlife.

"Let me make a little surprise for them," whispers one of the younger blades. He glides away and ties down a branch from a juniper into a bow. We scatter acorns beneath to trap rabbit and deer, but today we trap an Englishman.

They find it. They scratch their heads, they pace around.

"Beware," warns Red Hair. "It might be a trick."

A tall thin man who has fallen behind does not hear the warning and makes haste to catch up. He steps on the branch. It tightens around his ankle and, *whoosh*, he is whipped up in the air. He is upside down, yelping and twisting to get free. We almost give our hiding place away with our guffaws but the English make more noise, whooping with merriment. He is cut down, landing head first in bear shit. He does not enjoy being mocked.

It is a warning, they must understand that. We are in charge here. Their fate is in our hands.

A messenger summons us to the sachem Aspinet, chief of the Nauset tribe that rules the Cape. He is hunkered in his wigwam, surrounded by the symbols that connect us to the other world – a dead crow, a rattlesnake in a cage, a hawk. All is ready, should the gods choose to instruct us.

"Should we ambush these intruders?" he asks. "I have a hundred warriors ready."

"Not yet," say I.

He is suspicious. He knows that a sachem more powerful than he – Massasoit, chief of the Wampanoag – hates me. He rules the land from Pokanoket in the south to the border with the Nauset in the east, and last year he imprisons me for many months. Why should sachem Aspinet trust me, a nobody?

"You must hear my story," I tell him.

CHAPTER TWO

BETRAYED AND SAVED

MANY YEARS AGO, I MEET ENGLISH LIKE THESE. They are friendly. They take me to their country many, many, miles away. No eagle can fly that distance. A strange land of mighty stone buildings and more people than you can believe. But they are good to me. Six years ago, I return to my ancestral home in Patuxet on the other side of the bay. They need my help around the bays and rivers. I speak to the Indians for them.

In Patuxet – the English call it Plymouth – I meet an explorer called Captain John Smith, who comes with a fleet of ships to map our country and its coast.

He is a founder of another settlement many leagues to the south, which the English call Jamestown after their own grand sachem King James.

When Smith leaves, he hands over command to a ruffian called Thomas Hunt. His job is to trade with us Wampanoags.

He claims he has gold and trinkets to exchange for our beaver and he invites twenty-four of us on his ship for a mug of beer to toast the deal. The second we step on board, his men seize us, we are chained and thrown in the hold.

In the blink of a snake's eye I am torn from my homeland and my family.

A growl of anger from the assembly. I have their ears.

For two months we are kept below deck, allowed out only once a day. I do not recount the storms, the lack of food, the filth of the hold. The dishonour. That is for another time. But I hate this Englishman.

We sail to a city called Malaga in Spain, where Hunt sells us to rich folk for eight rials – little more than the price of a batch of beaver. We are treated like slaves, forced to live in cells in this hot, dirty city. One day, a holy man, a friar he calls himself, persuades our owners to free us and teaches us in the way of his god. In many ways he is like our own Kiehtan.

I escape and persuade a ship's skipper to let me work my passage to England. I hope I can find Captain Smith; maybe he can get me home. Malaga is a big city, but London – so many people, so much noise. Their homes are made of brick and timber and they have mighty halls of prayer. It is impossible to walk down a street without being knocked over by a horse and cart.

I am overwhelmed by the smoke and cloud that covers the sky. I hate the dirt. They eat disgusting food. Stews of fatty meat and boiled vegetables that make me fart like an autumn gale.

But I am lucky. I am found begging on a quayside and am given to live with a gentleman called John Slaney. He plans to build English homes in the land of the Mi'kmaq. Being English, he changes the name to Newfoundland. They change my name too. Tisquantum is too hard for them; they call me Squanto.

There is a low hoot of ridicule at their stupidity.

I meet again Captain Smith, who is angered by Hunt's cruelty. "Most dishonest and inhumane," he says of him. I meet another grand gentleman called Sir Ferdinando Gorges, an explorer who also wants to trade in these parts.

I learn their language so well that the gentleman asks me to be his interpreter and guide.

I tell you this to show that, like us, they have good men and bad. Most want nothing more than to be friends, to be peaceful. Isn't that what we want too?

"They will seize our lands," protests Aspinet. "Make us slaves like you. Kill us."

I reply, "No. They want to trade for our furs. Every man in London wears a beaver hat. Every woman too."

They laugh at that.

They will deal in guns and beautiful trinkets, spices and cloth. We have seen the power of their muskets; imagine how we can use them against our enemies. And they have drink, powerful drink.

They are scornful. What could be better than the juice of cranberries? But the young ones murmur in delight. Some have tried the strong water of the foreigners. It is to their taste.

I continue. When they realise I am from Patuxet and know this beautiful land of Nauset, they ask me to sail south with them to help them learn our ways.

Imagine my pain when I reach these shores to discover that the plague has killed nearly every single person; my wife, my brothers, my sisters, my parents, all gone. I am alone. What is a happy community only six years before is a wasteland, our wetus have rotted and fallen down, our fields are ragged with neglect. But worst, most terribly, the bones of the dead are left in the earth where they fall.

The sachem prods the fire, sending sparks flying like a thousand glowworms.

"You and Massasoit, you are enemies," he grunts.

A misunderstanding, I assure him. The good chief thinks these English are a danger and he ambushes them. I argue for their leader's release – he means no harm and is good to me – but Massasoit thinks I am a traitor because the Englishman escapes. It is not my fault. The chief understands that and now we are allies. We are of one accord.

I smile to myself. Allies indeed. If Massasoit and I have common cause, it is only because I am useful to him. He does not trust me, I have no respect for him but he needs me because I speak the language of these incomers so well.

To the sachem I say, "The white folk are different from us. We want to live quietly, follow the ebb and flow of the seasons, knowing when the herring arrive or the mallard fly, but they come all this way to make money. How will they do that without us? Can they fish, cut up grampus for its flesh? Can they trap and skin a beaver? They cannot. Will they grow corn without our skills? They will not. But with me, with us, they can survive, and when they do, we will grow rich and fat from selling our furs."

Dawn is breaking. At length, the sachem speaks.

"I agree with Tisquantum. We bide our time."

The crow on his shoulder cackles and flaps tempestuously into the dark night.

"But," the sachem holds me with his black eyes, "we must be wary. We cannot trust them. We must follow them day and night and be ready to strike if we have to."

A messenger races in to say the English are on the move. We follow.

They dig up three or four bushels of corn buried and stored in a basket and exclaim with pleasure over a wooden board, carved and painted to look as though it has a crown like the English King wears. They take baskets made of shells, they uncover bowls, trays, dishes and trinkets. In short, they take all the prettiest things. They start back when they dig up the bones and skull of a man that still has his fair hair and flesh hanging to his muddy bones. He is covered in a red powder, which mystifies them.

"It is a French captain," explains the sachem. "He came here three years ago but we burned his ship and killed the crew. We kept some as slaves," he adds with pride.

The English are moved to pity when they find the body of a child in the same grave. Its legs are bound with strings and bracelets of fine white beads. One of the men holds up a little bow. They take away the trinkets and cover up the bodies.

"They should leave well alone." Aspinet is angry. "Kiehtan insists the souls of the dead pass back and forth between their world and that of the living. No one can interfere."

I too am offended at the way they ransack our sepulchres. My fingers twitch on my bowstring. My name means 'divine rage' in Wampanoag, but I must stay cool.

"Now is a time to tread softly," I say.

A band of hotheads ignore me. I am woken at dawn by our war cry – woach woach ha ha hach woach – and the panic-stricken cries of the English as arrows rain down on them. They recover, load their muskets and fire back. A scream. One of our men is hit.

"Why strike?" I demand when we gather around the wounded man as he is treated with a poultice of raw cranberries. "Their weapons are more powerful than our arrows." We agree. "Watch and wait."

"They robbed the graves of my ancestors." He is defiant. "They take our corn and beans. Our food. If the chief will not act, I must."

"Be patient," I say. "This is not the time to avenge your hurt."

We follow them as they sail along the coast in their shallop, stopping here and there to see if they find a place to settle, whether it has a clear spring for water, fertile earth, cover from sun or snow. Nowhere is good enough.

Fifteen leagues they travel. The rain turns to snow. The wind blows harder and the sea roughs up. The men in the shallop are struggling. The rudder is broken and they are forced to steer with their oars. As the wind turns to gale, the mast breaks in three places. How they survive I do not know, but somehow they miss the rocks and land on the island by Saquish Head, a league or two across the bay from the mainland and my home of Patuxet.

When I was a boy, we would sail to the island and fish for cod and turbot.

In the calm of the morning, they row to the mainland and look for signs of life. We creep close. I can tell they like what they see – the woods of oak and pine, the spring that tumbles down the hill – but one picks up some bones, bones that were once someone I knew. Another throws a skull as if it is a ball. It is heartbreaking to see these strangers walking on the land of my ancestors.

Won't they wonder at the sad relics of the unburied dead? What do they make of the abandoned homes? They must see that these acres are haunted. Won't they be too scared to settle here?

This is not the place for them. I am tempted to walk into their midst and tell them: Englishmen, look elsewhere. The bay is too shallow, the land is poor, you will never be able to settle here. Keep moving. Head north.

Chapter Three

Cat and Mouse

THEY PACE AROUND, THEY MEASURE OUT PLOTS of land. I explain to chief Aspinet how much the English like order. Each family keeps to its own space. Not like us who move with the seasons, pitching our wigwams inland when the weather is warm, and near the coast and rivers in the winters for planting and fishing.

A messenger emerges silently from the scrub. A chief from the north is travelling through these parts. His name is Samoset. We meet in his encampment by the lake. Massasoit is there. He is the more powerful of the chiefs. He glowers at me.

"I have sixty brave men with me," Samoset declares.

"I can call on a hundred," growls Massasoit. "We are ready to fight if we must."

I see my opportunity. Massasoit may well boast of his power, but I know his people have been stricken by plague and are weak. I know too that he has enemies. A tribe from the south, the Narragansetts, are dangerous and greedy for Wampanoag land.

Massasoit needs an ally. He has not travelled twelve leagues merely to glower at me – no, he wants to make a pact with the English and he knows I am the only man who can make that happen.

He puts on a show of boldness. "We are much incensed and provoked against the English. That's why we kill them last year. You of all people know that." Again he scowls at me.

"You should stay your hand. You are mighty," I flatter, "but you are not strong enough. Although there are few of them, I have seen the power of the white man. They have guns that blow their enemies apart. But they are not strong now. They are on their knees. Many are already dying and more will follow. They will not survive the winter. That will be the time to strike. Come with me and watch."

We hide in a copse. It is as I say; the intruders stagger as they chop down trees; they are doubled up with coughing, they have to stop and rest every other minute. As we watch one falls face down in the ice and mud. He is dead. The English swiftly wrap up the body in a sheet and carry it up the hill.

A grave is dug, incantations offered and the grave filled in. It is all done in haste, eyes darting anxiously in case of an attack. I can see the mix of fear and grief on their faces.

"There will soon be so few left I will be able to defeat them single-handed," blusters Massasoit.

"Exactly," I say. I tell him the hand of death stalks them from the very first days of their landing when first a man then a child are buried in the dunes.

A woman falls overboard. "No one sees," reports our lookout. "The moon lights her up. Maybe she slips, it is hard to tell. Her body floats to the surface like a white flower and her hair spreads out like egret feathers, but we can do nothing. She is taken away by the tide."

The sea will rise in the spring and wash the sand away. The bodies will be ravaged by wolves.

How they suffer. I count more than twenty who die in the first weeks. On one day three of them are laid out. A mother clutches her baby and howls to the skies as the ravaged body of her man is taken away.

In time they become familiar to me. They are like players in a theatre Slaney took me to in London, where the dramas of life are played out. But here, the stage curtains are the trees.

There is an older man who leads their prayers and the thin man who we catch in the deer trap. He is still limping. Master Red Hair orders the men around, marches them up and down the hill, loading and unloading muskets.

One morning though, he too becomes one of the pitiful figures in my play. He stands beside a body. A lock of hair escapes from the shroud. It must be his wife. He is ramrod straight, head held high, but as she is dropped into the earth his shoulders slump and he holds his head in his hands. His tears flow unchecked.

Next day he is on his feet, marshalling the men as if nothing has changed, laying out the weapons, shouting instructions. Bristling.

"*Mawnaucoi*," murmurs Samoset admiringly. Strong. Very strong.

Something else too. I am sure I recognise one of them – a tall, sharp-featured man who often brings the men together to decide their tasks for the day. Yes, he visits Slaney with another gentleman, a preachy type. Slaney and his companions mock them. Pamphleteers and pests, they call them.

I say we must toy with them. Summon up the terror of

Kiehtan while they are weak. Let us provoke them by lighting fires. In this weather, the smoke will billow up and they will think they are surrounded, in mortal danger.

Samoset agrees. Massasoit grunts in reluctant agreement. Reluctant because it is my idea.

It has an immediate effect. Red Hair and his men come crashing through the forest in search of us, like bears confused by an early spring. They find the fires but they find no trace of us. Of course they do not, but they must know we are watching their every move. That frightens them.

To cheer themselves, they shoot an eagle and cook it over a fire. Too fierce a taste for me, like eating string dipped in urine, but the meal restores their spirits. I hear them laughing as they eat.

We watch them fish but they do not have the right-sized hooks. One of the sailors finds a herring alive on the shore.

They won't survive long on one fish, I joke.

I have to admire their steadfastness. I count six, maybe seven, men who are strong enough to do the work. Children help make the mud walls. Within a few weeks, they build several shelters. Tidy, in rows, like their London streets. They defy the frost and sleet to build a hall of timber, full twenty feet square. After three months the work is completed. Yes, I admire them. They will make good allies.

But not yet. "We must play cat and mouse," I tell Samoset. "Order two men to stand on the rise over there and wave at them to come to us."

They step out of the shelter of the forest. The English see them. They load their muskets but they hold their fire. They do not frighten me. They are not soldiers. They are merely young men more at home cobbling shoes or writing the pamphlets about their god that Slaney so mocked. No match for our warriors.

Red Hair and another walk steadily toward us. He keeps his eyes on our men, places his gun deliberately on the ground.

"A trap?" Samoset asks me.

We have men behind us ready to shoot their arrows. We can wipe them out.

"Stay still," I say. "It will bewilder them."

We stand in silence, both sides holding each other's gaze. "Now. Go back. Into the trees. Don't breathe a word or make a move that might incite them."

They fade into the shadows. Red Hair looks to come after us but the other man pulls him back. Another step and we would have cut them down.

Strange. Two men and their dogs leave the camp, bold as you like. Are they spies or fools? They chance on a deer, which the dogs chase, but it runs away before they unhitch their muskets. They are lost within minutes. They are fools. They wander around and, come night, freezing now, they huddle in the lee of a bank. They do not have any warm clothes and we hear their teeth chattering. They make the dogs come close to warm them. The only weapon they have is a sickle.

"We frighten them." Samoset lets out a wild shriek. "*Woach, woach.*" They jump out of their skins. Another cry from a knoll nearby, more shouts and shrieks from there, from here, from everywhere.

Terrified, they clamber up a tree, but they cannot balance on a branch – they're not squirrels – and scramble back down.

They stay there until dawn, hugging themselves, jumping up and down for warmth, clapping their frostbitten hands and groaning. At dawn they tramp past lakes and rivers, through woods and across a plain, all familiar to us but a wilderness of the unknown to them. At last they come to a hill where they see the bay and the smoke rising from the settlement.

They are greeted with jeers from their comrades. One of them has to cut off his shoes because his feet have swollen so much with frost's bite but no one helps.

We are almost sad to have our entertainment end, but it tells me how little they understand the perils they face. How easy it is for us to have our way. My way.

CHAPTER FOUR

HELLO ENGLISH

MASSASOIT SUMMONS ME TO A COUNCIL meeting.

"We must divine our purpose," he asserts as we gather in the ceremonial hall of Sowams, his village, deep in the swamp and safe from prying eyes.

He calls on the shaman and one of the clan mothers to deliberate. We have to humour these old women. They are humble but they have great power and influence.

"What do we do about these English?" he asks.

"Kill them," chorus the young bloods.

"Talk to them," say I.

For three days the shaman seeks guidance from Kiehtan. Only he can see him.

Our wise men undergo a ferocious trial to gain their wisdom. They must drink a bitter mix of herbs until they are sick into a platter. They drink their discharge again and again until it seems like blood. Foam comes from their mouth, their eyes roll. They are on the threshold of wisdom.

They are hardly able to stay upright but leave the wigwam to stand in the chill. Tribesmen beat their shins with sticks and they are chased through bushes and brambles. They return bleeding but strong enough to confront Chipi, the devil himself. Now they have earned the right to make decisions about war or peace.

We are silent as the shaman takes a draught of white hellebore, his crow perched on his shoulder. Smoke curls through the bark roof. He is in a trance. "I see great birds and wild wolves with teeth dripping blood. I have message from the bird and from the rattlesnake. I talk to Kiehtan in his home far westward in the heavens, the place where good men go when they die."

His eyes start from his head. "These men desecrate our land. You must slay them. Let us conjure up the shades of Chipi, send crows flying with poisoned beaks and unleash serpents into the swamps to wreak havoc and disaster."

The men chant, "*Cram, cram, cram*. Kill, kill, kill."

Massasoit looks to me.

I shake my head. "We kill some but they kill us too. Their muskets fire further than an arrow, even if it were carried by a hawk.

"We have many noble fighters still alive after the great famine." Samoset is eager for battle.

I step into the light of the fire.

I say, "It is true, the great Samoset has many brave warriors, but the danger comes not just from guns. These English have the power to spread the plague, which killed my people in Patuxet. As I say before, wait until most of them are dead. The few left will not have the strength to resist us."

Massasoit stays his tongue.

"Then we strike," I say. "But hear me. I do not believe these English want war. These are not like the fortune hunters who come to swap a few trinkets for beaver. No, I believe they have come to make a home here. Why else are there women and children? Are they going to set on us with their ladles and hoops? No. This is different. This is an opportunity for us. Imagine the riches."

Massasoit's eyes flicker.

I say, "If we become their allies, we become stronger than the Narragansetts. We beat them in battle."

Massasoit stamps his spear on the mud floor.

"We shall talk to them," he decrees. "We will be friends."

I have had my way.

"I shall go," announces Samoset. "My English is good."

His English is not as good as mine, not at all; he has picked up only a few words from traders, but I let him have his way. They will have use of me soon enough.

The chief strikes a fine figure. He wears only a leather breech cloth about his waist. His hair is blackened and hangs in a long tail behind. He carries a bow and two arrows.

We watch as he and his men walk tall and straight out of the cover of the forest, down the hill and into the encampment.

The English gape at him. One curses in amazement. The children are open-mouthed, their mothers too, hands in front of their mouths in shock at such a sight. The maids giggle. After all, the English keep their bodies covered in heavy fustian and thick linen. They never see naked men.

Red Hair reaches for a musket but the old man, the one who leads their prayers, gestures to him to be still.

Samoset halts, waits for quiet.

"Hello, English."

A hum of disbelief. Then the tall one, the one I fancy I remember from my years in London, steps forward and shakes him by the hand.

"Sit." He points to a chair that is brought forward and set like a throne in the centre of the gathering. Red Hair puts a coat around the chief's shoulders. A woman offers him a mug, which he drinks as if it was water, and he gasps with the shock of it. Brandy.

They feed him biscuit with butter and cheese and a slice of mallard. Samoset is enjoying himself. He babbles away, filling in the gaps of understanding with much hand waving. I am nervous. What if he is drunk and insults them? Or they upset him? It is time he comes back but he is in no hurry to leave.

He is welcomed into a home, where he stays the night. Is it a plot? Will they kill him? We stay in the dark. Ready.

In the morning he walks back to where we wait.

"As you told us, Tisquantum, they are friendly." He slurs. "They have a drink called brandy." And he sniggers.

I know all about this drink from the drunken sots who spit at me when I am a beggar in London.

He is clutching a knife, a bracelet and a ring. "Look what they give me." He burps quietly. "A hat, a pair of stockings and shoes, a shirt, and, here – look, a piece of cloth to tie about my waist.

"They want to truck. We shall go back with beaver skins."

Massasoit orders, "Tisquantum. You should go next time. You speak English language better."

I stride to the edge of the camp. The men cluster around. I wait. I enjoy being centre of attention.

"Good morning, Englishmen. Welcome to Patuxet."

If they are startled by another savage speaking their language, they hide it. That is their way. Tight of lip, polite. They offer me some biscuits, which are dry and full of weevils.

I tell them I live in London for many years and know John Slaney and Sir Ferdinand Gorges. For me – a savage, as they call us – to know such people impresses them. It makes matters warm between us.

I explain that it is another chief called Massasoit, not Samoset, who is the chief of the tribes in this country. He wants to parley with them about trade and friendship.

They nod, they are relieved. "We must know his mind."

One of their number says, "Take me to him. We have gifts for your leader."

His name is Edward Winslow. Ruddy of face, eager. I take him to where Massasoit is waiting outside his wetu. His braves lurk in the shadows, ready to strike.

Winslow puts down his musket in a gesture of peace. "Great chief, I come in friendship."

I say, "The white man has gifts. He wishes to parley."

Winslow presents the chief with two knives and a copper chain with a jewel. He offers him a bottle of brandy and biscuits. He is pleased.

"We must be friends," Winslow says. "Trade together. Become rich. Come with your men and talk. We can help each other."

He turns to me. "Squanto, explain trust to the great chief, how we must look after each other. We must not fight. This land is wide enough for all of us."

I like Winslow. Massasoit does too. He orders one of his wives to carve a venison steak for the Englishman and the men eat.

"Ask him for his sword and armour," the chief tells me.

Winslow refuses. "Not all men in this land are as noble as

you, great chief," he declares. "We have other, better, gifts for you."

Massasoit frowns. He finishes the bottle. He burps. "Better gifts," he repeats. "Good. Tell him I will come but he must stay here under guard. Just in case."

The chief comes to Patuxet with a great display of strength. He stands on the ridge overlooking the English encampment with sixty men in red and yellow paint, all carrying their bows.

I scorn the man, but he does carry himself like a true chief, unlike the English King who I see once in London as he passes in a carriage. A feeble figure. Massasoit has the trappings of power – a deerskin hanging from a brooch on one shoulder and a chain of white bones around his neck that carries his knife. He has broad black bands of paint stretching from forehead to chin.

He stands boldly in their midst.

Red Hair steps forward, puffs out his chest. He barely reaches the chief's shoulder.

"My name is Captain Standish," he booms. "Come."

We are marched with great ceremony between their guards and we enter a house, furnished with a green rug and cushions as if it was a withdrawing room like the rich have in England. The chief is impressed.

A blast of a trumpet and the beating of drums, and the tall, sharp-featured gentleman I notice before steps into the room. "My name is John Carver," he announces. "I am the Governor." To my astonishment, Massasoit, the great chief, gets to his feet and kisses his hand. Carver does the same. He is awkward. Lowering himself, perhaps.

"Welcome to New Plymouth." I am offended that the name of this place, my home, has been changed but I say nothing. He fills Massasoit's mug with strong water.

He proclaims, "We want to live side by side with you. We believe in friendship. We want to truck with you and your people."

I translate.

"We too desire a time of peace," the chief replies. "We live well until the plague takes our people away. Now we are weakened. We are threatened by a tribe of wrong-doers, the Narragansett, who covet our territory. Dangerous people. They would destroy you too."

Carver speaks up without hesitation. "We must make a treaty to look after both our interests."

He tops up the chief's drink and orders a deer to be roasted while they talk. I know this is the only food they have. They want to impress the chief.

They agree that the Wampanoag and the white men will live in friendship together and each protect the other.

"Here are our conditions." Carver leans forward to make sure there is no mistaking what he says. "First, if the peace is broken by an Indian, he will be sent here for punishment."

Massasoit agrees. "But if an Englishman does the same, he will be sent to our camp in Sowams."

They bump mugs in confirmation and each takes a mouthful.

"Second, when you Indians come to Plymouth you leave your weapons behind."

"You likewise," asserts the chief.

"Above all." Carver thumps the table, "if either side is unjustly attacked by another tribe or the French or Dutch, we will come to each other's aid."

"I agree," nods Massasoit. "Everyone under my rule will follow this."

He has not seen a pen before but he scratches a mark on

the parchment. Carver signs and grasps the chief by the arm in friendship. "Now we can make plans for us both to grow easy together and thrive."

We salute the contract with a beaker more of brandy. The moon comes up. It lights our faces. I see the English are relieved. Massasoit is pleased with himself. It is a better arrangement than I hope for.

CHAPTER FIVE

A MARRIAGE IS ARRANGED

I have to become a friend to the English.

The way to their hearts is through their stomachs. I learn that in London, where they never stop eating. Come with me, I say. I take them to a muddy creek where I tread out so many eels they cannot believe their eyes.

I will soon have them beholden to me.

I am woken one morning in April by cries of farewells. The *Mayflower* is leaving. I am glad to see it disappear into the horizon, for the crew are like all English sailors – hard as nails, greedy and dangerous. I know, I have suffered at their hands. The skipper is toughest of the lot.

That means fewer awkward folk to cope with. I reckon there are nineteen or twenty men, five or six women, several servants and about fifteen children, though some of those are babes in arms.

Only a handful are strong enough to take up weapons and actually fight. They can barely lift their feet, let alone their muskets, even if Captain Standish behaves as if he was leading a battalion of hardy warriors.

He is wary of me. He keeps his distance. So I make sure the old chap, William Brewster, is an ally. He is their father figure.

I remind him of Slaney, how we were in the same room. He looks me up and down and furrows his brow.

"Goodness me," he exclaims. "How extraordinary. So you were. You cut quite a figure."

He leads their religious ceremonies – dull affairs, with long prayers and longer speeches that go on until night falls come hail or sun. I see how much respect he is given. Everyone seeks his advice.

I must keep close to Master Carver because he is the chief. He recalls our meeting at Slaney's mansion, but he does not have the warmth of Brewster. He is disconcerted by me, as if the past should not be allowed to trespass in the present.

They come to me for help. Their corn does not grow. I teach them a trick we Wampanoags have known for generations.

I catch three herrings, to their great admiration, and show them how to build a small mound of earth, place the fish head to head in the soil and plant around them.

"Soon you celebrate first harvest," I tell them.

They do not believe how soon the green shoots appear.

"You are a special instrument sent from God," declares the thin man we catch in the trap. Master Bradford is his name.

I am flattered. They can see my worth to them. In April we have the first sun. Hotter than usual. Instead of shivering and wrapping up against the cold, now they shed their jerkins and throw off their hats. For the first time they smile and they sing. There has not been a death for two weeks; their dream of a flourishing plantation is coming true.

There is a cry from the fields. It is Master Carver. He is lying on his back, eyes staring, breathing heavily.

"Get him inside," I order. "The sun. It shocks his body."

For three days he lies in a coma. I do what I can with a herbal cure of sassafras and echinacea. I add lobelia. Bradford and Brewster fall to prayers, but it is no good. He is beyond saving.

This time they make no attempt to hide his going. I keep a respectful distance as they carry his body up the hill to the burial place. They stand by his graveside and fire a farewell salute. They weep but not for long. There is work to be done.

Bradford is made their new chief. I pay my respects. "A better leader it is impossible to imagine," I tell him. We laugh at him when he hangs upside down screeching for help but he is not a man to scoff at now. He is always very serious. I never see him smile.

He is as skinny as one of the hoes he tills the fields with, but he works like a man with twice his strength, sawing, chopping, hammering with the best of them. When he rests — not often — he reads and he talks and tells people what to believe. He is deep. He hurts himself working on one of their shelters and is taken away on a stretcher of timber, but I see him a few days later limping around with his saw. Determined.

I discover it is his wife who falls to her doom from the ship.

"It is hard when no body to grieve over," I say. "For us, when the soul leaves the body, it joins the spirit of relatives and friends in the world of the dead, which lies somewhere to the southwest. It can pass back and forth carrying messages between the world of the dead and that of the living."

He does not want to talk to me, a savage, about her. "She is gone." He shakes his head. "She lives in heaven and I must leave her there."

I am good friends with Edward Winslow. He is lively, clever. He too knows death. His wife dies two days after my first visit. He must be sad but he keeps his pain close to his heart. I notice him in conversation with the woman whose name is Susanna White. I see her before on her knees by the side of her dead husband. She is howling at the sky.

I am helping Edward dig a field ready for planting when he tells me, "I am to marry the widow White."

I am silent. It is sensible. There are so few women and they must breed if the settlement is to survive. But the heart, it thrives on love.

"We have a holy task to complete," he mutters but his eyes mist over. "It is our duty."

They are wed in May. The wind ruffles the waves in the bay, a buzzard soars, the sachim – little birds we revere for the way they fight off bigger birds like crows – chirrup in the dunes. It is a good omen.

The ceremony is short. Bradford reads a sermon and there is a toast of beer and slices of mallard. The new couple are like strangers. They stand apart. No smiles. Her eyes are like stone and I think he has tears in his.

I recall my marriage to a squaw from nearby Shawmee. We have a party with lutes, corn rattles and drums. How we dance. The crow hop, the shake dance and the ribbon dance. We frisk until dawn when it is time to do what all new couples do. For us, it is not a matter of duty.

CHAPTER SIX

GIVING THANKS

B RADFORD IS EMBARRASSED. "WE WELCOME your people coming to visit us. It is important that we get to know each other's ways but, let me be frank, we cannot cope with so many staying and eating our food. We have so little."

I see a chance to grow my influence. I suggest, "Let Master Edward and I visit the great chief. He explains the problem. As we travel, he sees our country and learns about our people. How we live."

"Take Stephen Hopkins with you," says Bradford. "Another witness will help our understanding of you savages."

The going is hard for them through the rocky countryside. Winslow admires the many small rivers, the wild woods of fir and towering chestnuts. Boys pester us for food. We are treated to shad and musty acorns by the good people of Namasket, lobsters in another village. We have a scare when two men hold us at arrow point while we are in the middle of a river. They think we come to plunder, but I shout, "Netop. Friend. We come in peace."

Winslow reaches into his knapsack and gives them bracelets of beads. They are all smiles. Friends indeed.

I stop to pray by one of the small markers of remembrance.

"What are they?" asks Winslow, always curious.

"When there has been a matter of moment, we dig a circle about two hands deep," I explain. "He who digs it has to recall what it was for and pass the memory on to his descendants."

"What sort of happening?"

"It might be a struggle, a birth, a marriage, an attack by wolves, anything that tells us of our lives before. I have a relative who was killed on this spot."

"I have much to learn," says Winslow. I respect him for that but Hopkins sneers, "Superstitious nonsense. What I expect from Indians."

I bite my tongue. I might need help one day even from this rude person but my patience is tested when we meet a group of women on a river bank.

"I want their furs," says Hopkins. "Tell them we'll buy them."

"They have nothing to wear," I say.

"Ask anyway," he insists. "They will not resist the offer of an Englishman." He holds out a handful of gems.

I translate and the words are scarce out of my mouth than they take off their clothes. They stand naked. I am shocked. Our women are usually so modest, their coats are long enough to hide their feet, but these covet the jewels that the white man is offering. What people do out of greed.

Hopkins sniggers.

"These beauties are worth more than a look, eh, Winslow." He makes a thrusting with his hips. "No need for beaver's tail here."

I ignore him. Winslow says, "Enough. We must behave with respect."

Hopkins will not stop. "Did you not hear about the beaver's tail? If our ladies knew what an aphrodisiac it is, they would want us to stop all other business and truck for that alone."

Winslow shakes his head. He is as disgusted as I am. Hopkins is still cackling when we reach the chief's camp. Children and women run to greet us and Winslow gives the chief a fine red horseman's coat. Susanna, the new Mistress Winslow, has added some artful lace that gives it a kingly grandness.

The chief is very pleased and poses with his men, such is his vanity.

"This is a sign of our boundless love and esteem," says his guest. "Squanto, explain that we are sorry but we cannot give his people the entertainment they deserve when they come to the Plantation. He must know that we do not have enough food for ourselves, let alone many other hungry mouths."

The chief is downhearted. He enjoys his visits to the Plantation. He likes the white man's brandy. But Winslow reaches into his satchel and brings out a glittering cluster of gewgaws. The chief is easily soothed. "Our men will no more pester you," he says, draping a shining strand around his neck.

He makes a long speech about the power he has over the tribes. Thirty of them pay him tributes, he claims, and he lists them all. The English yawn but I reckon, *every one of those tribes can be turned against this swollen-headed chief. By me.*

We are tired and hungry. We expect a welcoming feast – a roasted deer, corn, beans and squash – but there is nothing. Two days and nights we wait to be fed, instead, the mosquitoes feed on us. All Massasoit can muster is two striped bass which are shared between chiefs who have come to meet the English.

Winslow has had enough. "I must return to the settlement, if only to find something to eat."

I see an opportunity. "I go from here to all the villages owned by the great chief to tell what a fine gathering we have here. How you and the English come together to trade and live in peace."

The chief is suspicious – and rightly so. I talk to the sachems of the Mohegan and the Pequot, I meet the old women and the powwows. I talk to the medicine men. I tell them that I am the man who can do business with the English. I, not Massasoit.

Winslow cannot guess my scheme. He agrees. "Good idea, Squanto. You can tell them what they can earn in exchange for furs and corn."

He pours more beads and necklaces from a satchel. "Take these to them. We have plenty more."

The sight excites the chief. He helps himself to a gem of rich, ruby red.

"My thanks, Master Winsnow." Massasoit never speaks his name correctly. "In return, you will need help while Tisquantum is away, so I give you my most trusted brave. Take Hobbamock with you."

A stocky man steps forward and bows. I have met him before. I do not trust him; he does not trust me. He is Massasoit's man. A spy.

I say, "A wise idea, great chief." But I think, *I have to be careful. The English must never know I plan to turn the tribes against them. Massasoit would kill me if he had the slightest suspicion. But if I am cunning enough I will be the winner.*

Meanwhile I must convince the English that I am more than just a savage who can grow corn from the heads of herrings.

Luck is with me. A pesky boy called John Billington goes missing. I hear from my spies on the Cape that he has been handed over to the Nauset. This is dangerous. This is chief Aspinet's tribe. I have persuaded him to be friends with the intruders, but it is one of their men that the English wound when our hot heads attack and it is their corn they dig up and steal. Revenge is never far from his heart.

"I can help," I tell Bradford. "You will not rescue him without me."

As I warn, Aspinet is angry.

"Modoc." He comes right up to Bradford, his face an inch away. "You. Enemy."

I explain we come with gifts in exchange for the boy but an old woman, as wrinkled as a dried cranberry, grabs me by the arm.

"Tell them," she wails. "Tell them my sons were killed by these villains three years ago."

I share her grief but say, "These men are good. They are different."

I explain her bitterness to Bradford.

"We are sorry." He gives her a handful of glittering gewgaws and she is quietened. To the chief he says, "Take these knives and trinkets for the corn we take."

The chief is happy with the glittering pile. The boy is released and given a string of shells to wear around his neck. He has had an adventure. His father cuffs him around the head.

Bradford understands that only I can get them out of danger like this.

The settlers are happy. Not one has died for six months. Thanks to me the corn is rustling in the breeze. I teach them to cultivate beans and squash, they plant acres of barley and peas. I show them how to eat cranberries mashed with corn meal and bake them into bread.

It is the time of *paponakéeswush*, the season before the winter, so I tell them to prepare for the ducks and the geese to fly in. The English slaughter enough for one week's food.

Bradford says, "We should celebrate our good fortune. We must thank the Lord and rejoice together."

I tell him, "In our land every day is a time of thanksgiving. We give thanks to the dawn and the dusk, to the sun, to the moon, for the rain. We have many harvests – for wild berries, beans, corn. At this time of year, we celebrate the gathering in of cranberries."

"We shall do the same," he declares.

"Invite the great chief Massasoit and his people," I suggest.

It is a warm October day. The chief arrives with ninety braves and for three days sit down with the English to drink and eat together.

But first the Christians pray. They stand bareheaded in the weak autumn sun, heads bowed. Bradford speaks.

"We have been sustained by the spirit of God who heard our cries for help and saw us safe over the great ocean from the hand of the oppressor."

I see tears in the eyes of old man Brewster.

Bradford continues, "We have been delivered to this desert wilderness, hungry and thirsty, but we must thank the Lord for his loving kindness." *And thank me too*, I think.

Our women are busy cooking corn, beans and squash mixed with artichoke, pumpkin and zucchini. We call it the three sisters. The English roast deer and rabbit. Grouse and geese turn on spits. There are clams and eels; cranberries and plums; sweet, strong wine that Brewster has squeezed out of the grapes. Some of our men lose all restraint and dance, only to fall into a befuddled slumber.

The English make a stew of vegetables. "It reminds us of home," says Susanna, handing me a bowl. She balances the infant Peregrine on her knee.

"He is the first to be born here, Squanto." She is a strong, handsome woman with a bold chin. Not to my taste. "As old as Plymouth. He is the child that generations will remember, the one who proves we can make this wasteland a home."

It looks to me like she is with child again.

Her husband declares, "How lucky we are to be such friends. How trustworthy you and the Wampanoags are, Squanto, so quick of apprehension, ripe-witted and just."

"Thank you, sir," I say. "Together we make a success." I take too much of their strong water and am a little raddled – a word I learn in London from my trips to the drinking houses. "Yes," I say, "we prosper."

I speak too soon. The harvest is not so plentiful as they hope. They are soon short of corn and beans and have so little fruit there is not enough for a cranberry mash. The winter is on us. We are hungry.

CHAPTER SEVEN

SNAKE IN THE GRASS

"A SHIP. A SHIP IN THE BAY." THE ALARM IS sounded.

Friend or foe? Standish barks commands, the men load their muskets, the cannon is rolled out. The ship glides to a halt and we see the splash of the anchor. A flag flutters – two crosses, one red, one blue.

"English," declares Bradford.

"The *Fortune*." Standish squints through his telescope.

I count thirty passengers. Only one is a woman.

"Good," says Edward. "That more than doubles the number of workers here. Heaven knows we need them."

"Not enough women," grumbles John Howland. I like him. Young, vigorous. A man to trust.

"Next time," shrugs John Alden, the cooper, though he spends more time repairing roofs than making barrels. They both deserve a wife.

I tell the young men that our squaws make fine wives. They are eager to please, I tempt them, but they are horrified at the idea. I am offended. It tells me the white man looks down on us.

One of the passengers is greeted with warmth. He is Robert Cushman. I do remember him. He comes to Slaney's more than once with William Brewster. He is polite. He pretends to remember me.

He gives a sermon. I understand little. Something about love and the perils of the flesh. He upsets some, calls them drones – a word Winslow explains to me – but as he speaks, not all listen. Some mutter that he is brainless, others walk away. The new men from the ship play a game – lanterloo they call it – on the jetty.

I realise that the survivors of the first winter are not of one mind. I hear them argue amongst themselves about the way the corn should be planted, they dispute the rulings of the Governor. Some say the men from Leiden, like Brewster and Bradford, are arrogant and behave as if they are always right. Others hate the stern discipline that the settlement's leaders impose.

Take the Billington father. Always trouble. He berates Standish about the way he runs the militia.

"You don't know one end of a gun from another," he scoffs.

Standish is like a cauldron that boils over. He has the nuisance seized, his hands and feet tied together. The prisoner's wife, a fearful scold, curses Bradford and the anger simmers for many weeks until the rebel is released. He gathers the discontents around him to drink and gamble.

Two servants, duel over a mug of beer. They deserve their punishment: locked up in the meeting house.

That is nothing to the rumpus just after the winter solstice.

The new arrivals down tools for the day. They want to celebrate the birth of their god's son. Christmas Day, they call it.

"This cannot be," asserts Master Bradford. "Our faith does not recognise this day. It is a false artifice dreamt up by Papists and charlatans." I do not really understand what he is saying but I do know what he means when he hits the ground with his hoe angrily and declares, "We work like any other day, and when we finish we meet and pray."

"Your faith is not our faith." The men are defiant. "It is against our consciences not to celebrate the birth of our Lord."

Bradford glares. His authority is at stake.

"Very well," he spits. "But no gaming or revelling."

They disobey. They roast fish over a fire, drink beer, josh and lark about with a ball and a bat. Bradford seizes their toys and hurls them into the fire.

"I spare you working," his face is tight with anger, "but for you to be quiet and contemplative, not to play g—g—games. Is it fair that we wear our fingers to the bone while you turn the settlement into a rough house?"

Winslow is busy writing.

"What ho, Squanto." Shortening my name is his way of being friendly, I think. "Master Bradford and I are putting together some words to explain how we prosper here; how happily we live together and how easy it is to grow food. I am telling about our splendid thanksgiving celebration."

He reads: "'We had the happiness to be in one of the most pleasant, most healthful and most fruitful parts of the world. We have so much fish and fowl that fresh cod is but a coarse meat for us."

I am too polite to mock their fishing. Instead, I murmur, "But we starve. Half the people are in graves."

He grimaces. "I must explain to those in England who

belittle us because we are not sending home enough furs that there are too many people coming here without supplies and without the skills we need. You see these newcomers? Layabouts. We need to attract men who will roll up their sleeves and give their all to the Plantation. So, I have to make the place sound as close to an Eden as I can."

"Eden?"

"It is a story in our Bible. Where nature is in its untrammelled glory and the people free of sin."

"Ah. Kesuck, we call it. Heaven."

"And one we are creating here on Earth."

He is cheered when the *Fortune* leaves, loaded high with beaver skins, oak and sassafras, leaving behind pots, pans and trinkets to use for trade.

"That little lot is worth £500." He makes sure the sacks of sarsaparilla are carefully stowed. "I would get two shillings a pound in London for this. If only we had enough to fill the whole ship." He gives a sigh of satisfaction. "Still, this will stop the carping of the backers who claim we owe them money."

No sooner has the ship been lost over the horizon than a messenger comes from the Narragansetts. Their loathing of the Wampanoag is matched only by their hatred of the English.

He has a bundle of arrows wrapped in rattlesnake skin. The English are frightened.

"Does it mean war?" asks Bradford.

"Do not worry," I say. "This is a challenge. It is warning you to stay away. Keep the arrows but fill the snakeskin with bullets and gunpowder. Send it back. It will strike terror."

As I plan, the snake is passed from tribe to tribe, but it is returned untouched. As I say, they are frightened of the white man's magic, but the English are still concerned.

"We must bolster our defences," asserts Master Standish. "We must build a fort."

How they work, these English. Foundations three feet deep are dug, they chop down thousands of trees and lever the timbers into place with a great clamour of hammering. When night falls, they drop in utter weariness, desperate for the thin gruel the women prepare.

The wall is more than eight feet high and a league long.

"So strong," I say. "I cannot squeeze my hand through the cracks in the timbers." I do not warn that no wall is high enough to keep out an Indian.

Now I must stir the pot a little more. My scheme is to set all against the other; to incite violence against whom I will and make peace with whom I want. I have many wrongs against me. I deserve revenge for the suffering I endure from Massasoit and from the English who kidnap me.

First, I frighten the English.

I explain to Bradford and Winslow where danger lies. I tell about the Massachusetts who live in the wild lands of the north. They are weakened by plague but they are angry; "No friends of you," I say. When a fire breaks out in the palisade I hint – no more – that the Massachusetts creep in and light the spark.

I tell them that the Mohegans – the Wolf People, they call themselves – are also hostile to the English. They are not but it sows more doubt. Beware the Pequots to the south, I warn. They are many, they are strong, they will rise against you.

I stir the pot some more. News comes that Massasoit is seized by the Narragansetts, his men killed.

It is not true. The chief is unharmed. I know because it is my idea to spread this alarm. When they hear the chief is untouched, I warn the English that another sachem is trying to draw the hearts of the Wampanoag.

They are anxious, looking over their shoulders.

I frighten the tribes just as I scare the English. I tell them that the white men hide the plague in a barrel of gunpowder in their meeting house.

The sachems never lose their terror of the plague, how the rats spread the disease that turns the skin yellow, the pain and the cramping and the nose bleeds that tell us that there is no escape from death. I have them in the palm of my hands. I tell them, "It is I who offers better protection from the English than Massasoit, because I am closer to them. Pay me and I will make sure the English are your allies."

The English trust me; the tribes think I help them. A whisper here, a nod there. That's my game.

Chapter Eight

Spared

I hail Master Bradford as he comes in from the fields. "Fearful news; the Massachusetts plan a raid," I tell him. "Massasoit plots with them and the Narragansett to attack you."

"What should we do, Squanto? You know these people. You know their ways."

"Send Master Standish and his soldiers to crush them," I say. "I will be his guide."

But this is my game: I tell the Narragansett and other unruly chiefs that the settlement will be unprotected; only a few men, women and children to overcome. I tell Massasoit too.

If he does strike and is defeated, he will be hanged from the fort wall as the treaty rules. If he succeeds, I am the one who makes him victorious. Whatever happens, I am the winner.

No one will think to accuse me because I will be on the shallop, sailing with Standish and his men to do battle against the Massachusetts.

We are no further out in the bay than Gurnet's Head when the wind drops. We are becalmed. Standish curses. A cannon sounds from the fort. It is the English alarm. Standish swears again but orders the boat to be rowed back to the settlement. On the shore, a messenger is signalling wildly. Blood pours from his face. He is a relative of mine who knows my plans.

"I am struck by a Narragansett axe," he gasps. "They are coming this way. Massasoit too. They attack."

Now Massasoit's man Hobbamock shows his hand. He has so wormed his way into English favour that he and his wife are living with Captain Standish as his servants. Slaves more like.

The spy hisses, "Tisquantum is behind this. This man is his cousin." He points at the bloodstained courier. "He has secret meetings with our enemies and tries to turn one against the other and all against you."

"He is mad," I protest, "a treacherous toad."

Hobbamock cannot hide his loathing of me. "This traitor plans to replace Massasoit as chief. He hopes to make you fight your bravest ally and kindle a flame of hate that cannot be quenched. But the great chief will never strike against you. You can trust him. We Indians keep our word."

Bradford is distraught. He does not want to lose me. I am too valuable.

"The truth" he wails, "we must have the truth."

"These are lies, damn lies," I cry. "All I ask is for a life of quiet, to serve both you and the great chief."

Hobbamock is in a rage. He hurls a knife at me so close I can hear it whistle past my ear. It quivers in the door. "Shameless impostor. I will send my wife to the chief's camp. She will tell him what has occurred."

I stay calm. Or pretend to. This could mean the end for me. I am more frightened than the day I was kidnapped, more than the time the Spaniards threaten to cut off my hands. If I show the slightest fear it looks like guilt. My chest is tight, there is a pounding in my head and my bowels spasm.

I make a silent incantation to Kiehtan.

The chief comes. He carries a spear and a knife that would slice off a man's head with just the flick of his wrist.

Hobbamock's woman is with him. She smirks.

"This *wonksis*, this treacherous rat" – Massasoit points his spear at my neck – "has abused me. Do not forget, we agree that any man who betrays us has to die. It is in our treaty. I sign. You sign. I demand his head."

Bradford is dismayed. "Do not d—d—deprive me of our tongue," he begs. "He talks to the tribes for us, he teaches us to grow our crops."

"We have a pact," insists Massasoit. He sees Bradford's unease and lets out a halloo that echoes far into the forest. A band of braves stalk in. They have knives in their hands. They are to cut my head from my body.

Massasoit raises his spear, but Brewster speaks up. "We must not be rash. We must discuss this calmly."

I am locked in the meeting house. I hear raised voices, the booming of Standish, the high-pitched arguments of Bradford and the measured tone of Brewster. But the loudest voice belongs to Massasoit.

I am summoned. Massasoit's braves stand in a ring, knives still unsheathed, spears at the ready.

Bradford moans, "My love exceeds toward Squanto more than m—m—many, but we are agreed. We have to sacrifice him for the greater good of our two peoples."

The tribesmen step toward me.

"No!" I throw myself on the ground, prostrate. "This cannot be. After all I do for you. This is the work of one man." I point at Hobbamock. "He wants me dead."

The spy is triumphant.

Massasoit growls, "Give the traitor to me."

Standish prods me with the butt of his musket.

Hobbamock jeers, "On your knees, vermin."

The braves have ropes in their hands. They grab me round my neck and tie me, arms, legs, trussed like a fowl.

But then, a shout from Burial Hill. Everyone stops. They stare out to sea. A shallop is sailing across the bay toward us. They rush to the shore, guns ready. I am ignored. A miracle. Kiehtan be praised.

"Untie him," orders Bradford. "We will decide his fate later. They might be French come to assault us. We must have all the able-bodied men we can muster to resist them."

Massasoit protests, "This man is a traitor. He betrays me before and does so again."

"We will stay true to our word," promises Bradford. "We will honour the treaty."

The chief puts the tip of his spear against my throat. "You will die for this. I will cut off your head and pull your heart from your body."

My heart is thudding, my mouth is as dry as a bear's cave, but the English have a more pressing matter than two warring Indians. They watch warily as seven men splash ashore.

They announce that their sachem King James has permitted them to build another settlement in Wessagusset, a miserable place on a headland one day's sail away.

Bradford is pinched with fury. "The knave Weston is behind this. He has betrayed us."

I hear this name many times and always as if he is the devil himself. I ask Brewster why.

"He works with the rich merchants in London who give us money for this venture," he explains. "They sit in their moneyed ease and welsh on the arrangements we make with them but he does nothing to help. In short, damn the man, he has betrayed us."

I never hear him curse before.

I feel grateful to this figure of hate. Their anger at him helps them forget our little misunderstanding. But I must tread with care.

I still suffer the scorn of Hobbamock, who delights in telling me I will not escape justice. "Massasoit will come for you," he sneers. "Next time he will not leave the Plantation without you. Or your carcass."

Standish accuses me of falseness, of befriending the settlers only to betray them. He would have me strung up, that I know.

My life hangs by a thread. But once again the fates are with me.

The harvest fails. It is too early for the duck to fly to our waters and even now, many months later, my English friends have yet to master the art of fishing. The pumpkins die from mildew and the grapes wither.

They are at a loss. Hope is hard to find. They have been in my country for almost two years and they are as pitiful as the day they arrive. They are so hungry they complain of stomach cramps, their bones stick out, their flesh hangs loose. Mothers rinse their children's stomachs with warm water three times a day to make pretend they have food in their bellies. I hate to see Susanna tipping water into the mouth of baby Peregrine while he splutters and howls in misery.

The memory of their first thanksgiving is a mockery now.

Every night after a day in the fields, Winslow slumps beside me.

Like them all, his hair is matted, and he flicks away the lice that crawl over him.

"I could eat a deer every day for a week and still be hungry. I am so tired, my muscles and bones ache. My legs and arms weigh so heavy I can scarcely lift a hoe."

"Let me help," I say. "We must truck in new pastures. We go down the Cape – the way you come..."

"Sail through those rocks?" interrupts Standish. "I think not."

"Trust me," I say.

They look askance.

"You must let me prove my loyalty to you. I know the way. There are tribesmen there who will trade with you. They have much beaver. We must go before winter sets in."

They agree. I am safe. I offer a silent prayer.

> *Keihtanit*
> *Taubot neanawayean yeu kesukuk*
> Great Spirit
> I thank you today
> I thank you for Mother Earth
> I thank you for Grandmother Moon
> I thank you for Grandfather Sun.
> *Taubot neanawayean newutche yau ut nashik ohke*

I take the tiller of the shallop as we sail across the bay and around the great arm of the Cape. We are battered by the seas off Monomoy but I guide us into peaceful waters. I tell Bradford how I watch *Mayflower* from the heights when it is almost driven onto rocks. I hear the creak of the timbers, I tell him. I watch the men struggling to hold down the sails.

"I think you are about to drown," I say.

"So do I." He grimaces.

As I promise, the tribe's chief is happy with the trinkets.

Their women flash their eyes in delight. We celebrate with a meal of corn mixed with berries and acorns and boiled in water. It is the best food the English have had in weeks. Standish treats the chief to brandy. We are friends.

They trade us eight hogshead of corn and beans. Bradford is content.

My plan is going well.

I prove the Plantation cannot survive without me.

BOOK V

1622–1628

THE VOICE OF EDWARD WINSLOW

(RECORDED YEARS LATER ON HIS LAST JOURNEY HOME IN 1646)

A MAN APART

*Mr Edward Winslow, the Son of Edward Winslow, Esq;
of Draughtwich, in the Country of Worcester… Travelling
into the Low-Countries, he fell into Acquaintance with the
English Church at Leyden, and joining himself to them, he
Shipped himself with that part of them which first came over
into America; from which time he was continually engaged in
such extraordinary Actions, as the assistance of that People to
encounter their more than ordinary Difficulties, called for.*

Cotton Mather, *Magnalia Christi Americana*
or, *The Ecclesiastical History of New England, 1820*

CHAPTER ONE

A MISSION OF MERCY

MY BELOVED WIFE DIED THAT FIRST MARCH. It was an ugly end, her body arched in pain, eyes shut tight against the darkness that enveloped her. She gave a horrible cough, more of a grunt like an animal, blood poured from her mouth and she was gone, only twenty-four years old.

After William Brewster had led the murmured obsequies, he and Governor Carver took me to one side.

"Have you considered your future?" asked Carver.

The future? What did he mean? The present was too painful, let alone consider what was to come.

All I could think to say was, "There is much to be done around the Plantation."

Brewster was clearly embarrassed. "Yes, work, but we meant…"

Carver broke in bluntly. "You must marry."

I blinked in shock. Had I heard aright?

Brewster backed him up. "The Plantation needs children if it is to survive."

My wife's body was barely cold beneath my feet, yet I was being called on to provide the colony with heirs.

"No," was all I could manage. "No. Not now. Never. You ask the impossible. No."

"It is hard, but you cannot think only of yourself." Carver must have realised he had been too brusque for he gave a sympathetic cough. "Remember Master Cushman, how Pastor Robinson persuaded him to marry after he had lost his wife and two children in a matter of months. He was reluctant, he too was gripped by despair, but a new helpmate brought him consolation and revived his spirits."

They had obviously been rehearsing what they were to say because Brewster chipped in, "My dear Edward, I know it is hard, it may seem unnatural, but it has to be done. I love my Mary, she is my life, but if she were to die, I would do the same to keep the cause alive."

I stayed my tongue. I was going to remind them that Cushman had at least some months to recover his spirits and, to be frank, he had a choice of suitable wives among the maids and widows in Leiden. Unlike him, I was stranded in a wilderness where the number of women could be counted on one hand. *And anyway, I reflected bitterly, marriage should not be like bidding for a mare at auction.*

"It is a duty that any one of us should fulfil." Carver was unrelenting.

"What about Master Allerton?" I asked. "He is widowed; he and his three children would benefit more than I."

Brewster narrowed his eyes. "No," was all he uttered.

Terrible enough that my wife had just been taken from me, I was doubly oppressed by being cajoled to 'do my duty' in loveless service to the colony, for that is what it amounted to.

Worst of all, I was being steered into this unnatural union by Brewster, my mentor, the man I admired more than any. How could I resist him, especially as my head – if not my heart – knew he was right?

Who could make me a new wife? The choice was slight, to be sure. The orphan Elizabeth Tilley was only thirteen and was surely destined for another man another day. Mary Chilton, another thirteen-year-old, had lost both parents and was wide-eyed with misery. Priscilla Mullins was almost old enough at seventeen, but she too was grieving the loss of mother, father and her brother, and marriage so soon would be an insult to their memory.

As for the other maids, Desire Minter would not be appropriate because she was a servant – and anyway, she was a miserable little thing.

But the more I considered it, if this arrangement was to take place and to be a success, it had to be sensible and efficient. To be blunt, I would need a helpmeet in the house and the fields and, just as important, maybe more so, she had to be experienced in the ways of the bedchamber for this contract was about procreation, not love.

Only Susanna White met that measure.

I had liked her husband, a cheerful chap, a dab hand at the French game noddy who liked to josh around, and, I imagined, was pretty feckless when it came to business. Both Elizabeth and I had reckoned that she had been the force in the marriage.

My wife, my dead wife, had talked of Susanna's generous nature and I had noticed her fierce sense of what was right and wrong, how the children on the voyage adored her, and how even the toughest sailors were wary of her sharp tongue. Indeed, after she knocked out the obnoxious bosun, we were all a little in awe of her.

So, a strong woman, but not one who could hide her heartbreak. I still had the image of her on the shore by her husband's side, her face raised to the heavens, drowned in tears as she inveighed against his death.

How could she want another husband so soon, if at all?

For several days I concentrated on repairs to the meeting house, which had been damaged in a fire, trying to reconcile my unhappiness with what was expected of me. For the first time in my life I was bewildered and depressed. And I felt guilty – guilty that I would be betraying Elizabeth.

But duty, it was my duty.

"Elizabeth would understand." John Alden, the cooper, put a tentative arm around my shoulders. "She knew how this venture of ours might end and she would bless you and Susanna in this endeavour."

Brewster added to the chorus. "I shall ask Mary to have a word with her. I think she will be able to persuade Mistress White that happiness can emerge from pain and love can grow if there is respect."

"It will be hard for her, too." Mary had sought me out the following day. "She is a fine woman; she has a big heart. It may open itself to you and you to it."

For some days I avoided bumping into Mistress White by taking the long way around the fields if I saw her working, but it was impossible to pass her by when, one evening after prayers, I almost stumbled on her outside her house darning her lad's jerkin.

"Master Winslow," she murmured.

"Mistress White. Good day."

She gave a wry smile. More of a frown, if I am honest. I hope I can say without being accused of ignoble feelings that I had always considered her a comely woman, though not a beauty like my Elizabeth – for one thing, her chin was too pronounced, too square – but now her face was drawn, her eyes were dull, her mouth, which I recalled to be full of laughter, was clamped tight.

Such is man's vanity that I gave no consideration as to what she saw when she looked at me, but Elizabeth had joked that my cheeks, once ruddy and full, had become lined and grey, my beard and 'tache which I had kept modishly groomed were as straggly as a bird's nest, and my eyes started from a face hollowed by hunger.

There was no need to shilly shally. We understood what had to be done; we did not have to find feelings where none existed, and there was no benefit from lingering over the loves we had lost.

I had been a widower for barely four weeks, she had lost her husband a little more than two months before; but no matter, on a sunny day in May we were married.

"A toast to our first wedding." Brewster attempted to inject some sense of moment into our joining together, though a ceremony so devoid of note it would be impossible to imagine. I had an image of Elizabeth and I when we were wed in Leiden city hall – such colour and gaiety, the clamour of bagpipes, a surfeit of apple brandy – but I pushed it swiftly from my mind as we shared a few mouthfuls of mallard with dried biscuit. Standish produced a beaker of beer and we saluted our new life. Then I took her to my bed. It was not the way it was with Elizabeth, who welcomed my lusty enthusiasm for love-making. No, Susanna set her face and lay silently. We did our duty.

"Maybe we shall eventually come to take pleasure from the act," she sighed as she smoothed down her smock.

"I am sure we will," I replied, but I rather doubted it.

CHAPTER TWO

STRANGE MYSTERIES

I AM GETTING AHEAD OF MYSELF. WHERE TO begin? These jottings are being scribbled in 1646, twenty-five years after the gloomy day of my marriage. Here I am, fifty-one years old, sailing to London – not my first journey, by any means, but I believe my last.

The world has changed in all these years, of course it has, but who could have forecast the way that England is being transformed into a land of liberty and true religion. The King has been routed at Marston Moor by a heroic figure of sound faith by the name of Oliver Cromwell, and his archbishop, the Pope-loving William Laud, has been impeached. I trust the gallows will be his reward. For me, I confess, this England with all its fresh hope presents me with a new challenge. I am not sure what, but maybe it will be as profound as the day I knocked on Brewster's door in Stink Alley and asked to be his helper.

Bradford is annoyed that I am sailing on my own business, though he tries to disguise his displeasure, but he does share my joy at the news from the old country. "It is the Lord's doing," he exclaimed when the news reached us. "It ought to be marvellous in our eyes. May not the people of God say the Lord has brought forth our righteousness?"

Being the man he is, he most definitely includes himself in the number of righteous folk, but what of the rest? What of those who lived to build New Plymouth?

And what of me?

As I look back, I know that the vision that inspired so many of us to create a community in God's name has faded. I would not say that many died in vain, that would be to dishonour their name and their sacrifice, but as I reflect here in my cabin, I have to admit we have fallen short of our goal to create a free and independent society where all can live in harmony. It was a noble ambition, no doubt of that, but human frailty let us down.

I have been haunted by the question, would we have left Leiden at all if we had known that we would be praying over the graves of so many comrades? Would I have given up my fruitful career as a printer and a pleasurable life in Leiden had I been warned Elizabeth would die so soon? What about our first governor John Carver, who collapsed into a coma and never recovered, and his broken-hearted widow who followed him to the grave a few weeks later? I have never forgotten them. Nor have I abandoned the memory of good sorts like John Crackstone, Edward Fuller and his wife, Mary Allerton and her stillborn infant, Rose Standish, James Chilton and his wife, Degory Priest – what a card. All lost. Names that have no memorial, but names that only us few who remain remember.

Such was the toll that in the early days, perhaps only six or seven of us were fit enough to look after the sick. They were too weak to help themselves so we fed them with what little we had, dressed and undressed them and, not to put too fine a point on it, cleaned them up where they lay in their shit and piss – forgive my language – and washed their filthy clothes.

It was left to us to tame the wilderness, us men and the biggest of the children, who set to with our axes to chop down trees to use as frames for the houses and mix the soil and sand for the daub. Many were the days that we had to beg Squanto and whoever of his tribe he could muster to come to our rescue.

How much more difficult our struggle had become since his death.

Ah yes, he had died when we were trading with the Nauset on the south side of the Cape. One moment he was proudly telling me that he had come to a deal with the chief to exchange a sack of trinkets and a barrel of brandy for hogsheads of corn, the next he had collapsed and was stretched out on a mat in the chief's wetu.

"It is the end, Winslow," he gasped. "Blood from the nose means death." He gripped my arm. "Don't let me go, not until I have my spear, my bow and arrow beside me." His words came in breathless gulps. "Winslow, pray for me. Pray that I may go to your English heaven. There it will be sunny every day and the corn will grow high. There will be more game than I can eat in a hundred years. I will be content." His breath rattled. "*Nawhaw nissis.* Farewell."

I did pray for him. It was always our mission to encourage the Indians to reject their heathen beliefs and embrace our own but now, as the waves pitch and tumble me about, I have to tell you that the Indian race cannot be taught or converted; rather, it has become our enemy and one that must be snuffed out.

As for Squanto, he had no family to lament his passing and it was left to the old women of the village to sew a mat to wrap around his body, and in a touching gesture, the chief hung a coat of animal skin on the tree nearest his grave.

"It is our tradition," he explained.

I liked Squanto and I missed him. I had been amused by the umbrage he took when his rival Hobbamock came to live in the Plantation. He, and he alone, wanted to be our ally and the sole intermediary with chief Massasoit.

Standish, however, had been ill-disposed to Squanto from the moment he walked into our encampment and was adamant: "His ambition was to make himself great in the eyes of his countrymen by currying favour with us and I tell you, he did not care who suffered if it meant he had the upper hand."

I rather think Bradford and Standish exploited the pair of them so that each would spy on the other and that way keep us abreast of any mischief by our Indian neighbours.

Looking back, I am still not sure what games Squanto played. It rankled with Massasoit that he had not been executed as our treaty dictated, while Hobbamock never lost an opportunity to remind us of his treachery. But he too had benefited from Squanto's disgrace and won over Standish so completely that he lived with his wife in the settlement as the Captain's factotum for more than twenty years. He became a Christian, though I doubt he understood what it meant.

Maybe Squanto had been up to a trick or two but I am convinced his loyalty was to us English more than any other. Above all, he taught us how to stay alive in that blighted land.

It was thanks to Squanto that I understood the ways of the Indian better than my comrades in the Plantation. He and I would walk for miles along the dunes, deep into the forest, through swamps and across rocky plains. Often we would hunt together, he with his bow and me with a musket. He shot down many more birds than I.

"Everything has a use," he explained. "You English see this world as full of hazards, but we know nature is essential for our health and spirit.

"I have taught you about the seasons for geese and ducks, you know now how to tame the turkeys so that they come up to your doors and beg to be killed." He laughed. "Don't spurn the meat of wolves and beaver, they taste strong but they taste well. Just beware the long creepie, the rattlesnake. Only salad and herbs mixed into an oil can cure its bite.

"Look at the clothes I wear. Deer and moose skins make fine coats in winter and turkey feathers weaved together are as smart as any London gentleman would wear. And these boots – moose skin."

As we walked along the seashore digging out eels and picking mussels, he taught me the words that would make dealing with his fellows easier. Yes, *haha*. No, *matta*. Good morrow, *cowampanu*. Very good, *winnet*. Beaver, *tummunk* – and on one occasion, when he dragged me into the cover of a cave, *musq*, bear.

He was amused by our attempts to pronounce each other's languages as much as he was at our endeavours to catch fish, showing us, with an air of superiority, how to make the nets and tackle we needed.

Yes, I disagreed with Standish. I respected Squanto for his intelligence and humanity, as far removed from my image of a savage as I could imagine, but I was dismayed by the behaviour of some of my own Christian countrymen.

One year after the landing of *Mayflower*, another ship, the *Fortune*, arrived, and at first it seemed a blessing. There were thirty or so lusty lads on board, who we were happy to see because they meant extra hands in the fields. Best of all, it brought that honest comrade Robert Cushman with his boy Thomas, and William Brewster's son Jonathan. Bradford greeted him with unusual warmth, reminding us that he had grown up with him in the manor house in Scrooby, and I was amused to observe that Brewster was as delighted to see his son as he was by the delivery of a trunkful of books.

My younger brother John was with them. Lucky man, he wed Mary Chilton when she was of an age – about seventeen, I seem to recall. She has never stopped to remind us that she was the first to set foot in New Plymouth. Heavens, how time passes – as I write they have had their ninth child and share a happiness that I have never enjoyed.

Cushman was his usual anxious self.

"I have bad news." His tic had become more marked in the months since I last saw him. "I have a letter from Thomas Weston. He castigates you for not sending any furs or fish back on *Mayflower*. He accuses you of weakness of judgement rather than weakness of hands, and claims you spend too much time discoursing and arguing."

"What a wretch the m—m—man is," spluttered Bradford.

Cushman tossed the document to one side. "He warns that the Adventurers are impatient for a return on their investments."

"Does he not understand what we have endured?" My voice rose indignantly. "The deaths, the sheer bloody hard work of getting anything to grow in this wasteland."

Poor Cushman. He was merely the messenger.

But being the man of fierce belief that he was, he had something to say, and asked, almost apologetically, if he could share with us what was on his mind.

"The bane of all these mischiefs that arise among you is that men are too cleaving to themselves and their own matters and disregard and condemn all others." That caught our attention. "I charge you, let this self-seeking be left off; seek the good of your brethren, please them, honour them, reverence them, for otherwise it will never go well amongst you."

Isaac Allerton muttered, "Negligent fool. He thinks words are enough but when we need action, he fails."

Strange fellow, Allerton. Still so hostile to Master Robert after all this time. I glowered at him.

Cushman pulled no punches. He attacked men who sought ease or pleasure.

"They are like the scribes who sit by if the roof of their house falls in or Pharisees who refuse to move an inch if their fields become overgrown with weeds. A few idle drones will spoil the whole stock of hardworking bees. So it is here. One idle-belly, one murmurer, one complainer, one self-lover, will weaken and dishearten a whole colony."

One of the men newly arrived on *Fortune* sneered. "The man is a prating fool. I've had to put up with this rubbish all the way across the ocean."

To my disgust, the Billington family, followed by Hopkins and his wife, noisily walked out of the gathering. "Pah. Too busy to listen to this tara-diddle." Billington did not bother to lower his voice. Cushman flushed. The two servants who worked for Hopkins were not there at all, and most of the young men were playing dice on the jetty.

"Do not look for what others do for you but consider what you can do for them," continued Cushman. "Seek to please God, not yourself."

I congratulated him on his noble words but he cut a forlorn figure until the time came for him to board the *Fortune* and return to London. Only then, when he saw how much beaver and walnut we had loaded, did he cheer up – albeit only slightly.

"That little lot will go a long way to pay off the Adventurers," he judged. "My life will become a little easier."

He took with him a slim volume that Bradford and I had written, setting out our stall for the Plantation. Squanto had acutely observed that it was perhaps a rosy view, but I had little choice. I had to write in praise of the 'wondrous providence and goodness of God', I had to claim the country was healthful and hopeful. How else could I persuade other good, hard-working Christians to join us?

Maybe I went too far, maybe the good Lord decided to teach us a lesson by bringing us back to stern reality, because the year after the thanksgiving celebration, we were stricken by drought and by floods. The crops withered in fields cracked by the sun one day and the shrivelled remnants were swept away by rains the next. We were back to the beginning.

We struggled on – what choice did we have? But it did seem the world was against us, especially months later when we heard that *Fortune* had been seized by pirates off the coast of France and all its cargo looted.

"This is grievous news." Bradford held his head in his hands. "There was £500 worth of furs on the ship. Almost half our debts to London would have been settled."

Weston wrote to complain about the ship being taken. Complain! As if it were our fault. But that was not all that was sent to try us. Weston's letter arrived on a ship that brought another sixty men to our shores. They were hungry, mutinous and lazy. We did not expect them and we could not feed them. Why on earth had Weston sent them?

The answer came in a troubling postscript.

'I shall be setting up a colony a few leagues to the north of you on a fine plot of land, name of Wessagusset,' he wrote. 'You clearly do not have the skills to run a settlement and it is a waste of my time trying to help you, so it falls to me to demonstrate how to build a thriving community and grow wealthy from the beaver trade. Something you have failed to achieve. And one thing more: I have quit the Adventurers and I am quit of you – and you of me, for that matter.'

And this from the man who promised that he would never desert us.

Our anger was matched by our dismay. Like it or not – and we didn't – he was our conduit to the men in London who had the finances to support us, but now he was a rival for their backing and a competitor in the trade for furs.

"The sad truth is our hopes lie in the dust without his help," warned Brewster.

I cast my mind back to the first ill-fated meeting. "When he came to Leiden we asked ourselves if we could rely on the honesty of the man. How wrong we were. Now we know the promises he made were just wind."

CHAPTER THREE

FOXGLOVE AND MARSH MALLOW

S USANNA AND I WERE TRAPPED BY THE BURDEN of duty. We worked all day, we shared a bowl of pottage with her children and we slept the sleep of the dead, waking as weary as we had been the night before. When we had the energy, we would embrace as all married couples should. Duty. Damned duty.

We existed in a limbo of toleration that flickered into a kind of closeness when, in March '22, one year after the marriage, she became pregnant.

She was matter-of-fact about the news – the bright enthusiasm she had shown on the ship for life and for people had long been dimmed – but William Brewster was effusive.

"God is with you," he proclaimed. "This is a great day for us in the Plantation too, you know. This is the sign that God approves your contract."

He put his arm around me affectionately. "A child is proof that we will survive – nay, prosper. We are all grateful to you and Susanna and, I may say, the sacrifice you have made."

It sounded as though we had performed some function in good order, which I suppose we had, but in painful irony the child, a boy, lived for only a few weeks, his death mocking the very reason we had agreed to marry. If we felt any sadness, we did not show it; instead, Susanna merely pursed her lips more tightly.

"We shall have another."

We had scarcely buried the infant when a messenger arrived with disturbing news: Massasoit was close to death.

"Too late," gasped another distraught tribesman the very next day. "He has passed on to the *annōgssūe kesuk*, the starry heavens."

What was the truth? It was agreed that I should set off for his village immediately. If he was dead we had to form a new treaty with his successor. If alive, then my presence at his sick bed would prove that we cared for him and help cement our alliance.

As I prepared to leave, William Brewster came clutching a book.

"It's the *Complete English Huswife*. Take it with you – it has the cure for all the ailments you can imagine." He jabbed at a page. "This one might work. You need a quart of old ale – warm it and scrape off the scum, then mix in smearwort or round-leaved birthwort and wild celery or celandine. Boil it up and drain through a clean cloth."

"Dear William." I burst out laughing. "We do not have the time to collect the ingredients, let alone make such a cure. We must hurry."

He was crestfallen. "Well, at least take some hot clothes or bricks and lay them against the soles of his feet, and whatever you do, wrap him up warmly."

Susanna, more practical, handed me a knapsack. "Here is some foxglove and marsh mallow that I collected for the infant when he was ailing."

I took with me the Indian Hobbamock, who with the death of Squanto had become our go-between with the chief. We spoke little as we tramped furiously through dales and swamps, but after we had met a band from his tribe and shared a meal of pumpkin and duck, his tongue was loosened and I could not stop him talking.

"I am a *pniese*, what we call the bravest of the brave in the tribe," he informed me with great pride. "I have the power to conjure up Chipi, the evil spirit, what you call the devil. He appears to me like a snake or an eagle. He protects me from death and gives me the wisdom I need to advise the sachem. Bad people may knock at his door for succour but 'no', he orders; *quachet*, 'go away'. But not me. I am welcome."

"You are lucky to be so blessed." I reckoned he was bragging and paid little attention.

The Indian gave me a sideways look. "Tisquantum did have secret meetings with other sachems. I know it. He plotted to overthrow Massasoit."

"Surely not." I was not about to share my doubts about Squanto with him. "He was always loyal to the chief."

The Indian gave a contemptuous snort. "He hated the chief; the chief hated him. He wanted Squanto killed." He added obscurely, "We have poisons that no man can divine."

Was he hinting that Massasoit had plotted to kill Squanto? That added a twist to their often-rancorous relationship, but I was not prepared to believe everything Hobbamock said; after all, he was determined to destroy his rival's reputation and win greater favour for himself.

"Did you know Tisquantum had put the fear of Kiehtan into the tribesmen by telling them that the plague was buried in the store house?"

"I had heard that rumour." I spoke carefully. I knew it to be true and we had reprimanded Squanto, but he had sworn he did it only to scare our enemies.

"Not a rumour. The truth." Hobbamock was indignant. "It was a wicked trick to play and one he hoped would strengthen his power. He dug up the barrels to show them the evil powder within."

He did not speak for some minutes, worried that he might have upset me, but plucked up the courage to ask, "Was it true? Did the barrels contain such a terrible scourge?"

"No," I replied, but I decided to let the threat linger. I knew they contained only gunpowder, but how could ignorant savages know any better? "Our God does have the pox ready and can send it if he pleases to destroy our enemies."

We walked in silence for a league or two but as we neared the village, he began a eulogy of the chief, as though praising him would save his life.

"I have never seen his like," he affirmed. "He is no liar, he is not bloody and cruel like others. If he is angry, he soon calms down and is easily reconciled to those who have offended him. He governs his men without cruelty. I tell you, Master Winslow, you do not have a more faithful ally among the Indians."

I knew he was right and, more important, I understood how the chief's death might unleash forces against us that we would not be able to resist.

But he was not dead. Instead he was making a ridiculous fuss, lying on his palliasse groaning and moaning like an overgrown infant, surrounded by sachems, priests and the old crones of the tribe.

While they chanted and shed extravagant tears, one of his wives, Saunka, sat close by him while several women massaged his limbs to rid the body of the malady. I imagined some of them to be his other wives for, disgracefully, the savages wed as many women as they like, and we had quite upset the chief when we discussed our ten commandments. He accepted them all except the sixth – thou shalt not commit adultery.

"Just one woman?" he had protested. "Can that be true? That is against nature."

Massasoit pulled himself up, staring blindly.

"Who is there? I cannot see."

Hobbamock prostrated himself. "*Neen womasu Sagimus, neen womasu Sagimus*. My loving sachem, it is I, your servant. I am here with Master Winslow."

"Winsnow, welcome," gasped the great man. He never got my name right. "Is that really you?"

I held his hand and gripped it. "I will do what I can to make you better," I promised rashly, for what did I know of medical matters?

"Give me what you use," I asked the women, who produced a mess of corn, sassafras roots and strawberry leaves. I added the extract of herbs Susanna had given me and fed him tiny morsels with the tip of my knife, forcing the medicine through his clenched teeth.

He continued to groan; the cure was having no effect. I prised open his mouth to peer inside to find a tongue furred and stinking, reminding me of the horrible mix of dye extract and sewerage that spread like a green sludge on the canals of Leiden. Both those horrible odours stay with me today.

I suppressed a shudder and made him sluice water around his mouth before scraping off the gluey mess.

To everyone's relief, none more than mine, the chief sat up. He looked around, blinked in puzzlement and demanded, "Roast me a duck. I am hungry."

"Not a wise idea," I insisted. "Not in your condition."

"*Matta, matta.* No, no. Food. Give it to me." So I dutifully mixed up some crushed corn with a slice or two of duck, added a few more strawberry leaves and sassafras and warmed it into a pottage.

"That was good, Winsnow," he exclaimed. "So good that I must have more."

"Is that sensible? It is so fatty you will be sick again." He would not listen, gobbled down the fowl and promptly spewed it back over his bedding before falling back, holding his stomach and whimpering. He was bleeding at the nose. Dear Lord, no. I knew from poor Squanto's death that to the Wampanoags that signalled the end.

His men wailed in despair at the sight of the blood that dribbled from his nostrils for four long hours, but once he was asleep I washed him, and when he awoke he pronounced himself fully fit and dipped his face in a bowl of water, only to start bleeding again. Once more I was filled with panic, but the worst was over. In fact, he proved his recovery by squatting down right in front of us and producing three moderately sized stools.

"That is encouraging," I affirmed with a confidence I did not feel as we gathered around this proof of sound health.

"We must celebrate," he decreed. Fires were lit, venison roasted and the village rang to a heathen beat of water drums and gourd rattles, the stamping of feet and singing.

"Now we see how greatly the English love me," he declaimed. "I will never forget this kindness, Winsnow; we are enmeshed in the ties of obligation."

And he hugged me close, his noxious breath invading my mouth and my nostrils.

Chapter Four

A killing and a cover-up

B

Y THE TIME I REACHED THE PLANTATION THE happy news I brought about Massasoit had been overshadowed by darker tidings.

Two days after we had left the Indian camp, only a few leagues from Plymouth, Hobbamock had stopped me in my tracks and with an air of tremendous self-importance confided that Massasoit had warned him that a Massachusett chief by name of Wituwamat was about to sweep down the coast and wipe us out.

"He plan secret and villainous plot." Hobbamock whispered, though we were quite alone. "He tells the men at the Weston camp in Wessagusset that he is a friend to them. Join me, he say, destroy the Plantation. But he is no friend to any white man. He kill all of you in the Plantation then he tear down Wessagusset and rule these lands."

"We must strike first." Bradford was uncharacteristically excited when I told him. "Captain Standish will sail north, teach this scoundrel a lesson, and while he is there drive out Weston's gang of wastrels. We shall prove who rules here. We must strike fear and terror."

His fervour took me aback.

Standish was even thirstier for battle. His corselet gleamed, his guns were primed, his knife sharpened. "I shall cut off the head of this miscreant and bring it back here as a warning to all traitors."

Brewster smiled resignedly at the sight of our Captain in full flood. "He is a good man but as you know, if he is not properly used he can swiftly change from being a humble, often meek, comrade to a smoking chimney of ferocity."

There was no doubt which character had taken hold.

So it was that at the end of March '23, he and a troop of eight set sail with Isaac Allerton as his right-hand man and Hobbamock as guide, the Indian only too happy to destroy a rival to Massasoit.

We waited anxiously for news until a few days later we heard shouts from the bay and gathered on the shore to welcome the shallop as it hove into view. On the prow, like a Roman emperor glorying in his triumph, stood Standish. He jumped onto the great stone by the jetty and held high a sack.

"Behold the fate of any villain who defies us."

With a flourish he pulled out... what? What was it? At first I thought it was haunch of venison, its blood dripping onto the stone, but Susanna gave a gasp of horror. It was a head, a bloody human head, its hair matted, the tongue lolling as if trying to muster one last cry of defiance.

Standish shouted, "This miscreant threatened us with death. Now look at him." The dead man's blood had smeared his face and soaked into his beard. He was gripped with the ghastly exultation of his deed.

One of the onlookers cheered, then another, until it seemed that everyone was caught up in this gory triumph. Billington, Hopkins and the lads who came with the *Fortune* were bawling with the same ugly passion they would bring to a cock fight. I was dazed with disgust and looked to Bradford in the hope he would share my horror, but instead I was dismayed to see his eyes burning with a rapture as fierce as his blood-thirsty Captain. I had seen him gripped like this when he preached about forbearance and mercy, but here he was bringing the same blazing intensity to this act of savagery as to those fine qualities.

Susanna sat down in case she fainted. The children screamed but, intrigued, gathered round to stare at the monstrosity in their midst.

"Stick the traitor's head high," proclaimed Standish. "Let it be a flag of terror to all who oppose us."

"The honour and glory is down to God," intoned Bradford as he led a service of thanks. "We must let it be known that we did this only because of this man's treachery. It was not done lightly. But if anyone threatens us again, I vow we shall utterly consume them."

Standish boasted, "We tore Weston's settlement apart, smashed down their pathetic hovels and set fire to them. We seized their weapons and collected up all the trinkets they use for trade before we chased his pathetic gang into the swamps, shooting to kill any who showed resistance.

"'Come out and fight like men,' I shouted. 'Do not insult us by behaving like women.' We rounded them up, chucked them on a ship and sent them off to Maine. That's the last we'll hear of them, thank the Lord.

"As for him…" He gestured at the head of the Indian. "Now we have proved who rules in this country."

The young men gave a great huzzah and threw stones

at the head, cheering every time one hit the target. We had come that low.

Next day, Hobbamock came by the house with a net full of shad. "I have caught too many. Have some."

"You have had quite an adventure," said Susanna as she gutted the fish.

"Master Winslow, Mistress Susanna, you should have seen it." He struggled to find the words. "The shame. The terror. Such blood."

In his stumbling English he described what our men had found in the settlement. Weston's settlers had no food, their corn had failed, their pigs, chickens, all their livestock had broken through ill-made fences and disappeared into the forest. But, he reported contemptuously, they were so lazy that they had made no attempt to ease their hunger by gathering the clams or groundnuts that were there for the picking.

They lived in dirt – as he put it – which had shocked him, so familiar was he with our high standards. He was derisive at their failure to repair their homes, which were, anyway, little more than branches carelessly tied together and easily blown down by gales or wrecked by fire.

Perhaps what upset him the most was the way Indians and English intermingled. It upset his sense of order and, I might say, probity, which he had readily come to embrace in the Plantation; he as the servant, Standish as his master.

"For many months my spies say to me that my people come and go like they live there. They stay under the same roof. Weston men give them guns and blankets in exchange for oysters. If no deal they steal my people's food."

He shook his head in disbelief at such low behaviour. "And the women from the tribes, they spend time with the white men. You understand what I say?"

We did. And we shared his disgust at such immorality.

With increasing agitation he recounted how Wituwamat had come swaggering into the camp with a brave by his side. They each had a long knife hanging on a string across their chests. That meant one thing: they were eager to fight.

"Wituwamat make a great show," reported the Indian. "He puff out chest. He spits. He says, 'You think yourself a noble captain but you are but a little man, a dwarf. I am a man of great strength and courage.'

"He draws his knife and stabs it onto the table. A woman's face is on the handle.

"'I have another with the face of a man carved on it,' he boasts. 'I use it to kill the English and the Frenchies who come on our land. The two knives must marry.'

"Me, I would strike him down but Captain Standish, he stay calm."

The idea of our volatile Captain staying calm under such provocation made me smile at its sheer improbability but the Indian insisted that he was the very spirit of harmony.

"'We must live together in peace,' he declare. 'Come tomorrow and we shall have a feast.'

"The chief thinks he frightens the Captain. He thinks he will surrender."

I said, "That was his first mistake."

Susanna added dryly, "And his last."

"It was, Mistress Susanna. It was.

"When they arrive, I pour mugs of brandy," continued Hobbamock. "They talk of hunting and the harvest, the price of beaver fur. The chief boasts he kill a bear. Master Allerton gets to his feet to refill their drinks, but instead he slams shut the door. He crashes a beam across so it cannot be opened.

"The Captain leaps on Wituwamat. He has him on the

ground in a bat of an eye. His knife rises and falls, again and again. The chief yelps like a whipped dog."

The Indian paused. A shadow fell over his face as he relived the sound of the blade twisting, sinking deep into the chief's body, the choke of death deep within his throat, the sight of him convulsing and trembling like a rabid animal.

He shivered. "The blood leaked onto the mud floor from where he lay. You know that smell, the smell of slaughtered animals? It was like that."

He paused.

"And you?" asked Susanna. "What did you do?"

"Mistress, I did nothing. I hate the Massachusett but it was not my fight. I have been in wars. I have killed, but I was not prepared for the — what is the word? — the furiousness of the Captain. Like a starved wolf. He stood over the body and made the sign of your cross and cried, 'Rescue me, oh Lord, from evil men, save me from violent men, keep me, oh Lord, from the hands of the wicked.' I remember this from your prayers.

"He grabs Wituwamat's hair in one hand and hacks at his neck. Three, four blows, more. The head comes away from the body. So much blood. It spilled onto the ground and over his hands and arms. Some splashes on his face. I will never forget that moment."

The Indian was lost in the horror and the terrible thrill of the moment.

"I saw the might of you English."

CHAPTER FIVE

A RUFFLING

I F I WAS UNEASY BEFORE THE KILLING, I WAS utterly disheartened by Hobbamock's account. The pretence of friendship with the Indians showed a cunning that was not true to the way we English did things, nor did the glorying in the killing sit well with a community whose very aim was to live humbly in the shadow of a merciful Lord.

Even now, all these years later, I judge the assassination – a hard word, but that is what it amounted to – to be a turning point in the life of the Plantation. I still think of it as the moment we lost our innocence. After that we were tainted; a man had been killed not in the hurly burly of a brawl but deliberately and in cold blood.

But I must make a confession, one that I can safely make now that the terrible deed is far behind me and forgotten by most. Perhaps an admission is a better word. As well as my account of life in the Plantation, I wrote another chronicle entitled *Good News from New England*, which I modestly suggest earned me some praise. I devoted a few words to the claim that we had been threatened by Wituwamat and his Massachusetts tribesmen and explained that we had no option but to defend ourselves.

The astute reader will wonder how strange it was that Hobbamock mentioned this threat to me only a full two days after we left Massasoit. Why would he delay such momentous news? Why, indeed, did the chief himself not tell me? After all, I had just saved his life.

The truth is, the plan to attack had been made by Bradford and Standish before I reached the Plantation. That explains why the Captain was already armed and ready to avenge himself on those 'treacherous savages'.

Now, the purpose of *Good News* was to demonstrate how progressive and beneficial our settlement had become. How peaceful and secure. So I had little choice but to – how shall I put it? – reinterpret the events. Imagine the damage it would do our reputation to be perceived as bloody aggressors.

The real causes for the assault went back some months. Bradford, I do believe, was genuinely alarmed at the establishment at Wessagusset. He not only saw it as a trading rival but more, he was horrified by the dissolute behaviour of the men and disapproved of their religious beliefs, which he deemed too close to the King's Church.

"They are not fit for an honest man's company," he snapped.

It was personal too. He had grown to hate Thomas Weston and wanted retribution for the craven way he had treated us.

Then we had the hot-tempered Myles Standish. That too was personal. When our explosive Captain was bartering with the tribes along the Cape, he had fallen out with one sachem, who he accused of stealing trinkets – wrongly, it transpired – and quarrelled with other chiefs over deals that had failed.

He also had a set-to with chief Wituwamat, who he had confronted at the very Indian camp where Squanto had died.

"The scoundrel said we were such cowards that we whimpered like children when faced with death." As he recounted the confrontation, Standish became redder in the face with indignation than seemed possible. "He took out his knife, waved it in front of my face and crowed that he would ruinate the colony at Wessagusset before turning on us."

That might have ended there – a splenetic Englishman and an aggressive chief having an altercation – but add Bradford's loathing of Weston to Standish's lust to avenge a slight, for that was all it amounted to, and senseless destruction was inevitable.

The bloodied head stared down at us in angry retribution for many months.

To this day I feel unease about my chronicle's version of the killing, but Bradford never showed the slightest misgivings about his actions. Indeed, he took a grim pleasure in the sight of the head withering on the post.

It was still there being pecked at by the crows when we heard from Pastor Robinson in Leiden. Far from a letter of goodwill and cheery news, it was a rebuke couched in the severest of terms.

'How happy it would have been if you had converted some of them before you killed them,' he wrote. 'Once blood is shed, it takes a long time to staunch its flow. You will tell me that they deserved it, maybe they did, but the provocations and insults made by those heathenish Christians in Wessagusset, how bad were they really?

'You made your decision not on what they deserved, but what you wanted to inflict. I do not understand why you killed so many – just one or two of the ringleaders would have been enough. Bear in mind the rule – to punish the few to bring fear to the many.'

He had harsh words for Standish: 'I have to exhort you to consider the behaviour of your Captain. I love him and I know how much good he has done for you, but he needs to be used right.'

How true, I thought.

'If he is provoked he lacks a little tenderness when it comes to the lives of others. Never forget that in men's eyes, it is more glorious to be a terror to barbarous people than it is to the eyes of God. I fear this might draw others to ruffle the course of the world.'

The Captain stood stony-faced. He was hurt, I could tell. He had little in common with the pastor but he admired him – more than that, he loved him, and would have craved his approval.

Bradford pursed his lips and frowned. Much of his thinking had been inspired by Robinson who, though he was far away, was still the leader of our movement, and he would have taken the criticism as sorely as Standish.

But he would not admit publicly to doubt. "We had no choice," he said heavily. "I am confident that if Pastor John were here, he would see things differently. He would approve."

He insisted the skull stayed where it was during his marriage ceremony with Alice Southworth. What a surprise that was. Typically, he had shared nothing about his plans to take a wife until later that summer of '23, when he helped a woman in her thirties, handsome enough, down the gangplank of the *Anne* and onto the shore.

"Heavens, I remember her," exclaimed Brewster. "At least, I remember her being married to Edward Southworth when we were in Leiden."

"Me too," chimed in Mary. "I believe that was what made our young friend behave so oddly when it came to matters of the heart. I am pretty certain that she was his first love and he was distraught with the rejection."

I could not imagine a youthful Bradford in the throes of passion.

"Perhaps he felt more keenly for her than Dorothy," I wondered.

"Theirs was an unsettled marriage, true enough," admitted Mary. "But to conjecture what goes on behind other folks' doors is not fruitful."

We left it at that. We had endlessly wondered about Dorothy's death and been puzzled by Bradford's refusal to talk about it. Never a word; not a hint. He was much the same when his boy John finally joined him in New Plymouth in '27, demonstrating little affection for the ten-year-old. A slight, shy boy, utterly lacking the fierce determination of his father to change the world, he went on to lead a life of careful anonymity. He married, I think, a deacon's daughter, and moved away to Connecticut, leaving no mark on our community.

I never heard John mention his mother, so what he made of his father's new bride I could only guess. I felt for him as we gathered for the wedding. How could he possibly comprehend the rules that his father followed – fervently idealistic when it came to the word of God, coolly pragmatic when it came to the small matter of a partner for life?

The celebration was altogether grander than my perfunctory affair. A cloudless summer's day, everyone came, including Massasoit and Queen Saunka, though for decorum's sake he had left his five other wives behind. The chief had made an effort to impress with a black wolf skin draped over his shoulders and beads around his waist. His men paraded on either side, tall and imposing, their faces painted in crosses and bizarre patterns in black and red, yellow and white. We saluted them with a barrage of musket fire, which made them feel tremendously proud.

The Indians brought the Governor and his new bride three or four deer and a turkey to add to venison pasties, barrels of beer, bursting grapes and all sorts of plums and nuts.

It was a fine day, though the new Mistress Bradford looked somewhat askance – indeed I worried she might faint – at the nakedness of the braves as they danced with untamed abandon.

There were other unions to celebrate. Standish had also sent to England for a bride, one Barbara, though we knew little of her background. And I should perhaps mention that in the following year or two, Priscilla Mullins, the only survivor of the Mullins family, married the cooper John Alden, a cheery chap, and another credit to the community.

John Carver's servant John Howland had inherited a generous bequest from his master after his untimely death, but I am sure that had no bearing on the affections of Elizabeth Tilley, who waited until she reached seventeen before accepting his hand. A fine fellow, Howland. I had considered him a dry stick when we first met, one sound enough in the service of Master Carver, but little more than his book keeper and amanuensis. In fact, he was a hard worker determined to make the most of his life and, more importantly, he became a loyal comrade. The best. He and Lizzie made a pretty couple and swiftly had a daughter who they named Desire, after the servant girl.

The unhappy maid had hated every moment of our venture since she set sail from Holland, and had jumped at the opportunity to return to London with Thomas Cushman on the *Fortune*. As I recall, she was the only one of us to desert the settlement, and hopefully she has found tranquility in some cosy English village.

"She never recovered from the death of Master Carver," observed Brewster. "She also missed Dorothy badly. She had been kind to her."

The ship delivered many good folk from our old home, most welcome of all the Brewsters' daughters – Patience, now a pleasing, but still unmarried, twenty-three, and the younger girl, Fear, who was seventeen.

I remembered Fear as a serious child when I shared lodgings with the Brewsters in Stink Alley, though never too earnest to resist playing marbles or hot cockles with me. Now she was a demure, self-contained young lady who was understandably subdued by her new surroundings but not defeated, as a flash from eyes that were the same startling amber as her mother's signalled. I could not help noticing how her stillness made her the centre of attraction for the men in the settlement.

None, however, matched the hungry gaze of Isaac Allerton. He was a widower and he needed a wife to help him with his three children, so his interest was not improper – but he was twenty years older and that, I considered, made his attention unhealthy.

From the diaries of Fear Brewster
found hidden in her home after her death

It was two days before I noticed the skull. It was impaled on a stake, shreds of sinew hanging from it as it stared down on me through the empty sockets of its eyes. Boys were throwing stones at the birds that pecked at it. Horrible, horrible.

Master Winslow tried to justify the display by explaining that the dead man had been a treacherous chief who had threatened the Plantation, but I could tell he was troubled by the killing. Like me, like all of us in what was meant to be a God-fearing community, he believed we should treat people – including our enemies – with dignity.

If I was shocked by the skull, I confess I was utterly disheartened by the beggarliness of my new home.

When our ship, the Anne, had bumped up against the jetty, my sister Patience and I could not believe what we saw. Was this it? Surely this was just a small trading post. The main town with its sturdy houses and fields bursting with corn and barley, which we had read about in Master Winslow's book, must be beyond the hills.

All we could see was a cluster of wooden houses that were as rickety as chicken coops, a few acres of wilting crops and beyond, a dense forest no doubt roamed by the lions and savages we had been warned about. It was all so miserable, so small and barren.

But out of the coops and the forsaken fields came a rush of people. Was that Mother? Father? Our brothers Resolved and Wrestling? Yes, all there, filling the emptiness with the happy noise of greetings.

It had been only three years since we waved my parents God speed, but my goodness, how quickly they had become frail ghosts of their former selves.

Father's hair, which I remembered flecked with only the first traces of silver, was now white and he was so unsteady that he had to prop himself up with a stick while Mother clung to him, coughing and holding her chest. She was so frail I feared a gust of wind would take her away.

"Welcome, my dears." Father led us up a dusty path where pigs and goats wandered freely and stopped by their front door. "This is your new home." He tapped the walls proudly. "Cedar and chestnut. Built to last."

But the wind whistled through the cracks and the rain leaked through a roof of flimsy rushes. The room – the one room for all us six Brewsters and an orphan boy called Richard More, who Father had adopted – was filled with smoke from the hearth and guttering oil lamps, which mingled greasily with the smell of cooking. The floor was of packed mud, the table of crudely nailed timbers and chairs of splintery wood. As for the bed, it was made of unyielding planks, and it took me many restless nights before I became used to lying under what I learnt was a racoon pelt. I was close to suffocating from the musty, rotting smell of the dead creature.

The only reminders of happier times were Father's violet jacket hanging on the door knob, in which he had cut quite a dash in Leiden, but was now faded and frayed, and his library of books.

"I must have 200." He stroked their covers as if they had feelings. "My knees are so shaky these days I am not much use in the fields, so I can read without feeling guilty."

He took a tome from the shelves. "I am researching the best use for the herbs we find here." He ticked them off like an alchemist stocking his pharmacy. "There are strawberries, sorrel, yarrow and watercress. All good for health cures."

As a little girl, Father was a hero to me. He had defied the King, he had sent pamphlet after pamphlet of righteous fury spinning around the world. Now he was happy to sit on the step of his house and read about herbs.

It was a relief to find that Master Winslow had not retreated to a quiet life like his mentor. Together we walked up the hill that overlooked the settlement.

"You can see the world from here." We stood puffing for breath. In one direction, the blank monotony of the sea, relieved only by wave tops whipped into flecks of white by the wind. Behind, the forest, which stretched further than I imagined, hiding its secrets and dangers in an impenetrable darkness.

"Burial Hill, we call it," he murmured, gesturing at mound after mound of earth so slightly raised above the stony ground that I did not notice them until he pointed them out. "Maybe later generations will decide on a more appealing name."

He touched a patch of slightly raised earth gently. "Elizabeth."

We sat for a few moments in quiet.

He got to his feet. "Come. You must meet Susanna."

Susanna had been, if not a beauty, a woman who would have attracted many a youth in her younger days, but her gaze was dull and the lines on her face spoke of pain, not happiness. She was polite enough, poured me a beer and offered a plate of cold mallard.

"*What do you make of us?*" *she asked, but without waiting for my reply, she said,* "*You might find everything rough and ready, but when we landed here there was nothing. Nothing. Just fields of bones.*"

I flinched but she was not going to spare me.

She gestured with her chin toward the bay. "*I stubbed my toe on a skull just over there.*"

I struggled to find the words, but she did not need any feeble expression of sympathy from me.

"*We made it work. We had no choice. As for Edward and I, there had to be another generation if the settlement was to exist beyond our lives, and we did what was required of us.*"

I was cast down by her candidness but, if I am honest, what I found more dispiriting was the way the few survivors from Leiden, like my dear parents, had nothing on their minds but the day-to-day business of staying alive. Myles Standish, usually so jolly with us children, merely grunted when we met, and William Bradford, who had actually shared our home in Leiden, acknowledged me with preoccupied indifference. Isaac Allerton appraised me with the curious raised eyebrows that I remembered from when he stopped to pass the time with us girls – me, Mary the maid and Desire. Even at that tender age I considered him overly attentive. Desire loathed him.

They had become brutalised – could they not see that in themselves? Their faces were reddened and coarsened by the wind and sun but underneath their souls were grey.

After three years, I had accepted my lot. I no longer fretted at the rain dripping through the roof; I did not scream when the hogs escaped from their pen and ran amok through the allotments; I managed to eat the mush of corn and marrow, which was such a favourite of my parents, without wanting to throw up.

My lot also meant marriage. To Master Allerton. Once or twice when we walked together, he had helped me over a stile and given my elbow the slightest of squeezes and when we talked, he would hold my gaze with his watery eyes rather longer than was necessary. I did nothing to encourage his interest but I was not surprised when Father told me of his intentions. I was, however, distraught.

"I am too young," I protested, though at twenty I knew I was the ideal age. "He is forty years old," I complained. "I do not like him."

Father was unhappy about the marriage, I could tell, but he refused to relent, I turned to Mother. "Cannot love play a small part in this?" I begged. "As it did for you?"

She sympathised but she was as unmovable as Father. "Talk to Susanna. She understands."

The dutiful wife pursed her lips. "The men can hew down trees and build forts, shoot wild duck and kill savages. But only we women can guarantee the survival of New Plymouth. My dear, you know what you must do."

CHAPTER SIX

REVELS AND RETRIBUTION

WE CELEBRATED FEAR'S WEDDING WITH A modest meal. Old man Brewster stared fixedly to the front, her mother wept a little and I reflected somewhat sadly that just as I had been compelled to wed, she too had been given no option. Master Allerton, on the other hand, looked remarkably pleased with himself. No wonder. He had plucked a fine young bird.

Marriage, however, did not stop him keeping his eye on business. A few days after the wedding, he emerged from the secret delights of the marriage bed to call us together. He came straight to the point.

"This way of working as a collective, all for one and one for all, is not efficient." Before anyone could interrupt, he went on, "We would grow more crops if we worked for ourselves. That way, the enterprising will prosper and the hangers-on and the lazy will have to look to themselves."

"But," argued Brewster, "the Adventurers insisted that we

work together for seven years and when the time is up, the investors get their dividends and we split the assets between us."

"I do not think our colleagues in London will mind how they get their money as long as they are paid," asserted Allerton. "I do believe that if we give each family a parcel of land – say, between sixty and a hundred acres – and encourage them to grow as much as they like, it will prove profitable."

Brewster interrupted again. "Pastor Robinson always warned us that pursing private profit would unleash a deadly plague of greed."

Allerton, rather patronisingly, I considered, replied, "Dear Brewster, I am not suggesting we neglect each other, nor am I suggesting that greed is good. We will continue to labour in a comradely spirit on every other project."

And so it was. The Brewsters and Bradford were given land south of the highway, while Isaac Allerton and his new wife picked up a nice stretch to the south of the brook, toward the bay. I was given a patch to the north of the Plantation, across the way from Captain Standish, which suited me well.

It was remarkable how, as Allerton had predicted, with only ourselves to rely on, we did work harder and our crops flourished.

"Well," said William Brewster as autumn neared, "I have never seen such a harvest of corn. And what about the pumpkins? Enough for many months."

"I told you," crowed Allerton as he unloaded a barrow full of peas and beans. "One can still be a good Christian and work for a profit."

But we were to be tested yet again when we suffered a crippling drought. However hard we worked fetching and carrying water from the thin trickle of Eel Brook, the corn shrivelled and the peas and pumpkins turned brown and sank back into the dry-as-dust earth.

"Once again, we will starve," groaned Bradford, but Brewster would hear none of that defeatist talk. "No, we shall ask God to rescue us."

The entire Plantation gathered, even the sorry lots like Billington – after all, they too were hungry – and for eight hours we stood in the burning sun in what the old man dubbed 'a day of humiliation'. We prayed, we fasted, we talked about God's mission for us and we read encouraging passages from the Bible.

As dusk fell, I saw dark clouds rolling in over the sea. And then, miraculously, rain. It did not stop for two weeks. Our corn sprang into life. The harvest was saved.

We never experienced such a poor crop again. With God's goodwill, we had tamed the wilderness.

But we had not reckoned on the malign influence of man – or rather, one man.

Unannounced, unexpected, and most certainly unwelcome, out of the forest scrambled Thomas Weston.

I had had only the briefest of acquaintance with the man when he came to Leiden some seven or eight years before to persuade us to entrust our future to him, but what a change. The man who had visited us in Green Close, so contained and pleased with himself, was now an unkempt figure in muddied breeches and a ragged jacket. He was wild-eyed with anger and frustration and, I rather believe, embarrassment.

He was accompanied by various rapscallions, though one was smarter in dress and sharper of manner. Name of Thomas Morton. A superior type who sported the vestiges of a moustache and a beard too tidy for him to have spent much time in the wilds. He put his feet up on a table in an insolent manner and nonchalantly quaffed our beer.

It never occurred to us – why should it? – that he would prove to be the bane of the colony. But I shall tell of that anon.

Weston had some cock-and-bull story of crossing the Atlantic in a fishing boat, using another name and pretending to be a blacksmith.

"The shallop was sunk as we came ashore," claimed the so-called smithy. "The moment we were washed up, we were seized by Indians who stripped us of everything we possessed. We were lucky to escape."

Bradford was unmoved. "Do you expect us to assist you after all the harm you have caused?"

"You beg us for comfort, yet you built the settlement at Wessagusset," I added. "You planned to sabotage the Plantation."

Mention of his ill-fated venture briefly galvanised him. "I meant no harm. We could have worked together but instead you destroyed the place. Destroyed. All my men scattered to the wilds." He recaptured some of his familiar insolence. "For men who profess to be Christians, that was a sin. A cruel sin."

Bradford remained calm. "If you object so much, you are very welcome to leave. You no doubt heard the wolves howling as you hacked your way along the paths to reach here, and would have espied the savages sharpening their knives, but I am sure a man as clever as you will find a way to survive."

He quietened at that.

"You have to help me, I beg you. Lend me some beaver and I will sell it when I reach home and share the profit with you."

"Do you think we can trust you further than we can throw you?" Standish took a step toward him. I was sure he would pick him up and hurl him into the sea.

"No, no. Yes, you can trust me. That is unfair," gibbered the interloper. "You might think the arrangements made with the Adventurers were not to your favour, but let me tell you, without me you would not be here."

"Very well," agreed Bradford, who later, reluctantly, admitted that the scoundrel was right. "We will give you one hundred beaver skins, but make sure you repay us within the year."

"Thank you, thank you. The good Lord bless you all. I will never forget your kindness."

But of course, he had no intention of repaying us. The moment he reached London he sold the beaver for his own profit and wormed his way back into the favour of the Adventurers by undermining us with lies about our laziness and incompetence.

His behaviour was iniquitous, but the uncomfortable truth was that after four years, we were still hugely in debt to our London investors and constantly beset with complaints from them about the poor supply of furs and timber we were sending them.

"We must rebut Weston's lies," pronounced Bradford. "And we need to sort out our arrangements with our backers once and for all."

"We need to attract better people to join us here." Brewster gestured to a group who were playing cards and drinking rather than toiling in the fields. "We are being sent a weak lot; some are dishonest and the rest behave as though they are in a tavern. I would send most of them straight back if I could."

"We need more practical equipment like hoes, axes and spades, especially as most of them are broken." Standish held up a shovel held together with twine. "And our fishing tackle is useless in these conditions."

I interjected, "We need livestock too. Cattle and sheep, so we can farm like proper Englishmen."

"You are right, Edward." Brewster looked meaningfully at Bradford who nodded. "That's why we would like you to go to London and see what you can achieve."

"Work with Master Cushman," continued Bradford. "He is doing his best but we know, honest though he is, he is no match for those cunning devils."

"The *Anne* leaves in a few days," added Brewster pointedly.

Clearly I had little choice in the matter; I was the one to sort out our affairs in London.

In truth, the prospect of a change appealed to me. I rather hankered after the dash and vigour of the big city, and who would resist a break from the gruelling work of the Plantation? To be honest – and I am ashamed to confess it – I welcomed some time away from Susanna, for our arranged marriage was proving wearisome to me.

I felt she would feel the same but when I announced I had been given the task, she was unexpectedly tremulous.

"I think I might be pregnant," she whispered.

"I must stay to look after you."

"No, you must go. It is your duty."

Duty.

CHAPTER SEVEN

AN 'HONEST AND PLAIN' MAN

THE *ANNE* SAILED BACK TO LONDON IN THE autumn of '23 with me huddled for warmth between sacks of walnut and sassafras and piles of beaver and otter fur. Soon I was settled in Heneage House, an ancient jumble of timbered buildings in Aldgate with cramped rooms and dingy gardens scarcely worthy of the name.

Master Cushman was gripped by his habitual gloom, weighed down by his years in our service. He missed his boy, who he had left behind in New Plymouth, and was denied the consolation of his wife, who stayed in Leiden.

He had just returned from the funeral of Edwin Sandys, his sparring partner from the old Virginia Company.

"I know he had promised so much and delivered so little," he said. "But I think he meant well, unlike some of the so-called investors I am dealing with today. I have to tell you,

Master Edward, the Adventurers have all but broken up and without their backing, the Plantation will fall apart. They blame the confusion in the country. The King rules without parliament, which is an affront to lords and common men alike, but he has so little in his exchequer that he will have to recall his peers and that will cause further dissension. The people hate him frittering so much on George Villiers, his so-called adviser. Can you believe he has just made him the Duke of Buckingham? It's disgusting to have a sodomite – I do not spare my words – with such power."

Clearly Cushman needed cheering, so I invited him to a watering hole I used to frequent as a young print apprentice, called The Vintry. It was by a jetty on the river where the merchants of Bordeaux unloaded their wines. Over a bottle I showed him the draft of my book *Good News from New England*.

He approved of the title – "Good News, yes, direct and to the point" – and particularly enthused over my version of the Wessagusset affair.

"We need everyone to read this because Weston has been telling anyone who will listen how dishonourably we behaved in the killing of the Indian chief."

"I have made it clear that it is his behaviour that is the disgrace," I reassured him. "Here, I write: 'The settlers in Wessagusset had demeaned our faith. They had made Christ and Christianity stink in the nostrils of the poor infidels.'"

"Very powerful," he enthused. "Excellent."

"I reveal that Weston's men sold guns to the Indians and got close to their women – too close."

Cushman was delighted. "When the public read this it will help the cause no end, but first we have to convince a man by name of James Sherley. He is a wealthy goldsmith but more significantly, the Adventurers' financier. Persuade him and we persuade them all."

Sherley had small, narrowly set eyes, which glinted behind his spectacles, and his capacious chins spoke of a man given to ease. He exuded affability but as we were to find out over many years, it was a veneer. He was unrelenting in his determination to protect his interests and those of his clients.

We met in his shop on London Bridge, hard to miss under its gaudy sign *The Golden Horseshoe*, and as he poured us wine he boasted how he had two other houses and had earned his riches as adviser to London's leading merchants by searching for profit in unexpected corners.

"For example, I do a brisk trade selling ribbons, linen tape, plates and goat skins. Thimbles are popular."

We tried to appear suitably impressed.

"You might dismiss them as trifles," he continued, opening another bottle. "But try telling that to the lady of the house. She would insist they were essentials and, for me, anything that keeps the little woman happy and makes me money is worth doing. You must know some of the men on the *Mayflower* were in similar trades. William Mullins, the shoemaker from Dorking, made a steady living from selling oddments like these."

"Indeed he did," I acknowledged. "Sadly, he passed away soon after we landed, leaving his daughter Priscilla an orphan, but God in his mercy has found her a fine young man to marry."

But we were not there for pleasantries. He soon turned to what was on his mind.

"We investors have had many arguments about the best way to make New Plymouth profitable. Only last week I was convinced we would break up and end our dealings with you once and for all, but we talked, we argued in a benevolent enough way, and we are united once more to make your colony a success. Indeed, we toasted our agreement with a bottle of this Bordeaux, the best you can buy."

He took a draught of that unifying elixir. "God can turn the hearts of men when it pleases him, but I have to tell you that we are hearing complaints from the strangers, as you dub them. The ones who do not share your, er, purity of belief."

"Who are the people being so peevish about us?" I asked.

"There are many. I met a very convincing person only the other day by name of Thomas Morton, who visited you a year back. He claims that you are intolerant of those who do not share your convictions."

"Morton? I do not know him. You say he has come to the Plantation?"

"With Master Weston, I am told."

I searched my memory for a face and came up with the hazy image of the insolent young man who had drunk our beer while Weston begged for help.

Sherley went on. "Clever. A lawyer. He tells me the strangers are denied the sacraments and that family duties are being neglected on the Sabbath when, I am informed, the catechism is not taught or read."

"We cannot afford a school, nor do we have the teachers," replied Cushman.

"That is as may be, but the strangers feel differently," he riposted briskly. "Have you forgotten that there are more of them than you so-called Separatists, yet they are expected to work in the fields and fish the waters just like you? They deserve to be treated with respect." He glared at us over his spectacles. "Folk complain that there are thieves in the colony and that many are lazy and not pulling their weight."

I snapped back at such a ludicrous criticism. "If London had been free from crime, we would be free of it in the settlement."

Sherley ignored my sharpness. "Reports have it that the place is overrun with wolves, foxes and mosquitoes. The water is undrinkable, the people are starving. What kind of life is that? Why would anyone want to live in those conditions?"

"I have an answer for that too," I replied. "As you will see from my latest account – here, I have a copy for you – only people full of discontent and ill humour, and only those with their mouths full of clamours, complain of having to drink the water in our New Canaan. How could anyone be so simple to think that the fountains should stream wine and beer and the woods and rivers be lined with butchers' shops and fishmongers' stalls? If people are too delicate to put up with a few mosquito bites, they are unsuited to life in a colony like ours."

I warmed to my theme. "The book is called *Good News* for a reason; our lives are getting better by the day. Our houses are well built and the fortifications solid. The harvests are bountiful, fish and fowl are plentiful and soon we will supply enough beaver, fish and timber for your investors to make the profit they rightly yearn for."

He would not be impressed. "If you want more help from the investors, you will have to deliver more furs. It's as simple as that."

"That we shall do, Master Sherley," I retorted. "But there is more to it than fishing and furs. An issue just as important to us is the transport of the last of our brethren from Leiden. Furthermore, many of the flaws in our small society would be solved if our pastor and inspiration, John Robinson, was with us. I implore you to raise the funds to transport him and his family to join us. If they were in Plymouth we could hold the Lord's supper every Sabbath and baptisms when they are needed. All the criticisms by you and your associates, even by this Morton, would be met."

He took refuge in a bout of coughing and expressed nothing on that point, which made me suspect that he had no intention whatsoever of arranging transport for any of our people from Leiden – an impression that was confirmed in a letter from Robinson himself.

'The Adventurers have neither the money nor the inclination to help us,' he wrote. 'Only you can supply the funds but I know all too well that you do not have them. If I cannot join you in New England, maybe some other learned person will be sent. We will have to decide what is best when it happens.'

I tackled Sherley again and he made a show of cleaning his glasses before muttering into his double chins, "We may have a man in mind. He is honest and plain, not at all grand, and you can be free to use your own discretion about the role he has. He knows he has no right to any office with you, but perhaps with time and familiarity he may embrace your faith and forgo his own."

Cushman and I put this 'honest and plain' man out of mind while we busied ourselves buying supplies for our return on the *Charity*. We did not have the money for butter or sugar or any of the pleasures of life; instead, Cushman suggested that we buy useful equipment such as hooks and nets for fishing.

"You need to build up a small fleet of ketches for fishing," he advised. "For that you must have a carpenter. Think how useful a lighter and six or seven shallops would be to explore the coast in search of new trading posts."

We hired a salt maker too, but he was so unskilled that he produced hardly a grain of the stuff.

We bought bricks to build furnaces and fireplaces, nails, sheets of lead and steel, and sail cloth. We did buy some several quarts of brandy – very good for stomach ailments, claimed Master Cushman, the most temperate of men – but we had to forego the orders for shoes, stockings and shirts, and settled for the coarse cloth of Hampshire Kersey. No fancy, silk-lined doublets for us.

Our biggest purchase was of three heifers and a bull, which we pushed and chivvied along the wharf at Rotherhithe and onto the waiting ship.

"That's what we need." I took a rare pleasure in the sound of bellowing echoing from the hold. "Those beauties will change everything."

We were congratulating ourselves on our bargain when a woman with a gaggle of children stopped by.

"Goin' to New England." As much a statement as a question.

"Indeed," I replied.

She looked quizzically at Cushman.

"Name Jones mean owt to you? 'eard of the *Mayflower*?"

"Indeed I have, mistress," he replied.

"My old man was the skipper."

"What, Captain Jones?"

"The very one."

"My Lord. How is the good captain?" I asked.

"Died in '22," she replied briskly. "Got sick on that voyage of yours. Never recovered. A good husband too, as this little lot proves." She gestured at her offspring. "Seven of 'em, he left me with."

"I am sorry to hear it," I said. "And his ship?"

"Our ship," she retorted. "I 'ad a share in her but I sold 'er for scrap, got £128, eight shillings and precisely fourpence. Reckon they used the timbers to build a warehouse or, I 'eard, a smart new country mansion some place. I should've asked for more."

I bid her farewell and, to my surprise, felt a sharp twinge of regret at the loss of the skipper. The ship too. He had no great sympathy for us or our cause and we had many harsh words with him, but he is part of the story. If our names are remembered, so too will be that of Christopher Jones and the small ship that carried us across the Atlantic.

In a strange coincidence a few days later, when we paused for refreshment in a disreputable dockside tavern called *The Angel*, I heard a sailor talking about the *Speedwell*. Too flimsy to make the voyage in 1620, she was still in commission crossing the Channel with barrels of wine. Cushman and I shook our heads in rueful understanding; no doubt there was more money to be made in the wine trade than there was carrying a shipload of impoverished pilgrims.

As I was loading my trunk on board the day before we set sail, Cushman arrived to bid farewell and to introduce a shabby, hang-dog character in his mid-forties.

"Meet the Reverend John Lyford," he announced with no enthusiasm. "This is the gentleman Master Sherley, and the Adventurers have chosen to help the Plantation in its ministry. He has been working in Ireland."

I shook him by the hand. "Delighted to make your acquaintance."

The reverend was effusive. "I cannot tell you what an honour it is to enjoy the ordinances of God in purity among his people – good folk such as yourselves, stranded on a distant shore like my congregation in Ireland. My dear Master Winslow, how pleased I am to share this long voyage together. We can talk of many matters."

And we did. He spouted endlessly about his love for our movement and the pride he felt at taking on such an office. "I am the humblest person in the world," he claimed. "I cannot wait to join you and your congregation in the worship of the Lord."

His fulsomeness was tiring but my ears pricked up when he appeared to admit to sinful failings. It puzzled me at the time, but his meaning became horribly clear in the coming months.

"I can purge myself of the many corruptions that have been a burden to my conscience." His eyes glinted with a peculiar zeal. "All in the past and all misunderstandings…"

His wife had joined him on the ship, a slight, hesitant woman who kept herself to herself, though when he talked of past corruptions she gave him a glare that Medusa would have envied and his voice trailed off.

Susanna was waiting for me when I stepped off the *Charity*. In her arms a baby, my son Edward who had been born while I was away.

Once again we had done our duty. Once again the Plantation celebrated, but, as before, the boy lived for only three years, and the next child survived barely twelve months. There seemed little purpose to this marriage of mine.

We had to accept that our misfortune was down to God's judgement, just as we had to thank Him for our blessings. Josiah was born in the spring of '29 and is a credit to us.

We were by no means the only couple to ensure that there would be another generation in New Plymouth. As I write these notes, John Howland and his Lizzie have produced ten healthy children and John and Priscilla Alden have just had their seventh. I am sure they will have more; why not? They clearly care for each other.

I like to joke that they are in a competition to make sure the Plantation survives, and I am happy for them; but what still nags away at me – and I am not proud to admit as much – is that they married out of free will, while my marriage was out of obligation.

Duty does not necessarily reap as great a reward as love.

CHAPTER EIGHT

A TREASURE LOST TO GRIEF

T HERE WAS LITTLE TIME FOR SUCH introspection – or self-indulgence, as Susanna dismissed it – for within a few months we were plunged into a pandemonium of machination and deceit. I will be brief.

Bradford welcomed Lyford warmly, invited the preacher to join us on the council and, in proof of his goodwill, gave him a larger food allowance than any of us. At first, he won our approval by renouncing his former 'disorderly walking' – once again not explaining what that was – and we allowed him to teach at our Sabbath gatherings.

But despite his protestations, Master Sherley's replacement for John Robinson was not humble, not humble at all; he was a treacherous weasel. Within weeks he changed; he became argumentative and downright seditious, setting himself up as head of a faction of folk who were discontented with our church, including the egregious Billingtons, whispering and poking fun at me and Bradford – indeed, all the stalwarts of the settlement. Oddly too, he spent many hours locked away in his quarters. What was he up to? Brewster, suspicious of the preacher from the moment he arrived, took me to one side and together we wandered, oh so casually, past his quarters and peered in.

"Judging by the way his quill speeds across the parchment he is a keen letter writer," I reported to Bradford.

"Who can he be writing to?" he wondered. "What can he be writing about?"

"It can only be to London," reckoned Allerton. "And I do not suppose these missives are to sing our praises."

"He must be plotting against us." I recalled Sherley's shifty backing for the man. "I believe he is a spy sent to spread more calumnies about us."

"We must investigate," directed Bradford. "Now, the only way he can deliver his messages is by ship."

"The *Charity* will sail within days," I reminded them.

Bradford muttered something incomprehensible under his breath, but gave no clue that he was about to behave completely out of character. He waited until the ship slipped anchor and summoned me, Standish and Howland to the jetty.

"I need your help. I propose to chase after the ship, board it and find those letters."

We needed no bidding and caught up with the ship a league or two out. The skipper hauled us on board and handed over the letters. Twenty of them.

Bradford ripped them open. "They are full of slanders and false accusations which are designed to prejudice us here and lead to our ruin and utter c—c—collapse. He accuses us of being as dangerous as Jesuits in the inflexibility of our Separatist beliefs and urges London to send as many men as possible to overwhelm us and to stop more of our folk coming from Leiden. Above all, he begs that Master Robinson should be prevented from joining us."

For a second I feared Bradford would tear up the letters in his outrage, but he managed to control the impulse. "Hear what he says about our good Master Standish: 'If that captain you spoke of should come here as a general, I am sure he would be chosen, for this Standish looks a silly boy and is held in utter contempt.'"

The object of his derision turned white, then red. I was convinced he would go off on one of his furious firework displays but Brewster laid a gentle hand on his arm to restrain him

"We must take our time. Lay traps for him and when we are certain of his crimes against us – punish him."

Bradford insisted we make copies of the missives and, instead of reaching immediately for his collar, we waited to see what Lyford was up to as Brewster had suggested. Of course, the wretched man had no idea he had been rumbled and continued plotting with the same set of malcontents as before. Typical of Bradford – he made sure he had the evidence lined up so that 'these hedgehogs', as he called them, could be called to account.

At last, Lyford was summoned, the letters flung on the table before him. He turned white, he squirmed and denied he had written them, he plighted his loyalty to us, he flattered us, only for his wife, the melancholy Sarah, who had behaved with quiet dignity throughout her time with us, to find her voice.

What a tumult of rage and humiliation she unleashed.

"My husband, that man, had spawned a bastard by another before we were married. Even after we were wed, I could keep no maids but he meddled with them. I caught him in the act many, many times. He took cruel advantage of his position as a man of God and took a woman in the parish against her will." She gulped in her anguish. "Man of God? Spawn of the Devil, more like. The husband of the wronged woman and a band of his supporters hunted him down. That's why we had to leave Ireland, to flee the shame and the hurt."

She shuddered with bitter tears as she revealed how he had defiled her in the most unnatural way. I felt nothing but pity for the poor soul and Standish, still smarting at Lyford's insults, reached for his sword. I reckon he would have added the clergyman's head to the skull of Wituwamat, had not Brewster once more quietened him with a tug on the arm.

"Master Lyford, you have brought disgrace on this place," declared Bradford. "You are banished."

The wife begged, "Do not send me away with him. Please, I beseech you. I shall be befouled by the Indians, just as he defiled me and those other women."

Lyford, pathetic creature, wailed louder than his humiliated wife and begged forgiveness with such contrition that Bradford relented and granted him six months' probation – he even permitted him to preach again – but, unbelievably, we caught him sending more letters and this time he was expelled to the wilds. We made him run the gamut of our men, who gave him a good hiding with their musket butts as he scuttled through.

He was lucky to be so gently treated – "Just a bob on the bum," complained Standish, who had a more painful punishment in mind – but the wretched wife had no choice but to follow him into exile. Doubly punished for sins she did not commit.

Bradford urged me to return to London to berate Sherley for sending such a reprobate to the Plantation.

"He had been rejected by the godly in his own parish but had been deemed suitable for us in Plymouth," I seethed when

I found the financier comfortably ensconced in his rooms at *The Golden Horseshoe*. "How dare you pretend that he was an 'honest and plain' man, to use your words? He is a rapist. A beast. And, I rather think, a spy working for you Adventurers."

I have no doubt the worthy financier knew exactly the kind of man he was, for he did not look the slightest embarrassed, and when I asked yet again when Pastor Robinson would be brought to us, the goldsmith muttered that it was 'too expensive' to hire a ship and crew.

"The plague is cutting through the city like a scythe," he complained. "And that has rendered the market as stagnant as a duck pond. Trade has tailed off, which means there just isn't the money to pay for such expensive transport."

He refused, as usual, to countenance a loan, and warned that the Adventurers would send no more supplies. "Their opinion is that you are negligent, careless and wasteful." And in case we had not understood the extent of their objections, he added, "And unthrifty."

Cushman, his tic a blur of anxiety, did what he had been doing for many a year: he pleaded, he begged, and finally he persuaded them to deliver a small amount of goods.

"In return," insisted Sherley, "you send us as much fur, fish and timber as you can to pay off your debts – which, Master Winslow..." He made great show of looking at his ledger. "Which today stand at £1,400."

I gulped at that. "That is way beyond our means."

"You can do it," asserted Sherley, knocking out his pipe in complacent affirmation. "Go on, good friends, pluck up your spirits and acquit yourselves like men."

I was so depressed by my fruitless trip that I begged to be spared another. Instead we turned to Standish to be our representative, despite Bradford admitting, "Diplomacy, I confess, is Master Myles's least skill."

As we expected, he returned from his mission many months later empty-handed but bearing grievous news. He had barely put a foot on the landing stone when he blurted out, "Master Cushman is dead."

I recalled the days, the months, the years our selfless comrade had spent in futile negotiations with the Virginia Company. "He gave his life for the cause. I don't think we really appreciated how much good he did for us. He deserved better."

Bradford mused, "Think, if *Speedwell* had been seaworthy or he well enough to sail on *Mayflower*, his would have been one of the first signatures on the compact. He would have been with us every step of the way."

"He wrote a book that I was lucky enough to read when we were in London together," said Brewster. "At the time I rather considered he should have been spending more time negotiating with Weston than scribbling, as he modestly dismissed his endeavours. Indeed he was always reluctant to discuss it, humble fellow that he was. I have to say it is a work of deep religious import, which exposes the injustices of our society and shows how our faith can improve the lot of suffering people. *The Cry of a Stone*, he called it. It will be his epitaph."

"Nothing caused him more grief than not persuading the Adventurers to pay for our good Pastor to join us here," I reminded them.

Standish gave a strange, strangled sound, somewhere between a gasp for air and a sob. His mouth worked as he struggled to frame the words.

"I have more to report. Terrible, terrible news. Master Robinson. He too has gone."

Bradford stumbled and slumped onto a bench as if he had been struck with the butt of a musket.

"How?"

"He endured a week of sickness but made nothing of it, and continued to preach until he could do no more." Standish gulped. "He took to his bed with his family around him and went peacefully to his maker. He was buried in Pieterskerk, across the square from his home. He was only fifty. Too young. Too soon."

Bradford got to his feet and spoke with deep-felt sincerity. "We highly esteemed him in his l—l—life. How much more we shall esteem him now that he has gone. What a treasure we have lost to grief, how wounded are our souls." He broke off and covered his face to hide his anguish.

I recalled the short walks from the Brewster house in Stink Alley to gatherings in Green Close, past the children playing in the square, the sound of psalms from the church and the tinkling of the music teacher's piano.

Robinson would often open a window to let the sound drift in, and say, "How I envy him. Music expresses that which cannot be spoken. I wish I had that God-given talent."

Bradford recovered. "He had words, did he not? Words that inspired us in this great mission."

"It is hard to imagine that we have not seen him for five years or heard him speak," reflected Brewster tremulously. "Yet it has been his voice that has travelled the ocean, teaching, encouraging, and indeed, reprimanding us."

My mind went back to the evening when he addressed us six years before on the quay at Delftshaven as we waited to be taken away by the *Speedwell*. 'The Lord has more truth and light yet to break forth out of his holy Word. Even we Separatists, although we were precious shining lights when we first came to our beliefs, God has not yet revealed his whole will to us.'

Even then, five years later, we were still waiting to discover where His will would take us.

CHAPTER NINE

THE DEVIL HOLDS SWAY

W E HAD NEED OF ROBINSON'S WISDOM later that year. Almost as an afterthought, Standish had broken the news that King James had died and been replaced by his son Charles. James had always been hostile to our cause – 'brainsick' and 'pests' were his kinder insults – but Charles, we knew he would be a sterner foe. He had married the Frenchie trollop Henrietta-Maria, a Roman Catholic, which was bad enough, but worse, he had fallen under the influence of an ambitious bishop, one William Laud, who demanded strict following of the Book of Common Prayer, the wearing of surplices and bowing when the name of Jesus was used. Everything we stood against.

"A Papist by any other name," snapped Bradford.

Brewster quipped, "Give great praise to the Lord and little Laud to the Devil," but Bradford looked at him blankly. He never did understand jokes.

Allerton, as so often, was thinking ahead. "My guess is it will mean that hundreds, maybe thousands, will be scared of prosecution and follow our example by fleeing here to New England. The population will boom and that means there will be fierce competition for trade with the homeland. We must find new markets for our furs."

We paid slight attention to him at the time but he was proved right. And to our cost.

Within the year, Massasoit's spies brought us news that a settlement had been built in Mount Wollaston, a day's sail away to the north. The man in charge: a Thomas Morton.

"Who is he?" asked Bradford.

"He came with Weston last year." I recalled my acrimonious meeting with Sherley. "It turns out he knows our financier and is on good terms with many other notables in London."

"A fancy moustache," recalled Brewster. "He had all the slyness of a white fox."

Another colony so close was a threat to our trading monopoly, but a steady trickle of information from passing trappers and friendly natives revealed that the settlement was a menace to the moral standing of the territory. It had become a place of debauchery where drink was taken and the men lounged around playing cards while squaws brought them beer from a great barrel.

"The women sit on the knees of the white men and do nothing to stop their straying hands," one of Massasoit's men told us. "They have parties where the tribesmen beat their drums to rattles and lutes. They all dance and frisk hand in hand."

Most alarming, guns were being traded to the Indians for food and in return for them labouring in the fields doing the work they should be doing.

"The savages are mad for guns," warned Bradford. "They already have the advantage over us because they know the most secret haunts to hide in, and they are quicker and fitter. Imagine what bloodshed they could wreak if they were armed."

We became more concerned when we received letters from settlers as far away as Piscataqua and Nantasket, who were every bit as horrified at such lawlessness as we were and begged us to help rid the country of the renegades. Brewster, eager to find a peaceable solution, suggested we write in a neighbourly way to ask Morton to change his ways, but his overtures were met with a volley of abuse by the self-appointed governor.

'Mind your business and I will mind mine,' he wrote. 'You think yourselves so grand that you call your poxy council meeting a parliament. Only an illiterate multitude such as you could be so deluded to assume you have any real power, let alone over me.'

We decided to pay our unruly neighbour a visit. John Howland and John Alden, both of whom had by now become staunch members of the Plantation's inner circle, joined Standish, Allerton and myself to confront the scoundrel.

What a chaos of self-indulgence greeted us. The homes had been so badly knocked together that the timbers showed through the daub like skeletons and the thatch of the roofs hung in ragged clumps. The centre of the village was a muddy mess with open fires that smouldered feebly. The carcass of a half-eaten deer had fallen off a spit and lay charred and reeking of burnt flesh, and the allotments lay derelict with only a few heads of maize which had been left to rot.

But that was not what had us gaping in disbelief. Right in the middle of the settlement was a tree, a full eighty feet high, shaved of its branches and covered in ribbons of gaudy colours. On top, a pair of buck's horns.

A maypole, the symbol of Popery and excess, here on our shores.

Beneath it sprawled the languid figure of Morton, a mug

of brandy in one hand, a falcon perched next to him.

If he was taken aback to see us, he did not show it. Cool as you like, he took a swig.

"Welcome," he murmured. "A drink?"

"What is this?" demanded Bradford. "This stinking idol."

"This, my dear man, as you see, is a maypole. It will soon be May the First and I have decided to celebrate Merry Old England. I'm hoping a party will attract some Indian brides for my lovelorn men."

"It is unnatural," burst out Bradford.

"It is only unnatural to those who find no joy in life. That's why I call this place Merry Mount. It is an amusing play on the word Mare Mount, the mountain by the sea as I dub it – so much more mellifluous than Mount Wollaston, but, I imagine, a witticism too clever for you to grasp. Yes, Merry Mount, a name that fits the entertainment we intend to have."

I came straight to it. "We have heard you are selling guns to the Indians. You give them drink."

"It oils the wheels of commerce." Not a trace of shame. "And commerce is why I am here."

"But you must stop," cried John Howland. "Or else."

"Or else! Or else what, young man?" he jeered. "I shall trade with whomever I choose, as you do. There is plenty of beaver to go round and more otter and bear than the finest garbed ladies in London could hope to drape around their shoulders. As for the Indians, they have more humanity than many Christians and I get on better with them than some, er, others."

There was no mistaking his meaning – that we were inferior to the Indians. He raised a disdainful eyebrow, took hold of a ribbon and ostentatiously twirled himself around the maypole and began to sing, *"Lasses in beaver coats come away, ye shall be welcome to us night and day."*

Standish was so enraged that I was certain he was going to hit him, but he contained himself by striking the maypole so hard I feared he had broken his hand.

Morton laughed. "No one can stop me, least of all you hideous hypocrites."

He had faced us down, no doubt of that, but the story was not over, not by a long chalk. One glance at Bradford's face set with fury would have told him that. He summoned a council meeting as soon as we had returned home.

"As we have seen, the Devil holds sway in Mount Wollaston. Morton is turning the country into a school for atheism, with no respect for God or His teaching. We shall have to remove this p—p—pettyfogger and his sinful followers."

He strode back and forth in the meeting house, pounding his fist into the palm of his hand in anger. "They have revived the beastly practices of the mad Bacchanalians and we cannot allow the follies of the flesh to be so embraced."

Master Allerton, however, back from a scouting mission on the Penobscot River, took a more businesslike view of Morton.

"He and his crew are a bad lot, no doubt, but despite appearances, the settlement is successful." He brushed aside our indignation at the suggestion. "Morton has already made hundreds of pounds in Maine from the beaver trade, which is more than we have achieved."

"That is because they bribe them with guns and powder," I countered.

"That is as may be," retorted Allerton. "But, mark my words, his trading prowess will prove more of a threat to our future than his iniquitous goings-on."

Bradford grunted his disagreement. He was more concerned about the way Morton flouted the teachings of the Bible and the sinful example he set to the young than his prowess as a trader.

It was agreed: Morton would be driven out. We set off, Standish, me, Howland, Alden and six others, but found the place deserted, or so it seemed. The maypole still stood but its ribbons fluttered feebly.

"They must have had wind of our arrival," whispered Standish. I pointed to a tell-tale trickle of smoke that rose from Morton's quarters and he hammered at the door with his musket butt.

"Come out, you coward."

The door was flung open and a handful of men emerged, some running, some stumbling, others immediately ducking away into the cover of the forest. The few left behind were so drunk that they fired aimlessly, more out of bravado than any desire to wound, and instantly dropped their muskets when Standish sent a volley over their heads. They stood in bemused surrender but Morton was unperturbed, lolling in the doorway, cool as ever.

Standish gave a great hoot of triumph. "Master Morton, give me your carbine." He prodded the miscreant. "Hah, a fine soldier you'd make – this gun is only half filled with powder."

The captive was utterly unabashed.

"Oh, Captain Shrimp," he sneered. "What a posturing ninny you are. You're like a many-headed guard dog, the way you rush around, but without the brains to match."

Standish raised his musket to beat the man but restrained himself. Instead, he tied up his prisoner and ordered, "Watch this and lament the end of your pernicious project."

Howland took hold of a brand from a fire and hurled it into the house while Alden added to the pyre by chopping up the maypole and throwing the wood on the flames. Then, to the crackling of burning timber we set about tearing the place apart, demolishing the shelters and torching them. Within minutes, the settlement was a heap of charred debris.

I would like to report that our prisoner was bowed by the destruction but no, he was as insolent as before, with a smile of contempt that did not leave his face when we bundled him on board the shallop and took him to New Plymouth. Not a flicker of emotion crossed his face when Standish pointed to the pike where the last grisly scraps of Wituwamat clung and threatened, "You must die for your blasphemy."

"Such heroic sentiments, Captain Shrimp," sneered Morton. "You killed this luckless chief and drove away Master Weston and his followers at Wessagusset, and now you assault me and my men. So much for the Christian values preached by you malevolent moles."

"Hold your tongue," spluttered Standish.

Master Bradford hissed, "You are head of a t—t—turbulent crew. You live without common honesty, your men abuse the Indian women most filthily. You encourage d—d—drunken riot and other evils and you trade guns with the savages."

Morton stared at him quizzically.

"Ha," was all he bothered to say.

"We are sending you back to England for the safety of ourselves, our wives and our innocent children," decreed Bradford. "We shall take you as far as Piscataqua and leave you there until you are picked up by a passing vessel. We will keep your gun and your knife, but we will let you keep the clothes you stand in."

Morton shrugged. "How kind."

We watched as the shallop took him away.

"At least he is out of our lives forever," I declared.

How wrong I was.

BOOK VI

1628–1639

THE VOICE OF
JOHN HOWLAND
A PROFITABLE MEMBER

*A strong young man called John Howland, coming on deck,
was thrown into the sea; but it pleased God that he caught
hold of the top-sail halyards which hung overboard and ran
out at length; but he held his hold, though he was several
fathoms under water, till he was hauled up by the rope to the
brim of the water, and then with a boat hook helped into the
ship again and saved. And though he was something ill from
it he lived many years after and became a profitable member
both of church & commonwealth."*

William Bradford, *Of Plymouth Plantation.*

CHAPTER ONE

CRAFTY WITS

I NEVER CEASED TO WONDER AT THE QUIRKS OF fate that brought me to New Plymouth. The son of a grocer, who had travelled to London from East Anglia with no other plan than to help my brothers in the leather and cloth trade, the lucky lad who should have drowned, the luckier still to be introduced to Master Carver.

How much I owed him. When he informed me he was embarking on a voyage to the other side of the world and asked me to be his manservant, I did not hesitate. I was young, I was ambitious and I fancied the adventure. A life of ledgers and leather was not for me.

Of course, I could not foretell that when my mentor – for that is what he had become – was taken from us, followed so sadly by his wife, that he would leave his estate to me.

So, yes, fortunate indeed to be unexpectedly wealthy, but more so to be in the company of such committed and clever people as William Bradford and William Brewster, as colourful as Captain Standish and as cheery as Master Winslow, with whom I became sound friends. "Call me Edward," he insisted. "We will be sharing too many adventures to stand on ceremony."

I did not really belong to the world of the saints, as I jokingly called them, but I had to admire them for their bloody-minded tenacity in sacrificing everything they had owned and cared for to create their own Eden.

But in every Eden there is a snake, and in New Plymouth that was Master Isaac Allerton. I am not saying he was Satan incarnate, but the way he deceived his comrades was as shameful as the great betrayer in the Bible story.

Harsh words, I know.

I was wary of the man when I first met him on the quay at Southampton. He was one of the Leiden band's most eminent men and he had little time for me, a mere manservant. He had an air of certainty about his own superiority, accentuated by arched eyebrows that gave the impression he was about to ask a question, but hard grey eyes that suggested he already knew the answer.

There was something of the street about him as well. I was not the only one to be disconcerted by the way he set his cap at Brewster's daughter Fear, and my disapproval hardened after Edward had confided that the widower had flaunted his admiration for the old man's daughter in a most ungallant way.

"His lips became moist and his eyes gleamed as he listed the attributes of the maid that pleased him the most. We are men of the world, but I was mightily embarrassed by the way he savoured introducing her to the ways of Venus."

His trade was ordinary enough – he was a tailor – but he had done uncommonly well out of it and had amassed more savings than most of our company. Indeed, his wealth impressed us so much that he was elected assistant governor to Bradford for many years – with all the power and influence that came with it.

He was clever, no doubt about that. Let me give you one example: in one of the interminable debates about how the Plantation should pay off its debts to the Adventurers, he argued fiercely for a scheme in which eight of our leading lights would band together to meet all the colony's obligations and arrange the loans. I was immensely proud to be chosen as one of them.

"We will take the risks," asserted Allerton. "But we will earn the profits."

The Undertakers, we dubbed ourselves.

"Tempting fate," I joked.

He arched his eyebrows in disdain. "It will change everything. You will come to thank me."

A year or two before, in '23, he and Edward Winslow had travelled to London to negotiate a loan from the Merchant Adventurers, a loan we desperately needed if we were to afford to buy and ship the furs to sell to pay our debts, which in turn would give us the money to increase trade here – a vicious circle we did not free ourselves from for many tiresome years.

They returned months later with the good news that they had secured the rights to a trading post a few days' sail up the coast and deep inland on the Kennebec River. That pleased me no end, for it had been Edward and I who had first made landing in that wilderness and realised what a fine spot it would be for trucking with the Indians. So much so that we built a warehouse and a jetty, which was, admittedly, somewhat rickety but serviceable enough.

"James Sherley is still labouring away as the investors' financier and he is full of praise for Master Isaac," disclosed Edward. "'What a discreet fellow he is,' he insists, 'how well advised.' He has urged us to send him back to London next year."

Our negotiator smirked modestly but Brewster gave a tut of disapproval like a cork being pulled from a bottle.

"You have to admit he has an easy charm," conceded Edward once our much-praised negotiator had retired to his bed. "Unlike me, who finds the artifice of the withdrawing room a vexation, Isaac won us an introduction to Sir Ferdinando Gorges – and he is a man worth knowing, especially since he was granted control of the vast province of Maine by the King."

It was inevitable that the 'well-advised' Allerton would be chosen as our sole intermediary with the London money men and, to be fair, the arrangement was a success to start with.

"Here's proof of the Adventurers' goodwill," boasted our ambassador on his return. "You entrusted me with the task of settling our debts once and for all and that is what I have done. James Sherley has promised to loan us £1,800, and he has been persuaded by me that we will pay it off at £200 every year for the next ten years. Then we will be free of them and them of us. Isn't that what we have always wanted? A bargain, my friends, a real bargain. Furthermore, I have persuaded Master Sherley to finance the voyage of the remaining folk in Leiden to join us here."

"That is indeed a blessing," declared Bradford.

"At last, all happily together." Even Brewster enthused at that. "The Lord be praised."

Naturally, we toasted him as he deserved – or as we believed he deserved.

We should have realised sooner that our agent was playing his own game. For example, after a few missions to London I noticed that he stowed the goods in such a muddle that when they were unloaded it was hard to decide what belonged to whom – except the most expensive items, which ended up in his hands and which, we discovered, he sold at a pretty profit to other settlers.

"What about the hose, the shoes and the linen we ordered?" I asked on one occasion. "We gave you an allowance of £50 for them."

"Here." He opened a few boxes half filled with cheap stuff like Norwich gaiters, some woollen stockings, and a few bolts of shabby linen.

"Is that all?" asked Bradford. "What's in the crates?"

"I bought some good warm coats and rugs." He was all breezy confidence. "As well as shirts, some calf leather gloves and Monmouth caps. Gewgaws for the savages too."

"That is no use to us," I protested. "That is not what we asked you to spend our money on."

"What do I want with new caps?" demanded Standish. He pulled out a batch of hose. "These are lined with oiled-skin leather. We're not at court; we have no need of such luxury."

Allerton dismissed our concerns with a complacent wave of the hand. "I shall sell to others at a good price, don't you worry, and you will appreciate next year how the money will trickle down throughout the region and make you the richer for it. Remember the old adage, it does not make sense to spend a shilling on a purse and put six pennies in it."

Why did we not act when we saw that he was growing rich while we were running into deeper and deeper debt? Were we really so blind, so stupid, as not to notice how the money we owed London had shot up from £200 to £2,500 in only two years?

We were too trusting, that's the long and short of it, reluctant to accept that one of our number was cheating on us. I put it as bluntly as that – cheating. We had no option but to confront that uncomfortable truth when our Indian trading friends in the Kennebec region reported that Allerton had opened a post only twenty-five leagues to the north of our own base. Furthermore, and unforgivably, he had persuaded the Adventurers to back him.

We accused him of betrayal but, glib as always, he had a ready reply. "I do apologise for any misunderstanding and in future I promise to perform all the business according to your directions. I will mend my former errors, that I pledge."

He did nothing of the sort. With London's backing, but without telling us, he bought one ship and fitted out another, which he used to deal with other settlements which were rivals to us. One of the ships, the *White Angel*, arrived in Boston with £500 worth of enviable goods for the gentlemen of that upstart settlement, such as linen, small, well-stuffed mattresses and rugs, while all he set aside for us were bundles of Bastable rugs and two hogsheads of mead, most of which had been drunk. Outrageous.

But worse was to come, as we discovered when we received a letter from Sherley. There were four angry investors in London, he complained, who were owed £1,500 each by us.

By us! A total of £6,000. How could that be? In fact, as we ascertained after much probing, the debt had been run up by Allerton in the pursuit of his own profit, but here was Sherley expecting us to bear the burden of it. After all, the financier insisted, he was our man, doing our business. Furthermore to add insult to injury he had agreed to use the Plantation as collateral. As far as Sherley was concerned, we had no option but to pay up.

"I cannot understand why we tolerate this chicanery," I cried.

"He must be stopped dealing with the Adventurers on our behalf," decreed Bradford.

My indignation got the better of me. "He must be banished from Plymouth."

"Sadly, that cannot be." Bradford gave a shrug of regret. "I long to see the back of him but as long as he is married to Fear, we cannot upset or offend Master Brewster. He is a beloved and honoured father to us all and he would be distraught if his daughter and his new grandchild Sarah were parted from him. Fear is a sweet-natured young woman, as firm in the faith as her father, and I know she is in despair at the hostility toward her husband. She suffers it as though it is a smear on her own character."

"So, we have no choice but to tolerate him?" I was incensed.

"Sadly so," deemed Bradford. "But we must observe him closely. Him and those crafty wits in London."

Of all the crafty wits we had cause to mark, none were more of a thorn in our side than that scamp Thomas Morton.

We assumed we had seen the last of him, but no.

My wife Elizabeth was nursing our second baby when Bradford banged on the door and came crashing in without waiting for a reply, oblivious to Lizzie's undress.

"It's M—M—Morton," he gasped. "Here. With Master Allerton."

Impossible. I followed him out of the house to where a gaggle of folk had gathered around the agent and, bewilderingly, the man we had sent packing twelve months back.

Our devious go-between saluted us. "Greetings, my friends. I have returned from carrying out our business in London and, as you see, I have brought Master Morton with me."

He really did seem to relish the rare mix of amazement and anger that the villain's presence caused. "Thomas has been invaluable; he knows the key players in London and has helped me make contacts and suggest new avenues for trade. I have invited him to stay with me as my secretary."

Morton, as incongruous as ever in his foppish jerkin

and hose, gave a satirical wave. Calf leather gloves, I noticed. Probably a gift from Allerton.

"Salutations. What a pleasure to see you brave souls again." He held up a mug of beer in a mock toast. "Especially you, Master Bradford, and of course, you, Captain Shr—Standish."

The Captain reached for his sword but I held him back. Morton's blood was not worth shedding.

What sprite of malice had persuaded Allerton to ally himself with the charlatan and bring him here? He knew that the wretch was a threat to the colony; he had actually helped pull down the maypole and cheered as he was bundled onto the shallop, which had carried him away as far from us as possible. What was his game?

Most of the onlookers were insulted by Morton's presence, others were curious, but many of the more unruly youths gave a cheer. Sad to say, the shenanigans of Merry Mount were very much to their taste.

Thomas Morton and friends in conversation at the Crown Tavern, Strand, London, 1634

"*Those Separatists. Those saints,* soi disant. *What monsters of self-regard.*"

My companions nod in agreement, sound fellows that they are.

"*You should have seen their faces. What a scowling crew. They reckoned they had seen the last of me when they drove me out of Merry Mount but there I was in their very own homes, drinking their beer. I laughed, my, how I laughed! That pious streak Bradford, the old fool Brewster who talks of nothing but herbs and brewing wine. All of them, so superior. They persist in the canard that the savages are dangerous people, subtle, secret and mischievous, but you know, I was treated with greater respect by the infidels than the Christians.*"

I am sharing a drink with old friends, a clever cove by name of Ben Jonson, who has knocked out a play or two in his time and Sir Ferdinando Gorges. He and I go back a long way, as far as our childhood days in Devon. It was Ferdi who sounded the alarm when the Armada hove to in '88. A stout comrade. We trust each other and when we are in London we meet in the Crown to share a glass and discuss the matters of the day.

Ferdi leans forward and taps me on the knee: "So, my friend," he pours another glass of claret. "My dear old pal, I am a staunch royalist as you know. I hate Puritans but I hate Separatists more. I have every hope King Charles will renew my charter for Maine, where I plan a New England Council that would give me control of all the province to the north. Anything you can do to expose their wicked practices will be useful for my claims on the territory."

"Nothing will please me more than for you to prosper at the expense of those charlatans," say I.

My goal is to serve the great man as an attorney – his champion of liberty, no less – and with his power behind me, I plan to return to New England and build another settlement. I too want to see a humbling of those elephants of wit.

"I heard how shamefully they treated our good friend Thomas Weston," says Ferdi.

"Indeed. When I went to the Plantation with him back in '22, I found them to be suspicious and churlish. Later, after the bloodbath at Wessagusset, when Weston, perplexed by it all, went to find out why they had done such a terrible thing, they were all sweetness, congratulated him on his safe arrival, entertained him and fed him. Such liars. They blamed the savages for the destruction of the settlement, then they threw him to the wolves.

"Not content with destroying his livelihood, they set upon me like monstrous overgrown bears. Why? Because I held parties for our men who were lonely and homesick. Why should they not have a taste of merry old England, drink a yard of ale and disport themselves around the maypole?

"They sent an Indian to spy on me – as if I didn't spot him lurking about – and I utterly baffled him by declaiming my favourite pagan odes to Venus and her lusty children, Cupid, Hymen and Priapus."

"*Priapus, eh.*" *Ben snorted into his glass.*

"*They hate to see folk enjoying themselves and, as you can imagine, they worked themselves into a lather about my lads taking squaws for their comfort. Beautiful specimens by the way. The brethren conveniently ignore the fact that two of their number, Bradford and Standish, sent to England for brides as if they were a delivery of cattle.*"

"*Damnable hypocrites.*" *Ferdi thumped the table, spilling his claret.*

"*Did I not make merry sport with these — what do you call 'em? — Separatists in* The Alchemist?" *Ben pours another glass but spills some. He is not well, a stroke perhaps, and the claret dribbles down his chin.* "*Gross, shallow money grubbers, I called them.*"

"*You did, Ben, what a play. How right you were.*"

"*Go on, Thomas, continue.*" *Ferdi is impatient for more bad news from New England, not drunken nostalgia from Ben.*

"*Tell the Privy Council how they vilify His Majesty's church.*" *I fanned the flames.* "*Did you know they wink when they pray because they think themselves so perfect that they can find the highway to heaven blindfold?*"

"*Such arrogance,*" *splutters Ben.*

"*Let me tell you more: they sneer at the wedding ring, claiming it is a diabolical circle for the Devil to dance in. Believe it or not, one of their number, by name of Edward Winslow, conducted a marriage ceremony. Is he a man of the cloth? Has he been ordained by the King's true Church? He has not.*"

"*That is shocking indeed,*" *declares Ferdinando.* "*I shall inform my friend the Archbishop about this blasphemy.*"

He finishes his venison and spoons up a bowl of creamy frumenty.

"*How is the book of yours shaping?*" *he asks.*

"It will shake a few ears, I can assure you. I am calling it New English Canaan, a modest irony on my part, because these people have turned this promised land into a land of poverty and ill will, rather than a land awash with milk and honey."

"Excellent," enthuses Ferdi. "With your help and finely chosen words, we can denigrate these schismatics in the eyes of those who matter so that no one will invest in them. We will build new colonies that are fair, tolerant and kind to the natives. And we will become rich with our trading."

"Exactly," I concur. "Those benighted brethren are princes of limbo when it comes to trucking. You will have no difficulty supplanting them."

Ferdi ponders. "We need, as it were, an ally close to New Plymouth. Someone who knows their ways and can tip us the wink about their plans."

"They have only one man who understands where to find a bargain and make a profit. Isaac Allerton is his name."

"I remember him," says Ferdinando. "A shrewd speculator, I deemed. We met at James Sherley's shop last summer. We should encourage him to join us in our schemes."

"He would welcome that," I reply. "He and I already have one or two irons in the fire."

"A toast," cries Ferdi. "To irons in the fire."

"A salute to the New England Council and its great leader, Sir Ferdinando Gorges," I riposte.

We clink glasses.

"A song, my friends. I have a little ditty that I wrote when I was inspired by the muse. My men in Merry Mount enjoyed it no end.

Drink and be merry merry merry boys
Let all your delight be in Hymen's joys

Lo to Hymen now the day is come;
About the merry Maypole take a room.

"Huzzah and huzzah again." Ben claps me on the shoulder.
"Mine host, another bottle of claret for these good friends of
mine."

CHAPTER TWO

BROUGHT INTO THE BRIARS

LLERTON BOASTED THAT A CARGO OF BREAD, peas and cloth was cutting through the waves toward us but his blithe optimism was immediately contradicted by Master Sherley, who wrote that we faced another debt crisis caused by the cost of the two ships our agent had acquired.

'We have spent a fortune on them,' complained the harassed financier. 'If they had cost us only £400 or even £500 we would not be too concerned, but these ventures have cost double – nay, treble – for some of our investors.'

"This is nothing to do with us," I protested. "Allerton is entirely responsible for their purchase and fitting out."

"And we have had no benefit from their trading," added Bradford.

William Brewster was to the point. "He has got away with fair words for too long. We must put him on the spot."

We gathered in the meeting house. Master Bradford and Brewster sat by the table to the front, our so-called agent to one side with the council on benches, while Morton, still brazenly defying us, lounged at the back.

A shaft of sun filtered through a window onto a sheaf of documents filled with figures in front of Bradford.

He began. "It is bad enough that you, Master Allerton, mock us by bringing back this p—p—pettifogger." He pointed at Morton. "But you have gone too far with deals that do not b—b—benefit us."

Morton taunted Bradford's stammer, which often gripped him at moments of stress. "P—p—pathetic p—p—poseurs, you should be p—p—put out of your p—p—pain."

Bradford clenched his jaw. He would not be drawn. "This is your signature, is it not?" He held up a page of accounts on which we could see the cheat's elaborate handwriting. "These accounts are so long and intricate I cannot understand them, let alone examine and correct them, without a great deal of time and help, but what I do know is that our debts have risen since we made you our agent in London."

"You understand so little," scoffed the emissary. "How dare you doubt my motives?"

Bradford was not deterred. "To your shame, Master Sherley tells us you yourself have amassed debts so great that we owe some investors £1,500 each. £1,500! How have you wasted so much money? Where has it all gone?"

"I think we know the answer." I spoke up before he could interrupt again. "I was trained to read a ledger as well as the best merchant and you, sir, have charged for goods that you never saw and we never received."

He sat unmoved as we rolled out a litany of his trickery, only the arching of his eyebrows revealing his contempt for us.

I had to restrain myself. "You have lied to us about the interest rates. £30, you claimed we would have to pay, sealed with a clap of the hands you promised us, but by the time it reached us the charge had risen to £50."

Bradford weighed in. "You have screwed up your father-in-law's account to more than £200 because he assumed, after all his kindness to you, that these were p—p—presents to him and the children."

"Ha." Brewster could not contain his bitterness. "And you charged me interest too."

"Have you no sh—sh—shame?" demanded Bradford. "As if that was not heinous enough you have screwed us up as well, because you knew that we would never let our honourable elder be left with such a debt."

Allerton spoke for the first time, his voice dripping with sarcasm. "Maybe, Master Bradford, you fail to understand the accounts because you do not have a mastery of figures. I should remind the assembly that you are the least talented when it comes to financial matters. I seem to recall you lost all your money in Leiden?"

Bradford stared blankly at the mass of conflicting entries before him, his jaw clenching and unclenching.

Allerton came in for the kill. "It was a correction bestowed by God for certain decays of internal piety' was it not?"

His sneering disdain drew a gasp from those who knew the story and a murmur of puzzlement from those who did not. From the back of the meeting house, a yelp of laughter from Morton. Only later, when Brewster explained that Bradford had frittered away his inheritance in mysterious circumstances, did I understand how savage his tormentor had been. It also made me think a little differently about Bradford too. Decays of piety? Our rigorously correct Governor? That was not the upright figure I knew.

Bradford cleared his throat but he choked on his words, instead Master Brewster pushed himself unsteadily to his feet with his stick, reached across to the papers and spoke quietly but insistently.

"I have read enough of these figures – rather, I say, these fraudulent concoctions – to know you have wasted our money and resources, but what hurts above all is the disloyalty you have shown your old comrades. From the beginning, from the days spent in Green Close planning this brave venture with Pastor Robinson, we have striven together to create a world of freedom – and of trust. You, Master Allerton, are the kind of person who would cheat a lowly maid over a few guilders and you have duped us in the same way."

He paused, saw we were perplexed at this cryptic reference to an event we knew nothing about, and finished his damning judgement. "As the Book of Timothy states, 'For the love of money is the root of all evil. Those who covet it stray from the faith. They are pierced with many sorrows.' You cannot curb your greed. You do not belong here with us."

For once, the charlatan lost his assurance and stared around the meeting house for support, but only Morton gave him an encouraging nod.

"I would have brought yet more riches to these shores if you had listened to me," he blustered. "But, no, you are mired in debt and will stay so unless you take on other projects the way I have. In fact," he recovered his composure and added without a glimmer of embarrassment, "you owe me £300 for my latest delivery."

He picked up the accounts where they had fallen to the floor and arranged them carefully. "As for not belonging, I am going nowhere. As you acknowledge, Master Brewster, I have been on this crusade from the days in Leiden when we first dreamed of a New Canaan. My wife and infant son died here; our three children and my new family, Fear, Sarah and my son Isaac, are content here; I pay my taxes – £3 and eleven shillings last year – which is more than most of you. I have every right to stay in my home and every right to trade as I think fit. You cannot stop me."

A kerfuffle at the end of the hall had heads turning. It was Fear, the door crashing behind her as she stumbled out, face red with mortification, her children bawling as they fled.

Poor woman. She had to live with a husband who had become a pariah in the community. We wanted him to go but we knew that if she went with him, as duty dictated, her father could not endure such a loss. Either way, father and daughter would suffer.

The target of our outrage affected a blithe indifference. He stayed in his house on Town Street, tended his acres and took himself off on trading missions. How awkward it was to come across him and Fear together when the best we could manage were mumbled greetings and embarrassed pleasantries. For a young wife of only twenty-eight, she never smiled, she rarely spoke; instead, when anyone drew close, she hid from the humiliation her husband had brought down on her by scuttling away into their house.

He did leave once and for all in the spring of '35. Not out of shame, but because Fear died on December 12, 1634. He bundled his unhappy children into a shallop alongside his belongings and departed without a farewell. There was no longer anyone or anything to keep him.

CHAPTER THREE

GRIEF AND LOSS

WILLIAM BREWSTER WAS IN HIS SEVENTIES when Fear died. He never faltered in his conviction that his greatest responsibility was to the community and to future generations, and it was to that end he sacrificed his daughter to a marriage he knew repelled her. It brought him low but no lower than he was already. He had lost his zest for life some seven years before when he buried his wife Mary. The cough that afflicted her every winter became pneumonia. Thirty-five years they had been married. She was his soulmate.

His woes did not end with Fear's passing. He was anxious about his son Jonathan who had taken to alchemy and astrology, which the old man abhorred as godless, and further, he was hurt when the orphan Richard More, who he had looked after from the moment the *Mayflower* sailed, deserted him to work for Allerton, of all cursed people.

"I remember the night Fear was born," Bradford recalled

as we lingered on Burial Hill. "In the manor," he explained to us who did not know. "In Scrooby. Mistress Mary made so much noise I thought there had been a murder."

The older man smiled bleakly. It was an odd remark, but I understood that Bradford was reaching, in his clumsy way, to express a time when the bonds that brought them to this place were forged.

"Ah yes," Brewster murmured. "A time of fear. That's why we gave her that name, but we defied the dark shadows then and have done so ever since. For Mary and me, her birth was a symbol of that survival. Now, her death speaks of uncertainty and betrayal." He summoned up some of the old spark. "The only difference is that we are not being woken up in the night by the bishop's constables but betrayed by one man whose infamy has brought us into the briars."

If I am honest, we were embarrassed by our gullibility over the nefarious agent. Like the serpent in Eden, he was too clever for us.

Edward sailed to London to untangle what we hoped would be the last strands of Allerton's deceit, only to discover that Sherley himself was every bit as indignant at the way the agent had also cheated him and the Adventurers.

"How his opinion has changed since my last visit." Edward was amused. "Last year Sherley was full of praise for Allerton. 'Indefatigable', he called him, 'a person of uncommon activity, address and enterprise'. Now our good financier admits that the man has run a course to the 'great wrong and detriment of the Plantation.'"

"He fooled us all," lamented Bradford. "He was able to fold everything up in obscurity and keep it in the clouds."

"We can only guess at the extent of the deception he has hidden in those clouds," said Edward. "Sherley informed me that he made so much money on one venture that he was able to invest £400 in a brewery in Bristol."

"A brewery!"

"£400! Shameless."

"Worse, he has been working with Sir Ferdinando Gorges to set up trading ventures and stirred up prejudice against us from him and his cronies. A bad man to have as an enemy, the noble knight."

He took a letter from his trunk.

"It is from Sherley. Nothing but bad news, I'm afraid."

Bradford tore it open and read in stony anger.

"It appears Master Allerton has produced three books of accounts. His debts to us and to London come to…" He breathed deeply and blinked. "He owes £7,103, seven shillings and one penny."

Not for the first time, the man's deceit shocked us into horrified but helpless silence.

Once he had recovered his composure, Bradford continued. "Sherley admits he cannot make head nor tail of the figures because Allerton has deliberately made them as complicated as possible."

I could not help quipping, "Makes me wonder, if the accounts are really so knotty, how our financier manages to be precise down to the last one penny."

Bradford frowned. "He suggests we find what errors we can and charge Allerton for all the furs he has had from us." He brought the letter into the light to read more easily. "He writes that if we had allowed him to go on in this risky and expensive way one year more, we should not have been able to meet his expenses. He says that both he and the investors would have lain in the ditch and sunk under the burden."

What a mess – and one that was to get worse. Later that same year another letter came from Sherley, outlining what our erstwhile agent had spent. We were reconciled to more bad news but were aghast to discover how much of that huge debt we in the Plantation were accountable for. The total came to £4,770, nineteen shillings and two pence.

"But four years ago, we owed the Adventurers only £400." I grabbed the document from Bradford. "These include goods that have been double charged and I am sure many shipments from us have been ignored."

Bradford recovered sufficiently to insist, "We must go through every single ledger, letter and bill of lading we have sent and received from the very first day. Let us find out once and for all what the finances are; how much we owe – and are owed."

Bradford and I spent many days and nights examining figures going back almost ten years and lists of every deal we could find. My fingers were black with ink and my head whirring as we made an inventory of everything of value we owned, right down to the beads we had acquired, the knives, hatchets and cloth we had bought. We put a price on our boats and livestock – even the trading posts.

At last, I was able to announce, "By our calculations, in the past five years we have delivered more than 12,530 pounds in weight of beaver, and thousands more of black fox, mink and other skins."

"That must be worth at least £10,000," reckoned Edward. "That means that far from being debtors, we should be in profit."

Bradford arranged the ledgers in front of him. "I may not be a man with a head for figures," he began wryly, "but by my calculations, our debts were £5,770 in 1631 and the payments we have received to date amount to a mere £2,000." He checked the calendar to ensure the sums were correct. "As of this September, 1636, I declare that our obligations have been met. More, as Master Winslow suggests, we are the ones who are owed money. We shall pay no more. I will write to Master Sherley to inform him that we are fully acquitted, we are discharged of all actions and accounts, we are free of claims and demands. All of them without exception."

I couldn't help feeling that the financier, who had been the inexorable arbiter of our profit and loss for so long, would be as relieved as us that the years of wrangling were over — and I was right, thank the Lord. He acknowledged the grief and trouble that the 'mad Master Allerton has brought upon you and us' and the debt was signed off.

He stood down as financier for the Adventurers in 1636 and wrote to say how pleased he was that we had settled our affairs in 'peace and love'.

Of course, the quarrelling continued for years with one investor here claiming £500 and another creditor there insisting he was owed £400, but for us it meant we were free of constant demands on our funds and spared the never-ending carping about our skills as traders.

Brewster produced a bottle of herbal wine made from a blend of grape and sassafras, the women boiled chickens stuffed with parsley and flavoured with a juice of butter, salt and crab apples, and we allowed ourselves a drop of brandy. To much guffawing, Edward did an impersonation of Sherley, which he promised was true to life, by mumbling into his chins about the end of this 'long, tiresome and tedious business that was uncomfortable and unprofitable for all'.

That it was.

CHAPTER FOUR

A RECKONING

W E DID NOT SPEND ALL OUR DAYS AND nights fretting over Master Allerton and his tricks – far from it. We found time to farm, sell furs and raise our families.

But we were rocked by a deed that put the cheat right out of our minds – for a while at least – and one so terrible that it had an effect on me that took years to shake off. Maybe it was the same for all of us, for without doubt, New Plymouth was never the same again.

I was in Ducksburrow with John Alden, taking a break from picking the first of the pumpkin, when we heard a shot echoing from the woods that lined Jones River, followed by another. I assumed it was the lads shooting duck on the mud flats and did not give it another thought.

Minutes later, Standish and two of his men erupted from the undergrowth. At musket point stumbled John Billington.

"He's killed John Newcomen," cried Standish. "Murdering swine."

"Lies, damn lies," spluttered Billington. "He shot at me first."

"Shut your gob." Standish gave him a kick.

"Leave me be, you shiteabeds." The arrested man swung at him but tripped and fell.

Standish booted him again. "You'll hang for this."

Billington jeered. "You don't have the right, you turdy gut louts, you." But Standish jabbed him along with his musket to the meeting house, where he was locked away.

Edward said, "I heard them arguing this morning."

"They have been fighting over a strip of land for months." Standish polished his musket with considerable energy. "Billington says it is his, Master Newcomen claimed it for himself. The knave accuses Newcomen of shooting first and he returned fire not to hit him, he swears, but just to frighten him."

Luckless Newcomen, a perfectly decent companion, though we did tease him for his name. "So you're a newcomer, are you?" A weak joke but he took it in good spirit.

"Who do you think you are to set yourselves up in judgment?" yapped the villain when he came before us. "You, Winslow, false, impudent fool who married the first wench you could lay your hands on. Bradford, the wife killer. And you, old man Brewster, just a mealy-mouthed hypocrite. As for you, grocer's boy, you had no shame stepping into the wealthy shoes of a dead man."

We did not rise to his insults, though I was sorely tempted.

"You won't dare kill me," he blustered. "I'm too useful working the land. Look how well my crops grow. Who can shear sheep as well as me? No one."

We ignored him.

"He must be executed," ordered Bradford, his mind instantly made up. No shadow of doubt.

"We should be certain we know what happened," I cautioned, earning a glance of displeasure.

I was reassured when Brewster, too, struck a note of warning. "Remember, a man is innocent until proved guilty and bear in mind that though we may have the power to judge him, do we have the right?"

"Who will challenge us?" demanded Bradford.

"We have any number of enemies in London and here in New England who would be delighted to make us appear to be the transgressors," answered Brewster. "They could see this as an opportunity to disgrace us and land us on a charge of murder ourselves."

"I suggest we visit John Winthrop, the new Governor of Boston," said Edward. "He has only been in the colony for a few months, but he owes us a favour for the way we sent our men laden with medicines and food to help them fight the same plague that afflicted us. More important, perhaps, he has the backing of many men of influence in London, which gives him an authority we do not enjoy. I am sure we do have the moral right to despatch this villain, but his support would raise us above any legal quibbles. We should seek his backing."

I volunteered to go with Edward for I was curious to see what kind of man Winthrop was. A staunch Puritan, by all accounts, and a man of substance, he had seen the way the wind was blowing with the young King Charles, who had begun to persecute those who followed other faiths – above all, the Puritans. Winthrop had assembled a fleet of eleven ships and transported 700 frightened souls to the shores around Boston. Obviously a man of drive and determination.

I was impressed by him. A tall, slightly stooped figure in his forties, he was courteous, listened intently, and pronounced without further ado, "This man has committed a sin that cannot be forgiven. He must die, and the land be purged from the blood he has spilt."

That was what we wanted to hear.

We brought Billington before our grand jury and ignored his squawking obscenities. It was unanimous; the killing had been no accident. It was murder.

"Guilty," pronounced Bradford. "You will be hung tomorrow."

Then the killer became contrite, then he begged. Too late.

Soon after dawn he was dragged in chains to the gallows, which Alden had hastily hammered together. The entire settlement gathered in a silence that was broken only by his wife, who wept in ugly choking gulps.

As our Governor, it was Bradford's role to sign away the life of the doomed man. He reached for his quill.

Billington was on his knees. "Spare me. Spare me. Good Master Bradford. I will mend my ways."

Bradford paused.

He gave the slightest shake of the head as if coming out of a reverie, dipped the quill in the ink, and intoned, "You are guilty of wilful murder, by plain and notorious evidence."

I could hear the scratch of the quill on parchment as he signed.

Standish forced the felon at musket point to stand on a bench so that he could put the noose around his neck and, despite a caterwaul of pleas and curses from the condemned man, he kicked the bench away. A sharp gasp as his breath was choked out of him, the creak of wrenched muscle. Billington fought for many long minutes before giving one last ghastly rattle, and swung slowly around at the end of the noose. His head jerked up only to slump back toward his chest. It seemed he was glaring down at us in bitter rebuke.

"Praise be to God," intoned Bradford. The wife begged to have the body but the Governor stared past her without expression. Only Edward's wife Susanna reached out to her and gave her hand a squeeze in a gesture of rare sympathy.

The Governor limped off down to the shore and gazed out to sea. Maybe he was regretting his action. No, not Master Bradford. Ten years in his company and I knew regret was not a word in his dictionary. Doubt? Never.

I was surprised how sombre I felt after the hanging. When I first met Master Carver he had talked of building a society of quiet nobility but that vision had been diminished by the lazy drones and charlatans who had settled in our midst and was now besmirched by a murderer. We had suffered many jolts of cold reality in our years in New Plymouth, but this was the first time we had killed, not in the heat of the moment like the slaughter of the savage Wituwamat, but as a deliberate deed using all the trappings of the law.

Brewster shared my disquiet.

"We should try to understand that Billington was angry and frustrated by his travails here and that might explain why he was always so difficult," he reflected. "Do not forget his younger boy, John, died three years ago. I think he had reached a breaking point, like many of the strangers who have struggled as he did."

"If I am honest, I never understood why he joined the endeavour in the first place," I said. "I was fortunate to be invited by Master Carver, but Billington, what friends did he have who shuffled him into our company? He made little attempt to support our great undertaking; indeed, as you will remember, he tried to undermine it when we signed our covenant on the *Mayflower*."

Brewster, being the sound Christian he was, mused, "We cannot condone murder, of course not, but bear in mind that Billington and his like can never enjoy the peace of mind that we 'saints' – as he enjoyed mocking us – are lucky to enjoy, knowing that the Lord's hand is on our shoulder."

Perhaps His hand had reached out to me as well, for Lizzie and I had been married for six years by then and had sealed our love with the birth of our first daughter back in 1625. We named her Desire after the trusty servant and companion who had gone back to England. Four more children had followed in quick succession. No wonder, given the ardent way we embraced the lists of love.

I have to confess that Lizzie had caught my eye on the voyage. How could she not? A pretty little thing, though at thirteen too young for marriage, she was the first to my side after I had been rescued from drowning, and in the following days insisted on tending to the bloody weals seared into my back and arms by the ship's keel. I told myself it meant nothing, that she was merely doing her duty as a well brought up Christian girl, and stifled any improper feelings.

As I got to know her, I discovered she was no submissive doll – if I'd hinted as much, my courting would have fallen at the first hurdle – but she was pretty, no doubt of that, with a blaze of red hair and disconcerting eyes, one a lighter shade of green than the other, which to a simple country boy like me made her thrillingly exotic.

She was a more steadfast Christian than I ever was, finding inspiration from her Bible to stay strong in the first desperate winter when she lost her mother and father, brother and sister-in-law, every single person who was dear to her. It would have been unbearable for most but she stayed resolute. Instead of surrendering to grief she joined in the building of the colony and despite her slight frame, lugged the timbers, hammered and nailed with gusto and, rather than rest as she deserved, joined in the tilling of the stony earth.

"I do it for Mother and Father," she said. "Their sacrifice must not be wasted."

I did, however, often find her alone on Burial Hill, weeping by the graves of her lost family.

We were wed at about the time that my good friend John Alden married Priscilla Mullins. She too had been orphaned and John had been assiduous in comforting her and courting her – though not without hoydenish vacillation. The bashful chap was convinced that Standish, widowed in '21 but as self-assured as ever, was finding time from his military duties to woo the maid.

"Don't hesitate," I exhorted John. "Make your feelings clear. Captain Standish must be forty if he is a day, and no woman could fall for his bad temper and red hair."

"And he is short," laughed John, cheering up no end.

CHAPTER FIVE

KILLING ON THE KENNEBEC

S OME OF THE HAPPIEST TIMES I SPENT WERE UP
country in the station on the Kennebec River with
the men who had become my closest friends, Edward
Winslow and John Alden.

I had been given the task of running the trading post,
something I did for seven years to my immense pride and,
dare I say, with great success. We bivouacked in a timber
dwelling a good twenty feet square, which we had built onto
the warehouse, all surrounded by palisades to keep out the
wolves and bears. Though it was solid enough, the gales of
winter whistled through and as the snow melted in April, the
river water rose and flooded us out.

We had to roll up our sleeves, not just to catch our own
food and chop endless piles of firewood, but to gather the
beaver brought to us by the natives. We had to strip the fur
from the creature, a messy business that involved cutting off
the feet and tail, and when ready, pile high the shallop and

transport the haul back to Plymouth. It was tough, but I rather considered that while John hankered to return home to his family, Edward found our weeks away from the Plantation a welcome escape.

I could see his spirits rise every time we left the ocean behind and sailed past the sandy cliffs of the estuary and along the wide, placid waters of the river. The land on either bank was rich with maize and corn, vines and herbs, but above all, the country was teeming with the otter, wild cat, raccoon and beaver.

We traded with the Abenaki, a peaceable tribe whose lands stretched along Kennebec and far to the north. We rubbed along nicely. We would often beach our canoes by one of their riverside clearings, exchange gifts, eat oysters by the score and learn their ways. We tried to educate them too in the ways of the Lord. Though both Edward and I were friends to the Indian, and indeed admired much about them, they had to understand that we English were the superior race.

In exchange for their advice we gave them jars of cider. I don't think they liked the taste much, but judging by the singing and dancing that went on after a few mugs, they enjoyed the after-effect.

Our friendship with the Abenaki was so strong that Kennebec became one of our most profitable trading posts. Every year as the snow disappeared, the Indians came in their canoes laden with so much fur that our tiny jetty creaked under the weight. On one trip alone we exchanged a boatload of corn for 700 beaver, and after another memorable haul, we sent no less than twenty hogsheads of furs to England.

"And that," I crowed as we celebrated the deal, "works out at 140 beaver skins to a hogshead, and as each hogshead sells at twenty shillings, that's a mighty profitable winter's work."

"This would have been a better place for the Plantation." Edward and I were casting off the jetty to catch shad for our meal. "Richer soil, deeper rivers, more beaver." He frowned. "Still, nothing we can do about it now."

He had lost the ruddy-cheeked enthusiasm that had impressed me when we first met on the wharf in Southampton. He had been worn down by the tribulations of the Allerton affair and the fruitless negotiations in London but more, I felt, he had not fully recovered from the death of Elizabeth or found consolation in his hasty but necessary coupling with Susanna.

I never forgot the couple's set expressions when they wed, the most reluctant of 'I dos', the politest of kisses. Two strangers united for the good of us all in a rare sacrifice.

Susanna too had changed. Her independent spirit and lively looks had set her apart from the other women and I have to admit that we young men were drawn to her – though not, of course, in any inappropriate way.

I had been reminded of her generosity of heart when she comforted the Billington wife – a sharp-tongued hussy at the best of times – by squeezing her hand as her husband breathed his last, but that had been a rare flash of the old Susanna. For the most part, she went about her business with her eyes dulled and her mouth turned down in permanent disappointment.

Edward brooded. "We did agree to spend a life together so we cannot complain if happiness is too much to attain. I cannot shake Elizabeth from my memories, and I know Susanna has not let her husband, the first husband, slip from her mind. She visits his grave on Burial Hill every week."

Not for the first time, I reflected on the way the rituals of love and courtship had been debased by the pressures of our strange existence. How could any real affection, let alone lasting love, be nurtured by a handful of broken-hearted widows and lonely single men?

But the Plantation had to have children if it was to survive; that's why Edward had to wed, that's why Captain Standish had sent to England for the delightful Barbara and that need is what moved William Bradford to write to Alice Southworth.

Old man Brewster reckoned they had been sweet on each other many years before, but I detected little warmth from Bradford to his wife. I know it is presumptuous of me to judge another, but Alice, like tragic Dorothy, was a lost soul. I could see it in her eyes, beseeching if not affection, at least recognition from her man. Still, I may be wrong – after seven years of marriage they had produced three children. Their line was assured.

Edward could be forgiven for being envious of Lizzie and me. No doubt I would have been settled enough with some lass from Fenstanton had I not come adventuring, but meeting Lizzie in such unlikely circumstances was a happy serendipity.

She often came to live with me in the trading post, where the only the sounds were the gurgle of the water, the high-pitched squeals of bald eagles patrolling the sky and the grunting of bears crashing through the forest. We trapped rabbit and raccoon, which we roasted on an open fire, and had enough treats like biscuits, prunes and pickled fish to last through the winter – not to mention casks of cider and beer to keep up our spirits.

It was snug and we were so joyful in each other's company that Lizzie gave birth to three more children while we were in that oasis.

It seemed only right that I marked our time by naming my bark after her: the *Elizabeth Tilley*.

Our idyll was horribly shattered in April '34, just after we had returned to Plymouth with the latest consignment. No sooner were our backs turned than a gang of outlaws led by one John Hocking slunk into our territory from Piscataqua, a new settlement some leagues south. First, they did deals with the Indians by under-cutting our prices, but as they grew more confident they lay in wait for our boats as they came down river, boarded them, beat our men and stole our furs. Shamelessly, they sold the stolen goods to the highest bidder in Boston.

"These men are trespassers." Bradford flushed with indignation. "We have seen what damage renegades like Weston and Morton can wreak and if we have learnt one lesson from those two, it is that Hocking, whoever he is, must be snuffed out immediately. If he thinks he can steal what is rightfully ours, he is much mistaken."

Four boatloads of men pushed off from Plymouth with me, Edward, John Alden and a cheery servant boy called Moses, who insisted on coming for the 'adventure'. No sooner had we moored alongside the jetty than a raw-boned individual, ingrained with the dirt of the forest, stepped out of the shadows. He had a gun over one shoulder, a beaver fur on the other. A knife flashed on his belt. With him, a boy and two men carrying guns.

He pointed his gun at us. "Can I 'elp?"

"Master Hocking?" I asked.

"Captain 'Ocking to you. What d'you want?"

"This is our land. You must leave."

"And not come back." John Alden thumped the butt of his musket on the jetty.

"And 'ow do you intend to make me do that?" retorted the thief. "Cos I ain't shifting."

He walked along the jetty, as relaxed as a man strolling to the tavern, and jumped into the bark, the one I had named after Lizzie.

"See that pile of fur." He pointed to a stack of beaver and otter by the palisade gate. "This little boat of mine will be carrying as much of that as I can squeeze on board. It'll make a nice pot of cash for me and nowt you can do about it. You wasters can go hang."

"If anyone is going to hang it will be you," I shouted with a confidence I did not feel. "I give you one more chance."

He spat contemptuously into the muddy water but did not shift.

"I am warning you," I cried.

He gobbed again. "Flouting milksops. You can't outlick me."

But as he jeered, the current caught the boat and swung it bobbing and bouncing out into the river.

I yelled to Moses, "Quick! Get down the jetty and cut the rope. The current will sweep him away."

Three of my men dashed along the rickety timbers and hacked away at the ropes. They sliced through one – but too slow. Hocking pulled himself back toward the landing on the remaining cable.

"Now I'll teach yer." He raised his gun and before any of us could move a muscle, he fired. I ducked but the shot spattered the palisade and sent a splinter into my cheek.

As he reloaded, I yelled, "Shoot me, not them! They are only obeying my orders."

I must have been mad; I had no desire to be killed but I hoped I would confuse him with such a crazy notion.

By now he had reached the jetty. He grabbed Moses and rammed his pistol hard against the young man's head. His eyes were popping, he gibbered with terror. Hocking fired. Red blood, the white slivers of his skull and the ghastly grey and black of his brains were scattered on the jetty.

The lad toppled into the river, leaving a crimson ribbon on the water as he drifted off downstream. It had been his first and last adventure.

For a second we stood in appalled silence. A silence shattered by another shot.

A bullet smashed through the swine's head and he crumpled in a heap into the boat, his head lolling over the side. Blood trickled down over the word *Elizabeth*. His confederates ran like rats into the forest.

I cried, "Who shot him?"

Alden, grey with horror, choked, "I did not see."

"Nor me. Or me." There was a chorus of denial. No one had seen the trigger being pulled and if they had, no one was going to tell.

I had no choice. Wiping the blood from my cheek, I ordered, "We must say it was an accident. A gun discharged by chance. Above all, we must not incriminate one of our own."

Alden, usually so cheery and devil-may-care, spat, "The bastard asked for it."

CHAPTER SIX

THE CITY ON A HILL

I ASSUMED THE MATTER CLOSED. A MAN HAD BEEN killed on our lands but he was a thief and a murderer and he had been trespassing. It was rough justice, but justice nonetheless.

Governor Winthrop had other ideas. A few months later, Alden, who had been making his regular delivery of cattle to Boston market, was arrested.

"I have no option," insisted the Governor when Bradford, Standish and I sailed to confront him. "It was an outrageous assault committed on Massachusetts Bay territory. We must have law and order if the colony is to survive. The same goes for you in New Plymouth – even a backwater like yours – surely you can see that."

Bradford bit his tongue. A more assiduous keeper of the law it was impossible to find. Often, I considered, he was a tad too zealous.

The Governor insisted that Alden stand trial and to the

386

foot-stamping fury of Standish, he bound the Captain over as surety.

Still Bradford refused to be drawn into a show of anger. "The truth is that Hocking was trespassing on our territory and we have a patent to prove it. You and the Massachusetts Bay Company have no jurisdiction over Kennebec. Free our men immediately."

Winthrop was every bit as immoveable. "A shot was fired, a man was killed. Someone must know the truth. Someone is guilty."

He glowered at me. For a second, he contemplated arresting me too, I was sure of that.

"It was self-defence." I glared back. "The wretch had already murdered one of our number, just a boy, and was ready to shoot down the rest of us. For heaven's sake, the man was a villain."

The Governor shrugged. "Some assume your guilt." He raised an eyebrow sarcastically. "I pray you will find the testimony to prove your innocence."

By which, he meant quite the opposite; he had decided that Alden had committed the felony and would hang for murder.

"Master Bradford, I do, of course, respect you and the men of your community, but I have to say, on this occasion you are too convinced of your own rightness. Forgive me, but I worry about your judgment. I was appalled when I was told about the killing of the Indian chief Wituwamat and the cruel treatment meted out to the settlers in Wessagusset. Master Morton was another who was ill used by you."

I had not seen Bradford so exercised since the day he first saw that blackguard and the maypole, but once again he managed to control his temper. "They were evil men who threatened the very existence of the Plantation. We did what was right."

Winthrop shook his head in mock sympathy, as if anyone could be so mistaken.

If he had been less arrogant, he would have known the trial would end in farce – as it did. The arguments dragged on, legal documents were studied, patents and rights of ownership were called as evidence, but all they amounted to were angry accusations from Winthrop's lawyers, who had not a shred of evidence, and equally forceful denials from us. It was our word against... well, against nobody's, because we were the only witnesses to what really happened and even to this day, I do not know who fired the fatal shot. I never asked Alden, trusted friends though we were.

At last, the council ruled, albeit with much reluctant umming and ahhing, that Bradford was right – New Plymouth did have the full rights for exploration and trading in Kennebec. Winthrop had no choice but to accept that Hocking was trespassing and his death warranted.

He mustered as much grace as he could. "I pray we can be reconciled after this unhappy dispute for we will soon face greater trials from our enemies. We should not be cutting one another's throats for beaver. We should stand together."

Bradford accepted the judgement 'with love and humility', though as we sailed home, with John Alden safely on board and Standish cooling his indignation with a barrel of beer, he showed neither of those emotions; rather, he glowered with resentment.

"Remember how we helped them when they first landed here and they were stricken with plague just as we had been. We sent them our physicians and medicine and we prayed for their souls. Now we are rewarded with contempt."

That was the moment we understood that Boston had the upper hand in New England.

"Cast your mind back to 1630," said Edward. "Remember how astonished we were to hear Winthrop had sailed the Atlantic with 700 folk. How many of us were there in New Plymouth that same year? A mere 300. Thousands more have followed. It is Boston and the Massachusetts Bay Company that are attracting the brave and the bold, while the Plantation has become home to a pathetic lot who do little other than complain about the mosquitoes. At least, that is how they parody us in London. Now here we are in 1635 with 20,000 folk living in Boston while only 2,000 survive in New Plymouth."

Edward seemed determined to depress me with his catalogue of facts, but it was hard not to admire the way the city had sprung up alongside the rivers which flowed into Massachusetts Bay. It boasted rows of sturdy wood-frame homes covered with weatherboard and topped with steeply pitched roofs – quite a contrast to the Plantation which was just a group of rundown houses – little more than shelters. As for our farms, none could match Winthrop's grand estate on the banks of the Mystic River – something he never tired of reminding us about.

"Their streets are bustling," I had to agree. "Ships jostle for anchorage, laden to the gunwales with furs. Yes, Boston is prospering and at our expense."

Bradford added enviously, "Have you heard that they have built a college named after a benefactor, one John Harvard, a clergyman who trains priests to maintain standards of godliness among the heathen?"

The heat went out of our quarrel with Winthrop in time and we became regular visitors to Boston – well, we had to rub along with him, not least because so much of our business was with the city.

"You must see our printing press." Winthrop rarely missed an opportunity to crow about his achievements. "Allow me

VOICES OF THE MAYFLOWER

to present you with a translation of the Psalms that we have recently published."

Edward breathed in the smell of ink, stroked the texture of the parchment, and reminisced about the treatises he and William Brewster had published in Leiden which attacked the Church and, indeed, the King.

"The old firebrand." For once Winthrop was sincere in his praise. "I remembered his pamphlets well, and the writings of John Robinson too. Fine men. I may well disagree with their particular brand of belief, but I recognise men of principle."

"Our two settlements do have much in common," I asserted. "Governor Bradford has never faltered in his vision for a society based on a bond of love."

"Maybe you will still achieve that lofty goal," he murmured doubtfully.

I had been fascinated observing the way the two governors circled around each other. They were about the same age and both had made a pact with God to create a holy community in this wilderness, but while Bradford was the orphan son of an insignificant landowner, Winthrop was a scion of the gentry with a fine estate in Suffolk. It was obvious from the way he failed to disguise his scorn that he considered our Governor beneath his condescension.

"I do find him to be somewhat tight of vision," he declared indiscreetly. That I considered a discourtesy, but Winthrop was indifferent to what I might feel. "Some who come here may be rich, some poor, some powerful, others mean and subservient, but we need all sorts to create a sound community and for that we must bear each other's burdens like a company of Christ, bound together by love."

"We in Plymouth have always respected those qualities," I asserted.

He shook his head dismissively. "I do not think you can lift your eyes above the parapets of your palisades. Your Governor is so inward-looking that he has persuaded you the world owes you a living. It does not. For years it was Plymouth who rode the Bay horse, but now we have taken the reins."

I wanted to protest at his arrogance but he was in full flow.

"I believe that the God of Israel is among us here. Men shall say of succeeding plantations: May the Lord make it like that of New England. We shall be as a city upon a hill. The eyes of the world are upon us, so if we deal falsely with our God in this work and cause Him to withdraw His present help from us, we shall be made a byword for failure throughout the world. It is up to us to convert the heathens to our ways and our faith and if we cannot…" He paused. "Then we must drive them out."

"You mean the Indians?" I was taken aback. "We have lived in harmony with the Wampanoag from the day we landed here."

He ignored me. "Never forget who purified Canaan by exterminating the Canaanites. God understands the need to destroy evil by any means. By evil, I mean the savage."

"They are fine people who scorn all base dealings," I remonstrated.

He pursed his lips in disagreement and peered at me as if to say, *what can I possibly learn from a former manservant?*

"Surely you Plymouth brethren, of all people, understand that these savage people are quite content to get rich trading with us but cannot accept that we are growing in number and wealth? They rule over many lands without title and move their dwellings just as they please and where they fancy. How can you deny that we Christians should also be free to go where we will? God has given his people twofold rights to the Earth, the natural right that the savage enjoys, and a civil right. It is that second right that takes precedence. It entitles us to carve out new territory and build enclosures around our land. It permits us to seize whatever we need for our crops and cattle."

I was horrified at this ruthless disavowal of all we had tried to achieve with Massasoit and he must have realised he had upset me, for he softened his tone.

"Like you, I was a friend to the Indian. In my early days here, when we were hunting, I got lost and had to spend the night in a wetu. Only in the morning did I realise I was sharing the shelter with a squaw." He smirked in embarrassment. A rare moment of levity.

"But those easy days have gone. The Indian is a common enemy and cannot be allowed to stand in our way. We have God on our side and with Him, ten of us will be able to resist a thousand of our foes.

"We are saints for Christ and the enemy is the Indian."

CHAPTER SEVEN

A FINE BLACK COW

I LOST MY ENTHUSIASM FOR GOOD DEEDS AND public works after the Hocking affair. I had done my share; I had been elected assistant governor three times and worked hard to increase the beaver trade. As one of the younger, fitter men, I had been enlisted to help Standish train our soldiers, marching them up and down Town Street in an attempt to bring some order to their ragged columns.

To my great pride I had been chosen to be a freeman, though only after I had passed a rigorous test about my religious beliefs and moral standards. Clearly, I had come up to scratch for now I, John Howland, grocer's son and one-time servant, had the right to vote on matters of importance along with the likes of Bradford and Brewster, those most saintly of saints.

But it meant little. I could not rid myself of the image of the wretched Moses, his brains scattered on the waters of the Kennebec, and Hocking cackling like a mad man until he too was blasted into bloody oblivion.

The attempt by Winthrop to lay the blame at our door still rankled, as did his hostility to Bradford. I know our Governor was difficult, obdurate, often blinkered, but he was, above all, a man of principle.

To redress the balance, Edward sailed to London to explain why we were in the right over the Hocking business.

He returned almost one year later, simmering with anger and frustration at the way he had been treated.

"My feet had scarcely touched land when I was summoned by Archbishop Laud and Sir Ferdinando Gorges. They had been feasting on unfounded gossip and rumour fed to them by, guess who? Thomas Morton, no less. It transpires he is a friend of Gorges. They called him to their chambers to testify against us and what a banquet of revenge he enjoyed.

"He sneered at us, he poured scorn on our 'abominable religious practices' and our hypocrisy. He accused me of holding marriage services, which was quite true and nothing to be ashamed of, but Laud pounded the table, jumped to his feet and shouted that it was the work of the Devil. I rather think he enjoyed himself," he added wryly. "He had me jailed in the Fleet. Six months of stinking bedlam. The moment they let me out I was on the first ship home I could find."

His treatment confirmed me in my determination to settle for a life of ease and quiet. I was in my thirties, and Lizzie and I now had six children all under fifteen (we had two in quick succession in '35). What more could I want?

"Another child." She put my hand on her belly.

"How did that happen?" I was delighted.

At that time, in the mid-1630s, some of us had been looking beyond the Plantation's palisades to build new homes. Though we could have had no inkling at the time, the change had been inevitable from the day more than ten years before when Edward had sailed in with three heifers and a bull. In those days we had enough grazing ground for them, but very soon the sight of cattle being unloaded from ships and driven through the shallows to the shore had become commonplace, and the fields had become so crowded it became impossible to manage them properly.

After a cow had trampled over my allotment for the umpteenth time, I proposed to the council that we divided up the livestock between groups of about twelve or thirteen so that the animals could be kept under control.

Lizzie and I were well satisfied sharing a fine black cow and two heifers, as well as two noisy goats, with John and Priscilla Alden, though Edward boasted that he had been given the best of the red cows.

The arrangement worked well, so well that within a year or so we needed fresh fields for the livestock to graze.

"We should clear the salt marshes to the north," I suggested. "The meadows beyond Jones River will be perfect for the cattle and the soil is ideal for corn and peas. We can keep our pigs and goats on the uplands."

As we opened up new terrain, something else became obvious – New Plymouth itself was too small for us. More than that, the Plantation had become gripped with a sense of decay, a feeling that it could go no further physically or spiritually. We had no room to breathe. Our vitality was being sucked out of us. Too many of our citizens spent the days trudging aimlessly along the dusty streets to fields that delivered just enough to live on. Roofs had not been repaired, fences had fallen over and the meeting house had become so dilapidated it was more use to the chickens than people.

And something else. By then we had big families which could not be squeezed into our tiny dwellings. It was obvious: We had to move out and build new homes on the fertile acres we had cleared.

Bradford resisted the move. "It will be the ruin of New England if we desert the place that has been our home from the beginning." He was at his most inflexible. "It will destroy the church here and will provoke the Lord's displeasure."

Brewster, usually so placatory, riposted, "I have to dissent, William. I do understand your desire to keep the community together, but we have no choice. We have to expand. These days we cannot rely on the vagaries of London businessmen for commerce; we have to make the most of our living from farming and trading with Boston and the new settlements."

The Governor was outvoted and, to his dismay, we went ahead and divided the land between us. As a freeman I was one of the elite made up of the original settlers who, as we well deserved, had the first and best choices when it came to land. I picked up a few acres here and a stretch of meadow there until eventually I had eighty acres along the Jones River and down its banks to a pleasant patch by the creek where it spilled into the sea.

My labours redoubled. No more the life of ease and quiet I had promised myself. The land had to be cleared of rocks, the crops sowed and the cattle enclosed with stout fencing. There were trees to chop down, timber to saw, walls to build and thatch to gather for a roof. Soon our family were nicely settled in a fine, solid dwelling. Rocky Nook, we dubbed it. It felt like a home.

Across the meadows in Ducksburrow, Brewster built a modest place for himself and his two younger sons Love and Wrestling, while John Alden used his skills as a cooper to build one of the biggest of the houses in the neighbourhood – more than ten feet wide by thirty-eight long. He was very proud of the spruce cladding he had hammered on to the walls, which, he deemed, gave the place an air of refinement in that wild setting. Edward, always competitive, moved further afield to Green's Harbour, where he built a mansion — that's the only word for such a grand edifice — with at least half a dozen windows at the front and more to the sides and back. He was particularly proud of his tall chimney.

"No more smoke filling the rooms," he boasted. "And look at my apple trees — you did not believe I could sail them across the bay the way I did and replant them. What a crop. I am naming my new home Careswell, after the village I grew up in near Droitwich. Fanciful of me, I know, but sometimes when the salt air wafts in it reminds me of the brine flats that surrounded my old village."

Imagine my surprise when Bradford himself embraced life as a landowner. First, he bought a nice garden and three acres for the price of four goats, and the next thing I knew I was helping him lay a road that led from the bay to his farm, all 300 acres of it.

The Indian chief, Massasoit, was enthusiastic about the changes. "Let me prove my love," he begged, unloading cranberries fresh from his swamps for our delectation. "I have lands that have been neglected since the great plague. If the price is right, I will sell some to you."

An opportunity not to be missed. The egregious Stephen Hopkins bought an estate south of New Plymouth, and Bradford paid a handsome £16 and nine shillings for land on the curve of the Cape that we called Sandwich. The chief sold terrain to Standish at Mattacheese — we considered Yarmouth a more suitable name — for six coats, half a dozen pairs of small breeches, ten hoes and ten hatchets.

"Here," cried our Captain with typical impulsiveness. "Take these two brass kettles as well. And this one of iron. This is a bargain for all of us, my dear chief."

Standish was well into his sixties and though he still took command of the militia, he spent much of his time complaining about his kidney stones and, I rather think, he was just as content marshalling his book collection, which was almost as impressive as Brewster's. One volume always lay open: *Military Discipline or The Young Artillery Man* by one Captain William Barriffe.

"It tells me all I need to know about handling musket and pike and the exactest way to fight the enemy," he reckoned.

"Without him having to reach for helmet and armour," murmured Lizzie.

He was never far from one of his furious outbursts, however. Never more than the day he caught Morton – yes, Thomas Morton – trespassing on his land.

"Shooting my duck, damn the man," he spluttered. "He is one of the errantest rogues that ever trod on our shores."

Bradford snapped, "We cannot have that lord of misrule here. Get rid of him."

In truth, Morton cut a woebegone figure. The swagger had gone. We later heard many of his Indian allies had died from war or disease and that his benefactor Ferdinando Gorges had disowned him, but as he waited for the shallop to take him from our shores he roused himself for one last sally.

"You think you are saints. But you are little more than a gang of sly knaves."

We heard later that he fell out with Governor Winthrop and was sent home to kick his heels in Exeter jail. We shed no tears for him.

CHAPTER EIGHT

STREAMS OF BLOOD

I WAS CUTTING UP A WHALE, ONE OF THE MANY that were washed up on the shore near my home, when Bradford hailed me. He had been walking fast and his limp was more pronounced than usual.

"The P—P—Pequots." He struggled to catch his breath. "Winthrop has slaughtered them. Hundreds cut down and killed."

Winthrop had been warning us about plots by the Mohawks and the Narragansetts against the settlers for months, but the greatest danger, he insisted, came from the Pequot tribe who lived along the Connecticut River many miles south.

But what was that to do with us? We had our treaty with the Wampanoags and Massasoit was as staunch an ally as ever. Why should we become mixed up in any violence?

We still refused to take action when we heard the Pequots had scalped a settler and murdered eight others who were trapping on the river, but Winthrop did not hesitate and ordered the killing of savages in retaliation. A futile move, I reckoned, and so it proved. The Indians hit back with bloody raids on trading posts. Settlers were tortured, their hands severed and bodies dismembered. In turn, the Governor stepped up his attacks. A bad, bad business.

He needed our support but instead of a calm, well-reasoned request, he deeply offended us by his threatening tone.

He wrote, 'We would harbour ill thoughts against you if you do not join us in the fight. We would take it as a sign of bad will.'

"What weaselly words." Brewster was affronted. "'Harbour ill thoughts'. Pah."

The letter continued, 'It is not something that we would expect among neighbours and brethren.'

"He has a cheek," I exclaimed. "This bloodshed is as much Winthrop's fault as the Indians'. He has fanned the flames to spark their hatred. Who knows where it might end?"

"Agreed," chimed in Edward. "This does not concern us. The Pequots have not killed any of our people."

But fear is like a virus. We could not help but be infected with the hysteria as it rose across the settlements. Two men fishing were dragged from their boat and murdered with ingenious barbarity, not just stabbed a score of times but their hands and feet cut off; another pair were horribly mutilated and mangled before their bodies were split in two from head to toe and the parts hung up by the river's bank as a gruesome warning to other trespassers.

"'They flayed their captives, cut them in pieces and roasted them alive," reported Standish with unnecessary relish after another attack. "They slashed their victims' flesh with knives and filled the wounds with burning embers."

Now, when we drove cattle to Boston, we peered constantly over our shoulders and kept our muskets ready. Was that an Indian with a bow outlined against the snow or just the black skeleton of a tree? When we went hunting in the forest, were we being stalked by an enemy with a tomahawk or was it a shadow cast by the yellowing light of dusk?

Should we join Boston's campaign? Some argued yes; others a vehement no.

Brewster made one of his rare interventions. "Despite my reservations about Boston's warlike plans, I do believe we should help with men and arms for the sound reason that these are dangerous times. We assume we have the love of the Wampanoag, but that love is easily broken by the baseness of men. Remember, it is much safer to be feared than loved."

I was taken aback by his militant attitude. I had always taken him to be a man of peace.

"I suggest that you, Master Edward, make one of your trips to the Bay – take Master John with you – to discuss what can be done. Remember also these words from Master Machiavelli." He held up a copy of a book called *The Prince*. "'We are like the lion who cannot protect himself from traps and the fox that cannot defend himself from wolves. One must therefore be a fox to recognise traps and a lion to frighten wolves.'"

Winthrop came straight to it. He sat us down in his chambers and pronounced, "We are being tested. All of us. And that includes Plymouth. I have asked for your support because I know that you will need us to save you one day."

"We are secure, thanks to our treaty with the Wampanoag," I declared.

He was dismissive of our old ally. "They have little power compared with the Pequot. They have 4,000 warriors, some of the most ferocious fighters in the colony; if they attack, they will overrun you and Massasoit will not be able to save you. My friends, we cannot live in constant dread. I have listened to you many times claiming how full of moral virtue the savage is – but tell me, what is humane about the slaughter of innocent trappers? Make no mistake, they are trying to drive us out of our country.

"Only the other day, the savages in Mohegan territory complained when our cattle ate their grass and claimed our hogs spoiled their clam banks. *Their* grass! *Their* clams! The land belongs to us now. Surely you understand we are a more advanced people." He leant toward me, holding my gaze. "As I have told you before, our rights supersede those of the Indian."

His attitude made me uncomfortable and I was about to argue that we should respect them and their traditions, not to mention their rights, when to my consternation, Edward stood and banged the table.

"I have made many godly and precious friends in Boston and I am grateful, good sir, for your constant and long-continued love. I have listened to what you have to say and I undertake here and now that we will come to your aid. We will send thirty men to fight and another forty to man the boats."

I held my tongue. When did this change of heart take place?

He continued, "We are short of armour and weapons and would be grateful if you could supply us with what we need. We are willing to pay."

We pay! For his war! Edward was my friend, but this was craven. I knew that he had been spending more time in Boston as a go-between for our two colonies and, like us all, knew the importance of maintaining good terms for trade, but this proved just how much had clearly fallen under the influence of Winthrop. Needless to say, the Governor congratulated Edward for his 'good, sound sense.'

"This is a holy war." He clapped his hand on the Bible. "This is between God and Satan."

I waited until we were on the way home before I challenged my friend. "Now we are neither fox nor lion, Master Edward. Rather, the wolf has caught us in his trap. Do you really want to go to war to advance Boston's cause?"

He was a tad disconcerted by my directness. "We must stand together to create a godly nation across all New England. That, surely, should be the aim of all the settlements, including New Plymouth."

"But what about us?" I replied. "You yourself insisted it was not our fight. Don't you think that after all our years living peacefully side by side with Massasoit any new alliance threatens to create a country where trust and friendships are abandoned and, worst of all, bloodshed replaces negotiation?"

"I find it hard to be sure who is really a friend and who hate us." He was upset by my hostility. "Now, increasingly, I feel fear, and fear is easily turned to hate."

"But this is so out of character," I said.

He frowned. "I have been a defender of our treaty for all my time here. I love the chief, you know that. But my feelings have changed so much since I have got to know Governor Winthrop. I have been thinking of Pastor Robinson; remember his words? 'The Lord has more truth and light yet to break forth out of his holy Word.' Now I wonder if we will ever find that truth under the leadership of Master Bradford. He and Brewster are still wedded to the vision they had when I met them in Leiden – a vision they had shared for many years before."

I must have appeared shocked, for indeed I was, but Edward was in full spate.

"Who talks of Separatism now? When Robinson so tragically died, so too did the cause. I can say this to you because I know I can trust you. Master Bradford, noble Christian though he is, clings to the certainty of his beliefs even when they are doubtful to others. He is disturbed by contradiction; he cannot tolerate fresh argument.

"Now we must find a new truth. Governor Winthrop is a visionary who talks of love and comradeship, care and goodwill, just as we used to, but has the drive to make it happen. He believes that God has withdrawn his support from all the early English settlements – including, I'm afraid, the Plantation. This is about building a society that is bigger and bolder than anything we have managed to achieve and for that, we must come together and defy our enemies. The Indians are not part of God's plan."

We waded across a river that had burst its banks and did not talk for a while, but as the smoke from the farms came into view he continued, "I confess I do not feel the same passion for my life here as I did fifteen or sixteen years ago. I am out of sorts with many of the folk in Plymouth, some of whom have been spreading impudent reports about me, to my no small grief. I can only think they envy me my estate and my wealth, but God knows, I have worked for it. And there is Susanna…"

I let that go.

When we returned with the news of the agreement, Standish called us together. He was in his element, even if his armour was a tad tarnished and fitted rather tightly around his sturdy torso.

"Put out the order for every man and woman to keep their arms at the ready in case of a night attack," he commanded. "We must have warning signals. One shot will mean that a neighbouring township is being attacked, two that the Indians are attacking us here. Make sure you bring your arms to church on the Sabbath. Stay dressed when you go to bed. We cannot be too careful."

Lizzie was uncharacteristically fretful. "This is more frightening than our first winter." She pulled the children close. "Remember how the forests were alive with the cries of Indians and we never knew whether we would live to see the next day."

It was at the very moment that Captain Standish was readying our men for battle that Master Bradford came rushing up with the news of the victory.

"A bloody, merciless business it has been too." He was positively exultant. "To see them frying in the flames and the streams of blood dousing the blaze must have been horrible. Imagine the stink of death. The scent of it."

It made me uneasy to hear him jubilate like that. What a creature of contradictions he was. I had come to admire his leadership, the way he single-mindedly followed the scriptures and the rigid discipline he imposed on us all to make his vision a reality, but I had been unnerved by his ruthless reaction to anyone or anything that threatened the cause. His cause.

Brewster once recounted a story about him when they were fleeing England.

"He would have killed a constable had I not pulled an oar from his hands," he recalled. "He was only seventeen, usually shy and tongue-tied, but that day, he stood over the wretch ready to strike, screaming words of vengeance from the Bible. He was a man possessed."

I could well imagine. As news of the battle reached us, I witnessed the same unnerving glint in his eyes that he had displayed when Standish had brought back the head of the savage Wituwamat.

"Boston sent three vessels with more than 150 men to the Connecticut River," reported one returning soldier. "The first attack was repulsed by the Pequot but we hurled firebrands into the wigwams, which burst into flames and forced the enemy to flee straight into a barrage of lead. The ones who survived were cut down by swords and tomahawks.

"In one hour, more than 400 Pequots were killed but only three of us English were slain."

"Bravely done," enthused Standish.

"I say more savages perished," vouchsafed another. "More like 700."

Bradford gave an awkward tug at his collar. Perhaps the streams of blood had run too deep for his conscience to bear. But no. "The victory seems a sweet sacrifice," he proclaimed. "That false people have been destroyed forever."

How I hated his triumphalism. "I hear that not just men, but women and boys were rounded up after the battle and sent as slaves to the West Indies," I ventured. "Our kin in Boston are enthusiastic about this new trade and I am horrified to hear Master Winthrop himself has kept one for his own service. I say it is cruel to sell God's people as if they are chattels."

Brewster had been just as dispirited by the excess of the slaughter as I was. "How wrong for the victor to behave with such heartlessness. I have heard that the women and maidens were divided out among the soldiers like trophies."

"That is the case," I broke in. "One captain who desired a little squaw was granted his wish and a lieutenant lusted after another because she was tall and had three marks on her stomach. He boasted how exciting he found the embellishment. Forgive me for telling you of this, but it shows how war can degrade even those with right on their side."

Bradford shut his ears to such painful gossip.

"Sometimes the scriptures decree that women and children must perish with their parents and I believe there has been sufficient light from God for the way we have carried out our proceedings. Praise be to the Lord."

"Amen," I said. "But remember, not all the savages are our enemies."

"Do not be so trusting, John," broke in Edward. "If we do not snuff out their challenge to our authority, we will regret it."

"That is a far cry from them being discreet and courteous, as you once described them," I retorted.

"I know, I know." He was impatient with me for challenging him again. "Remember, it is the most stupid who stick tenaciously to their opinions, whatever the change in circumstance or evidence. It is God's will that we have prevailed.

"I believe that too many of the Indians behave as if they are the instruments of Satan sent to test us saints in our resolve."

Chapter Nine

Blessings

I confess the war had oppressed me. Of course, I would have taken up arms if I had been ordered to – but reluctantly. I was not a man of violence. I had none of Captain Standish's enthusiasm for battle – no, all I wanted to do was work the land and make my family happy.

It was a miracle to me that our rag bag of ribbon makers, reluctant weavers, small-time farmers and a retired postmaster – not to mention me, who had spent a year or two in the leather trade – had tamed the wilderness in which we had found ourselves almost twenty years before.

Who could have foretold that we would become so comfortably well off? And though I resented it because it cemented Winthrop's ascendancy over us, much of that comfort was thanks to our trade with Boston.

To my surprise and, I confess, my amusement, Master Bradford, the ascetic renouncer of wealth, the stickler who had condemned the move away from the Plantation as 'the ruin of the place, had almost come to enjoy the cut and thrust of market day. I say almost; Master Bradford was not given to levity.

"I was paid £20 for a cow and £3 for a goat," he disclosed with undeniable pleasure.

I encouraged him. "The prices are higher than they have been for years. I got £8 for a cow and £10 for a calf. I was lucky," I added, in case he thought I was trying to prove my cleverness at negotiation.

For me, the increase in business with our wealthy neighbours meant I had to work harder than imagined possible. So much for ease and quiet. I was in the fields from dawn to dusk, planting, harvesting, fattening up the livestock. Often John Alden and I would take our cattle to Boston – he, poor man, had to endure the black looks of Governor Winthrop – and hard-going it was too: dust and biting insects in the summer, rivers that burst their banks in spring, and in winter, drifts that hid treacherous ravines.

It was worth it. I earned enough to buy another six acres along the creek as well as forty acres by the bay and an island in Green's Harbour. What a spot that was to shoot duck.

But, as Bradford constantly reminded me, the hand of God was always there to remind us that our blessings were in his gift.

In the spring of '33, just as the earth was warming up after another long, hard winter, we were attacked by locusts. Locusts! I believed they were mythical creatures from the Bible, and there was indeed something terrifyingly apocalyptic about the creatures that appeared from holes in the ground making an unearthly yowling sound. So great was the cloud of insects that we could only look on helplessly as the creatures stripped the land of grass, the trees of their leaves and devoured every ripening cob of corn. The desolation they left behind was total; a year's labour wiped out in minutes.

But there was more. Who knows what horrible alchemy the creatures spawned, but in the heat of the following summer fever attacked the Plantation, killing twenty unfortunate folk, bringing back distressing memories of our first winter, and the fearsome pox spread, taking away scores of Massasoit's men as it swept through the territory claiming hundreds of lives.

"How horrible it is," lamented the chief when he came begging for medicine. "The pox breaks and runs and the skin of the afflicted sticks to the mats they lie on and is torn off when they move. Our people are dying like rotten sheep."

God had yet another test of our resolve, as if we had not been tested enough. We had recovered from the plague of locusts, the fields were once again full of burgeoning corn and the cattle fat, when an earthquake rampaged down the coast and hit us with the force of a hammer striking an anvil. At first we assumed it nothing more than a summer storm heading our way with great flashes of lightning and roars of thunder, but the ground shook beneath our feet and a rumbling erupted from the bowels of the earth. Lizzie and I clutched each other and the children as the house shook and plates, cups and saucepans were sent flying from the shelves.

The quake lasted only half an hour but it left a trail of shattered trees and flattened crops. The sea rose twenty feet and flooded our fields. Bradford had been at a meeting with folk who hoped to move away from the Plantation and judged that the turmoil was the Lord's way of showing his displeasure at such a plan. But, of course, he would.

But we were a resolute lot – hadn't we proved that over the years? We cleared the wreckage of the trees, shored up our defences against the sea, and rebuilt the sheds and roofs that had been torn down. We replanted our fields and made the best of things. So much so that after a profitable trading deal with a tribe of Indians up country, we raised enough money to build a prison – a building which Bradford was adamant would serve as a threat to those tempted by sin and a punishment for those who succumbed. After all, he insisted, were not our sufferings a signal of God's displeasure at our licentious ways?

The prison was kept busy. Francis Billington, the son of the murderer, was fined for smoking in the street and, a habitual offender, he spent many hours in the stocks for drinking, gaming and uncivil revelling.

Stephen Hopkins had to pay £2 for letting his servants drink in his house and play shovel board and, worse, was fined £7 for assaulting one of them. I could never work him out. He had served as assistant governor, a role heavy with responsibility, yet he often behaved like a common lout.

No doubt following his master's example, the servant Edward Doty cheated on the price of a flitch of bacon and was fined an extra fifty shillings for dubbing someone a rogue.

Many a drunken fool ended up with their hands and ankles held tight for a night and a day, while in Ducksburrow, the landlord of the township's first tavern was lucky only to lose his licence when he was found to be of an 'ardent temperament'.

"Fancy letting a man with a taste for drink run an inn," quipped Lizzie.

No failing or sin went unpunished but often I felt the restraints were too fierce. One summer's day the folk from Ducksburrow held a fair, a gentle gathering with an accordion and dancing, sweets for the children, a jug or two of beer and oysters for all. Some of the youngsters played a noisy game of hurling a ball to goal. It was harmless merrymaking, but all Bradford could see were the obscene cavortings of Morton and his drunken louts around the maypole and he was stirred to such a flurry of retribution that he confiscated the ball and ordered the stalls to be removed. In his anger, he broke one boy's kite.

I told Bradford that perhaps he had been too strict, too intolerant of folk enjoying themselves in innocent sport, but he would not have it.

"If anything, we should clamp down more fiercely," he insisted. "So much of our moral fabric is threatened by sin. I hear more and more examples of fornication, that most reprehensible of crimes. It must be stamped out with a whipping and a spell in the stocks. The husband should be thrashed in front of the wife – it will pain him and shame her."

The guilty could not hide their transgressions. Those who took to their beds before the marriage vows had been uttered had their sin revealed when a child was born within the natural nine months. Some mothers gave birth as much as two months before they were due but most reprehensible of all, some infants were delivered on the Sabbath itself, which, to Bradford, was proof that the parents had been shaking their sheets on that holy day.

There were scandalous examples. One wife was convicted of uncleanness with an Indian – an unimaginable trespass – and sentenced to be tied to a cart and whipped through the Plantation's streets wearing a badge with the letters AD – for adultery – inscribed on it.

"If she takes off the badge, I shall have the letters branded onto her forehead," declared Bradford.

He was convinced that his regime was restoring the stern morality of the scriptures to the community but he was rendered speechless when William Brewster's maid Elizabeth was caught with one of his servants. The old man had the young sinner soundly whipped and sent to jail to cool his illicit ardour.

Perhaps we spent too much time worrying about punishing the sinful and not enough energy teaching the young how honest endeavour and true friendship – and indeed true love

— can create a society in which the brief flicker of forbidden pleasure is readily rejected.

And, to be prosaic, Bradford's obsession with these delinquents deflected us from making enough effort to seek out new markets for our goods. To our cost.

Of course, none of us assumed the good times would last forever, but we were completely unprepared for a collapse in prices. It wasn't caused by earthquake, war or famine, but by King Charles, miles away in his palace in London. The monarch was bankrupt, Parliament was in constant turmoil and he was beset on all sides by good folk like us who hated his popish leanings. He could not allow a powerful force of 'heretics' to grow in a part of the world he could not control.

So in 1636 or thereabouts, with a snap of the fingers he closed English ports to any brethren who planned to settle in the colony and with that snap, he stymied the runaway prosperity of Boston. As the numbers of newcomers fell, so too did the amount of trade we carried out with our wealthy rival in Massachusetts Bay, and that spelt an end to our hefty profits.

"A cow that I sold for £20 a month ago now only fetches £5," I grumbled.

"I had to beg Governor Winthrop for a fair deal." Even Edward was finding it tough. "I had five cows that I valued at £18 but he would only pay £15. 'If that is too high,' I argued, 'especially at this, the most hard and dead time, truly I marvel at it.' He would not shift one jot."

Bradford had been listening glumly. "There is too much competition from the settlements that have sprung up in the remotest corners of the continent like Salem, Roxbury and Dorchester. We are surrounded by alien faces who are taking what should be ours by right."

CHAPTER TEN

OLD AND FORSAKEN

WE AWOKE ONE MORNING TO FIND ourselves in darkness. The sun had disappeared behind the moon, leaving us in an eerie twilight that had Lizzie, me and the children clinging together in trepidation. We were intrigued too; like the locusts and the quake, this strange event was beyond the control of us mortals, a mystery that only God could explain.

Bradford had no doubt what the eclipse foretold.

"As we read in Revelations," he declared, "there was a great earthquake and the sun became black as sackcloth of hair and the moon became as blood. And the stars of heaven fell unto the earth and every mountain and island were moved out of their places."

Chief Massasoit joined the lament. "The birds will fall from the sky," he wailed. "The wolves will never stop their howling and bears will leave their caves and attack us."

But as we watched, the moon slid slowly across the sky, revealing the blazing curve of the sun, and the land regained its shape, tree by tree, rock by rock. The only birds that fell were the ones we shot to eat in celebration of our survival, while the bears stayed deep in the forest.

Only Brewster had stayed calm, amused by our confusion.

"Surely you remember the comet when it shot like a great firework above the manor?" he asked Bradford. "How frightened the household was."

"It was a harbinger of change, you assured us." Bradford was embarrassed by his feverish reaction to the darkness.

"And so it proved," replied the older man. "Though I confess I did not foretell quite how." He permitted himself a reflective smile. "I had no truck with superstition then and have less now, but a happening like this does make me wonder if God is warning us that there has been too much change in the years we have lived here. Think back; we were able to make small things grow, because we were united by our common suffering, but now we have become small-minded and uncertain. Too many of us have lost the moral certitude that inspired us in the beginning. There is – how to describe it? – a coarseness about the place."

I concurred with that. "The shame of it is that today we suffer from too many ne'er-do-wells and second-raters, men without ambition who drink too much and fight and women who have grown lazy. I have never forgotten the words of Master Cushman about the drones amongst us who are mere scratchers and scrapers, interested only in their own comfort."

"Well spoken, John." Bradford straightened up, and tried to throw off the despondency that Brewster's words had stirred in him. "We have lost the sap of grace and have become mere worldlings. Master Brewster is correct. We have become fractious and paranoid and have allowed poverty to deflect us from the mission that brought us here."

We had gathered a few evenings after the mysterious

disappearance of the sun, and the elements were still playing tricks with us. A fog, deeper than usual, had rolled in from the sea, swirling around us and suspending us in a ghostly netherworld.

Brewster had a tale to tell. Of course he did.

"The Indians believe in a giant named Maushop, who fills his pipe with so much tobacco that he spreads a dark cloud over the region." He wheezed. "'It's old Maushop's smoke,' they cry."

We all laughed politely but Edward, who had been unusually quiet, rummaged in his knapsack and pulled out a sheaf of papers.

"Look, I found these scribblings which I made many years back and assumed I had lost in the earthquake. They say so much about the way we felt at the time. 'Plymouth is a community not laid upon schism, division or separation,' I wrote, 'but upon love, peace and holiness. Such love and mutual care for the spreading of the Gospel, the welfare of each other and their future generations is seldom found on earth.'"

He paused while we murmured our appreciation and I was cheered by such noble sentiments – only for him to dash them immediately.

"What an optimist I was. Have we really achieved love, peace and happiness? Do we care enough about the Plantation and the people in it or have we fallen into the trap of self-love, as Cushman so eloquently warned in his sermons?"

He tossed his writing on the table dismissively. "Maybe all we can do is look back and find peace in what we have accomplished and acknowledge where we have failed. But where does that leave us? Are we doomed to create nothing but a greater sense of failure?"

Susanna, who had materialised out of the dark to join the

group, gazed at him with a curious mix of pity and impatience.

We lapsed into a silence that was interrupted only by the dripping of moisture from the eaves, the snuffling of the cattle, somewhere unseeable in the meadow, and high above, the disembodied screech of a bald eagle.

Brewster broke into the quiet. "It is true that, for a while, we were like a candle lighting a thousand dreams." He gazed off into the fog. "But now that light is dimmed."

Bradford frowned. "We cannot resist what God has ordained in his merciless logic. How many good people have followed what they think are His wishes only to end in some futile enterprise?" He took a deep breath of the cold air as if to steady himself. "Master Edward, you sadden me. I pray the writers of history will not look back on this crusade of ours and say it was a failure."

Alice Bradford, usually a mouse in her husband's shadow, stopped pouring our drinks and stared at him perplexedly as though this reflective, almost humble, man was a stranger. Was this the inflexible husband she had married, the upstanding Governor who never showed a flicker of doubt?

I never forgot the first time we met. We were standing awkwardly together at the *Mayflower's* rail as England disappeared in its wake, and he obviously decided I needed a lecture on the importance of the venture.

Without so much as a 'good day' he began to lecture me. "I must explain why we are embarking on such a weighty voyage. We folk from Leiden have come together because we want a church closer to the primitive patterns of the first churches than any other has achieved."

I got as far as, "Master Carver has expounded to me something of your vision," but he was not interested in what a servant might have to say.

"We know we are pilgrims," he continued, staring beyond

me to the horizon. "We are like the Israelites seeking the promised land. Nothing will stand in our way." His militant tone was a contrast to the unsteady way his gangly figure struggled to keep its balance on the moving deck as he left me to reflect on his brief sermon.

But now, though he was as lean and upright as that day by the ship's rail, his eyes, everything about him, expressed an air of defeat – no, that is too strong, defeat was never in his lexicon – perhaps a misgiving that the certainties of his youth were not shared by the new generation in the Plantation.

"We cannot dwell on things we got wrong or wish we could undo." I tried to find some cheer. "We should treat those regrets as part of the characters we have become because to spend time trying to change that... well, it's like chasing clouds."

Brewster blew a puff of smoke that swirled like a ghostly sprite into the murk. "I pray so, Master John. We have been wanderers seeking the truth and whatever our failings – and there are many – I believe we have come close to finding it. God will be our judge, as he has been since we defied the King and his arrogant bishops these many years gone."

Another lull, interrupted only by the birds breaking out in a last frenzy of song.

I changed the subject. "The repair work has almost been completed on the church. John Alden is doing a fine job with the leaking roof."

I regretted saying it the moment the words were out of my mouth. The new church had been a blow to the very heart of Bradford's dream.

All of us who had moved away from the Plantation had become weary of the five-mile journey to the meeting house where the services had always been held.

"It is too far," I argued. "You know how bad the roads are, iced over in winter, muddy in spring and blowing dust into our faces in summer. Even those with an ox and cart find it an ordeal bumping along the track."

"I have made my feelings clear." Bradford would not be persuaded. "It means that those of us who have lived so long together in Christian and comfortable companionship will be divided." He added wistfully, "I used to walk twelve miles every Sabbath when I was a boy. Rain, shine or snow. I don't understand why our worshippers cannot manage that today. We have all become too soft."

"Dear William," Brewster interrupted impatiently. He had heard the argument as often as I had. "One church, two churches, they are only buildings. In Scrooby we met in village halls or humble front rooms and that was good enough for us, was it not? The important thing is that we all share the same beliefs."

The fog scudded away and as the sun filtered through the trees, a shot rang out. Probably Standish hunting for duck.

"Look. Listen." The old fellow ruminated: "Life is like this mist; it obscures the way then it vanishes, and once more we know the road to follow."

In the distance, smoke rose from the old houses in Plymouth and mingled with the last wisps of fog.

Bradford grimaced. "The Plantation is like a mother, grown old and forsaken by her children. Most of our old folk have been worn away by death, her children moved away. She is like a widow left only to trust in God. We had so many riches but now we are the p—p—poorer."

What could I say to cheer him? Even then, all those years after boarding the *Mayflower*, I was never wholly of their company, neither saint nor stranger. For me, there were no regrets, no laments over lost riches, spiritual or financial. I owned a house with hundreds of acres of fine land, I enjoyed a life far grander than I, the lad from the Fens, could have imagined in his wildest dreams. I had a glorious wife and brood of children – another on the way to make it eight. I was fulfilled.

"Master Bradford," I began. He looked at me with foreboding. "I have been proud to be one of the number who have built New Plymouth from nothing. What we have achieved is proof of God's approval. You should have no doubts about that. As for me, I resolved never to allow disappointment to cloud my life from the moment I fell into the Atlantic and woke up to find Lizzie tending to me."

She smiled, brushed the hint of a tear from her eye, reached out and touched my hand.

EPILOGUE

1644

A HUMBLE AND MODEST MIND

He that upheld the Apostle upheld them. They were persecuted but not forsaken, cast down but not destroyed, as unknown and yet well known, as dying and behold we live, as chastened and not killed – Corinthians 11, chapter nine.

Quoted by William Bradford at William Brewster's funeral.

T HEY STOOD QUIETLY AROUND THE BED.
Winslow poked at the fire, as much to fill the silence
as to revive the flames.

Howland said, "I saw him this morning. He was smoking his pipe on the doorstep and reading. He waved as I went by."

"He asked about the oxen." Winslow blew his nose noisily. "He reckoned one of them was lame."

William Brewster lay as still as one of the limestone effigies in St Wilfrid's, his old church in Scrooby, his hands clasped together, blankets up to his neck and a laced cap perched on his head.

The old man had taken to his bed at midday and though he insisted he was not in pain, when he did manage to open his eyes, his gaze was dim. They were not to see much more of this world.

Bradford stood stiff upright. Howland and Alden, the young men Brewster had encouraged, stayed in the doorway where his shabby red hat hung on a brass hook. Standish, a tad portly now that his fighting days were over, was at attention.

Winslow surreptitiously ran his fingers down the spines of the books on the shelves – Aristotle, *The Prince* by Machiavelli, *The Scourge of Drunkards* and one he had noticed before but had been too embarrassed to mention – *The Tragedy of Messalina, The Roman Empress*. Brewster must have known it had been acted on the stage in London and provoked a scandal. The old man had been surprising him ever since the escapade with the pamphlet that had seen him harried and hunted by the King. What glee they had felt at their effrontery. And what dread at being caught.

"You should have seen the library in the manor." Bradford was holding one of his Bibles. "He had taken delivery of this one just before we fled and hid it in the attic."

Silence. Just the pop and crackle of the fire. It was April, but a brisk wind came in off the bay making them shiver. Though that might have been the cold draught of death.

He was eighty years old so they should have been prepared for this moment but, reflected Bradford, a world without him did not seem possible. More than forty years he had known him; spring days in Scrooby, not unlike this one, tramping over the fields to hear the firebrand Richard Clyfton; the escape and their weighty voyage; the despair of those early days. He had been his inspiration through all that time.

"Remember when John Robinson preached at the Pentecost?" Bradford asked when his mentor had opened his eyes and was strong enough to speak. "The day the King came to the manor?"

The dying man roused himself. "James. Pah. The wisest fool in Christendom. Sparkles of affection..." A bubble of spittle hung on his lips as he managed a faint smile. "What of Mary the maid?"

No one remembered her.

"Bread and cheese," he croaked. "She brought me bread and cheese."

"His mind is wandering," whispered Winslow.

"Allerton cheated her of two guilders." He spoke clearly that time.

They blinked. So that was the cause for his hostility to the greedy tailor.

He muttered, "Francyse Wright… the vanities of youth…"

Bradford's eyes flickered in panic.

At about nine or ten o'clock in the evening, with the candles sending flickering shadows around the room, Bradford felt the slightest squeeze of his hand.

The old man gave a few short breaths and gasped, "Death is a delightful hiding place for weary men."

He gave one long drawn out sigh as if falling into sleep. He had left them.

"You have to say something," Standish urged Bradford in a loud whisper.

Bradford faltered. "It will be harder to exist in this world now he that made me has gone, but we can be sure that he has d—d—departed this life sweetly to a b—b—better…"

He gathered himself. "Our brother, our father, for that is what he was to you and to me, achieved much and suffered much for the sake of Lord Jesus and the gospels. Many of us were brought to God by Master William's powerful ministry. He was wise and well spoken, very sociable and pleasant to his friends. He had a humble and modest mind, though as a young man he could rip up the heart and conscience with his sermons. He did more in a year than many do in all their lives. But you know this. We all know this."

They shuffled out of the room to let the women prepare the body.

The next day they took the elder's remains in its shroud of flax in melancholy procession along the highway to Burial Hill, where his wife Mary and daughter Fear lay. So many of his comrades too.

To the cry of the eagles soaring like sentinels overhead, Bradford began his sermon.

"Everything is so much darker when the moon goes behind a cloud than it would have been if it had never risen but we are allowed to weep for anyone who dies and goes to his destiny. The only consolation we wretched mortals have is to let the tears roll down our faces."

He composed himself.

"I c—c—cannot match Master William for his eloquence, but he did encourage me to be true to a maxim I learnt from my grandfather: 'In the beginning was the Word…'"

WHAT CAME NEXT

THE PEOPLE

THE ENGLISH

John Alden died September 12, 1687, aged eighty-nine, in Ducksburrow (today Duxbury). He and his wife had ten children. Descendants include Henry Wadsworth Longfellow, John Adams, John Quincy Adams, Orson Welles, Dan Quayle, Raquel Welch, Martha Graham, Martha Stewart, Adlai Stevenson III, Dick Van Dyke, Julia Child and (possibly) Marilyn Monroe.

Isaac Allerton died circa February 10, 1659, aged about seventy-three, in New Haven, Massachusetts. He founded the town of Marblehead but died insolvent. He had six children by three wives. He is an ancestor of US presidents Zachary Taylor and Franklin D. Roosevelt.

William Bradford died May 9, 1659, aged sixty-eight, in

Plymouth. His account of the venture, *Of Plymouth Plantation*, was written between 1630 and 1651.

William Brewster died April 10, 1644, aged eighty, in Plymouth.

Stephen Hopkins died between June 6 and July 17, 1644, aged between fifty-nine and sixty-seven. Unknown burial. He had eight children with second wife Elizabeth. He was constantly in trouble with the authorities for selling alcohol and fighting. His servant **Edward Leister** left Plymouth and died in Barbados.

John Howland died February 1673, aged between seventy-four and eighty-one, in Rocky Nook. He was the last male of the *Mayflower* to die. He had ten children with wife Elizabeth Tilley. He had several brothers who also came to New England; one was an ancestor to Presidents Richard Nixon and Gerald Ford and another to Winston Churchill.

The orphan **Richard More** died between 1694 and 1696, aged about seventy-eight. He became a ship's captain and married three times. He died poor after being tried for 'gross unchastity with another man's wife'.

Thomas Morton died in 1647, aged seventy-one. After several abortive attempts to establish a settlement, he was arrested and accused of being a Royalist agitator by Cromwell and charged with sedition. His health failed and he was released only to end his days under the protection of Sir Ferdinand Gorges in Maine.

Edward Winslow died May 8, 1656, aged fifty-nine. He

returned to England in 1646 and worked for Oliver Cromwell. In 1655 he was on an expedition to the West Indies, but died of yellow fever and was buried at sea between Hispaniola and Jamaica. Winslow's portrait is the only likeness of any of the pilgrims taken from life. His descendant, Colonel John Winslow, drove the French-speaking population out of Nova Scotia in 1755. (Read the account in *The Scattered* by this author).

Susanna Winslow, date of death unknown, buried near family home in Marshfield, Plymouth. Her son Peregrine – the first child to be born in New England – died aged eighty-three in 1704.

John Winthrop died March 26, 1649, aged between fifty-eight and sixty-six in Boston. He is judged to be 'at once a significant founding father of America's best and worst impulses'. Many modern politicians, such as John Kennedy, Ronald Reagan and Sarah Palin, have referred to Winthrop's writings in their speeches.

The Native Americans

Hobbamock lived with the Standish family until he died in 1642 from a 'European disease'.

Chief Massasoit died around 1661. His grandson Metacom, called Philip by the settlers, was defeated by the English after a rebellion known as Philip's War (1675–78). The victory established English power in New England.

THE LEGACY

THE LEGACY OF THE MEN AND WOMEN OF THE *Mayflower* lies in the traditions they left behind and the spirit they represented. They established a model for self-reliance and resistance to authority, which was to become such an abiding characteristic of North America. They represent racial and religious tolerance, freedom and democracy.

But their descendants were also responsible for the destruction of the Native Americans, whose lands they seized.

Many acknowledge that the compact signed on the *Mayflower* was an inspiration for the US Constitution. The agreement to 'covenant and combine ourselves together into a civil Body Politick' was radical in the era of divine monarchy. The decision to make their own 'laws, ordinances, acts, constitutions and offices...' for the good of the colony, and to abide by those laws under an elected leader, paved the way to the independence of the colonies and underpins the governance of the US today. They established a religious liberty, free from the established Church, and rejected common ownership of land and livestock in favour of what today would be considered the kind of free market admired by most Americans and the Western world.

Nine US presidents trace their lineage back to the *Mayflower*. Others include astronaut Alan Shepard, baby care expert Dr Benjamin Spock, actors Humphrey Bogart, Orson Welles, Clint Eastwood and Richard Gere.

To claim the voyage changed the world is not an exaggeration; the men, women and children on the voyage laid the social, cultural and economic foundations for a nation that went on to dominate the twentieth century.

MORE BOOKS TO READ

Strangers and Pilgrims, Jeremy Bangs; *Of Plymouth Plantation*, William Bradford; *Making Haste from Babylon*, Nick Bunker; *Coming Over*, David Cressy; *The Cry of a Stone*, Robert Cushman; *The Mayflower Generation*, Rebecca Fraser; *Mayflower*, Christopher Hilton; *The Mayflower and Her Passengers*, Caleb H. Johnson; *New English Canaan*, Thomas Morton; *Mourt's Relation* Edward Winslow and William Bradford; *Mayflower*, Nathaniel Philbrick; *Mayflower Passenger References*, Susan E. Roser; *Spirit of the New England Tribes*, William S. Simmons; *Land Ho! 1620* W. Sears Nickerson *Saints and Strangers*, George Willison; *Good News from New England*, Edward Winslow.